SO I MIGHT BE A VAMPIRE

by Rodney V. Smith

LOST
bajan
PUBLISHING

SO I MIGHT BE A VAMPIRE
Copyright © 2017 by Rodney V. Smith

For information contact:
info@lostbajanpublishing.com
www.lostbajanpublishing.com

Edited by Nikki Barran

Book and Cover design by Rodney V. Smith

Cover photography by: Theik Smith

ISBN: 1775007272
ISBN-13: 978-1775007272

First Edition: February 2018

10 9 8 7 6 5 4 3 2 1

Dedication

For my wife Allison, who made me write it.
For my brother Ryan, who never got to read it.

"We don't like to hear the word "vampire" around here; we're trying to improve our public image."

-William S. Burroughs

TABLE OF CONTENTS

SO I MIGHT BE
A VAMPIRE

PROLOGUE

PROLOGUE

The cherry-red Camaro raced across the desert highway like a bat out of hell, a plume of dust rising from the road behind it. The dust served two purposes. One: it made the car look completely badass; and two: it obscured the coming light of dawn that threatened to burn the land and any really slow vampires that happened to be hanging around.

Any vampire with a sense of drama who was waiting for the sun to come up and explode its light across the land just like it does in the movies, was going to be very disappointed. The problem here is that the sun moves very slowly, drama be damned. You could almost say it moved "glacially" if you like that kind of joke. In any case, forget about that hypothetical drama-queen vampire; he isn't important, and neither is he real. Focus instead on the muscle car plowing its way across the landscape, its windows tinted a very illegal shade of black. If you wanted to meet any vampires, you would have to look no further than that car.

"Almost there Bobbikins! Two minutes and then you're going to *BURN*!"

This was from the crazed, and at the same time, extremely attractive blonde woman who drove the car as aggressively as she could. She was the kind of woman that this muscle car had no doubt been made for. The designer hadn't known it at the time of course, but if pressed he might have described a scene just like this one, where a beautiful blonde woman manhandled his well-designed and loud assemblage of machinery across a desert. He would, of course, have left out

1

the fact that this woman was dressed entirely in black from head to toe, including the leather gloves on her hands and the leather jacket that she wore so well. He would also have left out the fact that she was a vampire.

Since she isn't the one telling this story, and because I'm still very pissed off at her, I'm going to lie and say that she *isn't* that important. The reason I'm still pissed off at her, is that at that very moment, I was in the trunk of the car and it was getting very uncomfortable.

"I don't want to burn!" I yelled back, although it was doubtful that she could hear me over the noise of the engine.

I kicked once again at the closed trunk even though my past efforts over the past 15 minutes had been futile. The inside of the trunk was smeared with my blood, and my hands were almost hamburger by that point, but when someone is threatening to set you on fire, you kinda owe it to yourself to avoid that fate as much as possible. This time I kicked outward, having finally gotten into a position that while not entirely comfortable, gave me some leverage.

To my surprise, the trunk flew open with almost no effort, and I stared stupidly at the open space for way too long. I hadn't even had time to really process what had just happened and hadn't actually made any plans beyond getting the damn trunk open.

I somehow heard Beatrice swear, and the car began to power down as she took her foot off the gas.

I didn't wait.

I cursed myself for being an atheist since I didn't have any kind of god to pray to or swear at, and threw myself out of the back of the car.

There is a saying about throwing yourself out of the back of a moving vehicle traveling at what feels to be the speed of light. The saying goes something like this: "Don't do it."

If this were a movie, this would be the exact time they would do a hilarious freeze-frame of me flying through the air. This would be the split-second before gravity noticed that I was doing something that I shouldn't be, but at that moment, you could believe that man could fly. Yes, it was an awkward kind of flying, legs all splayed out behind me, hands still bound together with duct-tape, mouth open in a full scream that would inevitably end with a stream of cuss words that would brilliantly illustrate my pain to anyone watching. In the distance behind me, the car would be slamming on the brakes, a cloud of acrid smoke rising from the tires to join the dust cloud that had so eagerly followed the vehicle.

Go ahead and laugh. You know you want to. You don't have to deal with the pain of landing and bouncing down the desert road. No, that was my particular fate at that moment, that frozen moment that never happened because gravity is a bitch and has no sense of drama.

"Fuck!"

Bounce.

"Ow!"

Bounce.

"Shit!"

Roll and bounce.

"Ow!"

Splat.

"Rasshole!"

That, of course, was my progress down the road. It may have gone on a little bit longer than that, and involved a lot more Bajan swearwords I had picked up from my Dad. We had been traveling at well over 140 kilometers per hour and man, so that was a lot of rolling, swearing, *and* a lot of pain to deal with.

I was a mass of scrapes and cuts and bruises as I somehow managed to pull myself to my very unsteady feet. My head was ringing in that familiar "you just got a concussion" way, and my brain was telling me that all senses were buried in a thick fog. Something was screaming at me to get moving, don't look back, just get moving and run and for fuck's sake, don't look back—

I looked back.

Striding towards me at speed through the dust and smoke was Beatrice and goddamn if she wasn't the angel of death. The Katana that she unsheathed as she walked added to the ensemble in a way that said she knew exactly how cool she looked, but that was Beatrice for you.

"Don't run Bob! *Embrace it!*"

"Fuck that!" I yelled. "How about we do the complete opposite of that?" Beatrice only laughed and sped up her walk. I tried to implore to her good side. "How about we go someplace dark and talk about me not dying?"

"Blaze of glory Bob!"

I looked over my shoulder at the horizon where the sun was still promising an eventual appearance and then looked back to Beatrice, suddenly tired of running. Or maybe I was just too damn tired and beat up to run. Either way, it worked out the same: I was fucked.

I watched Beatrice rise into the air, sword held up to strike. It was a beautiful and well-rehearsed jump that sent her flying over the fifty feet between us. It was the kind of leap that would have been awesome in a movie, now that I think about it, especially with the sword raised like that. From my perspective on the ground though, it was utterly terrifying.

I could see that Beatrice's fangs were bared in a grin, and I knew she was getting a kick out of the violence she was about to inflict on me. Her brilliant blue vampire eyes focused on my own as she prepared to drive the sword through my heart.

At least I would go out like I tried to live my life: I raised my both of my battered and torn middle fingers, and flipped her off.

***

Shit.

Almost everything I just told you is a lie. Not the actual story, just more of a "fact-type thing" if you know what I mean. If you ask Beatrice what happened, believe me, her story would be completely different, and it would not even involve a car speeding through a desert! Like seriously? Who tells a story this epic and leaves out a speeding car in the desert?

Fine! Be that way then.

Look, facts don't matter here, only the truth, and the truth is that my story changes every time I tell it. It's not entirely my fault though. I mean it's not like I'm going out of my way to lie. I just end up editing stuff a little bit here and there, you know, so I look more badass. More like a hero. Everybody does it, just in tiny ways. Sometimes it's just about how you totally got the best of that jackass who cut in front of you at Starbucks with the perfectly timed snide comment (even though you only thought of it twenty minutes after the fact). Or maybe the story about how you finally told off Sara and walked out on her (instead of how you begged for her to stay and she left anyway and took the Xbox with her since she's the one who had actually paid for it). How you tell the story of it shapes how everybody looks at you, and you want to see the look on their faces as they imagine themselves in your shoes and think of how they would have done the exact same thing, only they, of course, imagine that they look even more badass.

People are strange that way.

So anyway, sticking to the facts: the desert thing never happened. The truth is, I'm from Toronto, and there are no deserts anywhere around here, at least not unless you drive a few hours away and even then there's still no real desert to speak of. It just doesn't sound so cool when it's the road to the Beaches that we're talking about.

I didn't escape from a car trunk either, although that would have been a lot cooler and less embarrassing than what actually did happen, and then there's the whole sordid mess of how I even got to that point at all. That's a whole story all by itself, and I can either give you the cliff notes version or get into all of the gritty detail, but nobody's got time for that, right?

Oh, you do? Of course you do.

Fine then. I'll try to be as honest as possible, but don't hold me to that. When there's a chance for me to look like a badass, I'm probably going to take that option, so I'm not making too many promises. Just as long as we both agree that everything I'm about to tell you is almost the complete truth.

Ready?

FRIENDS OF VLAD

Chapter 1

BOB THE VAMPIRE

"**I** want you to turn me into a vampire."

I don't know about you, but having someone actually say that and mean it is not exactly something I had ever expected to hear. And I definitely didn't welcome it. Yes, I *am* a vampire, and *no*, nobody had ever asked that of me before. I mean like seriously: *who actually does that, right?*

I was in the middle of trying very hard to get drunk and was desperately failing to do even *that*, so I wasn't being placed in exactly the best frame of mind. Cheap tequila is still expensive tequila when you're dead broke, and I wasn't looking forward to the moment the bartender tried to run my poor dented, and highly abused debit card.

"Fuck off," I said to the squirrelly little dude who had settled into the seat across the table and who had immediately made the insane request. The dude had almost no chin to speak of and wore a stupid fucking fedora much too big for him, and looked nothing like a gorgeous redhead with tattoos, so he instantly had all of that going against him. He also looked as broke as I was, one badly timed pay cheque away from being in the negative on the bank balance, so I knew there would be very little chance of getting any drinks out of him.

"*I know you're a vampire,*" he insisted. "I want you to turn me into one of you. Into *a vampire.*"

I took another look at the dude and realized that I had seen him sneaking curious glances at me about an hour ago, almost as if he recognized me or, at least, thought he recognized me but couldn't quite figure out who I was. The thought had occurred to me that maybe he was gay and was just checking me out and being stupidly obvious about it, but guys with his looks tended to be a little shyer.

Thing is, I had been getting lots of unwelcome attention ever since my eyes had changed color. It's not every day that you see a brown guy like me with the particular shade of intensely pale blue eyes that was unique among vampires. I'm mixed, half-black and half-Hispanic, so the contrast can't be ignored. Some people assumed that I was wearing contacts and dismissed me as pretentious, but they tended to be the exception. So I had taken to wearing dark sunglasses even at night. Unfortunately this had produced the opposite effect and people had started thinking I was a rockstar or something and would usually end up shocked when I tried to get them to pay for my drinks. That usually did not go down very well. I must say that the eyes did have a remarkable effect on women and I wasn't shy about using it to my advantage.

Squirrel Boy was definitely not someone whose pants I wanted to get into, and neither was he a friend. I didn't know who the hell he was, so the possibility that I owed him money or that he had been sent to kill me was pretty low. That had been a relief, especially after the events of the past week, and I really didn't feel like having yet another fight for my life. My future plans had involved me not fighting at all, but life has a way of hijacking all my plans.

I decided to try another tactic.

"That's your opening line? *Seriously* dude?"

Squirrel Boy swallowed hard and clutched his stupid shoulder bag even tighter than he had before. I knew almost instantly that he had some type of stupid ass weapon inside, that he intended to use to protect himself or to fend me off. I also realized I scared the shit out of him. I wondered for a moment what type of movie he had playing in his head where he had decided he was the lead and where I was the scary bad vampire man.

"Do I even know you?" I asked him.

"Not exactly. I mean, I *think* I sorta *know* you. I've seen you down at HTDK--"

I snorted. I just couldn't help myself. "Not likely. They like 'em prettier than you. No offense."

Squirrel Boy blushed. "I was waiting outside in the line…" he mumbled and I almost felt sorry for him. "I've seen you there lots of times. And then you started showing up here. *I know what you are,*" he whispered to me. "I could tell the whole bar, expose your secret."

I drained the glass and looked mournfully at the bottom and then looked even more mournfully at the empty bottle on the table. I still had no idea how I had managed to convince the bartender to give me the bottle, but I wasn't about to punch a gift horse in the eye. When life gives you tequila, you look for the lemons it gave you earlier. One of the problems with being a vampire is that it's impossible to go on a proper bender anymore. My body metabolizes alcohol too quickly and I end up sober with a throbbing headache before I even leave the bar… if I don't keep drinking. I miss the days of getting blackout drunk sometimes. Used to be a hell of a lot cheaper too.

That's one thing nobody ever tells you. Being a vampire is expensive in ways you never thought of.

I sighed deeply and looked blearily at Squirrel Boy.

"Go ahead then. Out me. Like I give a fuck."

Squirrel Boy licked his lips nervously, his bluff called. He apparently had seen this playing out differently. For a second, I considered telling him how lucky he was it was only me he was pulling this stupid stunt with. If it had been someone like Beatrice, she would already be beating the shit out of him in one of the bathroom stalls. And she most definitely wouldn't even bother with any biting, but there's no telling with a vampire like Beatrice.

"Look, what's your name. I can't call you Squirrel Boy all night."

"*Armand?*" A look of confusion crossed his face. "You haven't called me Squirrel B--"

"That's not your real name. If you're going to be obnoxious to me, you might as well tell me your real fucking name."

Squirrel Boy slumped and mumbled something under his breath, clearly embarrassed. "It's Sidney."

"Nice to meet you Sidney. I'm Bob." I grinned wickedly.

"Go get me some more drinks Sidney. Then we'll talk."

***

The first thing I want you to be aware of is this: being a vampire sucks.

It is definitely not like they show you in the movies or any of the books written on the subject. In the movies, the vampire is always such an intriguing figure and he always has his act together. He lives by the rules of the movie world and as rules go, they are relatively straightforward: avoid sunlight, dress in evening clothes, drink blood from the necks of nubile and attractive young ladies, be handsome and don't ever worry about picking up the check. So on that end, it's best to have lots of money and maybe a castle in someplace exotic and cold with significant thunder and lightning and preferably on top of a mountain somewhere. Also, don't look into mirrors and most of all, avoid any overly eager young men who happen to be carrying sharp pieces of wood with them.

I've broken every single one of those rules, even the last one.

***

When Sidney returned, I didn't ask any questions. I opened the bottle immediately and poured a shot for myself.

Sidney looked less sure of himself as he watched me drain the first glass, and then the second glass of tequila. He seemed a little uneasy after the bartender had actually given him the forbidden bottle with no questions asked. This was only after the bartender had looked over to my table and saw that the bottle was meant for me. If you want a genuine "what-the-fuck" moment, that one was definitely high on my list. Nobody gets to take a bottle from the bar: *nobody*. It looked like my run of good luck was still on!

If I was a nicer person and more of a pushover, I would have really felt sorry for poor Sidney. He had been expecting some kind of movie-type vampire and instead he had gotten me and my desperate need to have someone else buy my drinks. If he hadn't been such an asshole to me right off the bat, things might have gone a little differently. Here's a tip for you: if you're going to demand something from a stranger, at least introduce yourself and buy them a drink first *before* being an obnoxious dipshit. Protocol must be observed.

I poured Sidney a shot of tequila and slid it over to him.

"Why do you want to be a vampire Sidney?"

"Can you at least call me Armand? That's the name I've decided should be my vampire name."

I barely held in my laughter. "Fuck that. You're Sidney, so I'm fucking calling you Sidney. Now answer my fucking question. *Please.*"

Sidney hesitated and I noticed he was only playing with his still full glass of tequila. He was purposely not drinking it, perhaps in an ill-fated attempt to get me drunk. He really should have thought harder about this plan, since as I noted earlier, I was already trying very hard to get as drunk as possible.

"I want to live forever, but I want the power and everything that goes with being a vampire. I want to be cool, just like you."

"Is this about a girl? This is about a girl, isn't it?"

It's always about a girl. At the root of all our problems, it's always about wanting to impress someone.

"What's her name?" I asked.

Sidney considered lying to me, I could see it in his face, but he was already smiling, picturing the girl in his mind. "Dorothy," he breathed her name and I knew he wasn't lying this time. He turned and looked across the bar and I looked with him. "She's over there."

The girl was gorgeous. She was slim with a nice build for her small frame, dark hair and eyes and her smile lit up her face as she joked with her friends. She looked like a nice girl, the type of girl Sidney probably was too shy to be honest with and, consequently had probably ended up in the dreaded place called the friend-zone. She looked way too nice to be my type, unless she was one of those girls who got wild in bed and kept it hidden under that wholesome exterior.

"She looks nice," I said. "Why do you think being a vampire is going to make her like you?"

"Girls like her always go for the bad boys like you. There

isn't anyone who's a bigger badass than a vampire."

I have no idea how I didn't laugh in Sidney's face. *You gotta be fucking kidding me right?* He actually thought I was a badass! I thought of all the stories I could tell him about me definitely not being a badass, vampire or not. I wondered for a second if he maybe expected my skin to glitter or some shit, but then decided that he was probably more of a fan of the romantic kind of vampires *á la Anne Rice.*

Sidney was getting impatient.

"Look I bought you the drinks. Are you going to make me into a vampire or not?"

Well, that had escalated fast. And I thought we had just made a personal connection.

"Have we reached the part where you threaten me already?" I asked and poured myself another drink.

Apparently we had. Sidney reached into his man-purse and pulled out one of the biggest fucking crosses I have ever seen. He held it out in front of him triumphantly, apparently playing his trump card, bringing his knowledge of vampires from movies and books into the one thing that he knew would protect him.

Goddamn movies.

***

I'm going to cut to the chase here: you should definitely at all costs, avoid a vampire whenever possible.

See, the problem is that maybe 100 years ago you could actually do that, but these days, taking population explosion into account, maybe one person in every 50,000 you meet just *might be* a vampire. Avoidance might be a bit of an issue if you're that eager to not run into one, so yeah... good luck with that.

Imagine it. You're an ordinary guy, around thirty, which is my age, so you've grown up on a steady diet of rock music, horror movies, too much alcohol and withered expectations. I knew exactly where Sidney was coming from since I used to be that guy who believed on some level that the movies got it right about vampires, no matter how many times they contradicted themselves.

I was that guy, and you were that guy too. Or the girl. Whatever. Stay with me on this.

***

I noticed a girl at the bar glance over at us and look away, then she did a double take and her eyes widened, her mouth forming the words "What the fuck?" as her brain tried to figure out just what was going on, before deciding that she wasn't drunk enough for this shit and turned back to the bar.

So much for keeping a low profile.

Sidney's other hand was back in the bag and I knew it was clutching a wooden stake of some kind, either crudely made in Sidney's backyard or a prop purchased from the Internet. I thought about it and decided it had most likely been bought from some stupid vampire website that sold pieces of wood "*blessed by a priest and sprinkled with Holy Water*" to gullible people like Sidney. They weren't even hand-carved for a hint of authenticity, but instead were identical machine cut pieces of wood. Of course he had paid too much for it; it wouldn't be a proper scam if he didn't pay too much.

"Your negotiating tactics suck balls, I just want you to know that," I noted dryly.

"Fuck you, you fucking fuck."

Well it seemed that Sidney had a bit of a mouth on him. *Insults? So quickly? Wow man, just wow.*

I drained my glass and put it back on the table with an audible thud. I was determined to finish the bottle before I dealt with Sidney, just in case I had to leave in a hurry.

"No wonder you can't make it with Dorothy over there, Sidney. You have no game and you have no idea how to relate to people."

"*Don't make me compel you!*" Sidney said and then turned whiny. "I just need you to turn me man. I need this. Just bite me and make me one of you."

"Just bite you? Are you serious?"

"I know that's how you get turned. Everybody knows it."

I fucking hate the bullshit that Hollywood and bad literature has spread about vampires. Dude was hitting every one of my pet peeves, and the cross thing was just getting annoying. There were currently two options to get out of this so I could go somewhere else and drink until the sun came up, away from idiots wanting me to turn them into vampires.

Option one involved grabbing that stupid cross from Sidney and jamming it so far up his ass that every time he went to the bathroom after that, it would be the holiest place in the city. And I definitely wouldn't be putting my mouth anywhere near his neck or any other body part. I would however still have time to drain the bottle, you know: priorities and all.

Option two was probably going to be more entertaining…

I took off my sunglasses and wiped my brow, pretending very badly and overdramactically to be affected by the cross.

"Okay, you got me, I'm sorry, I'm so sorry, can you please move the cross now?"

I glanced at Sidney to see if he was buying my Razzy winning performance, but he had fully seen my freaky light blue vampire eyes and the reality of what he was doing suddenly crashed over him. Terror sweat had broken out on his upper lip and he started to shake in fear. The thought occurred to me he just wasn't prepared mentally to deal with the full reality of a real vampire. The reality that was me.

Congrats Sidney: you've just met your first real life vampire.

***

I looked Sidney directly in the eye and gently pushed the cross down. He weakly allowed me to do this, definitely terrified of me. Damn, my buzz was fading away, and I suddenly needed to pee very, very badly. Damn tequila.

"Crosses don't work. Neither does Holy Water, a chain of garlic, a silver bullet or whatever other stupid shit you've talked yourself into believing works. You have no protection from what I am, just because you read about it on the internet or whatever. *Think about it*, Sidney and for once in your life, get out of your head and into the real world. You are not the star of the show and for that matter, neither am I. I'm going to be a footnote to you, an interesting story you can tell your friends. Call it 'the night the vampire didn't kill me,' *because believe me, I can kill you and I'm not even the worst vampire you could meet.*" The part about me killing him was a lie, since I'd never killed anyone, but I wasn't telling Sidney that. "There are some really, *really* bad people out there, so don't you ever pull this shit again or you're going to wind up very dead. Just not by me and not tonight. You got me?"

He nodded mutely, still staring at my eyes, and I wondered if he had heard a word I'd said. It was almost as if he was hypnotized or something. That's not quite the word, but I couldn't think of a better one, so, like, whatever man. I was over it and the urge to pee was fucking killing me.

"Gimme the cross." He handed it over and I threw it into a corner where it couldn't insult anyone else. I held out my hand to him again.

"And the stake."

There were six of them, six inches long, smooth and identical, all from the internet *(www.wekillvampires.com)*. They still had the stickers on them.

I sighed deeply and looked Sidney in the eye again.

"Do you want to live Sidney? I mean, really live?"

He nodded and I sighed. I was done playing and I was on the verge of peeing my pants. I pointed over to Dorothy and her friends.

"*Then fucking live.* Go over there and ask her the fuck out. She's either going to say yes or she's going to say no, but at least get off your ass and get an answer and then you can move on with your life. And you'll get to ask another girl later on and maybe she'll say yes, because Dorothy there might not be the one for you and she'll probably say no, I mean *look at her*, but damn dude you gotta try, and I really gotta end this now cuz I gotta pee, so whaddaya say?"

Sidney nodded and stumbled to his feet. I got up with him, feeling the weight on my bladder of two bottles of tequila wanting to come back into the world a lot more diluted. I clapped him on the shoulder, and he turned wordlessly and walked toward Dorothy, a man on a mission of certain doom, but damn he was embracing his doom--

I never got to see how it turned out. I ran off to the bathroom and for a second I thought I wasn't going to make it to the urinal. I danced from one foot to the other, while trying to pull down a suddenly stubborn zipper, and finally I was free to pee the pee of the damned.

That's the problem with tequila: it always shoots right through me.

What? Don't give me that look. Just because I'm a vampire doesn't mean I'm suddenly a magical creature with no natural urges or processes. You try drinking two bottles of tequila and see if you aren't hosing down the closest urinal before you even get halfway through the first bottle. My pipes work the same as everybody else's.

If Sidney had bothered to even ask me what being a vampire was like, I would probably have told him the truth, although my total lack of badassery might have been a little too much for him to take in one night. One can only destroy so many dreams at once you know.

Truth is, I'm probably the *worst* vampire I know.

Chapter 2
THINGS THEY DON'T TELL YOU

I f you had told me a year ago that I would be sitting in a dive bar killing time before going to meet Claude at the diner, I would have definitely believed you, because that's an entirely reasonable thing. If you'd told me that I was going to be a vampire at the time, I would have just asked you to give me some of whatever you were smoking.

If you'd happened to mention that a few months *before* that, I would be spending my last night as a full-fledged member of the human species in the backseat of my Honda POS (literally means "Piece of Shit", but you already knew that), between the legs of a woman I'd only met ten minutes before, I might not have been able to stop laughing at you and your tomfoolery. If you also mentioned that said drunken chick was going to take a bite out of my neck in the throes of passion or whatever, I might have looked at you in all earnestness and asked what anyone normally would after this entirely odd conversation: "*So is that how I became a vampire? And by the way, about those winning lottery numbers…*"

You would have possibly run away cackling like a maniac. Past-you isn't very stable in my imagination.

Past-me was just as clueless as anybody else would be and due to that general cluelessness, would be getting it all wrong.

So just imagine for a second, me in all of my ignorance and the sudden shock of being bitten on the neck mid-coitus. I imagine for a male praying mantis it would be business as usual and if I had indeed been one, nothing would have interrupted me at the moment. Since I wasn't a praying mantis and instead just your regular average twenty-nine year old named Bob, I was definitely thrown off my stride.

"You bit me!" I gasped. "I can't believe you bit me!"

Her answer was to try to bite me again, and she was laughing while she did. I couldn't even remember the chick's name, Gloria or maybe Gladys or some shit like that. It wasn't important at the time, knowing her name, but that's a common theme with me. I suck with names anyway. All that mattered at that moment was that I hadn't had sex in three months, and this chick had been hot for me from the first time I bumped into her at the bar.

I had managed to spill my Vodka Seven all over my shirt and had been mourning the loss since I was *extremely* broke at the time and had just spent my last five dollars on said drink... which was now soaking into the front of my shirt. If I could have reached, I probably would have been trying to lick my shirt just to get a taste of some of that ever-so-important alcohol that just might give me a little buzz. The alcohol levels in my blood were dangerously low and I feared slipping into a coma of sheer depression.

"Did I do that?" She had asked, and I had nodded, already in mourning.

"Yep. That's alcohol abuse you know, spilling it like that."

"I can think of a much better use for it myself. Let me buy you another one to make up for it."

"I think I will let you do that," I said, and took a good look at her then, but my immediate attention was drawn to her generous cleavage which made it hard to look her directly in the eye. She was around forty and sure of herself. You could see it in the way she carried herself, especially with a rack like hers. Her ample curves spoke volumes to me in a sexy, husky voice that made a lie out of her decidedly corporate wear. Good God, the woman rocked a knee-length skirt like I've never experienced before or since. I managed to get all this in one glance at her and tried my best not to stutter. "Can't let you go around committing mortal sins like that," I managed and then almost kicked myself, but she smiled, charmed.

"Well, what kinds of sin should I be committing then?"

"The non-mortal kinds?" I grinned and shrugged. "I dunno. It sounded wittier in my head than it did coming out of my mouth."

Oh God, she was definitely interested.

"Don't you just hate it when that happens?" She asked, and she was giving me serious *"fuck me now"* eyes. "You should find a better use for your mouth you know."

"That's either a big come on or I'm being rejected without even trying."

"You weren't coming on to me?"

"No, actually. I was still mourning the loss of my drink. Hadn't had time to notice you yet."

"You're kidding, right? I thought you were ogling my boobs." She jiggled them, and they were quite an attractive pair. The half-chub that I had been trying to keep in check so I could try to walk away with my dignity intact was suddenly now well formed and ready for action. It was making it hard to think. Damn boobs.

"Well, I was," I admitted, "but I was also looking at the alcohol in my shirt."

"Shouldn't have put it there then."

"I didn't. I had been planning to put it into my mouth."

"I have something else you can put in your mouth..."

That's a line that us guys only ever dream of hearing. About ninety-five percent of us single guys will die without ever hearing those words uttered from the lips of a drunken bimbo in a corporate dress suit at a sleazy dive bar. I could now stamp my Man-Card and die a happy man.

"Now if I'm not mistaken, that one was a come-on line, wasn't it?" I asked, just to be sure. "And I do hope you're talking about breasts..."

"Definitely," she said and moved even closer, checking me out as she did. She smiled at the half-concealed bulge in my pants.

"Which one?"

"Both."

"You wanna get outta here?"

"I was going to say it, but I didn't want you to think I was a slut."

"Would it matter?"

"No, I'd fuck you anyway."

It wasn't until she bit my neck that I wondered what kind of freak I'd ended up with.

I managed to scramble out of the car as fast as I could, somehow pulling up my pants while not tripping over anything. I heard the bar door bang open, and the music and sounds from inside poured out into the night air for a few seconds as people either entered or exited the bar. They might have seen my naked ass or maybe not, but I didn't care at that point. All I cared about was that this woman had just bitten the hell out of me and I was probably going to be bleeding soon.

I kept an eye on Gloria as she exited the car, pulling down her skirt as she slid out, still giving me a saucy look.

"I thought you'd be into it," she said innocently. "We could always go back to my place and try it again. Or a motel and we can really get loud. No biting this time."

My stupid and possibly traitorous penis twitched at the thought and I made a note to shoot it for attempted mutiny. There was no way I was going anywhere with Gloria. It might not be my neck she was biting next time.

"Sounds great, but let's pretend that we did and call it a night," I said, still wary.

You're probably wondering at this point if Gloria is a vampire, so let's just lay that to rest right now. No, Gloria is not a vampire, and I wasn't about to turn into a vampire just because she bit me. Hell, the only thing I was going to turn into at this point was a more sober version of me since Gloria had never bought me that replacement drink.

Gloria reached out quickly, faster than a snake, and tucked something into the front of my pants before I could step away.

"Something to remember me by, lover." She blew me a kiss and sashayed away with significant extra sway in her hips, no doubt for my benefit. I'm not ashamed to admit I watched her every step. Crazy as she was, that was one hell of an ass.

"Don't stick your dick in crazy," I whispered to myself, more of a reminder to not go chasing after her to take her up on her offer; after all the deal was already sealed.

I pulled out whatever it was she had stuffed into my pants. Was I surprised it was her panties? Hell no. I almost smelled them, but instead, I wadded them up and pressed them against my fresh bite wound, the lace and tiny amounts of silk a reminder of just how the night had gone.

I trudged back to the bar, swearing at my bad luck.

***

I have no clue where we got this idea that a vampire bite would turn the victim into a vampire. Of course I'm going to blame the movies again since they get so much of it wrong, but it's also where a little common sense could do us all some good. If you stopped to think about it, how much sense would it make if your food came back to compete with you for the rest of the food out there? Pretty soon every steak you bit into would be stealing that nice juicy pork chop off your plate, just because you happened to bite it. The steak I mean, not the pork chop. I know it's a ridiculous image, but go with me here, okay? That sentient steak is just as ridiculous as the idea that a vampire bite will turn you into a vampire. I mean, it's not rabies. It's you *literally turning into an entirely new creature who just looks human*. I don't even know what the hell a vampire really is, but I can tell you, it's going to take more than being bitten by one of us, to *make* you into one of us.

Anyway, the food chain doesn't work like that.

If vampires used people as a source of nourishment like the stories all say, it would work out differently. What would happen is we people would be meat. Just meat. It's as simple as that. We'd be cattle who happen to walk and talk and cuss and kill stuff, but cattle nonetheless. Our self-awareness doesn't count for shit when we are what's for dinner.

Somebody did a calculation recently that showed exactly what would happen if every person bitten by a vampire turned into a vampire. Apparently it would spread like a disease and in about a month, there would be no one left to feed on. Everybody would be a starving vampire just imagining how tasty everyone else would be. Pretty much we would be back to where we had been before, all alike, one race looking for ways to not eat each other because *that's just gross*. Imagine that.

***

My usual crew of friends were out front somewhere. We had decided some time ago that this was going to be *our bar* but that had been when I wasn't so broke all of the time. For a moment, I considered trying to get one of them to buy me a beer. After doing a quick calculation and realizing that there was nobody there who I didn't owe money to, I shot down that idea and tried not to be too depressed about it. Damn, it sucked being broke.

So there I was, standing in the middle of the bar, Gloria's formerly white panties pressed against my bloody neck. I still smelled of sex and was completely sober. I still hadn't washed my hands and the smell of Gloria's sex clung to them. The last thing I expected was for some chick to be whispering in my ear.

"Why's there blood on your neck?"

That voice perked my mood up immediately. It belonged to the one person among my bar friends who I did not owe money to. You could not imagine the grin on my face when I turned around with a big one-armed hug for--

"Louise! Where the heck have you been?"

"Dude, you're seriously bleeding all over the place here. You have got to get a bandage on that."

Louise, the tall, dark-haired Castilian girl with the striking pale blue eyes and the not-taking-shit-from-you attitude was not about to take any shit from me.

"It's nothing, really--"

"Is that from a person? Dude! Are those panties?"

"Well—"

I swear she was going to hit me. She rolled her eyes at me instead and shook her head. Damn, it was good to see her.

"Jesus Bob, you have to get a tetanus shot. You don't mess around with bites like that."

"Serious? You're not even going to ask about the panties?"

"Yes seriously! Come on man, we have to get you to a doctor or something. And I really don't want to know about the panties."

"Does this mean you won't buy me a drink?"

She dragged me out of there, me faintly protesting all the way, drowned out by Louise filling me in on facts about bites and blood loss that I didn't need to know at the time. She was taking me to a doctor friend of hers who happened to live just around the corner. He would patch me up and get me disinfected. Only then would Louise come back to the bar with me and buy me all the drinks my heart desired. I made her say it so it *had to be true*. We both agreed that going to the emergency room was just going to suck even with her admitting privileges as a doctor herself.

So we walked the four short blocks to this guy's house, Louise on the phone part of the way, those huge retro-stylish sunglasses of hers on her face.

"Did you know that even though a bite from a person may not seem dangerous, it's anything but not-dangerous? You've got a huge amount of bacteria in your mouth so if you happen to bite someone, the risk of infection is extremely high. Your joints could get infected from even the smallest bite, and that's not even the worst of it. Blood borne diseases like Hepatitis-B and syphilis can be spread through bite wounds."

It was amazing listening to Louise spout off medical facts.

"You serious?"

"Deadly serious. I see lots of bite wounds. I know a lot about them."

For all of you paying attention, you just scored a point in a little game I like to call: "Spot the Vampire".

Surprise!

***

Dammit.

I was going to go on and tell you about how I became a vampire, but I'm beginning to realize that's *not the important thing here.* People already have this fucked up idea it's this great romantic thing, and God knows there have been a whole lot of stories written about becoming a vampire. I look at those stories and then look at my own account and it's just embarrassing.

I promise I'll get around to it. *Eventually.* But it's kind of not the point of this story.

The important thing here is that life as a vampire changes your entire perspective, but not like how you would assume. Even after you've put your assumptions aside, you realize the stories gloss over so much fine detail essential to everyday living. High adventure and save-the-world scenarios don't happen to all of us you see. For some of us, it's the day-to-day stuff that gets us.

They don't tell you the whole truth because it's just not sexy.

They don't tell you that when you become a vampire, you still have to hold down a job.

***

"You mean you actually have a job? What the fuck does a vampire even need a job for?"

I got this question on yet another night from this girl I had met in a bar. There's a whole theme going on here with me, bars, and girls with slightly more open attitudes about casual sex, so yes, I was in another bar, but this time slightly less broke than usual. This was about three months after I had become a vampire and I was hanging out at one of the bars my old friends would never ever go to. This girl had walked right up to me like she knew me and had said "I like your eyes," like it was nothing. She was utterly fearless and that was charming in itself. The fact that she was cute and a redhead also helped. I love redheads: they're my kryptonite.

"Oh, I got them when I became a vampire," I had said before realizing I was going to.

"Cool," she had said and that was that. "I'm Becky." We became instant friends in the way that strangers who don't want to fuck each other become friends. It was actually what I needed at the time since I was in one of my dark moods, and she had actually made me smile. We ended up sharing a joint while we walked to the next bar and it was cool to be honest with someone for a change. She and I would part ways at the end of the night and we would never see each other again, but for a while, at that moment, we had a connection and we were the best of friends.

"Well, I still gotta pay rent don't I?" I asked, but from the look on her face, I could tell she wasn't buying it. "Were you actually thinking that I lived in a graveyard somewhere, sleeping in a coffin and shit?"

"Well yeah. You're a vampire. That's what vampires do." Becky sounded a little let down by my admission.

"Sorry to disappoint?"

"You're really not what I expected a vampire to be like."

"I get that a lot."

"You tell a lot of people that you're a vampire?"

"Nah, only you. It's the other vampires who give me attitude. Man, the stories I could tell you."

To be honest, I get the "graveyard" question more often than not and people don't even think about the complications and total creep factor of hanging around graveyards. You probably think that's where vampires are supposed to live and I can't blame you. But can you imagine having the stench of death hanging on you? Ever spent a night in a graveyard? Believe me, there's a bit of a stench going on with all the decomposing bodies. And where would you even keep your clothes? This is where the whole smelling like a grave comes in, because clothes pick up whatever is in the surroundings and you're going to stink worse than a smoker. No thanks!

It's amazing what we've all been trained to think about how vampires live.

I live in the same place that I did before I got turned and I still have the same shitty job. Do I have a social insurance number? Check! I still paid my bills late, and when tax time rolled around, guess which guy was trying to find a way to not pay them on account of being a vampire, only to find out there is no vampire exemption clause anywhere. And I still hide from the occasional creditor by telling them that I'm dead. I'm still in the system, just another ordinary citizen, making his way through life, another face in the crowd.

"What about flying? Tell me there's at least flying," Becky pleaded.

"Sorry no. That's a movie plot device to keep things moving forward. I still take the bus which of course takes for-fucking-ever, and then on rainy nights, I drive my old piece of shit car.

And it's the same old piece of shit car I had before."

"Next, you'll be telling me there's no Easter Bunny or Santa Claus," Becky had pouted and passed the joint.

I inhaled deeply and passed the joint back to her, considering telling her that drugs no longer had any lasting effect on me, but then decided I didn't want to completely ruin her idea of vampires.

I could have told her what an elitist bunch of pricks vampires are. The old ones are the worst because they're the richest. They've had time to accumulate wealth, you see, and they consider it a prerequisite that to be worthy enough to be a vampire, first you had to be rich. Trust-fund kids are the best candidates for this, and the fact that so many of them are already rich assholes pre-qualifies them to be rich vampire assholes.

They say it's for their own protection and I see their point. It's expensive to be a vampire because you now have to actually plan for the future, get those investment portfolios rolling because it's no longer your grand kids you have to worry about leaving something for; it's yourself.

It's no wonder so many vampires are ecologists. If you don't understand this, then you're a fucking idiot and you ruined the earth. If you get it, please continue.

"You aren't just fucking with me are you?"

"I could be, but I think you can smell a bullshitter."

"Now you got me thinking," Becky said after a moment. "I was imagining vampires swanning about the damn place being all broody and shit and coming out at night to prey on people for blood…"

"Day in and day out. Think about it for a while, just think about doing that all damn day. Sounds incredibly boring right?"

"It sounds like the lifestyles of the rich and the bored." Becky agreed. "I never thought of it that way."

"You never thought of it at all. Don't worry: nobody thinks about it unless they're living it."

Not convinced? Fine: you decide not do the same thing that I did and not keep your job. You go off and have adventures, maybe even travel someplace exotic (or not, entirely up to you), or do something fun. That is assuming you have money saved. You do have a big savings account right? No? Then you're pretty much fucked and you're going to be bored pretty quickly… at least, until your landlord comes to kick you out for not paying the rent. Have you ever thought what you'd be doing if you didn't have a job to go to? Most people would just end up sleeping, overdosing on Netflix or porn and masturbating too much. Nothing beats boredom like tossing one off in the afternoon and for many people, going to work is the only thing saving them from the fate of being a compulsive masturbator.

"So what do you do for a living?" Becky asked.

Now *that* was one hell of a question.

***

Look, I'd love to tell you that I had a dream job to die for, and up until four years ago, I would have not been lying. I had been particularly proud of landing a job at one of the city's best tech firms. It was the type of job I had always dreamed about all through college, the kind that came with an enormous salary with one of those cool employer matching savings plans Canadians call a Group TFSA and the Americans refer to as a 401K.

We were based in the downtown core with an easy walk from the subway, and just knowing that I worked in that cool, shiny building in the financial sector made encountering any of my old classmates from high school an absolute pleasure. I was the jackass who took a particular delight in being a total shit to anybody I used to hate. You see them more than you think, rushing to and from work, sometimes commuting with you and trying to catch your eye, or maybe they're serving your morning coffee with a wry smile that you know is partly embarrassment and mostly annoyance. Some of them you like seeing and may even strike up a conversation or maybe have drinks with them later, whatever, but odds are, the ones you like, you don't see as often. If nobody sees you at all, though, that's perfectly okay. Sometimes it's better to be a stranger among strangers.

You don't know what vindication feels like until after you've wiped the smug look off the face of one of those assholes.

Then the company crashed and burned and we got laid off in batches that eventually claimed me as one of the victims and you know what? The smug look was gone right off my face. I ended up being the one avoiding eye contact and trying to hide behind a newspaper or even staring extra hard at the poster on the subway that I had read at least a hundred times since the ride began but was better to look at than at the people around me. Even on a good day, making eye contact is hard and ends up being either creepy or just plain uncomfortable and there I was suddenly broke and apparently unemployable, and aware that I was veering towards creepy.

I freelanced for a while, trying to get a new job and managed to survive from month to month. I ended up in the shitty basement apartment that I'm still in, telling myself it was only temporary; after all, I needed to save some money, but temporary has a way of sticking around if you're not too careful or too proud to admit it. Commuting turned into a once a week thing and as much as I tried to paint a positive spin on it whenever I'd run into any old friends in really nice suits, I just missed all of it. The familiarity of the daily grind among fellow commuters gave a sense of purpose that you don't get stumbling from your bed and over to your desk where you spend the next two hours reading Cracked.com and catching up on other people's lives over Facebook. Social media became my means of pretending that I was social or relevant until days would go by and I'd realize I hadn't actually spoken to anyone in a long time.

"You could always move in with me," Claude had offered, and I had almost taken him up on it, but life with Claude always seemed to be wildly unpredictable. He was my best friend of twenty years and was always there when I needed him, but remember what I said about pride? Yeah, pride has a way of making you make stupid decisions.

So I didn't move in with Claude and I found some new friends and went with the flow for a while.

These days I work in the shadow of the building I used to work in. It's a seriously fucked up combination porn shop/ head shop open twenty-four hours for some reason.

"You're gonna work the night shift," the boss had told me in no uncertain terms. "You work six days with one day off. Sort it out with Sammy and Matty, I really don't care which day, so whatever. You get here by eight and you leave at four when Sammy or one of the others comes in to relieve you. Don't steal from me, don't tell stupid lies to my face and don't fuck with me or the business and everything will be cool. If you feel the need to get high, don't do it in the store, and don't keep it in the store. That's what the alley back there is for, got it?"

"I don't do drugs—"

That was the first lie and he knew it.

"That's what they all say, kid. I can spot a junkie a mile away. Just let me know we have an understanding and then shut the fuck up."

"I got it."

"Good. Pay is ten fifty an hour, take it or leave it, and you can start tomorrow."

I took the job. Working freelance is nice but I was always hustling for the next job and the clients took forever to pay. One of the universities I had taken on as a customer had insisted on paying me ninety-days net with no deposit, only expenses paid and I was seriously up shit creek at that point.

My first day at work, Sammy, who was 100% not a dude and instead 100% 5'2" Chinese girl with a take-no-shit-at-least-not-from-you attitude, slapped the mop handle into my hand and pointed to the back of the store where the viewing booths were.

"Booths one and three need a little bit of love. You're going to need some gloves, which you'll find behind the counter."

"Wow, I thought we'd at least start with names first. Hi, I'm Bob."

"I'm Sammy. This is the bucket. You and it are going to be the best of friends."

"What about you and me?"

"Not fucking likely. Talk to me after you clean up booths one and three and then we'll see how much I don't not hate you, whaddaya say?"

The positive side of working in a porn shop is that porn

gets old really, really fast. You just lose your appetite for it after a while and almost nothing fazes you anymore, short of actual real-life violence. The downside is you get some real creeps from time to time and they make creative use of our viewing booths, which are little closed off booths in the back of the store with some seriously high-quality headphones attached. Yes, the Boss was a cheapass but apparently he was also an audiophile. Besides, the expensive headphones cancelled out even the loudest moans from the videos. When I first saw the booths my initial thought was *why is everything covered in plastic?* My first day at work, I discovered exactly *why* everything in those booths was encased in plastic of some kind.

I could have walked away and never looked back. Sammy was already back at the counter, reading a ratty, dog-eared Sandman trade paperback over which I was sure we would eventually geek-out about together. She likely wouldn't have given a shit if I stayed or if I allowed pride to have its way with me and walk me right out the door, and she would have probably applauded at my cowardice, but at that moment I had a sobering thought that realigned reality for me.

How the hell does any Asian girl even manage to survive more than a day in a porn shop without constant harassment and/or killing any of her fucked-up customers? I could get into the whole fetishization of Asian girls in porn and how creepy some of the customers can get about it, but then I'd be telling you a completely different story. Let's just say it's really bad and that some of you guys really need to knock it off. My point is that Sammy had found a way to survive and even thrive and that says more about her than you think you know.

"You got a spray bottle of bleach?" I asked instead, and Sammy grinned and tossed the bottle to me across the store. I fumbled the catch, but then shook my head and got to work.

"Just don't let any get on you and you'll be fine," Sammy said, and I could hear the smile in her voice. "And I'm not talking about the bleach either!" It seemed that I had gained some mark of respect in her book just for sticking around.

"Well it can't get any worse than this, right?"

"Wait until Tuesday. You're going to hate Tuesdays."

So I Might Be a Vampire

She was right: *I fucking hate Tuesdays.*
No I don't want to talk about it. Fuck Tuesdays. Seriously.

***

So yeah, that's the job I had when I became a vampire. I was still working at the store and it was easily one of the best jobs I could have had for my particular needs. Apart from missing a few days, there was literally no massive disruption to my work life, since I was already working nights and sleeping for most of the day. I sometimes think about what a clusterfuck it would have been if I suddenly had to find a job that allowed me to come to work after dark. Then I promptly realized there was a good number of them already out there. There was an entire sub-population that lived their lives after dark, all regular Joes, not a monster in the bunch.

Well, no monsters, except for me.

Chapter 3
TRUE LOVE HURTS

W hat about the love life?" I hear you asking. After all, vampires are known for their powers of seduction and their way with the young ladies, so surely there's got to be some kind of truth to that legend, right? The answer is a little more complicated than that. Don't get me wrong, I've had an awesome streak since becoming a vampire to the point where I can walk into almost any bar in the city and be confident that I'll be leaving with some gorgeous (and preferably *redheaded*) young lady in a very short time. But that's not love. Hell it's not even lust when you get down to it, just me enjoying the perks of finally getting over a six month absence of any sex whatsoever after Jaime had dumped my stupid ass.

I'm sure some of the women I slept with might have wanted to do the whole romance thing, but I never stuck around to find out. I'm a bit of a sucker for true love you see, believe it or not, and I was still in love with my ex-girlfriend.

***

So imagine you're me, and you're finally settling into the groove of your new life as a vampire. It's been two months since you first got turned and you've been through quite a few memorable (not in a good way) experiences that you have no interest in repeating, but if you were a better person, would have been some defining moment in your life. Instead, you're stuck being me, the guy who takes valuable life lessons as an excuse to try the same thing again but only harder, convinced this time it will be different.

That idiot up there, the one I just described? That's the same idiot who got in line at the supermarket behind a woman who looked remarkably exactly like how his ex-girlfriend Jaime used to look. She even had the same nice ass, the same tattoos on her arm and shoulder and yes: the same pissed off expression that became the default the longer we were together and the more I insisted on fucking up her life.

Oh holy shitballs: *it actually was Jaime.*

I should have known that mane of curly hair couldn't ever belong to anyone else. The beautifully striking face that was made more striking by the intense light brown eyes under those bushy eyebrows that were so naturally arched. When she smiled, those eyes shone with possibility and friendliness, but they weren't smiling at me now, reflecting only dull, flat anger.

"Jaime…" I said, and was I more than just a little happy to see her? You bet your ass I was.

You don't see the love of your life and feel nothing, even if she had decided that there was absolutely no fucking way that there was going to be a "we" anymore. Not even if the last time you had been face-to-face she had given you reason enough to hate her and for a while you had, but she was your true love so of course that couldn't last forever.

See? Told you I was a sucker for true love.

Of course, the memory of the restraining order she had filed against me should have wiped the smile off my face, but to be fair, this was the supermarket in my neighborhood. The bus dropped me right in front, and I only had to walk four blocks to my shitty basement apartment, so I counted this supermarket as being mine and not off limits. Jaime lived on the other side of town, so what the hell?

Restraining order and all, I should not have been surprised when Jaime wasn't that happy to see me.

"What the fuck Bob? Are you stalking me again?"

I threw up my hands in innocence. Even the cashier was giving me the stink-eye and was looking around for the non-existent security guard. My main thing was not to upset Jaime anymore than I had to. I should have known it was her. I could pick her out of a crowd at 100 meters, so why the hell hadn't I listened to myself when I saw her?

Maybe it was because I had not ever expected to see her here and was just content to daydream that it might actually be her. I'd already run into a couple of her doppelgängers, all sharing her same body type, 5'8", long legs, lean muscle, small but womanly boobs. I saw her on the train late one night, but her arms were devoid of tattoos, and the girl was with a couple of snooty looking girls Jaime would never be seen dead hanging out with; the second time had been at the airport and although a dead ringer for Jaime, the girl had been Chinese. So it wouldn't have surprised me to be running into yet another doppelgänger who would wonder why I was smiling at them so much.

Yeah… this time it was the real deal.

"I swear this is nothing like last time. This is pure coincidence! This time." I said, but Jaime still looked doubtful. "Hi?" I tried to not look threatening at all.

I looked around the supermarket, not exactly the most high-end of places, just a regular grocery store that sold all of the basic things I needed at just the right prices. I didn't even like the place most of the time but it was open 24 hours just like I needed and the cashiers weren't completely incompetent.

"I live right down the road from here. This is my neighborhood, my supermarket," I pleaded, trying to radiate innocence, "and in my defense, I didn't even see you there. Otherwise, I would have waited until you were gone. Really."

I looked at the cashier for backup, but I didn't recognize this one. Usually, there was a Pakistani girl working nights. Priya or something like that.

Jaime was hesitant, but she nodded.

"Right. Claude told me you had moved. I guess I should have asked where to so I could avoid you better."

I was getting the message loud and clear. Time to take my eggs and go hide in an aisle somewhere. I turned to go but—

A tired woman in a hijab had wheeled into the line behind me. She had already started unpacking her huge cart of groceries onto the conveyor belt and was blocking the narrow lane. Three small boys, aged maybe four to eight buzzed around her in the way that children do, with an almost complete disregard for anyone around themselves, caught up in their worlds of imagination and Ritalin overdoses. I shuffled uncomfortably, my avenue for a quick retreat now cut off.

"Don't worry about it Bob," Jaime said grudgingly. "You're right. Let's just ignore each other until I can get the hell outta here, okay? Okay."

I love how she didn't even wait for an answer.

A bro-dude, a total Chad if there was ever one, leaned over from next to Jaime to look at me.

"Is this the guy you were talking about? The shitty ex-boyfriend?"

"*Who the fuck are you?*" I immediately wanted to know. Then to Jaime. "*Who the fuck is that?*"

"None of your business Bob!" Jaime snapped. She focused her attention on the cashier, who was having way too much trouble getting a price on the box in her hands. "Is there a problem? We can just leave it. Really."

I suddenly saw what the cashier was holding in her hands, and before I knew it, my idiot mouth had gone down to the store, bought a backhoe and had started digging my grave.

"Hey! Those are my brand of condoms!"

Jaime slammed her hands down and stared straight ahead, never looking at me once.

"They are *a brand* of condom Bob. You don't *get to claim* a brand as your own, not now, not ever, and *especially not these.*"

Have you ever noticed how some people can say everything they want to say with all of the words they're not actually saying? With people you've been close to, you learn to read the signs, the language of those unspoken words. If you don't, then those words eventually get spoken, yelled, even, and it's all downhill from there since nobody knows how to listen when someone is screaming at them. But some words were never meant to be spoken, and you will do your best to avoid them when you see them bubbling under the surface, just dying to break through. I could see Jaime biting the words back and swallowing them. They were poison to her, and she swallowed them anyway even though the look she gave me spoke of how she was envisioning my brutal murder and was actively avoiding killing me. Hell, she could even use the hole I'd just so conveniently dug for myself to stash my body.

I knew that look, and I knew to back the fuck off. I wanted to reach out to this beautiful woman who had once loved me and ask her what I had done to make her hate me so much. I knew what I had done that had caused the split and I hated myself for it, but I had never expected to see such burning hatred for me. Seeing that look on her face made me want to curl up in a ball and hide and beat myself up for having caused that much pain.

Goddammit. Talking about Jaime is always difficult, especially the way it is now, so I'm just going to skip this part if it's all the same to you, okay? Great!

So what have we established so far? Oh yes: my ex-girlfriend hates my fucking guts and she's absolutely right to. I deserve all the hate, I freely admit it, but I still love her whether she wants my love or not. Love isn't something you just turn off when it's no longer convenient. You can love someone deeply and even after years apart, those feelings will still be there as strong as anything.

The cashier wasn't making things any better. She looked hesitantly from me to Jaime. "I'm going to have to do a price check—"

Jaime had reached her limit.

"Never mind. Come on Chad, we're leaving—"

I really couldn't help myself. It was always a severe case of foot-in-mouth disease with me when it came to Jaime.

"This douche-canoe's actual name is Chad? *Holy shit!*"

"Wait a sec babe, you can't just let him win—"

"MOVE IT CHAD!" Jaime yelled and shoved her way past the shocked Chad, who had seriously underestimated the dangers of getting in the way of my ex-girlfriend. That usually only happened once, and after that, you were pretty much toast.

As much as it hurt me to see Jaime storm away like that just because of my proximity… and my stupid comments, there was a little thrill of vindication that Chad the douche-canoe was not going to be sticking his dick into my ex-girlfriend anytime soon. Especially not using my brand of condoms.

I looked back to Chad to either give him a smug look that would tell him exactly what I was thinking, or to give him a shrug that said "women, right?", but he didn't give me a chance to decide to be a dick to him.

"You *fucker!*" Chad said and damn he was ready for a fight.

I whipped off my sunglasses and glared at him, ready to take him on. I was a vampire motherfucker! That had to count for something, right?

"*You should just walk away* Chad!" I growled.

Chad blinked rapidly, and all of the fight went out of him. He looked at me, confused and shook his head. "You're not worth it man. I'm-I'm just going to walk away now."

What the actual fuck was that?

I stood there utterly confused and watched Chad exit, my heart still hammering in my chest as the adrenaline surged through my body, wanting to be put to use, dying to *do* something. I shuddered as I felt the heat on my top lip, the heat of the adrenaline having nowhere to go and it still wanted me to lash out, break something or someone, so it was letting me smell it, that wavering heat as it dissipated and reminded me of how good it would feel to just let it out. I ignored it and tried to concentrate on breathing and not rushing after Chad to rip his head from his shoulders like it suddenly felt like I could before I had somehow convinced him

(scared him)

or Jedi-mind-tricked him into walking the fuck away.

I looked around, self-conscious now at the way the cashier looked terrified as she rang in my eggs, making more mistakes than she should have; the three boys were now huddled behind their mother, terrified that something they couldn't recognize was in their midst and it might well be a monster. All I could think as I paid for my eggs and exited the store was that I was glad Jaime hadn't seen that display of whatever the hell that was.

***

I admit it. I wanted to punch someone.

Jaime's jeep blew past me in the parking lot, and I don't think she saw me, but she was definitely driving angry.

But at least she was driving alone.

I saw Chad aggressively smoking next to a matte black Dodge Charger and had a momentary thrill that I had completely cock-blocked that douchebag. From the way he was angrily tapping at his phone, almost like he wanted to break it, he was probably posting something nasty about Jaime online, possibly involving the word "slut" several times. It's standard operating procedure for a douche-bro like Chad.

I considered going over and confronting him, but that was the punchy side of me talking, looking for an excuse to be unleashed.

God I really wanted to punch someone named Chad.

So I did the sensible thing and walked the hell away because my life isn't a movie full of epic fist fights and a questionable lack of assault charges, and as angry as I was, I still don't like the thought of hurting people, whether they deserved it or not.

Not even if their name was Chad.

***

Claude gave me a look as I slid into the booth. I just gave him a fake smile, and a thumbs up in response to his unasked question. Then and only then did I slump down into my seat and banged my head gently but firmly on the top of the table.

"You saw Jaime today?"

"I saw Jaime today," I confirmed. "Wait. How do you know that? Did she call you?"

"Yeah, she was a little pissed. A lot pissed actually."

"Why doesn't she love me anymore Claude?"

"Three possibilities, all of them being that you're a complete asshat," he said and took a big drink of his coffee. I glared at him.

"You're so not helping."

Claude was my best friend for over twenty years. We had met at school after I noticed him with a copy of Stephen King's Christine. Since I had only recently become a Stephen King fan and had started trying to collect every book he had written, I was more than happy to find a fellow aficionado and possible twisted mind. We had become fast friends with Stephen King as a shared interest and that had been that. Making friends as kids is a hell of a lot less complicated than making friends as adults. Less layers of complications when you're a kid. Claude had been through the shit with me and we'd always been each other's moral center and sanity control.

That being said, Claude had been the first person I had called when I had become a vampire.

To tell you the truth, Claude is the one who should have been the vampire.

He's the one people would automatically look at if you told them that one of us was a vampire, and no matter how much proof I gave them, they would still want to believe that it was Claude who was the vampire. I could rip their throats out with my teeth, and they would still be looking at Claude expectantly. Can't say I really blame them. I'd been always jealous of his cleft chin and chiseled good looks, although I'm good-looking in my own way. What Claude had was a more classic and rugged looking face, the kind of face that should be on magazine covers. These days he generally preferred to wear tailored suits that made him look more like a banker or broker than anything else, and even when he refused to wear a tie he still looked like the most respectable man in the room.

Considering that Claude was a crook, this was probably for the best.

A gentleman thief by definition, he did not entirely steal to get rich, nor did he steal from poor people or where someone might get hurt. He had very specific rules that he followed and very specific jobs that he hired himself out for. If Claude showed up with a new car, I always had to assume that it was stolen and the owner was not about to discover this fact for a very long time. I didn't even know if Claude actually owned the condo where he lived or if it belonged to somebody else like some banker in Hong Kong who used the condo once a year. Claude had access to certain circles you see, and he knew the right people, but even more importantly, he fit right in, and nobody ever questioned him. It was a big departure from the early days of sourcing cheap sunglasses or Walkman cassette players or whatever it was people wanted to get their hands on.

He had been there to drink with me and keep an eye on me after my cataclysmic meltdown when Jaime had dumped my stupid ass. He'd bailed me out of jail after that one disastrous night and was generally considered the "responsible one" when people thought about us. I was the sidekick, and I had no problems with that.

Claude raised his eyebrow at me now and flicked a toothpick at me.

"You were a dick to her—"

"I was a dick to Chad—"

He flicked another toothpick, and it caught me right between the eyes.

"She's dating a guy called Chad? Gross."

"I don't think it was any actual dating. They were buying condoms—"

"Doesn't matter what they were buying. Restraining orders are very specific." Claude thought for a second, then, "Seriously, his name was Chad?"

"I didn't know it was her. Besides, it's my supermarket." I was trying not to sound whiny and failing badly.

"You're right, and she apologized for that. She won't be filing any charges, but she's still pretty upset."

"I'm pretty upset. *She's fucking a guy named Chad.* Did I ruin her that much?"

Claude winced. "Sure sounds like it. Tell me he didn't look like a total dude-bro at least—"

I shook my head, and Claude grimaced, disappointed in Jaime's taste.

"Well, no wonder you were rude."

"Does this mean you're back on my side?"

"Dude, I'm *always* on your side. Why do you think I'm the one chewing you out?" Claude signaled the waitress. "So how's the vampiring going?"

"Vampiring is hard," I said and then thought it for a second. "You know, that would actually look awesome on a t-shirt…"

"You never got me those pamphlets you promised me. You

were supposed to do some research, remember? Get a little better? Find yourself a mentor…"

"I got busy. Besides, I don't even remember half of the people I met. People don't like it when you don't remember their names or their faces, and I don't remember anybody. That's how out of it I was when I was there. Nobody really wants to talk to me anymore dude. I've been rejected by vampire society. They don't love me either."

"Your mom loves you—"

"She has to."

"I love you—"

"Ew dude, ew."

"And I'm sure Sammy has some feels deep within that rotten black pirate heart of hers."

"She tolerates me, so I guess that counts. But I want *Jaime* to love me."

Claude looked disappointed. "Dude, what is the one thing I always tell you?"

"Never run from the scene of a crime since the cops always chase after a running man?" I asked, but Claude shook his head "no."

"Don't buy any cars with electronic locks since they're easier to steal?"

No.

"Put down the toilet seat, I was not raised in a barn?"

Another "no".

The waitress came over, and I turned my head to look at her. "Coffee, and a pot of hot water, please. Waffles, scrambled eggs —no pepper— and my one true love please."

"Sorry sweetie, we're fresh out of true love," the waitress said. Her name tag proclaimed that she was named MOLLY, and I wondered if I'd ever met any Mollys before. "Can I get you some freshly squeezed orange juice instead?"

I nodded and Molly gave me a tired smile. At least she didn't think I was an asshole. I think.

Claude waited until she was gone.

"So, if we're done talking about your love life--"

"You mean *lack* of love life," I interrupted.

"Whatever you choose to call it."

"I wasn't done talking about it yes," I complained.

"Well I am, so get suck it up Ginger," Claude said. "You gonna fill me in on the rest of your life or what?"

"Whatcha wanna know?"

"How's the recruiting for the club going? Anybody new showed up yet?"

That reminds me: did I tell you I started a support group for rejected vampires?

Chapter 4
VAMPIRES ARE PEOPLE TOO

I want you to imagine a packed line of beautiful people waiting to get into a big fancy nightclub. It's hugely popular, and everybody wants to get in. Do you see it? *Good.* Keep imagining that, but now, look *across the street from the club*, and you're going to see something that is a little bit different. See it? The one guy in the hoodie with the biggest sign he could find, the sign that says *"PRIVATE CLUBS SUCK"?* That guy is me. Or rather it *was* me a couple of months ago. In hindsight, it was possibly the oddest and loneliest protest in the history of protests, but dammit, it was my protest, so I'm actually proud of it.

I started the protest after I got kicked out of what everyone refers to as *HTDK*, but was officially known as the *Hall of the Drunken King*. While it might have once been clever, the name was a bit of a mouthful and hard as hell to market to the hip young crowd ready to spend cash. This was before I started the support group I was telling you about. Every week on my day off of work, I'd head down to the club and make a pain in the ass of myself.

Sammy and Claude both shared the opinion that it was one hell of a way to waste my day off, but since I only did it for about an hour just to make the point, I could easily justify it to myself. After all, I still had the rest of the night to work with, where I could make some pretense of being normal or whatever. For that one hour though, rubbing it in the face of the elite vampire pricks who attended the club that I was *still alive*, and there was nothing they could do about it, it was totally worth it.

It's my civic duty, really it is.

***

Claude came over one day while I was trying to make a new sign.

"I need a new slogan," I said as he entered the apartment. He gave it some thought and immediately grabbed the XBox controller from the couch. He had brought it over the week before but honestly, he played it more than I did, but at least it gave him the pretext to come over and keep an eye on me even if we both pretended that was clearly what he was not doing.

"Something obvious or sneakier, more subversive?" Claude asked.

"Subversive. I'm not looking to get my head ripped off by Harry for spilling any secrets."

Claude frowned at the mention of Harry's name. He didn't like Harry, but for completely different reasons than I had.

"How much can you really say on a sign anyway?" he asked. "You only have so much space after all."

"I once saw a dude who had all of the pages of Genesis from the bible on the front of one sign. He had to use really small lettering, but he made it all fit. Kinda had to squeeze to fit the last bit, but he got it in."

Claude turned his attention to his game and scoffed at me.

"Like people even read anymore these days." He turned back to me with an amused look. "I can't believe you're actually doing this."

"I'm making a stand for the little man: *me.*"

"What does Harry think of your little parlor trick?"

***

I could lie and say that Harry loved what I was doing, but I'm not that good of a liar. As a general rule, Harry hated everything that had to do with me.

"Bob, what the fuck do you think you're doing?"

Harry himself had come outside the first night I had shown up with my sign.

I had watched the human bouncers giving me the hairy eyeball from across the street, and there had been a lot of talking into their very discreet ear pieces, and lots of threatening looks thrown my way. Then a couple of the vampire bouncers had shown up, and the threatening looks had become promises of a sustained and brutal beating. I was beginning to rethink any life choices that had led me to think that this one man protest had ever been a good idea, when Harry emerged from the club.

He had stared at me for a long moment, and I had somehow managed to resist the urge to run away very quickly. I had suddenly developed the urge to find the nearest bathroom, but that was just my body trying to take over and give me an excuse to run away. To say I was shitting bricks is an understatement. I somehow did a very good job of not showing it.

Harry had asked his question almost conversationally as if he already knew the answer but was still considering beating it out of me anyway. I tried to look as unpunchable as possible.

"I'm just standing here, minding my own business," I said as innocently as I could.

"You're standing here *with a sign*," Harry pointed out helpfully.

"Oh, *this?* Damn, is that what *this* is? How did *that get there?*"

The sign that night had read "THIS CLUB SUCKS!"

"You're protesting the club," Harry said, and I had nodded.

"I'm protesting the club. You caught me."

"You think you're being clever with your little protest don't you?"

"But not *too* clever. I still remember the rules, and I definitely don't want to break any of those. I know how you are about rules." I conceded. I grinned my best hopeful grin. "You know, if you *let me back in*, I won't have anything to protest..."

"Not a chance. You pissed off a lot of people, and now you're pissing off *more* of them with this stunt."

"I'm pissing off a lot of people *just by living*."

"That goes without saying."

"You gonna shut me down?"

"You kidding? You're the best warning to some of these new kids about what might happen when they screw up."

"I could come in and give a speech, grab a drink or three..."

Harry was already walking away from me by that point.

"Stay on your side of the street Bob."

***

Claude just shook his head at me when I told him of my encounter.

"You're going to get yourself killed," he said.

"Since when has that ever stopped me? Besides, you'd never let me stay dead."

"Yeah, we really gotta talk about that. And by talk, I mean me yelling and you listening."

"Yell away. I'm ready. But can you really stay mad at this face?"

I made my most pathetic face.

"Oh, I can definitely stay mad at any face you give. Especially that one. But seriously dude: things have changed. We are so far out of the realm of normal that it's not funny. You're really going to get yourself killed if you're not careful."

"Dude, I'm a vampire. I don't stay dead."

"Yeah, but what happens if it's another vampire *doing the killing*? A vampire like Harry?"

"Let's burn that bridge when we're on it," I said, with a grin that didn't completely fool Claude or even myself.

***

The sign we eventually came up with was subtle.

"'Real Bloodsuckers Inside'?" This was a leggy brunette who had wandered over from the line. She seemed genuinely concerned that someone was outside with a sign. "What is that even supposed to mean?"

"REAL BLOODSUCKERS INSIDE!" was printed in bold red lettering on the front of the sign. It was as subversive and as juvenile as possible, and it was perfect. Unfortunately, it may have been a little too perfect and on the nose.

I jerked a finger at the sign. "Says exactly what I mean,"

I said smugly, and put my fingers to my lips. "Shh! I'm not allowed to say more than that, but beware and *heed my warning!*"

"You're weird," the girl said and gave me an odd look. She hurried back across the street to join her friends in the long line of people who were just dying to get into the club. They were more like lambs to the slaughter than they would have liked. The slaughter was of course metaphorical.

In a large city, the murder of a single person, or the disappearance of a lot of well-off white kids would raise a huge stink. So while they may have been marching into the largest and most well-funded lair of vampires in the city, nobody was getting killed, everybody was just having fun, and if they had a hazy recollection of just how the night had gone, you could always blame it on the booze and the drugs. HTDK was known for some killer parties, and the less you can remember, then the more fun was had, right?

Damn skippy.

About ten mintes later there had been a bit of a murmur in the crowd as if someone famous had shown up. If you've ever been to one of the bigger film festivals like we have every year with the Toronto International Film Festival, then you get familiar with that kind of murmur. It's different in tone and intensity and makes you want to turn and see who it is, if only to get a quick selfie as that famous person sprints by behind you.

This time it wasn't anybody really famous, at least that I knew of. It was a group of rich vampire dude-bros, and they were as cocky as hell, and they were looking for a fight. Specifically, they were looking for a fight with *me*.

There were about five of them, all skinny, pale and white in that classic vampire fashion as if they were auditioning to be the next great literary vampire. The crowd may have just seen some of the richest and most fashionable young adults in the city, famous simply for being young, rich and stupid, but I could tell that they were vampires. The eyes were a dead giveaway of course, but it was more in the way they walked, that swagger that said that they owned the city and more than anything, that they owned you.

Four of the five broke off from the group and headed across the street towards me. I just watched with that deer caught in the headlights look on my face, trying hard not to react. Harry had practically given me permission to be here, so this couldn't really be happening, *right?* Just in case, I quickly ran through the list of things I could have done that would have pissed off Harry, then when I realized that would take too long, I instead tried to figure out if someone had seen me while I was doing the thing that I should not have been doing.

Not that I'm admitting to anything of course...

"Hey Bob, you suck!" One of the frat boys hissed as he and his four buddies circled around me.

"Why don't you kill yourself you retard?" Another one hissed.

"Everybody hates you," the one with too much hair-gel whispered, and he had a definite kind of Lester-the-Molester look to him.

"Shouldn't you kids be in school," I responded. "Where are your hall passes?"

I noticed a couple of people in the line recording on their cell phones and shook my head. Kids in high school had better insults than these guys, and I had been out of high school for a very long time. They should have gone straight to emasculating me instead. So much more effective at any age.

"Seriously Bob, nobody wants you here."

"Yeah man, you're way too poor. Just go the fuck home."

"You will never be one of us. *Ever.*"

I noticed the fifth guy who had held back across the street. He looked kind of familiar, classically handsome in a punchable kind of way. He had hair that could only be described as lustrous and *that* at least seemed kind of familiar. I just couldn't put a name to the face, as punchable as it looked. The way he was staring a hole through me, with that level of smirk said that *he* definitely knew *me* and that I had *definitely* pissed him off.

Something about the way nobody had actually punched me yet suddenly clicked home and I grinned at the morons circling me, playing the intimidation game to the best of their limited abilities. Apparently, a grin was the last thing they had expected, and I was prepared for one of them to finally punch me, if it wasn't for one thing.

"You guys can't actually touch me, can you?"

They faltered and looked uncertainly at each other. Lester-the-Molester rallied.

"Oh, we can do more than touch you. In fact, we're going to *fuck you up*—"

"Then hit me!"

Lester-the-Molester raised his fist and lunged at me—

I'd like to say I didn't flinch, but I'd be a goddamn liar. Of course I flinched. Even though I knew he was only faking me out and that his fist would stop inches from my face, there was still the *reality of a fucking fist flying through the air heading directly for my nose*, and my body knew it was going to hurt. It's hard telling the body not to react, that it's all a big ruse when the body knows from past experience what kind of pain and indignities I've invited. So of course I flinched; you would have flinched too.

I grinned through my still unbroken teeth.

"Tell my friend across the street that this is all pointless. None of you can touch me, and you still don't scare me."

We both turned to look at the dude with the punchable face *(what the hell was his name anyway?)*, and he just glared at me even more. I turned back to Lester-the-Molester.

"Can you at least tell me what his name is? I'm thinking Lawrence? *Adolphus? Fuck-face?*"

Lester-the-Molester never answered me. He just flipped the bird, and then he and the other three vampires walked away from me, keeping up their bravado as if they had succeeded in showing me who was boss, but I could see their heart wasn't in it. Lester-the-Molester whispered something to my nameless nemesis, and I waved cheerily when he glared directly at me.

If I had thought he had been giving me the death glare before, I was definitely wrong. He gave me two middle fingers and there was some incoherent swearing in what might have been Italian, as he and his vampire crew made their way back to the club. With all of the noise on the street, it was kind of hard to hear, but I *think* it was mainly swearing.

A brunette who looked *almost exactly* like a popular movie

star except for her pale blue vampire eyes, was watching me from inside her Maserati, which had pulled up in front of the club at some point in the last few minutes.

"I like your sign," she said. "Way to stick it to the man. Ironic though since you're one of us."

Normally she would have had to yell, but she was a vampire, and she knew that I was a vampire as well, so she actually spoke normally, confident that I could hear exactly what she was saying.

"They didn't seem to appreciate it," I said, also not bothering to yell. This plays both ways, right? I could already feel the adrenaline ebbing away from me, my hands shaking and my stomach muscles clenching and unclenching, glad they hadn't been punched.

"Do you even know their names?" the movie-star vampire asked and I thought deeply.

"To tell you the truth, I can't even remember where I'm supposed to know these guys from but whatcha gonna do, right?"

"And yet they know exactly who you are." She winked at me. "Keep it real Bob."

"Wait, so you don't think I'm that bad?"

"I never said that. You're a *terrible vampire.* But is that such a bad thing?"

She left and no. I never saw her again because this isn't that kind of story where Bob goes off and dates some glamorous vampire, and all of the stuff you and I both wish would happen.

No, this is the *other* kind of story.

I continued my protest that night, but the encounter with those vampires had left me more shaken that I would like to admit.

Later that night, I chucked the sign into an open dumpster in an alley and just left it, wondering not for the first time if it was really worth it.

Oh, don't look at me like that, all sad and puppy-faced. It was not the first time I'd ever dumped a sign and had self-doubt about my purpose in life. It's kind of a weekly thing by this point.

But it was the first time I actually asked myself the serious question: Where were the other vampires out in the city who were just like me? And more importantly, *how the hell did I find them?*

Chapter 5
MISSED CONNECTIONS

I magine for a second that you were a vampire looking for a support group. Where would you look, and more specifically, what group would you be looking for? It's not like we vampires go around advertising what we are.

Trust me: *we do not advertise.*

If you happen to see someone boasting about how much they like blood and how they "welcome the darkness," and you notice that they dress in all black and are all gothy-looking and stuff, please for the love of all that is good, *avoid them like the plague.* They're idiots, *all of them.* They have no idea what they're talking about, and they just make us *real* vampires look bad. Those idiots go around and write bad poetry, all the while playing at the whole *romanticism* of it all. They don't know the whole truth behind real vampires, and most of them wouldn't have ever been *allowed* to join except as the occasional blood-donor.

The first group I checked out held meetings in the basement of some guy's house and everybody turned out to be just a bunch of kids who wore lots of black and way too much mascara. I was the first one there even though it was at 10 PM and by the time the host's very accommodating and *extremely flirty* mother had pointed me downstairs with the statement that "Leucetios will be down in just a second dear," I knew that it was a complete bust.

Any optimism I might have had was murdered in its sleep when I saw the snacks table at the far end of the room. There was no way I was going near that table, especially with the smell of the jalapenos from the salsa hitting me that strongly, kinda like mustard gas. That told me everything I needed to know about if there were any vampires around.

The room itself was pretty bad. In its defense, it was a great looking finished basement, the kind that with a little renovation could be rented out as yet another shitty basement apartment just like the one I lived in. What 'Leucetios' or whatever the fuck his name was, had done with it was absolutely shameful. The main theme seemed to be lots of black and leather, with trimmings of red here and there. A Rocky Horror poster with the iconic red lips on black dominated the room as well as a ton of poorly framed posters of various vampire movies.

It smelled of ass, rampant masturbation, and desperate shameful sex.

And salsa picante, the type with too much vinegar in it, the same type that was threatening to burn the nerve endings out of my nose.

***

Claude had already stopped using his beloved Tabasco sauce whenever I was around, especially after that disastrous diner incident, but I don't think either of us caught the full implications of my new sensitivity to spicy foods. Sure Claude may have treated it like a peanut allergy, but it wasn't like there was a vampire Epi-Pen that we could break out in the case of accidental exposure.

Much like a peanut allergy though, you soon find that spicy food is everywhere you go, just waiting to kill the hell out of you.

You know that thing about garlic repelling vampires? Well, there is some truth to it, but you don't just hang a bunch of garlic bulbs around your neck and call it a day. True story: garlic is most effective when it's been sliced or chopped. The finer it's cut, the more potent it gets. In fact, it can be *downright obnoxious.*

There is some kind of scientific thing going on which I'm not even going to bother to Google, but it's all true. More of those potent chemicals are released into the air, and normal humans can smell that shit, so just imagine what it's like for a hypersensitive nose. Now that you're picturing that, expand your imagination beyond just garlic, and think about all of the spicy foods out there.

You getting the picture yet?

There are whole streets downtown that I have to completely avoid. ChinaTown, Koreatown and various Mexican restaurants are now completely off limits to me. Hell, I couldn't even go to some of the chain restaurants anymore if I wanted to.

There's a reason Claude and I always end up going to a diner. Breakfast food is simply the safest and most accessible food for me now.

Pick any diner in town, and you'll find at least one or two vampires if you know what you're looking for.

***

"Pretty cool, huh?"

I turned, my hand over my nose, and I was trying to breathe through my mouth so I wouldn't pass out or throw up, but damn I could still taste it. *Jalapeño peppers and minced garlic,* a subtle cloud of vampire misery.

Leucetios was dressed in leather pants with too many zippers, a black shirt with silver buttons, various leather wristbands and yes, he was wearing mascara around his blue, but definitely *still human*, eyes.

He finally noticed my distress and frowned.

"Hey, you okay?"

I gave him the thumbs up, even though tears were streaming from my eyes, and then stumbled up the stairs and out the front door, gasping for air.

There was a small group of young men and women in their early twenties outside the house, smoking a combination of clove cigarettes and pot. They were all dressed in black and watched me with amusement.

"Just an allergy to the salsa," I managed to breathe to Leucetios, who had followed me outside.

"You're allergic to the *salsa*?" Leucetios said. "Fucking lame."

One of the girls looked at me funny, and I glanced at her as she desperately tried to get Leucetios' attention.

"I've seen him before," she said breathlessly. "Down at HTDK. He's one of the inner circle."

"You sure? I don't know—" One of the others said and he had that look in his eye as if he was trying to picture me holding a sign and marching on the side of the road like a damn fool.

"Just look at his eyes, you moron," the girl said, her own eyes wide in wonder.

I got out of there quickly, those kids yelling increasingly moronic things after me, promising to be my sex slaves. This was from both guys and girls, and they were genuine as far as I could tell from their hastily yelled proclamations.

I hadn't counted on being recognized, especially by someone who was not a vampire, but what did I really expect anyway? It wasn't like I had been keeping a low profile, yet another reason Harry had kicked me out. Harry didn't like attention, and I had a way of attracting attention to myself even without a sign.

***

I tried out a couple other groups and meetings, working my way down the list over the next couple of weeks. Shorter nights and one day off a week really don't work so well for me; social time is insufficient, and on regular days it seemed all I was doing was sleeping, avoiding the sun and then getting to work late. Rinse and repeat until Thursday where I could get out to the next set of groups.

The meetings that were scheduled too close to sunset I completely ignored, and I tried to look for other warning signs, but I somehow ended up in a few weird situations.

One was a bondage group where the members fetishized drinking human blood and spent a lot of time talking about the romance of blood and other bullshit. Some of them even had done some expensive dentistry to have fangs fitted onto their teeth and talking to them was a chore since fangs give you an instant lisp, so the mandatory shower that came with the conversation got tiring after a while.

That particular group appealed to me because of the readily

available blood supply, but one of the girls who seemed really into me... how the hell do I say this? Her blood *smelled bad*.

Remember that sensitive nose I was talking about? I could *smell* her the instant she walked into the room. I had resigned myself to just hanging out for an hour and then heading across town to the next group meeting for what would inevitably turn out to be more humans pretending to be vampires, but she kind of fast-tracked things for me.

Salvadore (the host) and I had been in a heated conversation about why I preferred Stuart Townsend's *Lestat* over the Tom Cruise version when he spotted her and waved her over.

"Lyssandra," Salvadore had called out, and I had just rolled my eyes. Of course, she had an 'exotic' sounding name. It seemed that most of them did even if they were white as hell and maple syrup ran in their veins. The only vampires I'd met with 'exotic' foreign sounding names had actually *been* from another country.

"Come meet our new friend 'Bob,'" Salvador had said.

Lyssandra had wrinkled her nose at my name. "What the hell kind of name is 'Bob' for a vampire? You should get that changed."

I went to shake her hand, but my nose was already in overdrive, telling me that there was something wrong about this girl. There was something sour under the layers of her perfume and natural musk, something that was almost rancid, and I just couldn't figure it out. It wasn't that she smelled bad in a haven't-showered-for-a-week way, since that would have been a shame for such a good looking girl. It was something different. *Something disturbing*.

She was a good looking Indian girl, tall and slim with gorgeous long black hair. She'd had specialty fangs made that she could easily slip into her mouth like a retainer, but I imagined gave her some difficulty.

I found out a month later while scrolling through the Facebook Group component of the meeting that she had been diagnosed with cancer. The group was devastated by the news, and I finally knew what it was about her that had smelled so wrong. I left the group soon after, disconnected myself from most of them completely. While some of the people had been nice, it definitely wasn't what I was looking for, and now I had the cancer-detection thing looming over me.

That was easily the worst part about finding out something like that. I could now recognize the smell on people and all of a sudden it seemed to be *everywhere* I went. Riding the bus was becoming torture when every time I got comfortable, there it was, that smell again. *Knowing* was the worst thing, especially one day when I smelled it coming from this beautiful little girl who couldn't have been more than six or seven. I wanted to say something, but how do you stand up in public and tell someone that they need to get their child to a doctor because they have cancer? *Oh, how do I know that? Because I can smell it on them?*

There is no easy answer to this question. I ended up scribbling a note and made some allusion to a bruise and slipped it into her mom's pocket, and hoped to hell that she did something about it. Even that felt like a cop-out.

***

After a while, I began to see patterns and realized that there was not a single vampire among these groups and even if there were, they would have been in deep trouble.

Those people only pretend to be vampires and aren't worth your attention if you're looking for the real deal.

The guy you ought to be watching is right next to you at the bar. He's the guy who looks perfectly normal, can actually hold his liquor and most times is a real jerk, the kind of guy you wish somebody would do something about, but nobody ever does. You don't see them too often unless they're like me, sick of the whole club experience and just want to experience something that more closely resembles real life. You have to know what to look for to really be sure, but when you spot them, you can see it easily enough: they carry the arrogance with them, and chicks dig it. No matter how jerky this real vampire is, somehow he always leaves the bar with some babe on his arm. It's just the natural order of things, *so get over it.*

This is the point when your vampire alarm should be screaming at you. You know that something is desperately trying to tell you that there is something wrong about this guy, but you can't quite figure out *exactly what*. All you know is that he is wrong but that's hardly something to make a judgment on, right?

He doesn't advertize, and he certainly knows how to blend into the shadows. Your more experienced vampire will have you convinced that there is nobody else as normal as him, forget the fact that he wears sunglasses at night. You won't know what he is until you wake up in the morning with a pounding headache and rapidly fading cuts on your wrists or neck that will be forgotten by the time you leave for work. The pounding headache you have is due to the reduced amount of blood pumping through your veins, and you're definitely going to need to restore some electrolytes. If your vampire is a nicer one, he'll have provided you with a nice tall glass of orange juice, and you'll be back to full strength in no time.

So a few things were working against me for finding or even forming the support group, but I was undeterred. I branched out a little and looked through a variety of standard support groups, from cancer to Goth suicide groups, to former altar boys with revenge fantasies.

Once at an AA meeting, I ran into another vampire.

"I'm Bob," I introduced myself.

"You're new aren't you?"

"Pretty new, yeah. Acci--"

"Don't care. I'm going to talk right now, and you're going to shut your face and listen carefully."

I nodded mutely. The dude scared the shit outta me.

"You listening?"

Another nod from me still pretending to be mute.

"Fuck off."

"But you don't even--"

Dude cut me off with a single look. I don't think I've ever actually seen anyone's eyes glow red before then or since and I gotta tell you that it's the most unnerving thing you've ever seen.

"Do you want to find out how much pain you can take before you die?"

"No."

"Then fuck off kid. Get the fuck outta here before I change my mind. Goddamn, junkie."

I left in a hurry.

I was going to have to start my own group.

Dammit

Chapter 6
FRIENDS OF VLAD

I was late for work one night, and my boss was busy chewing me out, telling me what an idiot I was, along with a whole bunch of etceteras that I was doing my best to tune out.

The Boss likes to go on the occasional rant, and it's often best to just stare off into the distance and imagine you're anywhere else while he finishes yelling at you. I know what you're saying, that you wouldn't take it if it were you and you'd rather quit, but there's another reality to consider. When you find a job where the owner doesn't give a fuck what you do as long as you're not fucking up the business or stealing from him, the freedom it grants to just fuck off for eight hours while getting paid comes with a price. The price was that the boss got to yell at me when I fucked up. I figured that if I couldn't deal with my own fucking attitude when I had fucked up, and couldn't recognize that I deserved the beatdown that I had just paid for, then there was something fundamentally wrong with me.

The thing is, I was late because sunset had been severely fucking with me. I had known the change in seasons was coming, but I hadn't realized just how bad it was going to be.

See, this is another thing that everybody fails to mention, that *where* you live in the world determines how many hours of daylight you have. I live in Toronto, and from the Fall to early Spring, it's an excellent place to be a vampire. With the sun going down around 5 PM and the nights getting longer as winter progresses, you really can't beat it. But that doesn't last forever and after Christmas, the days start to get longer and longer. By April, the sun is going down around 7 PM, and then right in the middle of summer, it's going down around 10 PM for some of the shortest nights in the history of ever.

Guess which dumbass had to go and get turned into a vampire around the end of March. The fact that it coincided with Easter wasn't lost on me, with the whole rising from the dead thing going on, but that wasn't my primary concern at the time. It was getting harder and harder to make it to work on time even with Sammy covering for me. Beatrice had given me a basic rundown on "day-tripping, " but I had mostly tuned out when I was supposed to be paying attention. Dumb, I know, but you know me. In any case, it was still incredibly hard to leave the house with the sun still up in the sky like it had any business being there. Most days I'd have to exit the house looking like a burn victim, all covered head to toe and trying desperately not to make eye contact with anyone.

When Claude got fed up and just paid a mechanic to fix the engine and the transmission in my piece of shit Honda, it made traveling to work a little easier, but people still stared at me. At least in the car, it was easier to just turn up the music and tune out anyone staring at me and pretend desperately that I didn't really give a fuck.

So I was getting to work later and later, and even Sammy was giving me strange looks like she suspected something was wrong with me. Didn't help that I had to rush to the store while keeping to the shadows, so I didn't get an accidental burn.

All of this was going through my mind while the Boss yelled at me and I just tuned him out, knowing I was going to keep on being late and all the yelling in the world wasn't going to change that. It was either pretend to be a burn victim or actually be a burn victim.

Goddamn sun.

It was while the boss was yelling at me that I noticed the sign on the board behind his head.

SPACE FOR RENT.
INQUIRE INSIDE FOR DETAILS.

"Is that for real?" I asked him, and he gave me a look that told me all I needed to know about my available bargaining power.

"Why you asking?"

"A friend of mine is looking for a place to rent is all."

"You're a bad fucking liar."

"I know. How much you want for it?"

I was screwed before I opened my mouth, so the next five minutes of negotiation was me putting up a token fight and then dropping my pants and taking it up the ass. Figuratively speaking of course. But I got the room, and that was all that mattered.

It was *all mine.*

It was a dinky little room with barely enough space for the ten foldout chairs that I eventually put there. Toronto has this thing with trash that they'd adopted from New York City, where people would put pieces of furniture they had no more use for out on the curb or beside the trash, instead of actually in the trash. It was with the understanding that someone else might find some further use out of it and it had even inspired some people with trucks to make early Tuesday morning raids to get the best pickings. You could find old computers, old television sets and old chairs out there if you were lucky and knew where to look. One time I had come across an old Mac Pro tower just sitting on the side of the driveway of some house in a nice neighborhood, and another time there had been a nice set of expensive studio monitors that were worth at least $600. So that's where I'd gotten all of my chairs: various street corners, and back alleyways giving up their goodies. They were all mismatched and in different stages of disrepair, but they didn't smell too bad, and you could at least sit on them.

I even made a sign:

FRIENDS OF VLAD MEETING
CALL 555-449-5478 for more info
Or email roberto.the.diego@gmail.com

I was proud of the wording for my little ad. I had worked

on it all night at the shop, writing and rewriting until it said everything I needed to say or at least thought I needed it to say. The random customers at the store didn't bother me; they shopped, paid for their stuff and left. It was the perfect symbiotic relationship where we had some hidden agreement to ignore each other until we actually needed each other. As far as I was concerned, as long as they weren't trying to cop a feel, blowing each other in the viewing booths or exposing themselves to anybody else in the shop, then they didn't exist. And yes, those are real examples of things that have happened.

What can I say? Midnight shift has its own brand of freakiness.

***

Sammy came in while I was printing off a bunch of fliers to take out with me. I was using the office computer, and the boss absolutely frowns on that kind of thing. Sammy loves to piss off the Boss though, so she was a natural ally.

"The fuck is '*Friends of Vlad*'?" she wanted to know.

"It's a club I'm starting. A vampire club."

"Cool. Can I come?"

"Are you a vampire?"

"No. What does that have to do with it? It's not like you're a vampire either."

"If I was, how would you know?"

"You haven't even tried to kiss my neck, let alone bite me, and I know I'm practically irresistible to vampires."

There is probably not a man alive, let alone a vampire, who could resist the urge to bite Sammy for very long. This is not just me being overly dramatic either. One of the nicer vampires I had met had ended up in the shop one night and had developed an instant crush on Sammy. He had been trying unsuccessfully to get her to go out with him ever since.

Let me describe Sammy properly: She was a steaming little hot body of sexual energy just waiting to be released, and she had the most beautiful neck, along with a predilection for tattoos. Plus she had the whole Asian thing going on, and we all know how fetishized Asian women already are. If there is one thing some vampires find irresistible, it is a gorgeous woman with tattoos. Sammy was beautiful, and she definitely had the tattoos to qualify as vampire-bait. She had a full-sleeve of the most detailed and kick-ass Chinese dragon you've ever seen and had confided to me that she'd spent about 40 hours just to get it completed. No, she hadn't minded the pain. It was one of her kinks, pain, but it was a pity that I'd never get to try that out. Total vampire bait.

"You haven't met very many vampires have you?" I asked lamely.

"And you have?" She flipped her hair at me and disappeared into the back room. "I'm going to make coffee. You want any?"

"Only if it's really, incredibly fucking weak. You know me and coffee."

"What you do to coffee is abuse, I hope you know that," Sammy said and flounced off to the back office.

She was right about the coffee. It wasn't by choice though. Before becoming a vampire, there had been nothing I liked more to start my day than a nice hot steaming cup of coffee, the stronger, the better. But like my situation with jalapeno peppers and spicy foods of any kind, coffee was now off limits to me. It depresses me to even think about it, so why don't I fill you in on that later?

"You wanna help me cut these out?" I yelled after her, and I got a raised middle finger in response.

I still had half an hour to go before I left for the night. Sammy liked to come in early just to torment me. She was cute in her own way, abrasive as hell but got away with it easily enough. By the time anyone realized that they'd been having a conversation where she had insulted them ten ways from Sunday while still having such a sunny smile on her face, they dismissed it as a trick of the mind. Sammy especially liked to fuck with the customers and more often than not teased the hell out of the poor slobs. She usually had the 4 AM to 12 PM shift, and of course, sales always seemed to spike in the morning.

So we spent the next half hour cutting out my fliers with the one pair of rusty scissors that the boss kept around. That is to say, I cut them out, and Sammy watched and drank her coffee.

"Is this meeting thing what you're going to be using the upstairs room for?"

"Mostly, yeah. I don't know if anyone will come, though."

"I heard the boss screwed you on the price."

"That kinda goes without saying. That cheap prick would screw his own grandmother."

"Eww gross! That's not the kind of imagery I want to start the day with. You can find enough of that shit in aisle three."

"Sorry."

"How you gonna get them upstairs?"

"What?"

"I'll repeat and use small words, just for you."

"Wow, thanks."

"Look around you, Bob. This is a porn shop, a seedy creepy place with more than ONE WEIRD AND UTTERLY DISGUSTING GUY JACKING OFF IN THE BACK AISLE TO THE "AFRO ANAL QUEENS VOLUME 17" AND IF HE DOESN'T PUT IT BACK INTO HIS PANTS I'M GONNA GET FUCKING HOSTILE ALL OVER HIS ASS!"

This last bit shocked the crap out of me. It also shocked the guy in the back aisle wearing the trench coat, who had up to that point been furiously masturbating in the middle of the aisle. He turned around to stare all guilty and wide-eyed at Sammy who happened to be on the store's PA system, so at this point, she was the voice of God.

"BUY SOMETHING AND GET THE FUCK OUT!"

The man was practically trembling now. He was terrified of Sammy, and I couldn't blame him. Some of these guys can't even talk to a woman without fumbling for words, let alone look them in the eye. Some of them were fearless and utterly shameless, like the one guy who came in every Tuesday like clockwork to get all of the new releases before anyone else could get them. That guy was special, and I could write monologues about him, but thankfully, most of them were just like our present masturbating pervert. I'm going to call him Trenchcoat Dude, just for clarity. Trenchcoat Dude now stumbled to the counter fumbling random items off the shelf and leaving a trail of dropped items in his path.

"SIR, PLEASE PUT THE PENIS AWAY."

Sammy then proceeded to ignore Trenchcoat Dude as he turned to zip up his pants. She turned back to me and smiled.

"My point is that it's a porn shop and the only entrance to the upstairs room is through the store itself. Anybody who comes to your little meeting is first going to have to brave our noble and austere customers."

"Oh." I hadn't thought of that.

"You did think of that, though, right?"

"Of course, I did." I'm such a bad liar.

Sammy rang up the one item that our embarrassed customer had picked up and tossed him a bag. Dude had penis fingers, and there was no way she was touching anything he had come in contact with. The fact that it was a 12" dildo didn't faze her in the least and the fact that poor old Trenchcoat had probably grabbed the first thing that came to hand out of embarrassment and shame after dropping the DVD he had grabbed first, didn't seem to matter. The store had a strict no return policy, especially on sex toys.

"Try to keep it in your pants, okay?"

"Sure," Trenchcoat mumbled and left in a hurry.

Sammy looked at me expectantly. "Well?"

"Well, what?"

"Do you have a solution to your particular fucking problem?"

Sammy had a point about the entrance to the room, and it was something that had been bugging me in the back of my mind for a while. I had probably been thinking about the practicality of the room when I took a look at the place and had only taken stock of the important things like the fact that it was relatively soundproof and had one tiny window that was quickly covered over.

I shook my head. *Whatever man, I give up.*

"Fuck 'em if they can't take a joke. Anybody who can get over themselves enough to come in here and then have to face you, they deserve to be here."

***

I thought about my new potential problem on the bus ride home and then eventually shrugged it off. It wasn't like anybody was going to come anyway. If anything, it would give me something to do on Thursday nights besides planning my weekly protests at HTDK.

So I went ahead and started to put up my little fliers on the way home. I only put up three of them, one at the bus stop since I was there anyway, another one at the Supermarket on the way to my apartment and then, just for kicks, I plastered one onto the side of the phone booth in the supermarket.

I considered hitting the late night diner for a quick meal, but the sun was coming up, and I had already learned that staying up to watch the sunrise was a pretty bad idea. I would put the rest of the flyers out tomorrow and look at the sunrise from someplace safe, like inside my apartment. Or even better, on TV.

As sunrises go, they're all pretty over-rated. Do you know how long you have to wait until you get a nice good look at the sun? A lot of people have never even seen the sunrise, so Hollywood is able to sell another lie about vampires without even trying.

For those of you who have never seen a sunrise, you really should make a point to do it. Get up early or stay up late and watch the sun come up one morning, and you'll realize it's nothing quite as dramatic or romantic as the movies make it out to be. Yes, being in the direct sunlight will *probably* kill me (eventually) since I now have a high sensitivity to direct sunlight. It's more of an advanced kind of rare skin cancer though, the kind of cancer that catches on fire and makes me have to take at least a day off to let the skin grow back.

One hundred percent nothing like the movies.

I don't think I can say that enough.

Sunrises tend to be slow affairs. It's more of a gradual brightening of the sky where you can make out shapes slowly, and then start to see more clearly after a while. A whole half hour can go by like this where it just grows brighter and brighter, but you know what? Even then there is no sun. You can wait an entire bloody hour before the sun even decides to make an appearance, and by that time any vampire in the area has sauntered off to someplace dark to continue getting completely piss drunk rather than wait around anymore. The whole story about the sun coming up and the vampire turning to dust? Yeah... Not likely to happen unless you have a really slow moving vampire.

Even at home with a bowl of Cheerios in my lap, I still couldn't figure out what to do about my meeting room. Then I just decided to say fuck it all and went to bed.

And no: I do not sleep in a coffin.

* * *

You can find anything you want on the Internet. Craigslist or Kijiji is especially useful for finding all of the stuff that nobody wants anymore, or for finding all of the weird people with foot fetishes and bizarre missed connections. Do yourself a favor and do not go down the rabbit hole that is Missed Connections on Craigslist; it might be days before you emerge, with or without your sanity. In any case, are you looking for some old junk, some new junk, or somebody to haul that junk for you? Then it's all right there. If you want, you can find people to smoke out with, people to hang out with, regular (but discreet) fuck buddies, or in some cases, not-so-discreet, if that is your taste. Anything you want, it's there. If you're lucky, you might even run across my advert from my Vampires Anonymous meeting. Go ahead and do a search and it will pop up. I know it's there. After all, I've been posting and reposting the same damn advert every single week.

I got kind of lazy and despondent after my first meeting where, as I predicted, no one at all showed up. Nobody had called or emailed me, so I knew that nobody was coming, but it still depressed the shit outta me.

So I read my book.

It was some story by someone I'd never heard before called "The Survivors." It was just getting good when Sammy popped up to see me, interrupting the vivid description of puke that the author was obsessing over.

"There's some dude here looking for you."

I almost fell off my chair.

"What? Really?"

"Nah, I'm just fucking with you. How's it going?"

Some days I found Sammy unbearably cute and sexy, especially the way she played with her curls when she was distracted. This wasn't one of those times, and I told her that.

"Yeah? Well, fuck you too."

I almost went after her since she actually seemed hurt, but in the end, I just sat there and went back to my book. It was either that or try to get into HTDK but I wasn't in the mood for a beating or humiliation.

Something is calming about an empty room. I don't know if this is a real calm or what, but I know for sure that every Thursday night at around 9 PM, I'd head up and it would always be reliably empty. No one was showing up to discuss their problems with being a vampire. Who knows, maybe other vampires didn't get depressed or question their mortality or lack of it, or maybe I was just defective. Either way, Thursday nights were reliably dead times, and I'd catch up on my reading. Sometimes Sammy would come up to keep me company when she wasn't torturing some poor schlub downstairs; other times she'd just stay away and let me have my peace.

She didn't know I was a vampire and I liked it that way.

I didn't want to see the fear in her eyes, thinking I was about to kill her.

"If I was a vampire, what would you do?" I asked her one day.

This was on one of the occasions that she was talking to me and was busy painting her toenails on the floor of my little room. The scent of nail polish would linger there for days afterward, but I didn't mind. She had probably broken up with her sometime boyfriend again and was reaching out for company in the only way she knew how to, but I wasn't about to ask. Hell, I appreciated the company, so I wasn't about to chase her away. It was better than any of the other rapidly rotating cast of employees that joined and sometimes quit in the same day.

Sammy paused and shrugged.

"I suppose I'd have to get a stake and drive it through your heart. Then cut it out and bury it in salt somewhere. I'd have to throw your body into the lake of course. In pieces, so I might need a chainsaw. Remind me to buy a chainsaw."

"Ouch, violent. Are you always this violent?"

"Only if you try to drink my blood. I like my blood exactly where it is thank you very much."

"It's not like you're using it you know," I offered after a moment's thought. "Blood is a renewable resource. Our bodies just make more of it."

"Look at the big brain on Bob. You've been reading some medical books or something?"

"Nope--"

"Then what the fuck do you know? Anybody tries to drink my blood, vampire or human is going to regret the day I was born."

Silence for a moment, then something occurred to me.

"Why salt? You'd have to buy a lot of salt you know."

"Shut the fuck up Bob."

"Shutting up."

Sammy had one hell of a mouth on her. I think her mouth was directly descended from pirates or something, but I liked having her around when she wasn't throwing things at me. It made Thursday nights bearable and less lonely. It was when I got lonely that I got restless, and when I got restless, well I just got into trouble and had to go feed my addiction. I'd been managing to keep it under wraps, and so far I didn't think that Sammy had actually noticed anything. Besides, as long as she had known me I was abusing some substance or the other. I think it was when I was actually sober that she thought I was freaky or something. She was good company though and for some reason, better company when I wasn't using.

And when she wasn't around, I had my books.

One Thursday someone showed up.

"Is this where the meeting is?"

"If this is one of Sammy's jokes then please just stop right now." I was busy digging through the stack of my books and magazines that I had collected and didn't even bother to look up.

"Well she said that you were having a meeting, but--"

So the joke was on this guy then. I wasn't going to let him suffer too much.

"Sammy has a really fucked up sense of humor-"

I stopped talking because I had turned around. I had stopped talking because my brain had caught up with the rest of me and an alarm was going off in my head.

The vampire standing in the doorway had the exact same reaction as me. He was a tall black guy, striking African features, like from Ghana or something, decently dressed and yes, pale blue vampire eyes. *Holy shit!*

"You're a vampire."

In the back of my mind all I was thinking how much tail this guy must be getting with the chicks throwing themselves at him, first for the eyes and then for the fucking awesome British accent coming out of his mouth.

"I've seen you before I think. You're that guy from the club. With the sign!"

Yes, I still went down to the club to protest. Nobody bothered me anymore and to be honest, it felt kind of pointless. I was surprised anyone was noticing.

"That's me. Standing up for the little guy. I was thinking of heading down tonight if nobody showed up here. You can come if you want…"

"Hard pass."

I shrugged and grinned. Not everybody wants to be a pain in the ass, especially if their face is visible.

"I'm Bob," I said. Then curiosity got the better of me. "You came here for the meeting?"

"Yeah, the 'Friends of Vlad' meeting? I assume its code for Vampires Anonymous or something like that?"

"Something like that, yeah."

"So here I am. When is everybody else getting here?"

"You know, I'm still trying to figure that out. I don't think they've heard of it yet, but they'll come around eventually."

There was a bit of an uncomfortable silence.

"What did you say your name was?"

"Oh, I'm Frankie."

"Want a name tag?"

"I don't think I'll need it. There's only the two of us."

"I'm really bad with names."

"Whatever you say mate." Something caught his eye, and he headed off to my book pile. "Is that 'The Survivors'? I've heard it's a bitching good read."

"It's kind of cool. Give it the paragraph test, and you'll see for yourself."

"What exactly is the paragraph test?"

The paragraph test is basically this: *take a book you've never read before and open it completely randomly.* Pick out the first paragraph you see and begin. In the middle of the book is usually the best place, because by that time the author already has a firm grasp on the story and is really into the flow of things, so you can tell a lot just based on that paragraph. You can usually get an idea about if you will enjoy the use of language and of course get a glimpse of some of the plot. More importantly, if you're still reading three pages later, then you've got one hell of a book on your hands.

Judging by Frankie's reaction to 'The Survivors,' he had one hell of a book on his hands. I left him to it and got lost in the book I was currently reading.

So there we were, our first little Vampires Anonymous meeting, and it looked more like a book club than anything else.

"I gotta ask you a question," Frankie said at one point, and I paused, knowing what was coming.

"Sure. Hit me with it."

"Does she know what we are? Your friend downstairs."

"I haven't told her, so no, I don't think so."

"Cool. Just checking."

***

When Frankie came back the next week, we nodded to each other and settled into our respective books. Every now and again we'd laugh out loud at something we read and then perhaps share the joke, but by the end of the night, we were friends. Cautious friends, but friends just the same.

We even went out to one of my old haunts afterward.

There were a bunch of my friends there, and they were a

little surprised to see me since I had all but fallen off the planet in the past few months. It wasn't like I had been trying to lose touch, but between working at the porn store and trying to first understand, then be rejected by vampire society, it wasn't that hard to do. Then, of course, I had my weekly protest in front of HTDK, and that was a solid hour of commitment. Besides, I had my habit to feed, and I didn't like doing it where I knew people, so I had mostly been hitting the dive bars on the other side of town. Much easier to be bad where your friends weren't watching and posting stupid pictures on their Facebook and Instagram feeds.

Craig and Danny bought me a drink. Well, *Danny* did the buying since he was the one who was an actual friend and had noticed that I hadn't been around as much.

"Dude, what's with the sunglasses?" Danny asked after shaking Frankie's hand.

"My future's bright man. You like 'em?"

"They'd look cooler on Bono. You ain't no Bono." This was Craig. He really wasn't a friend of mine anyway, more a friend of Danny's, and they seemed to come as a package deal these days.

"Fuck you too buddy-boy."

"I thought he was already fucking you." Craig jerked a finger at Frankie. Danny sprayed laughter and whiskey.

Things went downhill quickly after that.

There's a thing about friends of friends. They always seem to think that their friendship is more valuable to your friend, and as a result, they always seem to be competing to be the better friend, even if it comes down to fighting you. Especially if they don't like you too much, and the only reason you tolerate each other is because of said mutual friend. If you two are ever left alone, it's only a matter of time before a fight breaks out. Since I had been missing for months now, Craig assumed that my friendship with Danny was no longer an issue, and all alliances were off. I was now fair game, and Danny, of course, would automatically be on Craig's side in any altercation.

A bit of perverse logic, I know, but true nonetheless.

Now, of course, things might have been just a little

different if I hadn't all of a sudden, because of my "condition," developed actual reflexes.

In my defense, though, Craig threw the first punch.

It was one of those careless sucker punches that kids throw in Junior High, the kind of punch that geeks since the dawn of time never seem to be able to duck, even though everybody else could see it coming from miles away. Since I have thrown those kinds of punches, I knew it was coming, so I knew I could duck it, and I knew that I could get my own blow in.

I just didn't anticipate how fast I moved and how hard I kicked.

I should have remembered my earlier altercation with Julio.

I should have remembered that I wasn't human anymore.

But what I really should have done was kick a hell of a lot softer.

Craig was curled up on the floor, hands cradling his testicles and I could smell blood in the air. That was when I knew I had done some serious damage and my stomach dropped. The humor quickly left the situation, and I could only stare, aware only that Frankie was pulling me away, and trying to tell me something.

It was the look of betrayal on Danny's face that sold it to me, though. The betrayal and the horror on his face that clearly said I had gone way over the line. And all I could say was *What? I didn't even kick him that hard. Did I?*

Frankie hailed a cab, and we got out of there.

"I don't think you should go back there, dude."

I didn't know what to say, so I didn't. Say anything that is.

I had Frankie drop me off at the closest subway, but I didn't go home. I found the closest dive bar and went to get a fix.

***

I tried to make an effort to call or text my other friends from time to time, but word about Craig was spreading through some really long and insulting Facebook posts about me. I eventually had to shut down Facebook rather than responding. I was trying to keep my Facebook presence at a lurking level in order to avoid answering any serious questions, and responding would have ruined my perfect record. I fucking hate reading the comments section, especially when they were talking about me. Of course, it was an entirely fabricated version of what had actually happened, but it was out there on the internet, so it had to be true, right?

While turning into a vampire didn't turn me into a leper or a complete asshole, the altercation with Craig had nearly the same effect. All turning into a vampire had done was change my diet in huge ways, got me addicted to the smell and taste of blood, much like a junkie with heroin, and I could no longer see the sun.

For a while, I kept expecting the cops to show up at my job or to wake me up during the day at my apartment. Sammy could see I was getting jumpy, especially since I was hyper-vigilant for a few days, reacting to every customer that entered, and then in one case, actually hiding under the counter from a cop who just wanted to buy some specialty condoms.

"You're freaking me out, dude. Quit it."

After a while, when I wasn't arrested, I began to relax.

* * *

Anyway, fuck Craig and friends like him. If there was one guy I could always count on, it was Claude.

Here's the thing about Claude and me: we never actually manage to talk about anything serious. We may have had a total of five serious conversations, but that wasn't what the friendship was about. It was that we could talk about absolutely nothing, and it was cool because it didn't matter how bad things were. For a while, we could forget about the rest of the world. I could forget about my particular problems and just pretend for a while that I was normal.

"Pancakes," he said as I slid into the booth opposite him.

"Why pancakes?"

"Pancakes. They've got to be the perfect food. Well, not *entirely* perfect since they don't provide any actual nutritional value, but if you take it in combination with something else, scrambled eggs with ketchup, or bacon-"

"Gotta have the bacon."

"Exactly. You take it in combination with all of that, and you've got your salty and your sweet all right there on your plate, and it doesn't even trigger your taste buds too much."

"Have you ordered yet?"

"No, I was waiting for you."

"Really?"

"Nah. I got hungry, so I ordered some bacon. Love the bacon."

"Then I'm glad I'm not Jewish or anything." That made me think of something. "If I was Jewish, would that mean I couldn't take blood from people who eat bacon? And how would I tell? Do I go up to some chick I'm about to bite and ask her if she's Kosher?"

"Does biting hurt?"

"What? Yeah, of course, it does. You got some fangs in your neck, it's gonna hurt some."

"You know Kosher doesn't just mean 'no pork' right? For example, for beef to be kosher it means the cow was killed without feeling any pain, and then the body is checked thoroughly to make sure it had no diseases. So if the bite hurts or the person is sick, then biting anyone at all is definitely not Kosher."

"Then I'm glad I'm not Jewish. How do you know all this anyway? You dating some Jewish chick or something?"

"Nah. 'Hogan Knows Best' was on this weekend, and he was throwing a party where some Jewish people were going to be at, so he had to learn about Kosher, so by extension, I had to learn about Kosher."

"You're a fucking sponge for the oddest little factoids. You hear me over there? You're a sponge."

"And you suck. Literally." He grinned. "Pun definitely intended."

"Har-de-fricking-har."

It was one of our more intellectual conversations. There were times when we could go on for hours at end, but that was when some form of alcohol was involved. The amount of time between getting turned into a vampire, and me telling Claude? About three days, but that was only because I was so sick during the first two days.

"Have your fangs grown in yet?"

"No. See?"

My family was cursed with extremely short incisors. Seriously. They're about as short as the rest of the teeth in my mouth, not long like you see on some people, and I'd thought that one of the benefits of being a vampire, was that I would finally get some decently sized incisors. Nope. That was one battle where genetics won out over vampirism. My teeth had remained obstinately short, and I was forced to carry a little knife with me. I consoled myself with the fact that it was probably more efficient and definitely more hygienic.

"I thought you said the other vampires have like these massive fangs?"

"Not all of them. Just a lot of them. At least their teeth come to points, and they look the part if you know what you're looking for. Personally, I blame my dad."

"What does your dad have to do with this? He's not a vampire too is he?"

"Genetics. Short teeth. There's a whole conversation I was having in my head where this all makes sense."

"This is where you open your mouth, and sounds come out, and you tell me what you're thinking. It's called 'conversation.'"

"Still working on the brain to mouth thing. Is there a waitress around? I'm starving. And whatever smartass comment you're going to make, you can save it."

"I had a couple of good ones lined up. Instant classics."

"Uh huh."

I can't say this enough: breakfast food has been my salvation. It was probably the one thing that had shattered my perceptions of what it meant to be a vampire. Someday I'm going to make a list of every single thing that the movies and stories have lied to us about. Okay, maybe not lied, maybe they just got it wrong, but somehow I think that the guy who was making up all of these stories had himself been a vampire. It seemed very much like something a vampire would do.

We tend to be cocky like that.

"There was a Russian guy in the shop the other day," I said after I'd finally gotten the waitress' attention.

Claude went from relaxed to a state of alert relaxed. Nobody else but me would have noticed the difference between his two states of relaxation though.

I continued: "He was a lot gay though, like stereotypically over-the-top gay, so I don't think he's the kind of Russian you're looking for."

"Like movie gay or just flamboyant gay?"

"Just flamboyant and definitely not shy about it. Spent about three hundred bucks. Good quality stuff too."

"This Russian situation isn't a joke dude. You seriously gotta keep your eyes open."

"Dude, I see a Russian, any Russian at all, I'm going to let you know about it. You did say these guys were sneaky."

Claude had been away on the kind of job he always tried to avoid taking and had come back home with a justified paranoia of Russian assassins looking for him. That was the extent of what he'd told me about the Russians, and I'd never actually seen any of them, so I'd fallen into a basic routine of just watching for possible Russian assassins as a matter of routine.

It was kind of almost exactly like how Claude had fallen into the routine of looking for vampires, so turnabout is fair play I guess.

***

Here's another thing nobody ever tells you: you can't cut off connections to your old life, and most of all, you really want to tell someone what's happened to you. It's this huge fucking secret you're carrying around with you all the time, and it's such a lonely existence that you begin to *need* to tell someone. Especially if it helps you to reconcile with yourself that you are in fact actually a vampire.

***

It wasn't until the fifth Thursday after Frankie had shown up, that we started talking about our experiences. By that time, we'd had a third guy join us after two weeks of revolving characters. Benjamin was a bit of a mousy looking dude and had found us on Craigslist, and based on his attitude and shyness we weren't quite sure if he even was a vampire, but he had the eyes. He also enjoyed the books as much as we did, so we let him stay. There had also been this skinny but tough looking girl named Natalie, who had swung by the last Thursday, but we weren't sure if she was going to come back. She'd liked the comic books but wasn't completely sold on having to go through a porn and headshop to get to the meeting.

"Told you," Sammy had said, and I had glared at her.

"Oh shut up."

Banjamin had been waiting nervously in the store that Thursday and from the embarrassed look on his face, Sammy had been torturing the poor guy.

"What did you do to him? Ben, what did she do to you?"

"I think he's too sweet to be hanging out with you bozos," Sammy had said from around the lollipop she was sucking on. In the context of the store, this was an act of pure evil, but she made it seem so innocent.

"Aww we love you too Sammy," Frankie had grinned easily, apparently immune to Sammy's charms. He had thrown a protective arm around Benjamin's shoulders and guided him towards the stairs.

"It's okay Ben, we won't let the bad woman get you," I said, and Sammy shot me the double-bird as we headed up the stairs.

"The thing I really don't understand is the whole stake through the heart thing." This was later, and Frankie was looking for a new book in my meager collection of secondhand novels and comic-books. He seemed more restless than usual.

"What do you mean?"

"Well doesn't that work on ordinary people too? They say that it's the sure-fire way to kill a vampire: just drive a wooden stake through his heart, but dude, you do that to anybody, and they're definitely going to stop living."

"I personally blame the movies myself. They just start making all of this shit up that doesn't make sense at all. Like the whole mirror thing."

"Actually, I was kinda looking forward to the mirror thing. That was a bit of a disappointment."

"It's always a shame when basic physics ignores the stories. It's not like we're transparent, so why the hell should the most basic principles of physics ignore that for a stupid mirror trick? And don't get me started on flying. Did you guys try to fly? I know you did, cuz I sure as hell tried."

"Yeah." Frankie blushed. "I broke both my legs." A thought occurred to him. "My doctor was a vampire, and she wasn't too impressed."

"Blonde Doctor? Swedish name?"

"Yeah! You got her too?"

"Made me want to never go back there, so I guess she's effective."

We cracked up for a bit both of us, then Benjamin chimed in.

"I tried to turn into bats first. Spent all day trying to do that, but when that failed, I jumped off of a building downtown. They had a dumpster, so I figured it would at least break my fall, but some idiot had thrown some metal into the dumpster. I ended up impaling my leg because of some inconsiderate jerk. You're not supposed to throw that kind of trash into dumpsters, and there I was, impaled on it. It took me hours to get off of it and then I had to sleep for two days before I was able to walk again." He looked at us with pain in his eyes. "That's the one thing that nobody tells us. They don't tell you how much it hurts. Sure you heal eventually, but while it's doing that, it hurts... so... bad.

"Why doesn't anybody warn us?"

Something was bothering me about something Benjamin had said.

"Did you mean turn into bats, like multiple little bats, or just one big bat? Cuz I wasn't clear on that." Frankie shrugged at my expression.

Benjamin looked a little embarrassed. "I meant bats. You see it in the movies all the time. Vampire turns into a big cloud of little bats. Bats."

"Pretty fucking stupid now you think of it, yeah?" Frankie said, and Benjamin gave him the finger.

We were silent for a long moment then, each of us wrapped up in our own memories. Benjamin was staring solemnly at the floor. It was a long time before anyone spoke again.

"She never got a chance to tell me anything you know. I

barely knew what was going on at the time, I was so fucked up, and by the time I had a clue, she was already gone. No clues, no warning... Nothing really except a whole lot of confusion. Sometimes I wonder if I'd had some kind of warning, maybe, just maybe I would have stood a chance..."

I hadn't even meant to say that much, but there I was in the middle of the room that was our refuge from our own reality, and the words came tumbling out, surprising me as much as anyone else.

And at that moment, we all knew that everything had changed.

Vampires Anonymous had finally gotten off to start.

Chapter 7
THE DANCE MACABRE

SO ARE WE ALL CAUGHT UP on what being a vampire is really like?

Good. Glad we're all on the same page here.

I suppose I can't put it off any longer, so I'm going to go back and finish telling you about the night I got turned into a vampire. I know it's what you're really here for, so I might as well just get it over with.

Okay then: *here we go.*

***

Remember Louise? We were playing "spot the vampire" with her earlier. She had dragged me out of the bar while my neck was still dripping blood and had gotten on the phone with a doctor friend of hers.

"We are literally just around the corner," she said into her phone. The "doctor friend" she had called for help was apparently being a little difficult. "It's a stupid accident," she continued, "and I can patch him up in no time at all."

If you've already spotted her longer than normal incisors, kudos to you, but as far back as I can remember, Louise has always had long teeth. I'd always thought that it ran in her family. No stumpy incisors limited by genetics for her.

"Okay, fine, I'll see you soon," she agreed and rolled her eyes as she hung up. She grinned and gave me the thumbs up.

"Weren't you going to buy me a drink?" I asked her and Louise shot me a dirty look.

"Keep walking buddy-boy! Alcohol dilutes the blood and makes it harder to treat you. Just be quiet and let me take care of you, okay?"

I listened to her and kept on walking. Louise knew what she was talking about and I trusted her. Besides, I don't think she was going to let me escape.

Louise worked nights at one of those 24-hour clinics over on the Danforth side of town, and I never got to see her that much. I'd first run into her a couple of years ago when I used to hang out with Angus, and that had pretty much been that. We'd become instant friends over one of Angus's Super Fantastic Bongs and had kept running into each other after that. I even ended up crashing on her couch for a few weeks while I was between jobs and she was one of my first customers at the porn shop, just to see the look on my face. Louise had also been the person who had been responsible for me meeting Jaime, and since the breakup, I really hadn't seen her that much. I think she had been really disappointed in me and I couldn't blame her.

Besides, I worked nights, and she worked nights and the whole working at night thing sucks when your friends also work at night. Your schedules will never meet, so there's no overlap since one or both of you is always rushing off to work. I tried to make a note to myself to try to get her to meet me for breakfast one night after work so we could catch up.

I followed her as she led me out of the bar and away from all of the wonderful alcohol, none of which I seemed destined to drink.

"We need to catch up some time you know. Preferably over drinks." I said pointedly.

"I know. Let's get you patched up first, and then we can worry about that after."

"Sorry for ruining your night off."

"Hey, if you can't take care of your friends, then what does that tell you about yourself as a person?"

"Sorry though."

"You've not been taking care of yourself, Bob. This whole depression thing has got to stop at some point you know."

"I'm not depressed. Not that much. You make it sound like I'm suicidal or something."

"Are you?"

"Of course not."

I was lying, and we both knew it. Louise offered me enough grace and just ignored that little lie. She had been the one who had pumped my stomach that one night three months before, after all.

"So how far away is your friend?"

"Just a few more houses down."

"You dating this dude?"

"Nah. I've taken myself off of the meat market for a bit. Trying to figure out a few things in my life right now. You can call it a voyage of self-discovery if you want. I call it 'staying away from men for a while' myself."

"Good name. A bit long, but a good name."

"Good name for a rock band?"

"Nah, not rocking enough," I teased. "Kinda poppy, like K-Pop poppy."

Louise made a face and shrugged. "I like it anyway. You seeing anyone yet?"

"Nah. I'm just keeping to myself right now. A relationship is the last thing I need." I glanced at her wondering if I had created the perfect segue. Only one way to find out. "Have you heard from Jaime recently?"

Louise glances at her watch and smirks. "Five minutes, twenty seconds. New record for you Bob."

So much for the perfect segue. I blundered onward. "I held out as long as I could. I even made small talk, but now you gotta tell me: how is she?"

"Yes I saw her and in answer to the questions you're about to ask, *no you shouldn't call her,* and I mean *ever*; yes she hates your fucking guts - *her words* - you're an idiot - *my words* - and yeah… that should about cover it."

I really hate my friends sometimes. I made a silent vow to return Louise to the friend store for a full refund.

"You could have at least put a positive spin on it," I pointed out.

"That *was* the positive spin! Look, dude, you fucked up big time. My job is to tell you just how much you fucked up."

"I thought you were supposed to be the shoulder to cry on."

"That is Claude's job. How is the old crook?"

"Still evading incarceration. He's gotten really good at not getting caught. Can we get back to talking about Jaime—"

Louise stopped in her tracks and considered me for a long second.

"You still using?" She asked after a while. "Last time I checked it was prescription pills with you—"

"What does that have to do with it?" I asked, more defensively than I should have. Louise knew all of my bad habits. In fact, she was the one who had gotten me started on the prescription pills anyway. Doctors have access to the best drugs, especially the free samples.

Louise looked like she was going to haul off and hit me.

"It has everything to do with it, Bob! Everything! That was one of the many, many reasons Jaime left you or had you not figured that out?"

That one hit me like a ton of bricks. Stopped me in my tracks cold.

"Jaime left me because I was using? That's why?"

"*One* of the reasons, yes!" It's funny how much a statement like that tells you so much and evades so much at the same time. If you can pay attention, you could ask the right questions, but the other person usually presses on with the conversation…

Louise continued: "She never told you why she left?"

See what I mean? Expert evasion, and with that, I was focusing on the wrong thing.

"No! She just left one day and then refused to see me or talk to me. Even when she got the restraining order on me, not a single fucking word. Just a very unpleasant cop with a really bad attitude. Why do you think I've been so fucked up over it?"

Now Louise just looked pissed. She stomped around in a little circle in the middle of the street, making faces.

"I'm going to fucking *kill* her! I *told* her to let you know, but did she listen? *Oh no! Not little Miss 'He Should Have Figured It Out,'* no not her! Fucking girls don't know how to *communicate! Argh!*"

"You're a girl."

"How do you think I know?"

We just looked at each other for a moment, and then Louise cracked a smile. She was just cool like that. I was glad she was my friend.

"Come on, let's get that neck looked at. This is the house."

I followed her down the driveway to the little house with the well-kept garden. A Black BMW with black tinted windows was sitting in front of the garage door, stylishly cool. It spoke volumes about the owner, saying that he was coolly efficient, confident and just rich enough to think that he was ten times better than you, and if you were richer than he was, then it wouldn't faze him one way or the other. He probably walked around the house in a pullover or something equally as metrosexual.

His name was Robert, and when he opened the door, he was wearing a pullover. I hated him on first sight. Pompous prick.

In hindsight, I probably realized that something else was off about this guy, but I couldn't pinpoint it at the time. There was just some other reason that I didn't like him, and maybe if I had spotted the way he had of flicking his incisors with his tongue whenever he saw blood, I would have figured it out. Or maybe not: vampires were not real, not then, and were not something I used to be on the look out for.

"Is this him?" He asked Louise, indicating me.

I took my hand off my neck before Louise could reply and grinned. "I am him. He. Him. He..." How did it go again? Ahh, fuck it, it didn't matter anyway. "I'm the guy."

"Like he said. Robert this is Bob, Bob... hey wait a minute-I've got two Bobs." She looked back and forth at us, feeling clever.

"Let's just stick to Robert, what do you say?" Robert looked disgusted at that thought of being called 'Bob'. Nothing wrong with 'Bob'. I liked it just fine, thank you very much.

Louise shrugged an 'okay.' "You got the stuff right?"

"Yeah, come on in and let's get him fixed up and on the way."

Louise rolled her eyes at me as Robert opened the door wide. She could tell what I was thinking sometimes, I swear.

"Be nice, okay?"

"Being nice starting... *now.*"

I stepped inside and instantly forgot my promise. "*Holy fucking shit. It's Ikea!*"

Robert's house was almost an Ikea showroom. Everything looked like it had been lifted wholesale from Ikea, every combination perfect and complimentary. I was almost expecting a big blue and yellow shopping bag to be handed to me at any second before I was pointed towards the cinnamon buns and cheap 50-cent hotdogs.

"Sorry, about that Robert. I forgot to warn you that he's an idiot."

"It's quite okay. I get that reaction a lot."

I shrugged as Louise glared at me. "What?"

"You're lucky you're already bleeding."

That's when I saw it. The large Flarken Broj coffee table in the living room that was next to the Mjolnir combination couch and sectional had the largest *Gudaam Fuuken* pile of pills I had ever seen in my entire life. Tuinol and Seconal, Xanadrine and Setonicon, Oxytcontin and Fentanyl, uppers, downers, anti-psychotics, pre-psychotics, cocaine, morphine... it was like walking into 1980s Stephen Tyler's wet dream or bathroom. Remember what I said about doctors and prescription pills?

"Have I told you recently how much I love you?" I asked Louise, my eyes drinking in the drugs and plotting a course of complete annihilation. The right cocktail of drugs could kill you dead, but if you got the combination just right, you could party for a week.

"No drugs for you Bob," she said and damn she was *strong*.

Louise grabbed me and steered me away from the drugs down the corridor behind Robert to the bathroom. I protested all the way of course. I mean, goddamn! That was a lot of drugs!

The artwork was at least pre-Ikea and looked pretty expensive. There was a piece that looked like what could have been an early Rembrandt, but it had been more than a decade since I had studied art history, so excuse me if I was a little rusty at the time. Claude could have been able to tell me after he had stolen it and sold it to the highest bidder of course, but he's good like that. He absorbs all of the details about important stuff, but me, I'm almost completely useless without Google.

The bathroom was *(big surprise)* another Ikea masterpiece. I just bit my tongue and sat where Louise instructed me to. Robert disappeared down the corridor.

"You could have warned me about the Ikea effect," I whispered to her. "How do you expect me to behave when I'm walking into something like this?"

"You know I've really, really missed you. We should make a point of going out for breakfast after this."

"Yay breakfast." It occurred to me that I was broke. "Um…"

"My treat."

Have I mentioned how much Louise *ruled*? It's true. She totally ruled.

She inspected the bite on my neck now, slapping my hands away whenever she touched something sensitive, and I reacted. The bite was beginning to throb the more I thought about it and *what she was doing to me anyway?* Louise had obviously been right about infection.

"For someone unable to get over their ex-girlfriend, you sure don't seem to mind the one night stands."

"It was literally the first time in three months that I've actually had real sex. I've masturbated so much that my hands are about to sprout hair and I'm going to need a cane and dark glasses pretty soon if I keep it up. You know, for when—"

"When you go blind. Yeah, I know the joke. You need to take better care of yourself, Bob. How am I supposed to torture you if you're not around?"

Robert returned and passed some very medical looking supplies to Louise. He raised an eyebrow at me as he passed me a drink.

Louise: "That's not alcohol is it?"

"You know I don't drink… alcohol…"

I think both Louise and I must have rolled our eyes, but it got the first real grin out of Robert that I had seen. And the first real look at his incisors. This was a guy who was born to be a vampire. He passed Louise a bottle of water.

"You want me to do that?"

I could only imagine the look Louise gave him from behind my back. It must have been a doozy because Sweater Bob looked a little disappointed.

"I've got it, Robert. Thanks but I'm good at bites, remember?"

Robert looked from the bite to me, and I knew I *hated* this dude. "You should try to avoid getting bitten, *Bob*." He almost spat my name. "It's very unhygienic."

So there we were in Robert's house, Louise cleaning my bite wound and fixing me up, Robert watching from the doorway, and me wincing on occasion as Louise performed some heinous act on my neck. At least she wasn't telling me about the diseases a person could catch from being bitten by another human being. Nope. That was Robert, and it was practically a repeat performance of Louise's earlier diatribe. I swear it must be a doctor thing.

So I was practically dozing, off in my happy place where Robert wasn't talking at me, or actually didn't even exist. When Louise's phone rang from her purse out in the Lack™ living room, and she ran out to get it, I didn't even notice.

I heard distantly as she picked it up and started to talk, but I was reliving the best moments of this evening's grapple in my car and didn't care at the time. I didn't even care when Robert stepped behind me, presumably to look at Louise's handiwork.

I was still at the part where Gloria's head was still in my lap, when Robert made an incision at the side of my neck and began to suck on it long and hard. It happened pretty quickly, but by that time I was beyond caring. I was relaxed and carefree, off in the drug induced haze of whatever drug had been slipped into my coke. Apparently, Sweater Bob was also good at roofies. One of the additional benefits of being a doctor I suppose.

The bastard.

There were additional incisions with Robert sucking on each one with a determination and enthusiasm that I had only recently experienced with Gloria in the car. One of the things I found out much, much later was that it was a pain in the ass to drink non-arterial blood. The blood will flow quite easily yes, but once your friendly neighborhood vampire puts his mouth on you, the saliva in his mouth will cause the blood to flow even faster. But the instant they stop sucking, that same saliva has a tendency to cause the cut to heal, and fast. And for all of you who are asking why he doesn't just drink from an artery: are you even listening? The aim here is *not to kill your victim.* Cut into an artery and three times out of five you will have a dead body on your hands, and you're fucking up the supply.

I didn't notice how many times he cut me, but I do know that when Louise eventually came back, I was barely able to hold my head up.

Oh yeah... Louise. I hadn't even thought to tell her to run. That Sweater Bob here thought he was some kind of vampire or something.

Her reaction wasn't exactly the one I had expected.

"What *the fuck* do you think you're doing?"

"Having a drink. We can share."

"Robert you asshole! I didn't bring him here for you."

"You didn't?"

"No, I didn't. *Fuck.* You drugged him didn't you?"

"You sure you don't want some?"

"He's my friend Robert. My actual friend. He's a bit of a doorknob sometimes, but he's a friend. I do *not* make a habit of taking blood from my friends, *especially without asking.*"

"Hey, how was I supposed to know?" Robert sounded a little drunk. He was slurring his words like a crackhead who'd just gotten a fix. He sucked on my back for a quick second.

"Stop that!"

"You sure you don't want some?"

Louise just looked sad. She looked away.

"Yeah, I'm sure. Now, will you please stop that?"

"It's really good blood. Type A."

Liar. I was type-B Positive. So much for a discerning tongue.

Louise just looked tired, a look that I had seen before in the mirror. It was a look that usually followed an intense period of self-loathing and doubt, and sometimes one of my depressive states. It was a look that said, *"I'm going to fight this for long enough that I can convince myself that I really, really tried."* In short, it was the look of a junkie needing a fix.

One of the things that a junkie like me can tell you is that they can spot another junkie without even trying.

My friend Louise was a different kind of junkie, but she was a junkie just the same, as I was about to find out.

I didn't even know she was a vampire. I didn't even think of that. I was too drugged and too fucked up in my head to think clearly. I was in my happy place, and that was all that mattered.

Good roofies. Sweater Bob had access to some good shit.

"Hi Louise," I tried to say, but what came out was some weird and somewhat incoherent unintelligible mishmash of words that sounded more like I was drooling all over myself. Louise looked at me then, looked right through me, and I could see her thinking about it.

And her teeth... I could see them now.

When she started to suck on my neck, all I could think about was how pretty her teeth were.

After that, everything got kind of hazy.

I dreamed of *teeth*.

***

Here's the thing about vampires and blood: they don't need it to survive. They need it to get their *fix*. They're all blood junkies and like with a regular junkie, a little is never enough.

There is a curious effect that blood has on your ordinary vampire. I would later learn that it is very much like a drug that all vampires are hooked on to some degree. That was another point that the movies got completely wrong, labeling vampires as gorging on blood and feasting on it, needing it to live. There are, of course, a huge number of reasons that they list, like some quasi-scientific reason that because the vampire is undead, there is no circulation and no warmth, so the vampire needs to replace the blood in his own veins periodically...

That one cracks me up too. Just like the myth about not being able to see a vampire's reflection in the mirror. It's when the myths just get stupid and avoid any actual relation to physics and reality; those times get to me.

I cannot say this enough: *Vampires drink blood for the same reason that we smoke cigarettes, marijuana or a crack pipe.* It is simply because they *like* the effect it has on them. It is exactly like a drug, and they can't quite get enough of it.

I don't know how long Louise and Robert drank from my veins. I don't know if there were any regrets, or if they laughed like stoned idiots enjoying their fix. I don't know any of that. For a while, all I knew was darkness.

What I do know is pretty simple though. I know that there are about ten pints of blood in the human body. I know this because it was one of those weird conversations that Louise and I had had over a bong while she was doing her residency. It was one of the basic facts that all doctors have imprinted on their brains and they can spout off the details for different ages and weight classes if you were inclined to ask them. *Under no circumstances are you to ever ask them.* Trust me on this.

My point is that Louise and Robert *knew* how much blood there was. They both knew *exactly* how much blood a person could lose before death occurred.

I don't think *she* intended to kill me, but coming from my own experience as an addict, I know that what you intend has nothing to do with the actual outcome, no matter how noble or in some cases tragic. Addicts tend to fuck up everything, and they do it on a grand scale, and it's because they simply aren't thinking clearly.

You can lose up to four pints of blood before you die.

At some point, somebody decided he needed just one more fix. Just a little bit more couldn't hurt, could it? And besides, they were both doctors, so I was in safe hands.

Yet... somehow, they drank too much.

Way too much...

***

There was a taste of copper on my lips when I woke up. Like I had bitten my lip or something, and I could taste it. The taste practically *filled* my mouth.

When my eyes fluttered open, I could see Louise sitting curled up in the chair, just watching me. Her hand was wrapped in a bandage, and she looked like she had been crying her eyes out.

My throat was dry as hell, and I was exhausted. For a moment I wondered why and then it came back to me.

"You drank my blood, Louise. You and Robert. Dude, like what the fuck?"

"I'm sorry Bob, I really am."

"Since when do you go around drinking people's blood? Is this some weird new kink you haven't told me about?"

"There is something I have to tell you, and I want you to listen very carefully and not say a thing until I'm done. Can you do that for me?"

"Sure, whatever. Fuck, I'm sore all over."

"Bob..."

"Yeah, yeah. I'm listening."

"You died last night."

I hadn't expected that one. I had to fight the urge to laugh at her right then. What the fuck was going on here? Maybe I was still dreaming. It was a fucked up dream, but it would explain a few things.

"Robert... *Robert and I...* We got a little greedy, and you were dying of blood loss. I kind of freaked out a little, because we weren't *supposed* to have even taken your blood. That wasn't what I intended at all. I'd just wanted to take care of your bite. You've got to believe me on that. I didn't intend any of this to happen. I didn't want you to die, not like that. And especially not *because* of me. I didn't want to be responsible for the death of a friend, especially you. So I did the only thing I could think of."

She held up her bandaged wrist.

"You're going to be one of us now Bob. It was the only way."

"What the hell are you talking about?"

"Listen! *You need to listen*. In about two minutes someone is going to knock on the door, and I'm going to go outside to talk to some people. I expect that they're going to want to take me to have a talk with Harry, *about you*, and I really don't know what's going to happen after that. So I want you to listen to me and take me extremely seriously. *I'm not fucking around here.* I'm *deadly fucking serious* when I say that I am a vampire, and now… You're going to become one too. It's going to hurt, and you're going to be sick for a while, but as of right now, you're already one of us, and you need to know some rules. First, you're going to need some sunglasses--"

There was a knock on the door. A slow, gentle knock. Louise looked completely and utterly terrified.

"Louise-"

"I have to go, Bob. They're here."

"Who's here?"

"The Gentlemen. And you do not keep them waiting. " She tried to smile at me and failed miserably. "Goodbye, Bob."

And then she was gone.

Chapter 8
VERY BAD THINGS

The first three days I thought that I would have been better off dead.

They were the worst three days of my life at that point and I spent most of the time passed out on the bathroom floor, my pants permanently around my ankles. Vomit had sprayed around the toilet bowl, and I didn't even recall doing that, missing or even getting it in the bowl, but when your entire existence for three days is puking or shitting, then details are a little hazy.

Being on what I thought of as death's doorstep for three days brings things into clarity, but usually after the crisis has passed. Of course the better description would have been on death's toilet, since that's where I spent most of my time. I had either been puking or shitting my guts out, huge stinking and sometimes bloody masses. This was from either end mind you. I was usually doing both at the same time.

On the first night I had slept on the floor of the toilet, practically wrapped around the toilet bowl, never mind how cold it was. I had been sweaty and clammy, running a fever and in a definite state of delirium. Since Louise had disappeared I hadn't had much time for anything else, much less thought.

At times I wondered if she was simply having me on, but those thoughts never lasted long, and I'd either be puking again or passing into unconsciousness.

My dreams were no better, hazy fever dreams that left me feeling sick to my stomach.

On the second day when I woke up, I was still on the

bathroom floor, but someone had covered me with a wool blanket and I had clutched it around me while I slept. As I woke I was aware of someone in the room with me and tried to turn to see them, aware that my pants were still down around my ankles and my ass felt like it was caked with shit. Definitely not at my best.

"Louise?" I tried to say, but the movement was too much.

When I woke up again I was alone.

Oh the third day I dragged my weakened body into the shower, disgusted with myself for the state I was in. It took me almost an hour to get in there and another half hour to get the water on, but I was able to just lay under the water and after a while I began to feel human again. Only now can I appreciate the irony of that, but at the time, human was the only way I knew how to feel. I didn't know how long that feeling would last, but even if for just a little bit, it was more than enough.

It was the longest shower of my life and I made sure to take my time. It's not a good feeling to have shit caked on your ass, and I could partially relate to the disgust incontinent old people probably felt when they looked at a pair of Depends™. Hell at that point I could relate to an infant, who had no choice but to sit in their own shit until somebody cleaned their ass for them. However, I had a choice and I cleaned as carefully as I could.

I may have cried at some point. If I did, it's none of your business. And if I did cry, then I didn't know why, but it would have felt good to do so, just letting my despair out. But I didn't cry, and you can stop staring at me now.

Fact: showers have remarkably restorative powers. After a good hot shower you don't feel as shitty anymore, no matter how bad things are. You feel as if you can take on the world. You're clean and restored and you can feel good again.

That feeling only lasts as long as you're actually in the shower. The instant you turn off the water, it comes flooding back. The weakness and the doubt have simply been kept at bay by the water and as soon as you step out, they're waiting for you like old friends, ready to start the party again.

When I was able to step out of the shower, but very

carefully because I was so damn weak, I was a lot freaked out at the state of the bathroom. The stink was unbearable, more so than normal and my nose was a lot more than a little offended. I would have to get some kind of gas mask when I cleaned up this mess.

I stumbled out of the bathroom and caught a glimpse of myself in the mirror that had been awkwardly placed without any thought, next to the television. I crept closer to the mirror, not sure of what I was seeing there. When the towel fell from around my waist I didn't even notice. All I could look at was myself in the mirror and remember Louise's words to me and the absolute impossibility of it all.

But most of all, the only thing I could think about was, *what the fuck had happened to my eyes?*

The eyes looking back at me were not the eyes I had grown up with and looked at in the mirror every single day. Oh no, *those* beloved eyes had been a dark brown, deep and thoughtful, *soulful* as my mom used to say. They had never ever looked like this, these *freak eyes* that now sat in my eye sockets like they belonged there. *Damn them, what had they done to my eyes?*

The eyes that stared back at me, no matter how much I rubbed at them with my knuckles, trying to unsee what I was seeing, those eyes were a *pale blue*, almost luminescent in the dim light of the room.

This of course is the point where I freaked the fuck out.

Forget logic, forget pain. Forget sanity, just forget rational thought. Forget who you were or who you might have been. Forget everything, but remember these words because they may be the last words you hear. Forget it all because none of it matters. Forget the story, forget the songs, they were all wrong anyway, all lies planted like a seed of ugliness and fear, to feed the hunger, to feed the growing seed of myth that lies buried deep within. Forget everything you've known because it is a lie. Forget the truth and know that you are the truth. And know that *you are also the lie.*

"Louise pick up your fucking phone and talk to me dammit! Tell me what the fuck you did to me!"

I hate voicemail.

In between calling Louise and yelling at her voicemail, I'd stare at myself in the mirror, not wanting to see, not wanting to believe it. None of it. *I couldn't be a vampire.* This was just some huge fucking elaborate hoax, the onset of rabies or something exotic. Could you get rabies from a human bite? It didn't matter if you could or not, because I had *something* and it sure as hell wasn't normal.

When someone answered Louise's phone, I tried to calm myself.

"Louise you gotta talk to me. I'm freaking the fuck out here."

"Louise isn't here. Nobody by that name here."

"This isn't a wrong number. It's Louise's number."

There was silence and the sound of somebody fumbling the phone. Somebody mumbled something and there was laughter. I was about to says something when somebody *screamed.* It sounded just like Louise.

Click, and the phone hung up.

One thing that you can always remember, no matter how bad things may seem, is fear. It is your constant friend, waiting just out of sight, but always there, waiting to come back to be your best friend in the entire world. In fact, if it was your only friend, then that would suit it fine, just fine indeed...

I called back, my hand shaking as I listened to the phone ring. I prayed to a God I didn't believe in that maybe I had gotten the number wrong, but somehow I knew that I hadn't. I knew it deep in my gut, and when the phone was answered again, and all I could hear was Louise *screaming--*

This time I was the one who hung up.

I may have thrown the phone then, I don't know, but I started moving quickly, looking for my clothes, determined to find my damn pants and get out of there, get over to Louise's place as quickly as possible, I mean, she had to be there, *right*? And then what? *Then what was I going to do?*

I froze at the very thought, common sense kicking in. I stood there, one foot in my pants leg, screw the underwear, this was urgent! I realized that I was no action hero, I was in fact the worst person to be a hero of any sort. What kind of rescue was I going to pull off anyway? *My friend was screaming somewhere…* and maybe she wasn't even at her house. The best thing to do would be to call 911 and let them sort it out, right?

Fuck!

I spent the next few minutes trying to find the phone, dialing 911 and then hanging up, trying to amp myself up to be a hero goddammit, just be a hero for once, and then remembering the whole fucked up situation and the goddamn mess of the goddamn trashed motel room. Action is its own inaction and vice versa and *man I am so fucked up.*

I sat naked on the floor of that motel room, my cell phone on the floor in front of me and I just stared at it, afraid to use it and sure, just so goddamn sure it was about to ring and it would be Louise and this time she wouldn't be screaming, she would be okay and none of this would be happening because it was all a big fucking joke and there was no way I was a vampire—

I caught sight of my eyes in the mirror and the reality of it washed over me, the full possibility taking hold at the sight of those fucked up blue eyes in my head. I was beginning to really believe it now, or at least the possibility of it. I think that maybe my believing it freaked me out more than anything else.

"I'm sitting naked in the middle of a motel room and I'm losing my mind."

Claude had thankfully picked up on the second ring. We never ever said hello. We always just got straight to the point of what we had to say, kind of like continuing a conversation that we had interrupted the last time we spoke. No matter what I said, he always had the appropriate response for it.

"Maybe you should put some clothes on dude. Or at least sit on something. Those floors aren't known to be too clean you know."

He was right. I grabbed my towel from the floor and sat on the bed instead, the towel under my ass for protection.

"What would you say if I told you that I was turning into a vampire?"

"Is this turning, or have *turned*?"

"I think it's more turned at this point. I dunno for sure."

"So you might be a vampire," he said thoughtfully. "Okay, I can dig it. First thing I'd say is to stay indoors. Do not open the windows or go out into the sunlight. If you're a vampire, that will kill you for sure."

"Okay, I can do that. What time is it anyway?"

"Five oh five so the sun's still up. We might have twenty minutes till the sun sets, but don't quote me on that. Where the hell have you been anyway? Your mom's been trying to reach you for three days now. "

"I've been kinda busy turning into a vampire. Takes a lot out of a person."

"You need to call your mom dude. Where the hell are you right now? Do you know?"

I looked around the room and spotted the *Emergency Exit* map on the back of the door that all hotels are required to have. I peered at it myopically before realizing that I could read the writing from across the room. Definitely something I could never do before. I read the address off to him.

"The Motel Six on Lakeshore? What the hell are you doing all the way out there for?"

"I have no idea how I even got here dude. I'm still kinda freaking the fuck out at this whole situation."

"Hang tight and I'll come pick you up. I'm kind of in the middle of a job here, but nothing I can't cancel."

Click, and Claude was gone.

I peered out through the curtains and failed to be incinerated on the spot. It was pouring rain and there was no sun to speak of, so that might have had a lot to do with it, but at the time all I could think was how hungry I was. The possibility that I might have exploded into dust like a movie vampire (despite Claude's warning) didn't even occur to me.

It was another ten minutes before I had pulled myself together well enough to exit the room and then it was because my stomach was screaming at me that I needed to eat something and I needed to eat *right fucking now!* The last time that I could remember eating was three days ago, so you can excuse me for being a little single-minded at the time.

I stumbled out of the door, feeling the spray of rain that bounced off the metal rail lining the second floor walkway.

My head throbbed and pounded at me, stomach cursing loudly for me to feed it, so I couldn't even be bothered about getting wet. I stumbled down the walkway past identical doors, while digging in my pocket for loose change. I'd had an idea that there just might be a vending machine of some kind downstairs and I was determined to get to it.

There was a handful of change in my pocket and a couple of twenties that I couldn't remember owning, but I didn't care at the time. All I knew was the hunger that threatened to consume me.

I made my way down the stairs and looked around in the muted evening light--

Boom! There it was at the other end of the corridor next to what looked to be the registration office.

So, coins in slot, *no don't come back out...* okay fine, redeposit coin... and success. Punch code, wait for candy to drop... candy drops and retrieve... now rip open wrapper and eat.

I must tell you this: chocolate had never tasted so good in my entire life. It was an explosion of flavour, so sweet, so good, so goddamn *perfect*. It was everything I needed, and in a few quick bites it was gone.

Feeling the disappointment but also feeling just a little better for having had something to eat, I opened my eyes, ready to get out of there.

There was a teenage girl staring at me from across the corridor.

"Whoa. Nice eyes."

I didn't know what to say. I shrugged. "Thanks. I just got them."

"Cool. I want."

"Trust me, you really don't," I said. I bought another Snickers bar and headed to the parking lot, trying very hard not to look at the girl again, somehow afraid that she might suddenly figure out what it was I had become.

I hid from the rain and waited for Claude to show up.

***

Claude stared at my eyes, stunned. I shrugged, already

uncomfortable with the attention, and looked away.

"Did you bring the sunglasses? The light's giving me a headache."

I didn't even realize it was true until I opened my mouth and said it. But there it was, and true, every word of it. The lights from the diner, from the street lights, from everywhere, lights that we depend on every night, they were suddenly way too bright and sending piercing spears of pain through my head.

Claude brought out a pair of very expensive looking sunglasses and I took them gratefully, noting how much they cut the light down to something bearable that felt normal again. It was really weird being able to see in the dark like that. I felt a little light headed at the thought, and found myself fighting back what could only be described as an oncoming episode of me freaking the fuck out. I somehow managed to focus on the painful light that was serving as an overly annoying reminder that I might be a vampire.

"Thanks dude. You're a life saver."

"Yeah, and you're a vampire. Three words for you: *What the fuck?*"

Tell me about it.

"Believe me man: I feel the same way. It's as much a surprise to me as it is to you. Three nights ago, vampires did not exist, not in my world."

"At least you had time to get used to the idea. I only had an hour. Now, are you going to fill me in on this shit or not?"

"Buy me something to eat first. I haven't eaten in three days and just puked up my snickers bar."

It had been surprising and disgusting and left my mouth tasting of chocolate and bile. My mouth tasted like something had died in it.

"Why did you puke? Some kind of vampire thing?"

That hadn't occurred to me and I shook my head.

"No. I'm sure it's just because I haven't had anything to eat in three days and I ate that Snickers hella fast."

"Did you eat them both?"

I was confused and Claude read my confusion perfectly.

"Dude, I've never known you to just buy one Snickers bar."

I nodded and then shook my head.

We made our way into the diner, which was way too brightly lit in my personal opinion. Everything just seemed so bright, and so harsh... My headache had returned in full force by the time we were seated, and by the way my head throbbed, it was a headache that was promising to stick around for a good while, put its feet up and break some shit just for the hell of it.

"Hey you want some coffee?"

I had already sunk my head onto the table, and motioned for him to bring on the coffee. Coffee sounded like a really good idea at the time. Just the thought of it brought the strong aroma to mind and made me even hungrier.

"Can I just order right now?" I said to the waitress. "I'm really fricking hungry."

"Same here," Claude said.

The waitress shrugged and whipped out her notepad. "What'll it be then?"

A wave of nausea, probably from the hunger, hit me and I belched audibly. I could smell and taste the bile from my vomit with a few traces peanuts and chocolate. Claude jumped in to order for me.

"Scrambled eggs, lots of bacon, stack of pancakes, coffee. Same thing for my friend over here." Something occurred to him. "Or did you want a bloody steak instead?"

"You wanna make me puke? Pancakes. Please."

The waitress left and Claude just stared at me for a bit. Me? I just wanted to lay down and die. The stench from my belch was just hanging around in the air even with my feeble attempts to wave it away.

Claude slid some gum across the table to me and I tore into the packet, feeling the cool burn of peppermint all along my taste buds, appreciating the blast of sugar in my mouth.

"That should hold you for a couple of minutes," Claude said.

"Plus it will make my mouth not taste like ass," I moaned.

Wait a second. Something was wrong. I coughed and the gum flew out of my mouth, but the burn of the peppermint remained, hot and overwhelming in my mouth.

"What the fuck dude?"

I grabbed a glass of water and almost drowned myself by drinking it so fast. Some of it spilled but I didn't care, just chugged it down, feeling the stinging burn of the peppermint on my tastebuds and in my sinuses, finally begin to dissipate.

"What the hell was that about?" Claude asked when I could speak again.

"I can smell everything. That was way too much."

Claude looked at the pack of gum and then at me.

"Fill me in," Claude said. "Try not to skip anything important."

I took a deep breath to steady myself and began to talk.

You know in the movies how telling a story seems to take forever, and then hours will pass because the story is so long and involved? You know the reality of it. You know that unless it is some epic tale, that people just don't have that many words in them. It's different when you're telling the facts or even a story, than when you're writing it. When you write, it tends to take on a life of its own and you're able to think back and make clever statements and proper assessments. There is absolutely no relation to real life. In real life you don't embellish and describe everything. You simply tell your story and five minutes later, you're done.

The pancakes had arrived while I was talking, the waitress giving me a smile as she dropped off the plate and promised to bring the coffee. I shrugged and eagerly dug in. The sound of me chewing and the clank of my fork on the plate was the soundtrack for the rest of my story, but I was damned if I wasn't going to get some of those delicious smelling pancakes into my stomach.

"When that guy answered her phone, I was sure that it was Louise I heard screaming. Then I called you."

Claude paused at this and pulled out his phone. I don't think I've ever seen him look so serious before. It even made me pause from licking the syrup from my fork.

"You sure you heard screaming," he said and I nodded miserably. Claude continued. "Do you have any idea where she could be? I've got a couple of heavy hitters on speed dial who could be useful in a situation like this. All it takes is one phone call and they can get over there and get her out right now."

As much as I wanted Claude to call his heavy hitters, that wasn't going to be possible. I shook my head, 'no'.

"They took her from the motel so I don't think they went back to her house. I've been beating myself up thinking about it and I have no idea how to find her."

"Fuck dude." Claude hung up his phone, disturbed, and more than a little pissed.

"I've been trying to convince myself that Louise is a big girl, and has been around the block so she can take care of herself, right? Plus there's the whole her being a vampire thing…"

There was an uncomfortable silence but then the waitress returned with the coffee. Claude waited while I gleefully poured sugar into my cup. I could smell the coffee, rich and dark and promising to be a real treat. I could practically taste it. Four packets of sugar went in one by one.

"Lemme see your eyes again?"

"Oh come on dude. It's embarrassing and still freaking me out."

He just gave me a look and I took off the sunglasses and threw them onto the table. The coffee would have to wait for a second or two.

"Wow man. That is seriously fucked up."

"Thanks."

"And it's because of the puking and the eyes that you think Louise wasn't messing around? That you actually are a vampire."

"Well yeah… I mean, this doesn't happen. You don't ever hear of any disease or anything that causes people's eyes to completely change color and if there was some kind of pill for it, you'd be seeing ads for it all over the place instead of Cialis."

"Side effects might include nausea, diarrhea, death, bloodlust and an aversion to crosses."

"Get your Vampiralis today. Yeah, that would sell real fast."

I took my coffee and inhaled the flavour, ready to drink. Claude pulled out a small velvet bag from his jacket and dumped it onto the table. I stared at what appeared to be collection of religious symbols. Claude now grabbed a crucifix and held it up.

"Aha!"

I was nonplussed. Didn't quite know how to react.

"Nice crucifix?"I ventured and Claude deflated. He put the crucifix down on the table and now held up a Star of David. I shrugged, unimpressed. It looked expensive. Maybe he was trying to sell it to me or something, I dunno.

"It's very nice, but I'm not Jewish you know."

"Dammit dude, you're ruining this for me."

"What am I ruining?"

"Vampires are traditionally afraid of religious symbols. It's a well known fact. If you're any kind of vampire, you should be outta here by now, not just sitting there drinking your coffee."

"I'm not actually drinking it yet. It's hot so I'm blowing on it."

"Well don't you feel anything? Anything at all?"

"I feel like I need my coffee. Does that count?"

Claude held up a Yin and Yang. I shook my head. A Star and Crescent was next. *Nothing.*

"What's that one?"

"Hands of God from Slavic Neopaganism. You feel something?"

My stomach grumbled noisily and I belched. "Nope. Just thought it looked cool."

"How about the Torii?"

"What's that?"

"Shinto religion?"

"Nope."

"Oh screw this: I give up."

"Nice collection though. Very expensive looking."

"Should be. I had to borrow them from the museum." He rolled his eyes at the look on my face. "It's not like they were using them anyway. Don't worry. I'm taking them back."

"Maybe it doesn't work like that anyway. You're an atheist. Hell we both are, so maybe the person with the symbol has to believe for it to work."

Claude watched me for a moment and shook his head. I

didn't quite like the look in his eyes. It usually meant that I was about to become a guinea pig, whether for the betterment of myself or just for fun. Claude usually claimed it was to help me out, but ever since Sara Jeffers had slapped me in ninth grade because of something Claude told me to say, I didn't quite believe him.

Claude almost poured a whole bottle of Tabasco sauce over his eggs and I paused eating, watching him. I could really smell the pepper from where I was sitting. It tickled my nose and for a few seconds, a sneeze threatened. The urge to vomit came back rather strongly and I found myself shutting down my nostrils in defense and just breathing through my mouth. *Damn,* why hadn't I ever noticed just how toxic the smell of the Tabasco was?

"Do you feel the urge to bite anybody?" Claude wanted to know.

"Well, is this like the blood sucking kind of biting, or is this the biting someone because they're irritating you and not letting you eat your pancakes?"

"I choose door number A."

I determined to ignore Claude for the moment. My food was really, really good and I was getting overwhelmed by the flavours. Oh the sweet, sweet flavours... And damn there was that fucking smell of Tabasco sauce again, somehow made worse by Claude slicing the egg and eating that horrible mess—

"*Your Tabasco sauce is seriously fucking with me dude.*"

My voice came out all cracked and hoarse and I coughed, surprising both Claude and myself. I could hear my breathing catch in my throat and felt a tightness across my chest as if there was a four hundred pound gorilla named Paulie sitting on me. Almost exactly like an asthma attack.

Fucking Tabasco.

Claude looked from me down to his eggs swimming in the Tabasco and in one movement, he threw a napkin onto the plate, then grabbed the plate and walked it over to the counter, but more importantly, away from me. I felt the gorilla on my chest ease up a little, allowing me to get a little bit of air and to fumble a glass of water to my mouth.

Claude returned, looking cautious. He slid his plate of pancakes over in front of him. For some reason the waitress had brought him the pancakes on a separate plate, so now with the Tabasco sauce plate gone, at least he still had something to eat.

"So the Tabasco sauce has more effect on you than any of the religious symbols," he finally said.

I drained my water and slammed down the glass on the table.

"Let's not do that again, shall we?" I said and Claude nodded, but I could tell he was filing that information away for later in that way that he always did.

I blew my nose and wiped my watering eyes before polishing off my pancakes, rather than looking at him. I was relieved to be able to breathe again.

"These pancakes are fucking delicious. Have you had your pancakes yet? Best fucking pancakes I've ever had."

"You're kidding right?" Claude poked at his own pancakes. "They taste more like sawdust than anything else."

"This guy, this cook here is a chef. He's a fucking chef, that's how good he is. Way too good for this place."

"Are you on crack? It's just ordinary diner food."

"I'm ignoring you dude. In fact, I'm going to just drink my coffee."

And I did.

Flavour exploded onto my taste buds. Caffeine raced through my system instantly, *pure electricity* coursing through my veins—

Everything went white as deep in my brain, synapses fired and then fired again and again and again and again—

It was all a fog to me, and somewhere I could hear someone screaming faintly but I was too busy, wrapped up in the fog to care who it was or even to tell them to stop.

***

This is what happens to a vampire who is exposed to an overabundance of flavour: the brain literally shuts down from the overload. The tastebuds on a vampire are apparently extremely sensitive, and while the most fragrant and delicious of foods will be doubly delicious, it is also too much for a vampire to handle. The taste sensation is more like an atom bomb, and every single receptor in the mouth is screaming, singing HOSANA at the top of their fucking lungs.

I had dodged the Tabasco bullet and run directly in front of the coffee train.

It was the "Starbucks Effect" in full force.

Reality came back, much like a brick to slap me in the face. One minute I was in a happy place with clouds. The next minute, I'm waking up in Claude's car, barreling down the freeway at horrendous speeds.

A minor spasm hit my body then and I turned my head to look at my friend, my eyes not wanting to focus, having a tendency to wander just a little bit. I tried to focus but my eyelids didn't seem to want to cooperate.

"Wha's happ'ing?" I managed to slur. Apparently my mouth was also taking a vacation. Upon further inspection, it seemed that the rest of my body was as equally unresponsive.

"I'm taking you to the hospital man. You just had a fucking seizure back there. Some dude was saying that you might have had a stroke or something." He looked worried now. "Your eyes and ears were bleeding dude."

Something popped in my ear then, and I was finally able to focus on Claude. There was a tingly feeling in my body as nerve receptors started to fire again. I somehow managed to reach up to massage my neck.

"I feel like shit. Like I overdosed or something."

"How would you know?"

Shit. That's right. That's the one thing that I'd never shared with Claude. It was probably more embarrassment than anything, and he probably suspected that I smoked a little weed or popped some pills from time to time, but he might have never guessed about the heroin. Hell, I would never have guessed about the heroin myself. It was one of the drugs that I had sworn never to take, along with any chemical drugs like LSD or Meth or even Acid. When it came to cocaine, I didn't even want to go there because they all felt so manufactured. With marijuana, I at least knew where I stood, and until my first taste of heroin, that had been my drug of choice.

So, needless to say, I remained mute on that one and massaged my neck, letting the feeling return to my body. Claude drove on, shooting me a look of suspicion.

"Maybe you should lie down dude. At least until we can get a doctor to look at you."

"I'm feeling better already. Really." That was in response to the look he was giving me. "Maybe you should stop speeding."

"I'm still taking you to the hospital."

"Do we have to? Last doctor I saw sucked all of my blood out and turned me into a vampire. I'd rather not go through that again."

Claude gave me another look, and I leaned back, giving in. He can get really fractious when he's pissed. "Fine, let's just avoid the ones with the intensely blue eyes, okay?"

By the time we got to the hospital, I could move my entire left side again, and my right side was fully recovered. Claude nevertheless managed to commandeer a wheelchair, and having dumped me into it with more force than necessary, pushed me into the Emergency Room, while humming the tune to the "Facts of Life" under his breath.

We spent the next three hours roaming the limits of the Emergency room, with me making the occasional bid for escape, but Claude wasn't letting me get away. He'd just chase after me and wheel me back into the ER.

I have a theory that boredom was invented in Emergency Room waiting areas. I'm serious. It's got to be the most boring place on earth. Within the first ten minutes, I'd already gone through the magazines twice and had rescued a snoring man from falling over and crushing his cigarettes. This was in the hopes that I could point out that I'd saved his cigarettes and then he'd offer me one, but no, it was not to be. He just crossed his arms, snorted and kept on snoring away, this time leaning severely over to the other side of the chair. When he fell over rather loudly, ten minutes later, I was already in the middle of *"Better Living Through Gardening"* and was rather enjoying the engrossing article on potting soils. It even had pictures.

Boredom I tell you. *Boredom.*

***

"Claude?"

"What is it Bob?"

"I hate hospitals."

"Me too. They always feel like places to die to me."

"Yeah. I know what you mean... I'm not dying am I?"

"Only if you have more coffee."

"This is seriously going to fuck with my diet."

"Maybe you'd feel better if you bit someone. Like her over there."

"Which one? The blonde?"

"She's cute. At least I think she's cute."

"Well, her back is cute. Shapely... What are you doing?"

"Well, Bob ol' buddy, I'm using my mental powers and I'm willing her to turn around."

"I don't think it's working."

"Wait, she's turning..."

"Fuck."

"What?"

"She's a vampire."

***

The vampire's name was Iva Mendelssohn and she happened to be my doctor. She gave me the once over as she entered the room, looking at my chart.

"What seems to be the problem? Mister—" She glanced at my chart. "Mister Diego."

"I had a bad reaction from some coffee."

"You're obviously new. Freshly minted are we?"

"First night. What gave it away?"

"The fact that you're here in the hospital. Our kind usually don't end up here unless they're clueless or helpless."

"Are you really a vampire?"

"See the eyes? The horrible bedside manner and the inability to give a shit? Good. Glad we're on the same page. Any more questions?" She looked at Claude as if she was seeing him for the first time. "You. Why are you here? You guys related?"

"I'm either the moral support or just here to keep him

alive. That part is still in discussion."

"Yeah," Dr. Mendelssohn said way too doubtfully. "Good luck with that." She turned back to me. "Do yourself a favour Mr. Diego. Go home, stay indoors during the day and try to stay out of trouble while you figure out exactly what it is you've gotten yourself into. First thing I would do is to get whoever turned you to teach you the basics."

"That's not as easy as it sounds," I said, thinking of Louise. "Look, maybe you can help me out here—"

"Nope. Not my job to train you. I assume you're smart guys, so better figure something out."

I was a little taken aback by this. Somehow I'd expected my fellow vampires to be more welcoming. Dr. Mendelssohn just looked tired and overworked, pretty much like all of the other doctors out on the floor tonight. Sure she was the least tired looking one, but she was tired anyway.

"What? No words of advice?"

"I just gave you all the words you need."

"Oh."

She turned to leave and stopped at the door. "Oh and Mr. Diego?"

"Yes?"

"One teaspoon of coffee to three cups of water. It won't kill you, and you can still get to enjoy it. My gift to you."

***

Claude drove me home in relative silence. I was thinking about Louise again so didn't really feel like talking much. Claude and I had spent several hours just waiting in the emergency room. It was one of the longest times I'd seen my friend in years. Pity it was because I was freaking out about being a vampire.

"So what now?"

"I dunno. I was thinking about everything and I suddenly realized that I had never seen the sunrise. I'd always just fallen asleep waiting for it."

"It's overrated."

"But it is one way to find out for sure what I am. What I've become..."

Claude nodded and shrugged.

"We're going to need a fire extinguisher."

***

I had never once seen a sunrise in all of my thirty years on the planet. I had talked about it from time to time, about going to see it, but that was usually to either get into some girl's pants or simply because I was drunk. Either way I would either be passed out or too busy by the time the sun was actually in the act of rising. From what I've heard it's supposed to be something pretty spectacular, a life-affirming experience that makes you glad to be alive, but I usually passed on it, mainly because I wasn't that into life-affirming things anyway.

So it was ironic that it would be the experience of becoming what might be a vampire (and my encounter with the lovely Dr. Mendelssohn was a kick in the nuts type of affirmation) that spurred my first sunrise experience. I was hoping that it wouldn't be my last sunrise either, but I just had to know for sure. I had long passed the point where someone telling me would be enough. What I was going through was a life changing experience, as fucked up as it was, and I had to know the absolute truth of it.

So I sat on the back porch of my apartment with Claude at the ready with his fire-extinguisher and a blanket, and watched as dawn slowly lit up the darkness. And I do mean slowly.

Claude had gotten a six-pack of beer from the trunk of his car, where he apparently kept a few in a cooler for emergencies. I didn't ask him what else he kept back there, since he had also gotten the fire-extinguisher and the fire blanket from there as well. I was just glad for the beer, and for the first time in my life I actually enjoyed the weak taste of American beer. Now that's what you can call irony.

"So irony is bad beer. That makes sense."

"Right now, I'm just glad that I can *drink* beer. I've been trying to make a list of any spicy foods that I'll have to avoid, and so far my options are diminishing really quickly."

"But that's only if you really are a vampire."

"I don't think there's any doubt about it. Not after the

night I've had. The coffee thing is kinda freaking me out a little, even more than the eyes."

"Yeah, I was gonna mention something earlier but I kinda forgot."

"What is it? Did I grow horns or something?"

"It's about your eyes."

"What about them?"

"They kinda glow in the dark now."

"You're fucking with me, right? Tell me you're fucking with me."

"It's not that bad really. It's actually kind of cool if you're into that sort of thing."

I was looking at myself in the glass of the porch door by this time, and I could kind of see what he was talking about. If I tilted my head just so, my eyes caught the light and reflected it back, just like a cat's eyes.

Whoa. Freaky.

"I don't think I'll ever get used to that. *Man.*"

"Have another beer."

I dug one out and opened it, inhaling the flavor of the beer I had previously hated, actually enjoying the smell of it now. I was getting a kick out of the smells. I noticed smells so much more now, everything an explosion of sensation that was practically colors in the air, waiting to be inhaled. The beer in my hand right then was incredible, a virtual powerhouse of waiting flavor, and I wondered what a good German beer would taste like. It would most likely give me another aneurysm or whatever the hell it was that happened to me earlier.

"You gonna tell your mom?"

That one came out of left field. I just gaped at Claude, and he took a deep swig of his beer.

"What am I going to tell her exactly? This isn't like some bad career choice or dating some girl she hates you know. I can't go home and say 'Hey guess what mom? I'm a vampire now.'"

"Why not? Your mom's more understanding than you think."

"Dude, I'm a *fucking vampire.*"

And then it hit me completely and totally for the first time. There would be other moments over the next year where reality would come back and hit me in the nuts, but it would never be the same. This first one was a doozy, and it hit right where it hurt.

Here I was watching the sun rise slowly from my back patio, and it was very likely it would be the first and last sunrise I would ever see. Three days ago, when I walked outside complaining about the sun, I had never taken the time to enjoy the sunlight and enjoy the day, never knowing that it would be the last time I would see the sun. The last time I would ever look at the sky. It was a tragedy because I couldn't remember the last time I'd even looked at the sky apart from a quick glance to see if it was going to rain. Nobody looks at the sky anymore; nobody ever looks up, and I was one of the nobodies.

"I'm scared Claude."

"We can call this off you know. You can go inside and wait it out."

"No. I need this."

"I'm scared for you too dude."

It was completely light out now, and there was still no sun, just a lightening of the sky, a sky that I now looked to, sunglasses in my hand. I looked about, seeing the light and felt a little foolish at my fear and nervousness.

"Nothing going on here."

Claude relaxed his hold on the fire extinguisher. He grinned, possibly as relieved as I was.

I turned back, sunglasses going onto my face, and the sun peeked over the tree line. I had started to laugh, laugh at the foolishness, and laugh out of relief, sheer unadulterated relief.

My laughter turned into screams as my exposed skin began to blister and boil. I staggered back, pain shooting through me, trying desperately to find cover, and I could smell something sweet like barbecued pork. Something was burning, and that something was me.

A blast of foam from the fire-extinguisher hit me, covering my skin and granting temporary relief. Claude somehow managed to throw the fire blanket over me and wrestled me back towards the door trying to get me inside where it was safe, and I could hide from the sun. He was yelling something at me, but I wasn't listening, just concentrating on the intense pain that was my skin.

Even as he slammed the door behind me, and I collapsed on the floor, still dripping fire extinguisher foam, I knew it was over. My tears couldn't take back the awful truth and the look on Claude's face echoed the truth.

Dismay.

Shock.

Horror.

Fuck.

Fuck me.

I was a *vampire.*

I was a fucking vampire.

Chapter 9
THE PROBLEM WITH VAMPIRES

D epression was quick in rearing its ugly head, and I didn't fight it. To tell you the truth, I was a little too busy just dealing with the burns on my face and hands to notice. The pain was immense, especially from my head, which Claude later told me had actually caught on fire.

My eternal thanks to the inventor of the fire-extinguisher and Claude's ability to not completely panic even in the most fucked up of situations and use said fire-extinguisher with skill and a good aim. It's not every day that you watch your best friend spontaneously combust from being in the sunlight. Okay, so maybe *'spontaneously combust'* is a little too strong a description and a little more than inaccurate, but I must point out that my hair *did* catch on fire, and when a man's hair is on fire, are you actually going to argue the finer points of actual spontaneous combustion? *Didn't think so.*

I had managed to fumble my way to the kitchen sink, and with Claude's assistance, had soaked whatever towels I had. After carefully cleaning the remains of the fire extinguisher foam off (*ow ow, pain, motherfucker that hurt*), I had pressed the towels to my seared and swelling flesh. My hands weren't so bad, just red and cracked and raw and only just beginning to swell. It was my face that felt like it was on fire, and the last thing I wanted to see was what damage had been done.

Claude left me lying on the couch while he went to get some burn ointment, which he happened to have in his fantastically well stocked car. I just lay there, wet towels on my poor skin.

I had been lucky to have been wearing my jacket at the time, and quickly ruled out any sunbathing in the future. At least that was one of the myths about vampires that stood up to the testing, and now I hoped that the myth about the quick healing was true.

"Remind me never to do that again." I managed to say when Claude returned.

"Never do that again." He handed me a handful of pills. "Vicodin. Take them all."

I popped the pills into my mouth without arguing.

"How bad does it look?"

"You don't wanna know."

"I'm asking aren't I?"

"Yeah, but I figure if you really wanted to know, you'd be asking me for a mirror instead of for my expert opinion."

"This fucking hurts man."

"That doctor did warn you."

Have you ever tried to apply burn ointment to yourself, while the hand you're using to apply said ointment, also happens to be burned? Try it sometime. It's self-fuckery at it's best. Claude could only watch me fumble and swear at myself so long, before he took the ointment from me and slathered it onto my face.

"Hold still and let's just get this over with."

"If you weren't you I'd almost kiss you, but my lips are burned too."

"Easy solution. No talking and definitely no kissing."

Claude put the rest of the ointment onto my face in relative silence and did my hands. I just lay back and waited for my depression to come creeping over me. My skin was itching like crazy, like there were ants under the surface, and they had all decided to not like me anymore, but the Vicodin was already kicking in. Claude was saying something to me, and I could barely see his lips moving.

Sleep claimed me and for a while I was able to rest and not think about anything at all.

I had the most fucked up dreams that day. I don't even remember what they were, but I remember waking up thinking about how fucked up they had been. What also got me was the fact that I didn't hurt anymore.

Of course I told myself that it was the Vicodin doing its job, but it wasn't until I stood over the toilet pissing my heart out, that I realized I could use my hands. The swelling had gone down, and as I flexed my hand, the skin was no longer cracked. It itched a little, like from a well formed scab, but that was all.

I *had* to look. So I spent the next five minutes taking off the bandages that Claude had wrapped my hands and head in, feeling way too much like a plastic surgery patient. I took them off carefully, just in case they needed to go back on, but after seeing my first hand exposed, I no longer had any doubt. I still looked like a lobster, but now the burned skin was peeling off in huge flakes where it had cracked, revealing completely new healed skin underneath. I wasted no time in ripping the rest of the bandages off, especially those on my face. I was relieved that my face was intact, just bearing the appearance of a bad sunburn, and I had to resist the urge to pick at the loose skin. My hair was quite another story. It was still burned, of course, and stunk the way that only burned hair can. I was going to have to shave it or cut it in order to get rid of the damaged bits. Apart from that, I looked like I could have just spent way too long in the sun.

I heard someone entering through the front door and turned, wondering if Claude had taken my keys, but then remembered that doors weren't the type of thing that got in Claude's way.

"Dude tell me that's you," I called out.

"Yeah it's me," Claude replied. "How are you feeling?"

I still itched, so I guess the healing process wasn't completed yet, but *holy fucking shit!* From burn victim to sunburn victim in eight hours. *Wow.*

"A little meh," I said, which was the understatement of the year, but I was being cautious and didn't want to jinx myself too much.

"You were on fire yesterday and now all I can get out of you is 'meh'?"

I walked out into the living room and for the first time

noticed exactly why the whole place was feeling so dark. It had been bugging me in a low grade way, the feeling that something was a little bit off, but I had been unable to see it until I was looking right at it.

Claude had been busy while I was sleeping and had duct-taped black trash bags over all of my windows, living room, kitchen and bedroom included.

"You did all of this? The windows?" I asked, stunned.

Claude stared at me as if I had risen from the dead or something. I raised my healed hands and grinned as best I could. The skin was still tight and felt a little tingly, so grinning wasn't exactly comfortable.

"Whoa," said Claude.

"Whoa," I nodded in agreement.

Claude shrugged and continued unpacking the crate of groceries he had gone out for. He produced an apple and bit into it.

"Nice job on the windows," I said as he threw an apple to me. I of course fumbled it, since my burned hands were still being stupid.

"Can't have you bursting into flames on me, buddy," he said.

"Or turning into ashes."

"Ashes wouldn't be good, but I don't think you're in any danger of that, not unless you kept burning and even then, you'd have to burn for a very long time."

I flexed my hand and winced a little at the residual itch. "I'm a vampire," I whispered. "Either that or Weapon X."

Claude wasn't convinced.

"Let me see the claws then."

I flexed my fists and adamantium claws completely *failed* to rip their way out of my hands, no matter how hard I wished.

"So vampire?" Claude grinned at me.

"Vampire it is," I took a moment to breathe it in and live with it. "Wow. I'm a motherfucking vampire."

I had to say it. I had to hear me say it. That was a point that I would later bring to bear in the Vampires Anonymous meetings, because it was quite possibly the most relevant, and the only way I could come to terms with what I had become.

I was a vampire, simple as that, and there was no turning back.

I looked up at Claude, an idea forming in my head.

"I wonder what else I can do."

***

So this is the montage part of becoming a vampire. In the movie there would be some insanely catchy pop song that would serve to tie together the series of wacky incidents with me and Claude. The reality was a little more mundane and one step at a time.

Claude wanted to take baby steps, and he actually started making a list, but I was full of the sort of nervous energy that bad decisions are made of, and couldn't sit still for the life of me. I kept peeking out the window, not really listening to Claude, but knowing that whatever he was saying was really important.

It was an overcast day, the kind that you get during the screwed up days of late Winter in Toronto, where Spring wasn't so much a season as a moment of relaxation that all of the snow had finally melted and was definitely maybe not coming back this time. *Maybe.* It might be a full two months before Summer blasted its heat at us, anxious to make up for all of the lost time, or it might be just a single week, but there were two things you could be absolutely sure of: when it rained, it was going to suck, and you were going to be glad it wasn't snow anymore.

It was one of the days where the weather hadn't quite decided to soak all of us and was in fact teasing the rain with the occasional gust of wind that shook the trees in the front courtyard like it had every intention of ripping off the limbs, and the thick, heavy grey clouds that were definitely waiting to make sure that nobody had bothered to bring an umbrella along. It wasn't malevolent weather, just really *sulky* weather. The kind of weather that hid the sun behind a perpetual blanket of cloud and suck.

I could still hear Louise's screams in the back of my head and somewhere I was entertaining a fucked up fantasy of mastering my vampire powers like a badass and going to rescue her with Claude tagging along as my sidekick this one time.

The big problem was that apart from burning in the sun and healing fast, I didn't seem to actually have any proper powers to test out.

I had opened the apartment door and was slowly making my way outside, sure that I was going to burst into flames at any second.

"You haven't listened to a word I've been saying," Claude said from somewhere behind me. It wasn't even a question. He already knew how my brain was working. "You know, about taking it slow and figuring out what we're dealing with here?"

"I'll tell you what I'm dealing with," I said, still fascinated by the lack of burning skin. There was a slight tingle, but nothing more, nothing out of the ordinary. "Indirect daylight seems to be okay... so far."

"We've definitely ruled in direct sunlight, so I hope you don't have any plans for the beach."

"Oh man, summer is going to suck so hard," I suddenly realized. "My mom was trying to get me to go back to Barbados to see my Dad this summer."

"Have you called your mom yet dude?" Claude reminded me. "She's kinda really worried about you."

"What am I supposed to tell her?"

"Nothing you idiot. You're just supposed to call her."

"I'll call her, I promise," I grumbled, and stepped out further into the muted light of the overcast day. *Suck it vampire legends!*

A thought occurred to me and I turned back to Claude.

"I think I might be able to fly."

***

"This is a bad idea," Claude said.

"Yes it is, but fortune favours the bold, man!"

"Fortune is a sadist. Your currently unbroken bones favour you taking a few baby steps to begin with. The smaller the steps, the better."

"I've got the fast healing thing man! I got this covered!"

"Are you serious or are you telling me what you want on your tombstone?"

"Yes!"

"Which one?"

"BOTH! I'm going to do it!"

"You really shouldn't!"

"I'm doing it!"

"So… I notice you're still here…"

"I'm doing a countdown in my head. I'm still at twenty!"

"I really don't think we should be trusting things we read on the internet dude! *Especially* about vampires!"

"If I can fly, it's going to be *so awesome!*"

"And if you can't fly, it's just going to hurt!"

"You only live once!"

"Or twice according to you!"

Fuck it. I ran for the edge, going full tilt and then I was sailing off the edge of the roof, daring gravity to grab hold of me in all of my defiance and for a moment, just a moment, I was invincible and I could do anything in the world.

The one thing I couldn't do however, was fly.

Damn you internet.

✳ ✳ ✳

Dr. Mendelssohn wasn't impressed at all with my lack of flying ability. She was even less impressed with the broken leg I had sustained from jumping off the roof.

I had bounced off the side of the building facing the alley I had failed to fly over, and had somehow managed to push myself back with enough force to hit the opposite wall, before falling haplessly in a decidedly downward direction. If I had been a cartoon character I would have pin-balled from wall to wall all the way down and staggered away with stars and birds circling my head. Since I clearly wasn't a cartoon, I managed to first break my fall and then my right leg when I landed awkwardly and with great force.

"I told him it wasn't a good idea," Claude said, and she just glared at him as she examined my leg. She had already discarded of the makeshift splint Claude had made from a piece of metal, shoelaces and his belt and her examination was not gentle in any way.

"Just shoot him next time," she hissed at Claude. "Much easier to deal with than this mess."

"He might have a concussion as well..." Claude said awkwardly.

Dr. Mendelssohn just shook her head and took a deep breath.

"I wouldn't worry about that one so much," she said. "The bleeding on your brain should have stopped quickly. Once the bruising heals it might actually make you smarter Mister Diego... but I wouldn't hold out much hope for that."

Well that was a disappointment, but I was in too much pain from my leg to care.

"I thought I was supposed to heal quickly!" I yelped. Ow! Pain!

"That's the problem, Mister Diego," Dr. Mendelssohn snapped. "You heal quickly, but if the bones aren't set, then they heal broken. They don't magically straighten themselves. That's *my* job."

Dr. Mendelssohn suddenly did something painful to my leg and I spent the next two minutes, or maybe it was an eternity, trying desperately not to scream. Finally she was done and I dared to look down at my abused leg, wondering if I should tell her about the other parts of me that were in pain.

"You didn't have to make it hurt so much, " I managed to gasp.

"I have to make sure you never want to come back here," she said, still not smiling. "Jump off another building and you will see the true meaning of pain, are we clear?"

I gave her the thumbs up, then grimaced at the itching in my leg. Something was going on down there and it hurt like hell.

"The nurse is going to fit you with a boot, but you need to stay off the leg for at least another twenty-four hours. You snapped the   tibia and the fibula, and the only reason you aren't screaming right now is because you're a vampire, so please don't do this again."

"Thanks Doctor," Claude said.

"Instead of experimenting, get him to talk to his mentor," Dr. Mendelssohn said to Claude. "It will save a lot of pain in the future, okay?"

"She isn't around—"

Dr.. Mendelssohn interpreted my forlorn look perfectly.

"No Mister Diego: I will not be your mentor. I've got enough fuck-ups in my life at this point and you sir, are a complete mess."

Dr. Mendelssohn pulled back the curtain and motioned for a nurse to take my chart.

"And get a haircut. Hair doesn't heal from burning."

***

11:22 PM is one of the worst times to get a haircut. If you really need a haircut at that hour, you're just going to have to do it yourself.

Claude bought a buzzer from the nearest pharmacy, which was pretty close to a McDonald's, and since we needed a power source and a mirror (plus I was hungry and wanted an apple pie), McDonald's was the best choice.

So I shaved my head in the McDonald's bathroom. It was far from the oddest thing I had ever done in the bathroom of a fast food restaurant, but it was strange to watch the burned clumps of hair fall into the sink as the skin of my head emerged from under the scruff of black hair that was just getting long enough to get a little curl to it.

There is something relaxing about having a freshly shaved head. The ability to run your hands over the skin in one direction and feel the smoothness and all of the previously hidden bumps saying "hi!" to the world, is a completely alien feeling to most people. Some people have only ever had a trim or a cut of their hair, never even thinking about taking a buzzer and going right down to the skin. They will never feel the alien landscape of their freshly shaved heads that on a simple change of direction in stroke, turns from silky smoothness to a prickly and strangely arousing experience as every single sheared follicle is pushed in the wrong direction. That right there, that feeling was the reason I never liked a lot of people rubbing my head on those times that I did shave it.

I normally kept my hair on the shorter side, since at a certain length it stopped growing thick and straight and it started to get curly. I had grown it out as a teenager and had ended up with a badass afro of thick curls, one of the benefits of a black father and a Mexican mother. A lot of the girls had loved it at the time, so that look was pure gold for a teenager. I had first shaved my head when I hit twenty-one and had then kept it short over the years. The shorter hair was just easier to deal with, especially just shaving it all off, letting it grow a couple of inches and then repeating the process.

My blue eyes stared back at me in the mirror as I ran my hand over my head and I just stared at myself for a very long time. I wondered who the hell this stranger was on the other side of the mirror.

It was disorienting to see those alien eyes again and not for the first time I wondered if the sunglasses weren't a means of self-protection, at least at first. Part of me wanted to claw at my eyes, to rip them out in sheer panic because they sure as shit weren't my eyes—

Okay, deep breathing, clam yourself.

After a moment of deep breathing with my eyes closed, I managed to look at myself in the mirror again, but I was very careful not to look myself in the eye.

The manager burst in at that moment and there was some confusion as he looked from the hair in the sink, to the still vibrating buzzer, to my face and then back down to the hair, still trying to figure out what was going on.

"Someone said you were shooting up in here. You can't do drugs in my bathroom pal."

"I'm just cutting my hair—"

"I don't care what you're doing buddy. You're done."

It was strangely ironic that I had done drugs in quite a few bathrooms and here I was finally getting kicked out for cutting my hair.

***

We ended up at the diner on Bathurst Street.

I was concentrating on making Judy-the-waitress turn away from talking to the young family that was currently taking her attention. The little girl was trying to climb over the back of the booth to get a good look at me, while the father was valiantly wrestling her back down, and the little boy was repeatedly stabbing the menu and loudly repeating his order of "and fries!" while his mother ordered for everyone. If I had any mental powers at all, they were being overridden by the chaos of a small family trying to order dinner.

Claude was looking up vampire powers, courtesy of the fount of all knowledge, humanity's version of the Hitchhiker's Guide to the Galaxy: the internet on an iPhone. Unfortunately, the internet was full of questionable sources and flooded by any idiot who had $12 to buy a domain and whatever it cost them to host a webpage that contained their particular brand of idiocy. At least he wasn't looking on 4Chan or we would have been besieged by a good dose of racism to round off the night.

"Standard vampire powers are supposed to include turning into bats, or small mammals," Claude read, somewhat skeptically.

I rubbed my temples and narrowed my eyes as I tried to concentrate on the waitress. I had seen someone somewhere do something like that once so it had to work, right? No, not the bats: the concentrating. I think it might have been David Copperfield, or some other stage magician. Those guys were worth millions of dollars so maybe they knew something that I didn't.

"More shit from the movies. Is this the same article that said I could fly?" I asked, still concentrating. "Because fuck that guy."

Claude grimaced and typed on his screen.

"Okay, this next site looks more promising…"

There was something logically wrong about what Claude had said and it bothered me enough to make me break my concentration on the waitress, who had almost escaped the family but now had to deal from the spill the six year old boy had caused when he had kneeled in his seat to insist that she acknowledge his order of "and fries! Please!"

"And is that like a single big bat or tiny little bats? How the hell is that even supposed to work?"

Claude shrugged, as confused as I was.

"Don't shoot the messenger. I'm just reading what I see. Here's a promising one: you get to come back from the dead."

I looked for Judy but she had already ducked away into the back. Damn she moved fast. I looked back to Claude, not impressed with his Google powers.

"We already know that. Kinda the whole thing behind being a vampire. I had to die to get here didn't I? I'm one of the undead."

"You have a heartbeat and you bleed. Like a lot. I don't think I've seen anyone bleed as much as you, so I think it's fair to say that you're not dead."

"Good, cuz I don't feel dead."

I didn't either. I wondered for a second exactly how being dead was supposed to feel and if I'd even know the difference.

"But if you die again, you get to come back."

I raised my eyebrow at Claude and played with my empty glass of we-don't-have-Coke-is-Pepsi-okay. The ice cubes clinked restlessly into the bottom of the glass and I stared at them as I tried to form the words that I wasn't quite able to get my mind around. Finally I looked at Claude and just shook my head.

"I don't think we're going to be testing that one out," I said cautiously. "First of all, I'd have to die and then we have the question of who's going to kill me. I can't let you do it, because if it doesn't work, then we're both fucked and very important here: I'm fucking dead. I'm too chickenshit to even try offing myself and if it doesn't work, it's really going to suck, what with me being fucking dead. Besides it could be as much bullshit as the turning into bats thing and I really, *really* don't want to die."

"Considering it's on the same website, maybe I should go to the next site?"

"Clickety click!"

Judy the waitress was back with drinks for the family and I resumed directing my mental energy at her, really concentrating now. Claude fought back a laugh and then, as seriously as he was able: "How about those psychic powers? Any luck yet?"

"If anything I'm making the waitress stay away… which is the exact opposite of what I want. I might as well throw a pen at her for all of the good it's doing."

"Or you could, you know, call her over."

"I *am* calling her over. *With my mind!*"

I gave up and just raised my hand when Judy glanced over my way. Believe it or not, she saw that instantly and nodded at me, the universal waitress sign for *"I see you and I'm coming, but this family is driving me crazy, okay?"*

Claude smiled and flashed his phone at me. There was a lot of red and black on the site. Lots of black. Talk about bad design.

"This site mentions compulsion—"

"Which doesn't work. Next?"

"Telekenesis?"

I tried and failed to knock over the salt shaker with my mind. I reached out and gave it an assist from my hand instead.

"Next!"

"Pyrokenesis."

"Well you're not on fire and I've been trying since we got there. Sorry not sorry."

Claude threw his phone down in disgust. "So what can you do dude? What kind of vampire are you?"

"Apparently the wrong kind."

I lowered my head onto the table top, suddenly exhausted and tried not to think of my broken leg. Claude was deep in thought, obviously vexed that he didn't have any answers for me. He liked to have answers to everything. It made coming up with an escape plan a lot easier when you knew exactly where you stood.

"I hate to break it to you dude, but I think you need Louise, or at least another vampire, to figure this out."

"And here I was hoping I could learn my vampire powers and be an instant badass so I could go and rescue Louise…"

"We don't even know where she is dude. I'm sorry, but I'm officially out of ideas."

We were quiet for a long moment and I just stared out the window, trying not to let the sounds of Louise's screams echo through my head too much. The thing is, they were already fading in my memory and that was the worst of it all, the guilt that I wasn't panicking anymore, somehow getting used to the memory, which should have cut me deep for a very long time. When Judy came to take my order, I barely noticed, so she just refilled my Pepsi and walked away.

I felt a wave of depression coming in the way that it always did, slow-building and inevitable, sucking all of the air out of the room and making even the simplest task seem impossible. I grinned haplessly in the face of it, tried to not go under.

"Maybe there is a guidebook or something on its way in the mail right now…"

Claude looked a little uncomfortable and placed his phone down onto the table, face down. Uh oh, this was going to be bad news…

"I've got one more bit of bad news…"

See?

"Let me have it."

"I have this job-type thing that I've been setting up for a couple of weeks. Which means I'm going to have to fly out to New York in the morning."

Panic. Don't panic. Don't react. Damn, it was hard not to react at all, and Claude could see the look on my face, could see me trying to deal with it like my world wasn't coming to an end. Until that point I hadn't realized just how much I was depending on Claude to be my sanity and help me through this whole vampire experience. It was useful to have him to talk to and try to figure things out, to avoid the insanity of the situation. We were a team, unstoppable once we got rolling and once I finally started listening to him, but now how the hell was I going to figure things out on my own? I knew myself and how much I managed to fuck things up without even trying.

I tried to smile again, tried to make a joke out of it, but I wasn't buying it and neither was Claude.

"You're abandoning me? At a time like this? Hashtag *what the fuck?*"

"Unfortunately yes. It's kind of a big deal, otherwise I'd bail on it… what are you doing? You look constipated."

I had my fingers to my temples again and I had been concentrating super hard at Claude, enough to give me an instant headache.

"I'm compelling you to stay."

"Look, you can stay at my place while I'm gone. There's plenty of food and fast internet—"

"And great big windows to let the sunshine in on mornings."

Claude looked like someone had punched him in the gut.

"Oh. I kinda forgot about the sunlight thing."

I smiled.

"Don't worry about it dude. I'll figure it out. I'm a big boy."

* * *

I didn't let Claude help me inside when he dropped me off at my place. I insisted on hobbling in and asked him if he was going to also kiss me good night and he allowed me to escape and pretend to be tough.

I was trying to not be an asshole about him leaving, since I was mainly freaking out. Besides you don't want to be an asshole to your friends, not really anyway, especially if you want them to stay friends. Yes the occasional mean jab happens, is in fact practically required, but you don't cross the line into asshole behavior.

Claude had to leave and that was that. It had nothing to do with me and I couldn't take it personally. Besides it was only for a couple of days, right? *What could possibly go wrong in that time?*

This is of course where Julio *"everything that could possibly go wrong"* Hernandes, enters the picture.

Julio was the drug dealer who lived in my complex. He was coming back from a car across the street as I hobbled away from Claude. Julio kept a careful eye on me as Claude's car pulled away and then he seemed to finally recognize me, cast and all. He broke out into a huge shit-eating grin and some more swagger instantly entered into his walk.

"Hey Roberto, mi amigo. What the hell happened to your foot man?"

I shrugged and looked down at the boot on my itchy foot.

"Stylish right? All the kids are wearing them these days,"

137

I joked. I jerked a thumb at my building. "I fell off the roof earlier. Broke my damn foot."

"Oh that's harsh man. Better to hurt *a los pies* than *la cabeza*, yeah?"

It took my brain a second to catch up. I spent 99% of my time speaking English unless I was around other Spanish speakers, and I still had to switch gears. When you're thinking in one language it's hard to stop translating everything and to just *think* the words.

"Damn straight," I said and fell into step with Julio, more hobbling than anything as we walked back towards my unit.

To call it a complex is a bit of an overstatement. The original owners had purchased a huge lot and had built 10 semi-detached houses with a shared courtyard in the middle. They had then sectioned off the basements to have their own entrance and small sunken balcony in the back and had rented them out as separate units. Some of the houses were divided even further with an upstairs and downstairs apartment as well. I lived in the basement, since that was cheapest and since I wasn't home at night, I didn't have to listen to people walking around above me all the time.

Julio lived in one of the other upstairs apartments with his girlfriend Sheila and a constant revolving cast of colourful and potentially dangerous characters. When I had showed up, I think he had been glad to see another Latino in the neighbourhood. I had been happy to know where the drug dealer was, so we had become instant bros despite the fact that we had nothing else in common.

"I don't owe you any money do I?" I asked him cautiously, and he just laughed and shook his head.

"Nah man, you're good, you're good. Got a little opportunity if you'd like to earn some cash though."

"How illegal is it?"

"Same deal as last time yo. Technically it's not illegal if you don't get caught, so just don't get caught, alright?"

I considered and shrugged. Why the hell not? It's always a good idea to be on the "nicer" side of your neighbourhood drug dealer, especially if you could score some drugs out of it… Besides, all I had to do was stash whatever bag he was going to give me and make sure he got it back. Easy money all around.

"Throw in a little something extra for me and you got a deal."

Ten minutes later I was inside my apartment and was seriously considering taking my boot off to see how my foot was doing. The big black bag Julio had left in my questionable care was open on the floor in front of me, full of clear-wrapped bricks of drugs that I was not to touch under any circumstances.

"I'll cut off your fucking balls and feed them to you," Julio had threatened, and he hadn't been kidding.

I had given an enthusiastic thumbs up, especially since he had provided a special brick just for my own entertainment.

What are you looking at me like that for? I already said I had a substance abuse problem, so *none of this* should surprise you. Did you think I was kidding?

I'm not ashamed to say that I prepared to shoot up and I was really looking forward to it, but even as I waited for the drugs to flow through my veins, waited for that feeling of euphoria, I had time to wonder what my new vampire senses were going to make of the experience. I had every reason at the time to expect the *ultimate* high.

What I didn't expect was a sudden rush of numbness and then… nothing.

I shot up again, thinking that maybe the drugs were defective, that maybe I was doing something wrong, but there was nothing doing, just the inescapable feeling of definitely *not* being high. The third needle had the same effect, the same desperate lack of anything at all. Thinking that Julio had somehow duped me, I did the unthinkable and opened one of the other bricks in the bag, the ones which I was *never* to touch on pain of death, but I was desperate dammit. It was only after I had injected twice from that new batch that I was finally convinced of the awful truth sticking out of my veins.

Drugs no longer had any effect on me.
Fuck.

Chapter 10
FIVE DAYS

D<u>ay One:</u>
Claude was long gone by the time I woke up. His flight had taken off at 7:15 AM and he had sent a couple of text messages, which I had pretended to ignore, but he saw right through.

-While you're ignoring me: Call your mom and let her know you're alive.

I'm an asshole. I didn't call my mom. Instead, I spent the day watching daytime television which only convinced me of one simple fact, and it's this: there needs to be a "Pimp My House" for vampires. Seriously. Do you know how expensive it would be just in curtains alone, to convert the ordinary apartment or even a house, into a vampire-safe home environment?

You've got all of these shows about people flipping houses, changing lifestyles and clothes, and they're all so cheery and bitchy and smiley and grumpy and not broke at all. I hated them all after an afternoon of TLC and MTV. Sure I had hated them before, but now this was a different kind of hate, the kind of hate that is spawned from not being able to go out into the sun and not having Claude around to bitch at and remind me not to go outside.

So I peeled my scabs, finally caving into the urges, and ended up watching back-to-back episodes of House of Cards for a couple of hours just so I could at least feel a little bit smarter about the world. While I did that, I wondered idly about how much a nice heavy curtain would cost to replace the garbage bags Claude had thoughtfully stapled over the windows. If any home needed to be flipped, pimped or made-over, it was my place.

Around 4 PM, still waiting for the sun to go down and cursing at it to move faster dammit, I poked around my nearly empty fridge and finally settled on making a fried egg sandwich with ketchup on the egg. Those were always good and cheap as long as you had bread.

I tried to call Louise, but the phone just went to voicemail. Then on a whim I called Jaime, glad to have an excuse to hear her voice again. I had rocks in my stomach even as I dialed her number. I was afraid I'd turn into a stuttering fool, but her phone also went to voice mail.

Feeling more relief than I should have, I hung up without leaving a message and stared at the phone for a while. I texted Claude.

-I think I'm dying.

-You're a liar. How are you feeling?

-I'm all healed up. Just peeling scabs.

-Sounds gross. You call your mom yet?

-Scared to. Plus she always asks about Jaime.

-I left a cheque for rent on your fridge. Make sure you give it to your landlord.

I looked over to the fridge and sure enough there it was, pinned to the freezer door by a magnet. Damn Claude couldn't give me enough ammunition to hate him. Instead I felt horrible for being so selfish.

-Dude, you didn't have to do that.

-Yes I did. You've been missing for six days. You might not even have a job anymore.

Oh shit. That hadn't occurred to me at all.

When the sun went down three hours later, I headed straight for the store, the reality of still having to pay rent and buy food staring me straight in the very empty wallet.

Needless to say, the Boss made me beg for thirty minutes before he relented. The fact that he hadn't immediately kicked me out should have clued me in that he was going to give me a second chance, but I didn't care. All of those late graveyard shifts were looking very attractive around that time.

"I'll work graveyard shift from now on," I pleaded.

"You already work graveyard," he pointed out.

"But I mean only ever graveyard. You know how everybody always tries to get out of graveyard? I'm volunteering to be the graveyard guy."

"Deal."

He made me work the rest of the night as penance, especially since I asked for an advance on the week's paycheque, and he exited the store grumbling loudly. I didn't mind it.

Sammy tortured me when she had come in an hour early and found out that I was back. She had assumed I'd finally gotten fed up of the whole mess and either offed myself or run off to Mexico.

When she saw my eyes, she literally squealed and spent the next ten minutes examining my eyes trying to figure out what I'd done to change the color. Sammy is resilient on her best days, and it wasn't until she had finally peeled my eyelids back, her nails almost digging into my eyeballs, that she was convinced I wasn't wearing contacts. I told her it was some kind of genetic thing that ran in my family.

"That's a kind of fucked up genetic defect. Did it hurt? Is that why you were gone for six days?"

It had never occurred to me to try to play it off like that. I seized on it immediately. *Thank you Sammy.*

"That's exactly it. I thought my brain was going to explode it hurt so much."

"It's a good look for you. Can't say the same for your head though. That was dumb."

I winced, still a little self-conscious about having a shaved head for the first time in four years. Some people are made to have bald heads with the perfect shape to just look cool. My head wasn't one of those and I couldn't wait for my hair to grow back in. *Stupid sun.*

And that was it. Things went back to normal from there, and I got on with my new life as a vampire. To my great disappointment it was almost exactly like my life before I was a vampire.

***

Day Two:

Nothing much happened.

Okay, that was a goddamn lie and I'm sorry, but in the big picture way of looking at things, nothing much really happened.

I mean I kinda freaked a little bit and went by to see Sweater Bob, since that fucker was the only other vampire I knew about at that point, but that was a complete bust.

When I got to the house, he was rushing out to his car with a couple of bags and man he was in a hurry. It was as if he was being chased by the devil himself or something. When he saw me, he didn't even pause, just threw the bags into the car and then jumped into the driver's seat.

"What the fuck do you want?"

"Have you seen Louise? She's kinda gone missing—"

"Get the fuck out of my way or I'll run you the fuck over!"

I jumped back as he gunned the engine.

"Do you know what happened to her?"

"The same damn thing that's going to happen to me, which is why I'm leaving."

"Is it the Gentlemen? Louise mentioned something about them before she vanished. Is it them?"

From the way Sweater Bob reacted, I was dead on.

"Sorry about the whole killing you thing pal," he said, and then Sweater Bob pealed off into the night, leaving me in front of his empty house wondering just who the fuck the Gentlemen were.

***

Day Three:

After work and a relentless half an hour of staring at Sammy's ass in her too short leather mini-skirt, I came out of the store to find that some moron had broken the back window of my Honda POS. The fact that the doors weren't locked hadn't deterred them, although I wondered what they thought they would find inside. It was probably just kids.

And now I was going to have to get that repaired. Fuck! At least I had Claude's cheque to take care of rent, but if he hadn't been that thoughtful I would have been completely fucked. It's one of the disadvantages of being as broke as I was. I went from paycheque to paycheque, barely making it through most weeks, and any sudden expense like some moron breaking the windows of my car, tended to be catastrophic. I didn't have any savings and all of my credit cards were completely maxed and two of them were already in collections, so there was literally no safety net.

I had time to wonder just how things had gotten so truly fucked up but then shook it off and drove home with the wind buffeting at me from the back of the car.

I somehow managed to make it home without getting a ticket, glad for being able to drive at a time of day when the cops weren't interested in you unless you were really fucking up. I was going to have to get some plastic to put over the hole in the window before it rained.

I went home and passed out for a bit. When I woke up, the Gentlemen had come to pay me a visit.

***

When they come for you, you are almost always asleep.

Wakefulness comes slowly, the pain in my joints a reminder of the awkward position in which I had somehow managed to fall asleep. I am still on the couch, and I can feel the tingling sensation of my nerves waking up and screaming at me, from the formerly numb side of my body. I have fallen asleep in front of the television again, some long ago battle being fought and discussed on the History Channel fueling my hazy and horribly detailed dreams. So I guess the first thing that I notice is that the television has been turned off.

It is entirely the wrong order of priority for me, because the very first thing that I should in fact be noticing is that there are three extremely scary looking men in the apartment with me.

One of them is currently making tea.

The small one, the one I will later come to know as Mr. Flynn, he is simply scaring the shit out of me.

The really fucked up part is that I'm not even sure if I'm actually awake or still dreaming some half-formed dream where my nightmares have followed and have manifested in the forms of three extremely well dressed men who I am dead sure are vampires.

I turn my head slightly and realize that the third one is perched on the back of the couch like an animal, intently studying my every move, his eyes dark, his teeth sharp and pointed and ready to bite.

This definitely has the feel of the dream to it and I will myself to wake up, to fight it, just close my eyes and open them again and it will be okay because these men are not real. This is how the dream always goes, where I'm not sure if I'm dreaming at all or if it is possible to ever wake up again.

I close my eyes and count to five. When I open them, the men are still there and yes, they are still scary.

I freeze and slowly look back to the small man, the one who scares me the most and is not inches away from ripping my face off.

I know that if I attempt to move without his permission, I'm probably a dead man. In fact, I'm already dead but for the grace of Mr. Flynn. I don't know how I know, but the fact is that I do, and that is enough for me.

"This is most unfortunate that our presence be required here." Mr. Flynn's voice is refined and extremely British. It speaks volumes of his years of experience and wealth, more so than his very expensive suit.

"You Mister Diego are an accident. Not meant to be."

He pauses as his second henchman returns with a cup of tea. It is a delicate china cup, with an equally delicate saucer, and the only reason I notice this is because I do not, or have not ever owned a delicate china anything.

"My employer does not like accidents and neither does he tolerate them."

He sips, his little finger held out ever so delicately.

"It is in your best interests that from this point forward, you will act deliberately, and you will be extremely careful in your actions. Every single action. You are a vampire now, accident or not, and you will not bring dishonor onto our old and esteemed house."

He smiles at me now, and I can see his fangs, long and sharp.

The large one reaches under the couch and pulls out Julio's bag of drugs as if he has always known that they were there. He places the bag onto the kitchen table and opens it but I don't care; I only have eyes for Mr. Flynn.

"Do we have an agreement Mister Diego?" He asks and nods his permission. "You may speak now."

"Just so you know, those aren't my drugs," I manage to mumble and instantly regret it. Apparently some part of me is aware of just how fucked up my entire life is about to be and how much of a bad dream this isn't, no matter how much I want it to be.

"The drugs do not matter. The attention they may bring to you and thusly to us… well that is entirely our concern. Do you wish to bargain for their return, Mister Diego?"

"No," I whisper even though I want to say yes.

Mr. Flynn, smiles broadly. He is after all, a reasonable man.

"Now, that wasn't so unpleasant as it could have been, was it?"

He smiles and sips at his tea. I watch numbly as he takes his time to finish the cup, smiling as if we were at a dinner party instead of my crummy old apartment. And every moment he is here, I pray for my life.

When he stands, it is crisp and deliberate. He hands his teacup to one of his associates and in one fluid motion, produces a business card from his coat. He holds it out to me and barely concealing my fear, I reach for it.

"Your presence will be required at nine tomorrow night. Do try not to be late. My employer dislikes tardiness in any form, and if you are late, one of the gentlemen here will have to have a word with you about it. I assure you that you will not enjoy it.

"Should you let fear take hold of you, and decide to absent yourself, you can be rest assured that I will be the one who will be having a few words with you."

The gorilla holds Julio's bag loosely in his hand as he stops and looks down at me, a terrifying figure. He watches me as Mr. Flynn exits; he leans over me, his breath rank and foul like the lair of some horrendous beast.

"Be late. We'll have fun, I promise."

***

Day Four:

I hadn't expected any of this, whatever this was.

It was an office like all of the other offices in the downtown core, except this office was populated with a variety of what

I assumed were vampires. Everywhere I looked on this floor, I saw the same familiar blue eyes in the faces of perfectly normal and to be honest, perfectly attractive people, who all looked moderately wealthy, even the interns.

The building was two blocks down from where I used to work, and it was one of those buildings that didn't have a name. It was simply 55 Queen Street West, the name and address, the one and the same. The kind of mystery that you never think of as a mystery until you have to wonder exactly who had their businesses in the building. I hadn't even been sure where to go when I entered, there being three banks of elevators to choose from. The concierge had pointed me to the third bank and I'd had time to wonder if I was even in the right place since all I saw were perfectly ordinary people. Even the armed security guards were perfectly normal, if not looking for a reason to make my day less pleasant since I looked like the type they usually kicked out with extreme prejudice. I was beginning to regret not having kept the cast on my leg so I could at least get the sympathy vote, but since the pain in my shin had died down, I'd felt confident enough to leave home without it. Stupid over-confidence.

Entering the elevator, I began to feel extremely self-conscious and had the thought that maybe I should have at least shaved. Guys like me are probably the reason they put full-length mirrors into elevators like the one I entered. Everything about the elevator said that I was about to enter into a world of corporate business and expensive suits, and you'd better not be wearing jeans and Doc Martens unless you're the delivery boy.

Yeah... I was wearing jeans and Doc Martens. I could feel the tightness of the cheap jacket I was wearing that was honestly the nicest thing that I owned. Unfortunately the nicest shirt I owned was a red Hawaiian type shirt covered with skulls instead of leaves or flowers and the combination was hardly flattering, especially with the stained blue-jeans and aforementioned Doc Martens. Most of my nice clothes had been stuck in my storage locker ever since I defaulted on the monthly payments, so there was no getting those back in a hurry.

There were no buttons in the elevator, just a flatscreen on the panel which lit up as soon as the doors closed. There wasn't even a door-open button or a call button, which I'm sure was extremely illegal, but I was getting the idea that whoever ran this operation was far beyond giving any fucks whatsoever. I was essentially trapped in the elevator that now seemed to thrum with a waiting energy, almost like a lurking beast itself.

I noticed the tiny camera above the screen and leaned over, sure that I was about to completely fuck this up for myself.

"Um, hello?"

The screen lit up and the extremely attractive receptionist stared out of the screen at me. She was black, young looking and her piercing blue eyes told me everything I needed to know.

"Do you have a card?"

I froze, my hands automatically going to pat every single pocket that I knew didn't have the card before my brain kicked in and reminded me to stop looking stupid and just get my wallet out.

"Card?" I asked stupidly. "I have a business card that the gentleman gave me. Tall, skinny, scary British guy."

"Please hold the card up to the camera."

I dug the card out of my wallet and tried a smile, seeing if I could lighten the mood a little.

"Yeah I got it here. Lucky I brought it with me too—"

"Just hold the card up sir."

Right then. Message received loud and clear. I shut the fuck up and held the card up to the camera. Something went beep, the elevator clicked and thrummed, and I was suddenly being propelled upward in the smoothest and scariest elevator I had ever ridden in.

The receptionist smiled from the screen.

"Take a right as you exit the elevator and I will see you there Mister Diego." The screen went black and I was alone for the rest of the extremely fast and extremely short ride, completely aware of the growing distance between myself and the ground. This distance was something I was acutely aware of, especially as my ears popped from the pressure change that's your body's built-in sensor, specifically designed to signal you when you're too damn high.

Floor forty-four was too damn high.

I exited the elevator and turned right as instructed, walking past a pair of women in tailored grey suits, neither of them with a hair out of place, their blue vampire eyes flicking over at me, examining and then looking away as if I was of little interest. They headed through a glass door that opened soundlessly and for a brief second I caught a glimpse of cubicles and offices beyond the door. It was just an ordinary office to all appearances, just very expensive looking.

The hallways were a shiny brown wood-grain, accented by steel or aluminum fluting with the baseboards and the ceilings lit with warm lights that made the black granite floors feel slightly more welcoming. The receptionist waited for me at the end of the short corridor, the wall behind her desk dominated by gigantic aluminum letters that spelled out The de Biers Company.

All it all it was very impressive and looked extremely legit.

Whatever the vampires of the company were doing for work paid very well. I had a fleeting hope that maybe I would be offered a job there, maybe in the mailroom or something, and approached the receptionist a little more timidly than I had been intending.

She just smiled and waved me over to a comfortable looking waiting area that looked out over the city.

"Harry will be with you momentarily," she said and then she was gone, finger to her ear as she answered a call. "The de Biers Company. How may I direct your call?"

I had discovered the floor to ceiling tinted windows in the waiting area that seemed more like a death sentence for any vampire on the floor. Since the sun had already sunk below the horizon, it seemed safe enough so I had approached the view tentatively and had been grateful there was nothing to make me explode into flame.

That had been fifteen minutes before Beatrice had showed up.

I had enough time to appreciate the view from forty-four stories up, a view that very few in the city ever got to see, but I was growing more hopeful that it was a view I would be seeing more often. The lights in the city were turning on here and there, yellow and white spots of illumination, distant signs of life in the humming city below that reminded me there were real people out there oblivious to my existence. Oblivious to the world I was about to enter.

If this was the way they lived, being a vampire might not be such a bad thing after all.

"I'm a daytripper you know," Beatrice had said as she had stepped up to the window to look out at the view before us.

Since this was easily the oddest thing anyone had said to me in a few days, I had to look to first make sure she was talking to me and not her phone or someone else who I hadn't noticed come in, and then to really make sure she was real.

She was about 5'8", slender with lean muscle that was definitely not from a gym, and she looked like she was in her early twenties. That is, until you got to her light blue vampire eyes and found yourself taken aback by a certain weariness and depth that you wouldn't see in a person that young.

"Hi Daytripper," I said. "I'm Bob."

She looked at me with a half-smile. "You're not half as funny as you think you are. Cute, so I'll give you a pass."

"So about this daytripper business—"

"Goggles, Bob. Polarized and coated with U.V. protection. Just like this window here. You could stand here in the direct sunlight and never even feel a tingle. It's the one thing that makes everyone feel truly alive you know: *sunlight*. The goggles I wear are extremely useful for protection against even the hottest midday sun. They're part of my outfit because you gotta have the rest of the outfit, otherwise you will burn. *Burn like a motherfucker.*"

"Like a motherfucker."

"Damn straight. A lot of the others are scared to try it you see. I've told them about it and they just look at me like I'm crazy. Do I look crazy to you Bob? Can I call you Bobby?"

"No you don't and no you can't—"

"We have all of this wonderful modern technology at our fingertips Bobby. This company has got shares in the latest sun protection creams, in sunglasses etcetera, etcetera. A hell of a lot of etcetera, if you know what I mean. It's in our best interest as vampires to be protected and to invest in ways we can walk in the sun. These fuckers here only dream of walking in the sun. Instead of standing inside a room and pretending, I actually do it. I've got a mask and all of this other gear and I don't let the sun stop me, because *fuck the sun,* you know?"

Holy shit, she was intense.

"Don't you look strange putting on all of that stuff? Don't people stare at you?"

"Let them stare. They don't know it's me under there, so why do I give a shit?"

I looked out over the city, not really knowing what to say. It sounded a little bit nuts, but she did have a point.

"It's kind of like changing the way you think about being a vampire, huh?" I said.

She smiled then and there was a quiet sadness, but at the same time a cheerful gleefulness in her eyes. There was something broken about her, something deeply flawed that was almost scary because she knew it and she wasn't scared of it.

"You should try it sometime Bob," she said intently. "You don't have to live your entire life after dark, no matter what they tell you."

BOOM! A door slammed open from across the hall, and we both turned to look, me startled out of the spell that I had been placed in, Beatrice with a more bored expression.

"BEATRICE!" A man's voice boomed around the office and all at once we were wrapped up in the wide wonderful world of Harry de Biers the third, Vampire extraordinaire, bastard son of a fucking bastard.

I hated him on first sight, but he already had me beat. He hated me way before ever meeting me, but that was just Harry. He went straight for Beatrice, who had by this time taken a few steps forward.

"Harry, you motherfucker!"

Harry wasted no time. He grabbed Beatrice by her ever so lovely blonde hair and punched her in the face, one, two, three times. It was fast and brutal and I didn't even have time think about blinking. Beatrice staggered backward from the assault and her head collided with the dark U.V. glass, cracks spidering up from the point of impact. Beatrice jumped forward, fists flying at Harry, but he blocked them all with ease before grabbing her by the throat and then in one swift move that would have looked more at home in a televised wrestling match, yanked her off her feet and slammed her bodily down onto the granite.

Beatrice moaned, coughing blood and spitting teeth and Harry got to his feet, holding onto a fistful of her hair.

This had all happened in the space of three seconds. I was still frozen in shock, staring stupidly at Harry and Beatrice as if trying to tell myself that I wasn't seeing this. All I could see was blood and broken teeth, and at the sight of the blood, part of me wondered if vampire teeth. Priorities, right?

Harry fixed his pale blue eyes on mine and smiled. His fangs were huge.

Oh, what big teeth you have, Mr. Wolf...

The fangs slid back up before Harry spoke to me.

"You. Come with me."

And with that command, Harry turned and walked back the way he had come, dragging a feebly struggling Beatrice behind him by the hair, leaving me to follow. Panic, my old friend, flooded back, bringing a whole chorus of 'oh shits' and 'oh fucks' with it, all yelling for attention in my head, all trying to be first.

"Oh, fuck me," I finally decided and raced after Harry, definitely not wanting to see what would happen if I didn't follow. I considered standing up for Beatrice for one millisecond, before deciding that it would get me deep into a world of pain and misery.

The receptionist nodded to me and closed the door behind us as we went through into the next hallway, and more than anything her lack of reaction was the scariest thing of all. It was all just business as usual here at the de Biers Company, have a nice day.

I followed Harry down the wood paneled corridor, past a few expensive looking paintings and caught Beatrice glaring at me, her look telling me to do *something dammit,* but what the hell was I going to do? Her face was flecked with blood and her teeth looked all broken to shit, and all I could think of was just how fast Harry had moved, at how good he was at personally delivering a very effective beating. Definitely not a man I wanted to be fucking with, no matter how much Beatrice begged me with her eyes to do something—

"What are you going to do to her? Sir?" I ventured.

Harry looked over his shoulder at me and laughed humourlessly, but he didn't break his stride.

"I was thinking of nailing her to a wall and letting her bleed out," he said.

This was the point where reality took a firm but definite leave of absence, because none of this could be real, could it? I had exited the real world where stuff like this doesn't happen, and when it does happen, somebody tries to stop it or at least says something about it... right?

Right?

"I don't think I can let you do that," I said, and instantly regretted it.

Harry stopped in his tracks, turned, and looking me directly in the eye, pulled Beatrice toward him and punched her in the face like it was nothing.

"Every time you say something," he said and punched her in the face again, her head rocking back limply as blood sprayed from the impact. "I'm going to hit her more," Harry finished, and punched Beatrice one more time for good measure.

Beatrice drooled blood and slumped down so suddenly I thought he had killed her on the spot.

"More pudding please," she mumbled.

Harry nodded to me and if I hadn't been scared before, I sure as shit was scared now, if not for me, then for this formerly beautiful stranger Harry had chosen to demonstrate his particular brand of brutality.

"Keep it up son."

Terrified beyond belief, I made the zipping motion across my mouth.

This was the fucked up scenario, Harry dragging the mostly unconscious Beatrice down the corridor by her hair, leaving a trail of blood and drool on the floor, and me meekly following and seriously reconsidering any job offer that I was now hoping was not going to be made.

I followed Harry into a huge leather themed office where he finally let go of Beatrice's hair, dumping her onto the carpet. He walked towards his gigantic desk without a care in the world. Beatrice stirred and spat blood out on the carpet and caught me looking at her poor fucked up face.

She smiled at me through jagged teeth and tried to wink with an eye that was mostly swollen shut.

"How you doing sailor?" She slurred, and failed to adopt a sexy pose. The swollen, bloody face was a little disturbing anyway.

"What you think I should do with her Bob?" I was startled to hear Harry even bothering to talk to me. He was sitting at his desk idly playing with a sharp looking katana and I wondered briefly if this whole thing was just a really fucked up show put on for my benefit—

One look at Beatrice made me reconsider that.

Harry continued. "That is your name, right? Bob?"

"Yeah, that's me."

"So what you think I should do with her?"

"With all due respect sir, I only just met her and I don't have a clue about any quarrel between you-"

"That's not what I asked you. Do you think I should kill her or let her live?"

Beatrice tried to sit up and slumped over instead. She looked at me with pleading eyes, and I got the idea that someone was playing for keeps, and it wasn't her. Saliva rushed my mouth then, as my adrenaline surged, and my heart pounded in my ears. I could feel my sphincter tighten as I stood there, not knowing what to say.

I chose my words carefully.

"I kinda like her, so maybe definitely not kill her? Please?"

There was relief in Beatrice's eyes now, and she tried a crooked smile, ruined by her swollen lips and a broken, bloody mouth. Harry never took his eyes off of me.

"You're absolutely correct. Of course, the choice isn't up to you, and I could decide that mercy isn't such a wise choice especially when it comes to little miss Beatrice here."

He looked at Beatrice now, and she looked to him with pleading eyes. "Wait outside Beatrice. We're going to have a talk when I'm done with Bobby here."

Of course I could have corrected him and told him that nobody but my mom ever called me 'Bobby' but I don't think he would have cared. So I just watched Beatrice stumble and then when she inevitably fell, drag herself out the door. I wondered how much damage and shame and humiliation I was going to suffer before I got out of Harry's clutches.

Harry was a very large man. He reminded me of Tony Soprano, but it was mainly because of his stature and those beady little eyes that watched you ever so carefully, as if telling you that they knew every little secret you tried to keep, and they knew that you weren't worth shit. His suit was probably more expensive than my mom's house, and he wore it casually, no tie for this man. His shirt was blood red, and it suited him just fine since it probably did a great job of hiding the blood. This was just a predator in an expensive suit, and he knew that you knew, and he was *glad.*

The predator watched me from his desk for a long moment until I got more uncomfortable than I already was, even though I hadn't thought that was possible. I met his calculating gaze, afraid to take my eyes off of him.

When he put the sword down on his desk I barely stopped myself from flinching, but I think he saw me despite my best effort.

"I hope that Mister Flynn and the Gentlemen treated you well when they delivered my invitation."

It was bullshit, and we both knew it. Anyone who met Mr. Flynn knew exactly what to expect from him.

"Very... um... courteous. I would love to have the opportunity to avoid spending any more time than is strictly necessary with them."

Harry grinned then, humourlessly. "They took a real liking to you. Mister Bryce commented on his excitement about seeing you again. I could call him up if you wanted, rekindle your friendship."

"That won't be necessary. I might just pop in to see him on the way out."

"Are you always this full of shit, Bobby?"

"Yes sir, I'm afraid so."

"I don't like you Bobby. Nothing personal, but you're an accident, and I don't like accidents. Too many of them happening these days. " He sighed. "Louise filled me in on what happened with you."

"You've seen Louise? I've been trying to reach her all week."

"She's been sent away for a while."

"Look, I heard her screaming on the phone! I just need to know that she's okay! You have to tell me—"

The look he gave me was less friendly than before.

"You're not here to ask questions or make demands Bobby, so shut the fuck up."

"Can I at least sit?"

"No. "

Okay then, so that was how it was going to be.

"You're here because Louise fucked up and decided to make you into a vampire. That is the sole reason I have to carve out a significant chunk of my day to deal with a loser like you.

"So you're a vampire now Bobby. Big fucking deal. It's not like it used to be in the old days. Back then we were a little more selective about who got the opportunity to become a vampire. It was something you had to earn, and by God you earned the hell out of it. Now, times are changing and we're trying to change with them, so we have a few people like you who don't know the first thing about us or even how to be one of us. Up until a week ago, you didn't know that we existed outside of stories and it was because that's the way we want it to be. Now here you are, standing on my goddamn carpet and I don't know if to kill you myself or welcome you… I don't even know if you even deserve to learn how to do things our way."

"Can I say something?"

"You just did. Speak again without permission. Go ahead. Please."

The charming part about Harry is that he never offered alternatives. There was never an "or else," never an option to chicken out, never a chance to run. So I did what I was told to do, and you would have done the same. Anyone would have. I shut the fuck up and listened.

"Well at least you can listen, I'll give you that. So I'll give you the benefit of the doubt and trust you not to fuck it up."

This just goes to show how well Harry had done his research on me. What works on paper and through facts is easily spoiled by being around me for a couple of days. I hate to say it this way, but I have a talent for disaster, especially when I'm trying really hard to do well, so I could already see how this was going to go.

"Here's a few basic rules for you Bobby boy: do not ever draw attention to yourself and by extension, to us. We vampires do not exist, and we do not advertise our existence. It is how we work and so far it's been working for thousands of years. Do not fuck it up."

I am so fucked...

"Don't go around killing people. That's not what we're about and besides, it breaks rule number one. You start acting like a psycho killer, then Mister Flynn and Mister Bryce will *find you.* They're very good at finding people. They will find you and then Mister Sinnel will make you disappear. He's very, very good at disappearing people.

"Do not under any circumstances, ever, EVER make another vampire. There is careful consideration that goes into who becomes a vampire and ultimately the decision isn't up to you. You break that rule, then all three of the gentlemen will be coming for you. I guarantee that. Nothing short of death will stop them, and even then I don't think they'll be satisfied.

"You're a vampire now Bobby. Welcome. Now get the fuck out before I change my mind about killing you."

I took the chance to ask about the one other thing that had been bothering me since Mr. Flynn had so kindly visited me.

"Look, Mister Flynn took a bag from my place last night—"

"Right. The drugs. Two kilograms of heroin and a lot of unwashed underwear. Okay, I really have to ask: does hiding the drugs in dirty underwear actually work?"

"You'd have to ask Julio, since they're his drugs... and his underwear. Emphasis on his, not mine. Personally I wouldn't want to be touching some dude's dirty underwear so—"

"Get the fuck out of my office. And I'm keeping the drugs."

"Julio is going to kill me if I don't have them. As in *literally kill me.*"

Harry looked at me as if I was stupid and I wondered if I was.

"You're a vampire now Bobby! Figure it out. Sink or swim baby, but you gotta figure out quickly what being a vampire means."

I started to leave, absolutely dumbfounded and mostly freaking out about my impending death, but I had to stop. Something was hurting me inside, and it was named Louise.

"What happened to Louise?"

"I already told you what happened to her."

"And you were lying then. I just want to know what happened to my friend."

Harry watched me for a long moment and finally nodded.

"She was a good friend of yours then?"

I nodded.

"Then she was a better friend to you than you deserved."

It was the past tense that drove it home for me. The finality of those words marking the transition of a person from a someone to a thing, that's something you never really want to hear. Louise had gone from an "is" to a "was" and it was because she had tried to help me. It was because of me.

***

I took that knowledge with me as I left, and I may have well been shrouded in a cloak of misery.

Beatrice was blowing bloody snot rockets at the wall outside the office and turned to look at me, her half-clotted globs of blood-snot painting a slow and disgusting trail down the wall. I was shocked to see her previously swollen eyes were just now black and blue. Her open wounds were closed, vicious red lines on her face the only sign that they had ever existed. Her broken teeth were jagged though and I wondered if she would have to pull them out and if they would grow back.

"*Beware the Drunken King,*" she whispered to me and I wondered just when she had lost her goddamned mind.

"Beatrice! Get your ass in here!" Harry roared, and she waggled her fingers at me.

"I'm gonna go bleed *all over* his carpet," she said as she

backed away into Harry's office. "He loves it when I do that."

The door slammed shut behind her and I was left alone in the hallway with my misery.

"Mister Diego?"

I turned, startled and the skinny intern in the thousand dollar suit who had snuck up on me like a goddamn fucking ninja, stepped back, aware that I might just hit him.

"The fuck did you come from?"

The intern led me out of the office, talking all the way to the elevator as if this was such a great day. I tuned him out even though he was saying things that sounded important, the only thoughts in my head being those of Louise in a definite state of dead. Memories of the times we'd spent together came unbidden and I found myself fighting back actual tears, fighting back the misery that threatened to roll over me and crush me under its weight because it was all because of me that my friend was dead. It was all my fault and this asshole was talking to me. How dare he? I considered taking a bite out of his jugular just to shut him up. He didn't know about Louise, and if he did, she'd meant nothing to him and he didn't care and *I hated him for it.*

"What happens when we die?"

That caught him off guard and stopped him in his tracks.

"What? What do you mean?"

"If I killed you, would you come back?"

The intern looked cautious as if he didn't know if I was joking or not. To be honest, I have no idea if I actually was joking either, so kudos to him.

"Maybe you should talk to your mentor about that. She should have given you some pamphlets, some reading material about it. I have some of them here if you'd like. Harry seemed to think you needed them—"

"What? Like the 'Benefits of Becoming a Vampire' and 'Welcome to YOUR After Life,' pamphlets like that?"

The prat thought I was serious. He looked mildly amused as he led me over to the elevator, rifling through the folder in his hand. He found what he was looking for and handed me a thick stylish black envelope that looked more like a set of documents you'd get from signing up for a chequeing account at a bank.

"Well, you got the titles wrong, but yes, pamphlets like that. You'll find the materials in here, standardized agreements, rules, a little bit of history—"

Okay, I was definitely not in Kansas, or even Oz anymore. What in the sweet name of Aunt Bessie was this idiot on about? They actually had pamphlets on how to become a vampire, like it was a fucking country club or something equally stupid and elitist. And this stupid gentleman's club mentality, these stupid rules was why my friend *had to die*?

The intern must have seen the look on my face, especially after I didn't take the package he was handing to me. Or maybe he saw the vein that was violently throbbing in the side of my forehead. He slowly started to back away.

"Maybe we can mail them out to you instead—"

"Fuck off you fucking pendejo. My friend is dead, and you're talking to me about pamphlets?"

"I'm sorry for your loss—"

"NO YOU'RE NOT! YOU DIDN'T EVEN KNOW HER, SO DON'T STAND THERE AND TELL ME HOW FUCKING SORRY YOU ARE!"

It seemed to get through to him. He nodded and tried on a smile that didn't quite fit. I felt sorry for him. Dude was just trying to do his job and here I was yelling at him.

"I lost some of my friends too. I know how it is," he said and I immediately felt like shit. He might be a vampire, but he was still human first, and last I checked I still felt like a human myself. Just an extremely fucked up one right at that moment.

"Sorry, I yelled at you. I just… I really don't feel like talking."

He rode down to the lobby with me and I recognized that he had probably been instructed to make sure I left the building, but I was too tired to care. In the lobby, he gave me a couple of printed glossy passes. I recognized the HTDK logo instantly. After all, it *was* the hottest club in town and had people lining up around the block to get in. The black plastic passes, like the ones I had just been given, were probably worth their weight in gold, especially on eBay.

"I am sorry that you lost your friend," the intern said.

"I'm sorry too."

"When you get a chance, come on down to the club. It will give you a chance to meet a bunch of us."

"What do you mean 'a bunch of us'?"

The intern looked surprised, then let me off the hook.

"Harry owns the place," he said. "It's a place for us vampires. Welcome to the club."

***

I went to see Jaime.

Or at least I intended to, but I wussed out at the last minute. There is something magical to a restraining order that inspires that kind of wussing out. So I didn't walk into her store and tell her the news that our mutual friend Louise, the one who had brought us together, was dead

Instead I stood in the alley across from her store and tried to cry for Louise and all that we had lost. As easy as the tears had come earlier, they were decidedly less forthcoming at that moment, so I stood there, stalking my ex-girlfriend and was completely unable to cry for my friend. The alley had the perfect combination of shadows and the occasional homeless person that allowed me to stand there long enough to catch a glimpse of her through the window without ever being seen.

After a while, feeling like a complete fraud because I couldn't cry for my friend, I stumbled off to work.

***

I was still in a state of depression, especially after I realized that I didn't have any pictures of me and Louise. Sure she had a bunch of her pictures up on her social media accounts, so I had those to remember her by, but I didn't have any of the two of us together. In fact, I couldn't remember taking any pictures of the two of us. I was always the one behind the camera, and now *nothing* was all I had to show for it.

By the time, Sammy showed up I had gotten to thinking about how I was going to tell my friends that Louise was dead, in fact, what I was going to tell them about her death. This had quickly led to the fact that I couldn't *actually tell* anyone that Louise was, in fact, dead, without telling them how I knew for sure, *oh and by the way, she was a vampire and now I am one too*. That wouldn't go down very well.

Maybe they would figure it out after a while when she failed to update her Facebook page. The last time had been the night she had met me in the bar and then nothing after that. Just the picture of her and her eternally sunny smile on her timeline banner. The picture had been taken at night in a bar somewhere.

In fact, all of her pictures had been taken at night.

There are some points when you ask yourself exactly how well you know your friends. How much do you really, really know about them, and how much of it is truth? How much do they actually want you to know, and how much can you know before you begin to judge someone? In all of my memories of Louise, I now realized that I had never once met her during the day. All of our encounters had been after dark, but that was just the nature of the friendship, and I hadn't thought twice about it. She was just one of those friends that always seemed to show up in dark places. Even when I had crashed on her couch for a couple of weeks when I was trying to find a new place, we had never gone outside during the day and the curtains had always kept the place dark, which was fine by me.

Now I wondered exactly how long she had been a vampire.

So that was what was on my mind when Sammy showed up, steam practically coming off of her.

"I hate men!"

"I'm a man."

"Well, I hate you too, but that's different. That's a personal hatred. This is more general and a lot more vindictive."

"Lucky me."

"What the fuck is wrong with you? Somebody died or something?"

"Actually yes."

"So remind me to care in about twenty minutes."

Anger. Genuine anger and hurt. How well do you know your friends, and if you knew them well enough, would you actually care?

"You're a fucking asshole Sammy. I want you to know that."

"I think you meant to say bitch," she snapped back at me.

"No," I replied. "You're definitely a *fucking asshole.*"

I didn't speak to her for the rest of the night. She eventually tried to apologize, a real heartfelt apology, but I wasn't listening at the time. I just wanted to get away from her and be depressed and think deep and depressing philosophical thoughts.

Most of all I just wanted to mourn for my friend in peace.

***

When I got out of work, someone had stolen my car.

I stood there looking at the space in which I knew I had parked my Honda eight hours before, and I felt so lost, so alone. I didn't even think to look anywhere else since this was the spot that I had parked it in. This was my spot, the only place I ever parked. It even had a minor oil stain about the size of Texas from the everlasting leak in the bottom of it, so there was nowhere else to look at all.

I should have laughed and been cheered up. After all, someone was obviously broker and more fucked up than I was. So fucked up that they had to take my car...

When I turned around, I spotted my car parked in front of the store, lights on, engine running. I knew it was my car. I had been driving it for years now, and it was one of twenty in the entire city and besides, my POS had a particular lean to it, just like the one in front of the store.

I got pissed then. I mean it's one thing to steal my car, but it's another thing entirely to steal it and then flaunt it in front of me. I had enough of my own problems right now, with my best friend abandoning me to my own devices when I needed him the most, me being an extremely broke vampire and my other friend dead because of me, and I couldn't even mourn her in peace. So yeah I got pissed, and before I knew it, I was walking towards my car, fists clenched, ready to fight tooth and nail over what was mine.

I was ready, adrenaline pumping something fierce and about halfway there I started to run. I had a passing thought about if vampires had any additional strength like in the movies, since something like that would come in useful right about now.

My bubble got busted when the car door opened, and Claude stepped out into the light and waved at me.

Have you ever had one of those moments where your emotions are suddenly switched, and you're left holding the bag and you're caught up in the momentum of whatever it was you were doing? That was me all around. I couldn't stop running, I tried to, but I literally couldn't stop myself, and I couldn't stop running either. Claude had this moment where he was smiling and then saw me still coming at him, and the look on his face went into "oh shit" mode. And then he took off, running from me, not knowing what the hell was going on. I ended up chasing him around the car, but by that time I was laughing more out of relief than anything else.

"Dude stop chasing me!" he managed to yell, and that broke the spell. We both stopped then, looking over the car at each other, me completely out of breath. Claude grinned. "Good to see you too man."

"You stopped texting me dude! I thought you got arrested or something!"

"Never! Getting arrested is for amateurs," he grinned. "How's the vampiring going? Bitten anybody yet?"

That was the funny thing. I hadn't even had the urge to bite anyone and had just been eating regular food, if you can count expired cereal and egg sandwiches as regular food.

"Actually no. I haven't. I've been wondering about that, and I really gotta talk to someone about it."

"Yeah, I thought it was one of the basic tenets of vampirism. Goes with the teeth, the sleeping during the day, the coffins, the lusty young maidens…"

"Well, I still don't have a coffin and last time I checked, still no lusty young maidens."

"Any word on Louise?"

I nodded, not able to say the words, suddenly unable to breathe, and finally there with my best friend in the world I was finally able to cry for my dead friend Louise.

I don't know how long I cried for and it didn't matter. Claude let me cry and didn't say a word. It didn't even feel like I was crying for her but for all of the things I never got to say to her, all of the time I had wasted doing other shit than appreciating her while she was still there. She had been my other best friend, and now she was gone and it wasn't fair, *none of it.* I should have been the one who was dead and I knew it. I'm kind of embarrassed to say that I was also crying for myself, the thought of everything I had gone through, all of the hard times and all of the things I had lost. I cried and was horrified for even being so selfish that even then I couldn't make it all about Louise, but I guess that's what human is being about.

And I wasn't that anymore and I knew it.

So I cried and fuck you if you think any less of me for it. You would have cried too.

Claude handed me his phone while we sat on the curb drinking the six-pack he had brought with him. I looked from the phone to Claude and thought I was going to cry some more. Finally, I just took the phone and flipped through the photos I had been looking for.

Pictures of me and Louise.

They were exactly what I needed to be able to say goodbye.

***

Day Five:

I woke up around 1:30 PM, the kind of waking up that's more like being jerked out of sleep with the feeling that someone else was in my apartment.

This is true: most people can tell when their house is not empty. Every house has its own feel, smell and sounds and it's something we all become attuned to. You know exactly what it's supposed to feel like at 3 AM when you suddenly have to pee so badly that you've almost wet the bed. You know what it's supposed to sound like at 9 AM when people are moving around outside and traffic is buzzing about and even that sound is so different than how it sounds at 5 PM. The house sounded different when there were six people inside, and it was such an alien feeling that if they stayed too long, you began to get a little itchy for people to get the fuck out so that the house and you could feel normal again.

The house especially feels wrong when you wake up in the middle of the afternoon and there is someone else there who isn't supposed to be.

I jerked out of sleep, my heart already pounding in my chest even though I was barely conscious, and I was aware more than I had ever thought was possible of someone else in the apartment with me.

The television was on and I could hear the sounds of someone playing on the XBox console. They weren't doing so well and I could hear the impatient sounds of the controller being tapped and jerked around, but underneath that, the sound of a heartbeat that wasn't mine. It was the first time in days that I had been so acutely aware of my vampire senses, and as I focused on the intruder, it occurred to me that I could smell him, a mixture of sweat and cologne and… a lot of marijuana?

I fumbled on a pair of sunglasses and stumbled to my bedroom door. I carefully peeked around the corner at Julio.

"Dude, what are you doing in my house?"

"Playing XBox yo. I was going to wake your ass up but then I remembered that you work the night shift you know? That new Super, Oscar, he opened up for me. A bit of a *pendejo*, but nice guy."

On the screen Lara Croft missed a jump and plunged to a grisly death. Julio grimaced and then turned to me, laughing.

"Man this game is fucked up! You seen this shit?"

My heart was still pounding, more from the rush of adrenaline that was surging through my veins due to the clear danger of Julio, and I looked around my apartment, trying to get a full bearing on the situation and hoping against hope that Julio had not come to pick up his drugs.

"I'm gonna grab some cereal," I said. "You want anything?"

Julio looked me in the eye and he smiled slyly. "Naw, I'm good amigo. Just got back from a fucking sushi lunch. All-you-can eat is my favorite, you know? You get to choose from all kinds of good shit but I always go for the fucking *unagi*, you know?"

Julio resumed the game and I made my way over to the kitchen, still calculating my chances of making it out of the situation alive.

"I don't get much of a chance to go out for sushi these days man. That shit can get expensive and my job doesn't pay shit."

"Plus you got a drug habit to support, right Bobby?" Julio laughed a little at that and I hated him for it. Cocky bastard. "I feel you my hermano. It's all fucked up until it isn't, correcto?"

"One hundred percent," I poured a bowl of Rice Crispies and added just the right amount of milk, or at least so I hoped. Getting the right milk to cereal ratio is humanity's next great holy grail, and after achieving it once in my life, I was forever chasing that happy accident once again.

"What's with the windows Bobby?" Julio asked. "You trying to keep the light out? Or trying to stop people from looking in?"

"There's a funny story about that—" I said as I turned around.

BLAM! The cereal bowl exploded in my hands and I jumped, startled, as hard plastic fragments, milk and puffed rice flew everywhere.

"Holy shit! What the fuck dude?" I yelled and looked up at Julio, who was still pointing the gun at me, smoke rising from the barrel.

"I'm going to ask you once, and then I'm going to shoot you again when you lie to me, so don't fucking lie to me Bobby. Tell me the truth and I might even call you an ambulance and get you patched up, okay?"

"What do you mean shoot me 'again'?" I asked and Julio gestured at me with the gun.

I looked down at myself and for the first time I noticed the bullet hole in my shirt and the slowly spreading bloodstain as my body and brain caught on to the fact that I had just been shot.

Here's the funny thing about getting shot. Everything that you see in the movies about getting shot is about 99% bullshit. It's similar to vampires in that aspect. People don't get shot and go flying backward or flipping through the air like you see sometimes. It all comes down to physics and the fact that a small piece of metal is being powered by an explosion which sends it moving through the air so fast that you can't see it. It is so fast that some people report hearing the sound after they had already been shot, and in some cases they simply didn't have a clue that they had in fact been hit until well after the fact. That's just how fast bullets move, and everybody reacts differently.

I should have felt pain, should have felt something at that point, but there was nothing and it was almost comical to me. I had been shot in the stomach and all I wanted to do was laugh at the sheer absurdity of it all.

"Where are my drugs Bobby?"

I laughed then, a short barking laugh that caused fresh blossoms of blood to appear on my shirt, but still there was no pain at all.

"I knew it! I fucking knew that was why you were here!" I grinned but Julio didn't grin back. He either didn't get or like the joke. "I don't have your drugs Julio! If you want them, you'll have to talk to Harry but good luck with that one, let me tell you. I don't think he wants to give them back and I even asked nicely."

Julio really didn't get the joke.

"I can't figure out if you're lying to me or deliberately fucking with me, " he said. "Where are my fucking drugs?"

"*Harry* has them! Swear to God! You want his address so you and he can talk it out?"

"Who the *fuck* is Harry?" He shook his head. "Fuck it. It doesn't matter. I'm just gonna have to fucking kill that *cabron* as well. I actually trusted you Bob, you know that? You're a dumbass, but didn;t think you were actually stupid. Especially stupid enough to go and sell my drugs out from under me? That was worth at least fifty thou easy, so you better had gotten a good fucking deal."

"See, here's the problem Julio. Harry's guys didn't *buy* the drugs as much as they *took* the drugs…"

Julio looked like he was going to cry.

"Doesn't matter, since you're just going to shoot me anyway!" I said and what the fuck was wrong with me anyway? Why was I in such a good mood after I had just been shot? It felt kind of like after I'd had one cup of coffee too many, the point where the jitters begin but before the shits kicked in.

"You're goddamn right," Julio said and shot me again.

Or at least he tried to shoot me again. I saw him aim and squeeze the trigger and I was already moving, jumping to the side and *holy shit*! I had actually *dodged the fucking bullet!*

A hole had appeared in the wall behind where I had just been standing. Not in me, but in the wall, because I had *dodged the bullet!* I looked from the hole to Julio, and he looked as surprised as I was.

"Did you see that?" I asked him excitedly. "Did you *fucking see that?*"

BLAM! Julio fired again, and I jerked my shoulder back as the bullet whizzed by and smashed into the wall.

Julio stared at me, astounded. "*Chinga la madre,* what the fuck is up with you?"

I felt amazing and wondered if this is what Harry had meant when he talked about figuring out what being a vampire was. It was a pity that Claude wasn't around to see this display because I knew he would have been as amazed at it as I was. I wondered just how fast I was moving. Maybe I was so fast I was just a blur like in the movies. Who the hell knew I could dodge bullets now? *Why didn't somebody tell me about this shit?*

I looked up at Julio and grinned the grin of a bastard son.

"I got bad news for you Julio. Only one of us is walking out of here alive."

Julio wasn't convinced. "*I still got the gun dumbass!*"

"And I can dodge bullets, you fuckstick. *I'm a vampire now.*"

Julio just looked at me like I was stupid, but then something clicked in his brain and he looked around the apartment at the blacked out windows.

"Is this why you taped up the windows? *Pendejo* motherfucker! Holy shit man, *what the fuck happened to your eyes?*"

I had whipped off my sunglasses and Julio had finally given the response I had been looking for. About fucking time!

"I'm a vampire motherfucker. You can't kill me!" I announced triumphantly.

"*Chingado* motherfucking *chupacabra!*" Julio yelled and he was freaking out, just like I wanted, just like he should freak out when faced with a fucking vampire. God it felt good to get the right reaction; it felt *good just to say it* and have it out in the open and actually mean something.

Unfortunately, Julio's method of freaking out also involved trying to make a run for the door, while unloading his gun at me. The first two shots were very panicky shots and would have missed anyway, but the remaining eleven bullets found their mark, ripping through various parts of my body as reality reaffirmed its hold and reminded me what a bitch it was.

I looked down at the multiple holes in my legs, arms and torso and wondered what had happened to my sudden power of dodging bullets. I had been doing so well and now my body was just filled with so much pain. Pain and holes.

"Ow," I said and spat up blood.

And then Julio shot me again.

This time, that motherfucker shot me right between the eyes.

Chapter 11
DEATH AND ALL HIS FRIENDS

As a vampire, death is something that happens to other people.

Everybody's got some kind of opinion about death. Go ahead and pick a random person out of a crowd and they will have some kind of personal connection to death. Maybe they will even pretend to be blasé about death or say that they don't *fear* death, but this one thing is true: death has touched us *all* in one way or another.

Maybe it is some ancient family member that everyone is finally relieved to be able to stop checking in on and lying about how well they're looking, and *no you don't look old at all Nana, no one can guess you were one hundred and thirty years and will you just die already dammit?*

Maybe it's a friend they've been meaning to catch up with and can never seem to make schedules match with until they hear one day that there's been *an accident* and of course they promise to make it to the funeral, but in the end are either too *chickenshit* to go or once again, *schedules* don't match.

Maybe it's someone closer, a friend or a brother who they never expected to be gone just like that and it's *just not fair goddammit. That kind of pain…* they will carry that with them for the rest of their lives, that *knowledge* that they can never again hear the laughter of that loved one, and that soon even the *smell* of them will be forgotten.

Or maybe it is a pet that stuck around way too long but was such a huge part of their lives and saying goodbye is like losing part of themselves.

In the end, death touches *everyone.*

Except for vampires.

Yes it touches us and yes we die, but it's not in the way that people and pets *die.* For vampires death is more like a holiday or a weekend trip. It's something we always come back *from.*

The problem is that the act of dying still *hurts like a sonofabitch.*

***

"Hey buddy. You owe me ten large for saving your ass."

That was the last thing I had ever expected when my drawer was finally pulled open and I blinked into the bright fluorescent light, wishing desperately for my sunglasses, and just shielding my eyes as best I could with my hands. As it was, it saved me from having to look directly up Vern's hairy nostrils as he leaned over and breathed into my face.

"You wanna know what they do to you down at the morgue? They cut you open and pull all yer organs out before bagging 'em and putting 'em back inside, along with a ton of other nasty brutal-type stuff. Luckily you're here, where we make sure all yer bits are accounted fer, and then we lovingly put you back together so yer all nice and shiny and *alive.* All o' this for the low, low price of ten thousand dollars. So whaddaya say?"

Now, the normal reaction in a case like this would be simply to stutter "What?" and look completely confused, which is what I almost did. But since this was hardly a normal circumstance, being that I didn't come back from the dead every day and since I wasn't enjoying the experience all that much, my response was more in the lines of:

"Fuck you buddy!"

Luckily, that was more Vern's kind of language, and he just shrugged.

"All right then. Fair enough, fair enough. I expect you'll be wanting some clothes then. It's fucking cold in here, what?"

The 'here' that Vern was referring to was a brightly lit morgue, and it gave me the creeps, especially since I had until a few minutes ago, been one of the more *silent* residents.

The whole being dead thing, that didn't return to my memory yet. I think I was a little too traumatized at that point for my mind to want to start poring over that particular highlight of my otherwise dull and pointless life. I hadn't been planning to die for a good while, and even being a vampire, it was an experience that I had been hoping to put off for a very long time. I had been specifically avoiding mobs with pitchforks and torches due to their vampire killing tendencies.

And now here was this old dude extorting me for ten thousand dollars.

Okay: for the sake of clarity, let me back up a little bit, to about ten minutes before.

***

My initial reaction when I had woken up in the semi-darkness had been anger. That had of course quickly been replaced with a good dose of fear mixed with a lot of "what-the-fuck?"

There was a low-wattage light in my box, and an iPad installed in the roof of the box. The note taped on top of the iPad said the most helpful thing that anyone could have said, given the circumstances.

DO NOT PANIC.

Now here's the thing about coming back from the dead, at least for me: It was just like waking up. Of course, some people will wake more violently, depending on their various methods of death, or perhaps because of the very last thing they remember. People who died violently like I had, you know with the whole *rain of bullets* plus the bullet to the brain type of thing, would be a little more traumatized by the suddenness of the entire affair. Others who died more slowly would have longer memories and more pain to remember. They, in fact, may not have wanted to come back. See, the absence of pain is a wonderful thing. In fact, it is the natural state of being for all of us, and we would like to remember those times when there was a lot of the whole lack of pain thing going around.

I would have hated to die slowly.

So I woke up, not yet completely traumatized, and the first thing I was aware of was the note above my head. It said not to panic, so I took its advice, after all, there was probably a very good reason why someone thought I might panic and didn't want me to, right? Or was that the *exact reason to panic?*

I started to freak myself out a little bit there. Comes from thinking too much.

I felt the familiar strains of panic reaching at me, and then read the note again, thinking that maybe a little positive affirmation would help, but there's something about being enclosed in a metal box that just *drives the panic right home.* I had finally gotten a bearing on my current location and despite the iPad above my head, it was definitely very box-like and not very reassuring, despite the note--

Hey, there was more to the note. It had been simply folded over, and there was more writing on the inside.

Curiosity being such a huge part of human nature, I stopped freaking myself out and opened the note.

"Greetings. If you have taken my advice and have not panicked, then I would like to apprise you of your current circumstances. You have been placed in storage while your body regenerates from the extensive damage caused by the manner of your violent death. There is a communication system next to the iPad-"

I checked, and there it was. Funny that I hadn't seen it before.

"--so please feel free to alert us when you are awake. Someone will be by shortly to let you out. In the meantime, feel free to watch television on the provided applications. We have full subscriptions available to premium services in all of our boxes, including Netflix, HBO and Showtime, so please, enjoy while you wait"

I hesitantly tapped the screen and after a moment of confusion, figured out which app to select for Showtime or SyFy.

It wasn't for another twenty minutes that I realized I hadn't actually used the intercom to tell anyone that I was back from the dead yet. Then again, I don't have Showtime and HBO at home, either.

"Um... hello?"

There was no answer.

"Hello? I'm done being dead now. Can I be let out, please?"

Still no answer.

Dammit. I went back to watching the SyFy Channel app. Rather appropriately, they were offering full seasons of '*Dead Like Me.*' I spent the next hour being amazed at how they'd managed to take all the cuss words out and apparently half of the humour as well. It was a lot funnier with swearing from what I remembered, but then again I come from the school of thought that everything is funnier with swearing.

It's amazing how watching television can take you away from things. I was getting comfortable and wishing I had some snacks when someone came knocking at my box. I paused the screen and listened.

"Hello?" I said into the intercom.

"You ready to come out yet?"

"Can I just finish this show first? It's got like ten minutes left in it."

"I suppose so. Tell you what, I'm going to get some tea and muffins from the kitchen, and I'll check on you then, how's that?"

"Can you get me a donut while you're at it?"

"Fine, but I'll have to charge you."

So I watched the last ten minutes of the show, devoid of thought for a while. What a charmed existence, you must think, that I was able to get comfortable in a drawer at the morgue. Given the circumstances, I think I was just glad to be able to get comfortable at all, especially considering the alternative of freaking out and trying to claw my way out of a metal drawer. Like that would have been productive. I was just glad I wasn't claustrophobic.

What happens if you get a claustrophobic vampire?

I shudder even to think about it.

***

Are we all caught up now? And in case you're wondering, no: I have no memory of death, no stories of tunnels of white blinding lights and certainly no angels with harps or even a solitary demon and a single match with which to torture me. All I knew

(blam!)

was that I had been dead and now... I wasn't anymore. Is there life after death? *Yes there is.* There is life after death, and *it's your own...* but only if you're a vampire.

Everybody else is fucked.

Vern disappeared from sight as I tried to position myself to get off the side of the drawer, wiggling my legs over the side and trying to get a bearing on my situation. I finally got a good look at the rest of the place, and it completely blew my mind.

For a morgue, it was very nice. It looked like it had been designed by whoever designed Harry's office, all leather and wood and marble wherever they could make it work. It was rich and gaudy and beautiful all at the same time. Even the Latin etched into the floor above the Coat of Arms told me everything I needed to know. Of course, I didn't understand it, since Latin is one of those languages that they just don't teach in school anymore, but just the fact that they would put it in Latin said a basic fact: *"we're richer than you and we have a* Coat of Arms *motherfucker."* That was all I needed to know.

EN CRUOREM NOS PARTIR.

Impressive right? The Coat of Arms was identical to the one in Harry's office and had the smell of very old money, maybe older than most other old money, and would most definitely stand out here in Toronto. You only found that kind of old money in some moody old European country. This Coat of Arms had a bat and a wolf on it. Do I really need to say more?

"Yer clothes are over 'ere."

I looked over to Vern, past the rows of identical wood panelled boxes similar to the one I had just gotten out of. Vern was standing behind a desk in the middle of the room, a slender looking computer in front of him. Everything in the room matched, even Vern... at least until you looked at his *shoes.* They were the only non-elegant or inexpensive thing in the room and clearly were a very old and very comfortable pair of shoes that were never intended to match his very expensive suit. They were the kind of shoes that had been good sometime in the 1970s and had been polished and treated with love even as they folded themselves to fit the shape of Vern's feet. They had been repaired more times than I could guess and said so much about the man that wore them that I could have written a book about his life. Loyal and steadfast, even if he was a little opportunistic… and a little smelly. The smell of tobacco that engulfed me as he leaned over told an even louder story and his long and strong fingers, stained yellow from nicotine, told of a lifetime of hard labour. The thought occurred to me that maybe Vern's little extortion deal wasn't going exactly to plan.

"Has anyone ever actually paid you to get out of this box?"

Vern considered it for a moment.

"There was this one gent, he was ready to pay, him being afraid o' the dark and all, 'specially since I'd turned out his light. But Madame Vera wasn't having none o' that. I only tries it on the young 'uns like yerself. Bit more willing you lot are. The older 'uns'd just rip me throat out and call it a day they would."

Something occurred to me then, and I blinked with surprise.

"You're not a vampire?"

"Wouldn't want to be, the condition some of you comes in looking. When I goes, ain't no coming back that I'll be wanting. Couldn't afford it if some bloke was asking me to pay up y'see."

"Can I have my clothes now?"

I turned to get dressed and Vern went to the computer to do whatever the hell it is he did here. I half expected him to type slowly with one finger, but Vern was amazingly adept at using the keyboard and the combination touch screen.

The clothes weren't mine. It was a brand new suit, Italian, according to the label, and it looked like a year's salary to me.

"These aren't my clothes you know."

"Oh, I knows it. Madame Vera bought them for ya seeing as how yer old clothes were full o' blood an' holes an' the like. I wouldn't worry about it if I was you."

Well okay then. If Madame Vera didn't want me to worry

about it, who was I to turn down a $600 pair of pants?

I got dressed and turned to find Vern waiting for me.

"So who is this 'Madame Vera' anyway?"

"She owns this place. I just runs it, make sure yer kind are comfortable and the like."

"And ten grand poorer if you had your way."

"You know what I could do with ten large? One day lad, one day..."

Vern led the way out of the morgue, and I followed, pausing only one minute to wonder if there were any other dead vampires in the process of healing inside the drawers. It made me uneasy to think of it and

(gunflash)

there was a moment where I felt like throwing up when my ears

(bang!)

rang like I had been standing I front of a concert PA system all night, but then it passed, and I followed after Vern, wondering what the hell was going on.

There was definitely way too much marble in the place for my liking and by the time Vern led me into the office where Vera was waiting for us, I had stopped trying to count the number of hideously expensive paintings on the wall. By that time, none of the surroundings mattered anymore. Nothing mattered anymore, just *Madame Vera*.

"Hello Robert," she said and I couldn't help but smile weakly.

Madame Vera was utterly exquisite. She was perfect in every single way, and she knew it, but then she'd had an extremely long time to practice. She looked to be in her early forties, and had the kind of exquisite beauty that all women hope to have at some point and that all men got an instant woody over. She was at least six feet tall with long slender limbs that were all toned muscle, her flawless olive skin a perfect complement to her piercing vampire-blue eyes and dark brown hair that would have been dyed black if this was a vampire movie. Truthfully, my first thought was that Catherine Zeta-Jones was a vampire, but then I realized that this woman was more flawlessly beautiful than any woman who had ever appeared on the movie screen. There was no denying the effect she had on me, possibly had on all men. In fact, with Madame Vera, there was no denying anything at all.

"Hello," I said back, and found myself wanting to bow or something absurdly gentlemanly that I had no idea of how to be. I just wanted to scream out *'Holy shit you're fucking gorgeous!'* but that was behavior that would get you in the doghouse, and that was the last place you wanted to be. Oh no, you wanted to be in Madame Vera's good graces all the time.

"Welcome back among the living Robert. I trust you won't make dying a regular habit."

"If it means getting to see you again, it's a habit I'll have to take up."

That one failed to make any points. I'm sure she'd heard it before, and there I was making an ass of myself.

"Come along now Robert, I have an eight-thirty appointment and we're already running late."

And with barely a pause, I was caught up in the whirlwind that is Madame Vera, hustling along behind her, barely keeping up as she swept me through the corridors of what now appeared to be a convention-sized mansion.

"You're about twenty minutes overdue, but we'll excuse your tardiness this time, after all it is your first time here, but we must make sure to do better next time and not keep everyone waiting."

"Who is everyone?" I managed to stammer, and Madame Vera beckoned for me to open the door for her. I did, and she bustled her way through, mesmerizing and intoxicating in every fibre of her being. I was sure I was in lust, if not in actual love.

"Oh, silly boy, your guests of course. They've come to pay their respects to you."

Guests? Respects? There was the overwhelming feeling of being completely out of my depth, and I didn't quite know if Madame Vera was a circling shark or a friendly dolphin. With those teeth of hers, she was looking more like a shark every minute, albeit a very sexy shark who could bite me anytime she wanted…

"Where are we going again?"

"Oh dear, dear Robert: we're going to your *funeral.* Come along now."

This last was because I had stopped dead in my tracks and was fairly boggling at her. I had to run to catch up because Madame Vera didn't stop for anybody.

"How can I have a funeral? I'm not dead anymore." I had to think for a moment. "Am I dead?"

"Don't be silly Robert: not at all. This is your first death however, and you must celebrate your rebirth in style and class. Don't worry about a thing: I've already made all of the arrangements and even rented you some friends for a half an hour or so. "

"You rented me friends?"

"Well of course I did. I wasn't about to go find your real ones. Besides, real emotions are so difficult to deal with. These friends will do very nicely and for a half an hour they'll be your very best friends in the whole world. Only the best for you, darling."

"Suppose I don't want a funeral?"

She just raised her eyebrow at me and I felt the quiet fury of countless years of dealing with idiots like myself staring down at me. I wanted to punch myself in the face right there just so she wouldn't have to do it herself. Madame Vera knew what was best, and that started with me shutting up and doing exactly as she told me to.

"Of course you want a funeral," she said rather pointedly. I could read the subtext loud and clear and endeavoured to shut the fuck up. Madame Vera continued. "I've already made all of the arrangements, so you just listen to me and everything will be over before you know it. It will be *mostly* painless, I promise."

She hustled me into a darkened room and there, at the end of the room in a mound of flowers, was a casket. It was very expensive looking, all polished brass and rich mahoganies or whatever it was made of. It was also very empty, clearly waiting for someone (me) to take up residence. The problem is that someone (me again) wasn't exactly sold on the idea of actually needing a coffin and was entertaining the idea of running away very quickly. My rented friends, a couple of girls and three guys who looked like they came right out of an Abercrombie commercial, started to sniffle on cue. I had to admit, at least my friends were pretty.

The organist struck up a tune, and Madame Vera hustled me to the casket.

"Now into the nice coffin you go."

I hesitated, and Madame Vera smiled reassuringly.

"Trust me, it's remarkably cathartic. I believe one client referred to it as 'healing… relaxing' and she's got very good taste. Hurry now darling, we must not let your nice friends wait."

And that's how I ended up at my own funeral, lying in a casket and wondering what the hell I was doing. Two attendants had shown up almost out of nowhere and Madame Vera ordered them around like the general she was, getting them to fix the flowers and making sure everything was perfect. I just grinned and bore it, wondering how the hell anyone had managed to talk me into the macabre ceremony.

Madame Vera looked down into the coffin, something clearly on her mind.

"Oh, I forgot to ask. Did you want a Priest or a Rabbi? I've gotten Father Macklin to pop by, and if it isn't any bother, I'd prefer if we just went ahead and used him if it was all the same to you."

I sat up in the coffin, more out of shock than anything.

"You got me a priest? Is he a vampire?"

Madame Vera gently pushed me back down.

"Of course he's a vampire. Now lay down. You're technically dead."

Something was bothering me. I popped back up, hoping to get a look at the vampire priest.

"What does God think of that arrangement?" I wanted to know, but Madame gently and forcefully shoved me back down.

"I have no idea Robert. Next time you see him, why don't you ask him?"

I had one more question. I popped back up and Madame Vera smacked me in the forehead with the palm of her hand, clearly at her wit's end.

"Talk to the priest after the ceremony Robert."

"But I have questions—"

"Great!" Madame Vera said, sending the message loud and clear that we were done. "Now that our corpse has agreed to stay in the coffin, we'll just start with the viewing..."

I had a few minutes to look at the beautifully carved wooden ceiling, wondering if I dared to get up and make an exit, but Madame Vera would probably just wrestle me to the floor before I ruined her perfectly prepared funeral. I still wanted to get a look at the vampire priest but had a feeling that Madame Vera was prepared to nail me into the coffin and have a closed casket funeral if that's what it was going to take.

I actually started to relax and wondered at what Madame Vera had said about how healing this experience was. She may have had some very good logic and insight behind this whole thing. I started to come to terms with my entire existence and how much it had changed. I made a vow to ask the priest about the whole God and the meaning of life thing.

The first of my rented friends showed up, a gorgeous blonde with expensive jewelry. I winked at her, but she was fully into the role and ignored me.

"I'll miss you--"

"Bob," I hissed at her.

"--Bob, so very much."

And then she was gone, replaced by two of the guys who were sobbing inconsolably. This went on for about a full minute, probably because Madame Vera was directing everyone from out of sight somewhere, and the rented friends were gone. The last one, a Puerto Rican looking girl with dark hair, kissed me deeply. She smelled of some expensive perfume and that was heady and overpowering as I enjoyed the surprise tongue in my mouth and the sweet taste of her lips. What surprised me even more was that she had also slipped a card into my hand, presumably with her number on it. It was cool and weird and sexy as hell and almost made up for the weirdness of the whole situation.

The priest was a bit of a surprise. He was definitely a

vampire. He was a good-looking fifty, and had a whole George Clooney thing going on that no doubt had him neck-deep in panties at every service. Not like that would matter to a priest, right? I wondered for a second if they stayed celibate after becoming a vampire, but one more look at the sexy motherfucker who was about to conduct my service convinced me otherwise. Dude winked at me and grinned, clearly enjoying himself.

It was the shortest ceremony I had ever been through.

"You were dead, now you're not, be blessed under God, ashes to ashes, dust to dust and welcome back." He held out a hand. "Need a hand outta there, son?"

I took his hand and pulled myself out of the coffin. As I did, I noticed Madame Vera looking very sad and crying, actually crying, as if this was all for real, and my heart went out to her. The rented friends were already filing out, and the cute brunette waved to me as she went out the door. I made a note definitely to call her later.

"Thank you father," I said and he smiled at me. "Does God know you're doing this?"

"Beats me. I'm still waiting for him to tell me otherwise. In the meantime I still have my faith."

"I would have just thought that you couldn't be a vampire and be a priest at the same time. Seems a little hypocritical if you know what I mean…"

"God works in mysterious ways son. Can't be anymore mysterious than in the face of vampires, now can it?

Madame Vera came over and slipped her arm through mine and once again I was in love as she leaned into me, her smell wafting over me. It was instant woody time all over again. Damn she was sexy.

"Thank you father," she sobbed. "That was a lovely service." Madame Vera started to guide me away, and I waved to the priest as she swept me away again down a different set of corridors.

"That was not so bad," I said and she smiled.

"Oh, course not. It's a very healing ceremony, an acceptance of our lives after death, *despite death* in our cases and it allows us to understand our very place in the world. We're vampires, and we should be *proud* to honour that."

We'd reached a door now, and I was guided outside, feeling thankful for having met this wonderfully sexy woman.

"I can never repay you for this Madame Vera."

She smiled, total benevolence and I wanted to jump her bones right there and then.

"Don't be silly Robert. Of course, you can. Here's your bill."

The door slammed very solidly in my face.

***

Madame Vera had a car waiting for me, courtesy of Uber Black and no doubt already added to my humongous bill. I rode most of the way back into town in pants-shitting terror, my eyes occasionally seeking out the invoice in my hands and instantly finding that huge number of twelve fucking thousand dollars and a few odd cents. I don't think I have ever seen that much money in one place, not even after cashing out my 401K after I had gotten laid off.

Somehow in my state of panic I managed to call Claude.

"Dude! Are you okay? Where the fuck have you been?"

"Dead. Dying. Mostly dead. I'm not anymore."

"I have so many bad words to say to you, but right now I'm just glad that you're alive."

"I guess that's one test we don't have to run anymore. It's official, I'm one hundred percent not dead anymore. I'm a vampire."

The driver jerked in his seat and I could see him looking at me in the mirror, clearly disturbed.

"Chill out dude," I said to the driver. "It's just roleplay. I'm not going to bite you."

"What?" Claude said. "Since when were you biting people?"

"I'm not. I was talking to the driver. He's dropping eaves pretty hard right now," I said, and lowered my voice a little, deliberately looking out the window at the passing scenery. "I'm going to need a huge favour—"

"If this involves money to pay off the dealer who shot you in the head, then *you've got to be fucking kidding me.* I mean I'm glad you're not dead anymore and everything, but no."

Fuck. He knew about Julio and apparently Julio had been talking. A lot.

"No," I said and I heard Claude exhale in relief. "This is about money to pay off expenses with the vampire morgue. I apparently owe them twelve thousand dollars?"

Silence, then: "Did I mention all of the bad words I have to say to you?"

A wave of helplessness and desperation hit me hard then, and looking at the bill for confirmation didn't help at all. I found myself gritting my teeth and could feel my temples throbbing as I realized just how fucked I was. I looked down at the expensive suit that I was wearing and peeked at the bill to see how much the suit had cost me. I almost teared up when I saw a $7500 price on the suit, but the very next line was "*Complimentary -$7500*", so maybe Madame Vera had taken it easy on me after all.

"Dude, I really need your help here. Do you need me to beg? Is that it? Because I will—"

"Meet me at the Thompson Diner in twenty minutes."

I stared out the window, watching the trees turn into apartment buildings nestled among even more trees and steadily encroaching concrete, and I had a particular flash of clarity about the exact moment my life had gotten so fucked up. It wasn't when I had gotten turned into a vampire, or even when I first burned in the sun, but instead something much more insidious and perfectly ordinary, at least if you were me. It had been when I had chosen to take those drugs from Julio. Everything had just gone all fucked up from that moment and I knew it. I wondered what else Julio had been saying about me, if he had been ranting that I was some kind of vampire. I wondered if he had run from the scene of my murder and if some kind of high speed chase had followed that had ended in a blaze of gunfire worthy of a scene in a movie.

My phone buzzed, a text from Claude.

-*Don't panic dude. We'll figure this out.*

-*Panic over and done. Mild freaking out to begin in 5…*

-*As long as it's mild. See you at the diner.*

I suddenly realized that the driver was watching me again,

probably wondering exactly what kind of psycho he was driving around.

***

For me, and millions of other people, coffee is sanity.

Dr. Mendelsshon was right about the coffee. I was still training myself to go through this ritual instead of pouring and drinking and enjoying the resulting embolism, but it was fairly easy to remember. In restaurants it earned me some really weird looks but I had decided that I really didn't give a fuck, since all I wanted was to drink my coffee. So the waitress would bring me four cups, one empty, two filled with hot water and one filled with coffee. First I poured one third of the coffee into the empty cup and then filled the rest with hot water. Add sugar, stir and blow before I scorched my lips off.

It was a new ritual and one I would come to know very well over the next year, so much so that it was almost automatic, but as it was still new at the time it was one I was still struggling with. The waiter, a skinny dude with a name tag that said "Jimmy" gave me an amused look as he took food to the booth behind mine.

Claude slid smoothly into the booth across from me, startling me with his sudden entrance.

"Dude, where the fuck did you come from?"

Claude got straight to the point.

"Do you know that your shooting didn't even make the news?"

That got my attention in a hurry. I paused from stirring the sugar into my heavily diluted coffee, the clink-clink-clink of the spoon on the mug coming to a sudden stop, then resuming ever so carefully after a moment as I let that particular fact sink in.

"How's that even possible?" I eventually asked.

"Is there something you're not telling me Bob?" Claude wanted to know. "Something happen while I was gone? I ask only because I'm completely in the dark here and I really want to help you, but I can't do that if you're keeping shit from me."

"Maybe…" I said, thinking of Harry and my encounter

with the Gentlemen. I had meant to tell Claude everything, but had only loosely filled him in on the barest details about Harry. I hadn't told him a thing about the Gentlemen because even thinking about those guys made me extremely and irrationally terrified that they would show up just by the mere mention of them. Please note that I did mention how irrational that fear was, and yet there was something about it that I really didn't want to test out.

Oh and of course I hadn't told him about Julio and the drugs because frankly that was none of his damn business… except now that it was.

"If it wasn't in the news, how did you find out about it?" I asked.

"Oscar, the new apartment supervisor gave me a call. I've been paying him to keep an eye on you." Claude nodded to Jimmy and mimed drinking a glass of water. I could only stare at Claude in astonishment, my jaw practically hitting the floor.

"You're spying on me?"

"Only since you got turned into a vampire. Somebody's got to look out for you ya know."

Jimmy came over and Claude ordered the burger and a I'm-Sorry-All-We-Have-Is-Pepsi. Jimmy hustled away and I glared defensively at Claude.

"I can take care of myself."

"You just got shot in the face by your drug dealer Bob. How is that taking care of yourself thing working out for you?"

Fuck you dude. I didn't say that, but I thought it really hard.

"Well I'm still here, aren't I?"

"The only reason you're not dead is because you're a vampire, you idiot! If the whole coming back from the dead thing wasn't real, who do you think would be the one making the call to tell your mother how you died? Who do you think would be the one scrubbing your blood off the walls and wondering how his friend could be such a fucking moron? To die in such a pointless way?"

Holy shit.

I must have blinked maybe ten times out of sheer panic

that I was getting this reaction from Claude.

How the hell do you respond to the unvarnished truth? How do you respond when you can still remember the pain of the bullets slamming one by one into your body, even though it's a memory you keep looking away from and denying that it even exists?

"Well this got heavy all of a sudden," I tried to smile, but Claude wasn't smiling with me. His usual happy-go-lucky attitude was gone, replaced by earnest caring. That earnestness made me nervous, but honestly it was more the greasy, queasy feeling of rock hard guilt that was making me squirm. "Come on man, at least crack a smile. Relax. I'm not dead anymore."

"Tell me about it then. Tell me why you suddenly owe someone twelve grand?"

"Only if we agree to put the Julio incident behind us. That was stupid and reckless and really, I mean really stupid—"

"You said stupid twice."

"Well that's just how stupid it was. It bears repeating. Good news is that drugs no longer have any effect on me, so I don't have any use for a dealer anymore, not even if he's not going to shoot me in the face—"

"He ran you know. *Julio.* The cops had an idea he was involved, but he had taken off long before they figured it out. By the time I got there, your body was already gone but I was hoping that it wasn't you, you know? But I knew, and all I could feel was just this… this *rage…*" Claude looked me in the eye and it was scary how calm he was. "I… I know some bad people you know. Truly *horrible* men. I tend to meet them from time to time in my line of work and I always make a point to never work with them again. I don't need that kind of fucked up karma in my life, you know? Well it turns out that these… *horrible men…* these guys know how to find people. The cops couldn't find Julio, but these guys did. I got the call while I was still trying to track down where they had taken your body, but it was like you had vanished. There was no record of your body anywhere, but you know what let me know your powerful vampires had gotten involved and that maybe you were still alive somewhere? The official police record of your death didn't exist. They had it down as a domestic disturbance, like it never even happened."

Claude saw my stunned expression and nodded.

"But my guys, my *horrible men*, they caught Julio and he told them that he had done us all a favour, that they should be giving him a *medal* because he had killed a fucking *real life vampire*. He had shot that fucker right in the face. He told them everything, because that's what happens when you get caught by these kinds of horrible men…" Claude trailed off in thought for a moment and then looked back at me, a fake smile cracking his face. "So I'm going to sit here and smile and I'm going to put the Julio incident behind us, because I don't want to think about what I had to do to find the man who killed my best friend."

I didn't want to think about it. I didn't want to ask about it. Everything was screaming at me to *stay in the dark and just don't ask!*

"What did you do?"

"I did what I hope you would do if you were ever in my place. I got vengeance."

"Claude, I'm sorry—"

"By vengeance I mean we turned him over to the cops."

"Oh. Well that's a relief—"

"*Eventually.* We turned him over to the cops eventually. I mean you're a vampire, so you had to be coming back, right?"

If I were a complete sap, I would have almost cried at the raw emotion and honesty coming from Claude and the realization that he really did love me in the way that we men never like to talk about. With that kind of emotion, we beat our chests and make idiot noises and never tell each other the simple words that we tell rather easily to a series of women over the years. He loved me and I had disappointed him. Since I wasn't a complete sap though, I didn't tear up or even tell my friend of twenty years that I loved him right back and I'm sorry I was an idiot. No: I did the thing he and I always did when emotions came up and I made an idiotic joke about it.

"If you were a chick I'd kiss you right now."

See what I mean? Anyway, Claude just rolled his eyes at me, but he played along. This was familiar ground after all.

"If you kissed me I'd have to slap you. You're just not my type, dude."

"That's only if you were a chick."

"Still slap."

I had to ask the question that was hanging over my head, even more than Claude's disappointment in me for being a complete idiot.

"So… can you help me out with the twelve thousand dollars?"

"Is someone going to break your kneecaps if you don't pay?"

That hadn't occurred to me to ask.

"If I don't then Madame Vera might be very disappointed in me and as sexy as she was, I don't think I want Madame Vera disappointed in me. Just a feeling in my gut, you know?"

"I need to pee. When I get back, there are going to be lots of words. First we're going to talk about the suit."

"It was for my funeral. You missed it."

"Funeral? How was it?"

"Expensive."

"I can tell by the suit. Fill me in on the details when I get back."

Claude slipped out from the booth and I breathed a little easier, finally allowing myself to relax for the first time since Madame Vera's. If you don't know the giant weight placed on your shoulders due to owing an exorbitant amount of money to a very dangerous person, then you can count yourself lucky as hell. It's similar to the weight placed by not paying your taxes or your cellphone bill, and knowing that your service is going to be possibly cut at any minute… just a hell of a lot more dangerous. I hadn't even felt that kind of pressure when I had lost Julio's drugs because I figured I could talk my way out of it somehow or the other and to be honest, I had been a little bit overwhelmed and just didn't care as much at the time.

Jimmy the waiter brought some food over and I barely noticed. I was too busy staring out the window, watching a gorgeous and expensive looking blonde exit a black town car and walk towards the diner. My brain was working overtime trying to figure out how and why I would know this woman, but it was coming up blank... *wait a minute*—

I had time to turn in my seat as Beatrice entered the diner and walked directly over to my table. I realized that my heart was pounding hard in my chest, the blood surging as every sense told me to run away, run away, while my brain interjected and tried to calm everything down with common sense and logic. There was no reason to panic and besides, she was gorgeous.

She was also kind of freaking me out since she seemed to have completely healed from the beating Harry had inflicted on her. Even her teeth all seemed to have grown back.

But what is she doing here?

Nothing good! Now start running you fucking idiot.

By that time it was way too late to do anything other than to watch Beatrice approach in her white designer suit. She slipped into Claude's seat and took a long sip of his soda, her eyes never leaving mine, daring me to say or do something.

"Harry wants to have a chat," she finally said.

"Is this about Madame Vera? Because I'm just about to get the money—"

"Harry says you shouldn't worry about the money, but if I were you, I'd *really* worry about it, if you know what I mean. Past experience, you know? But I also know you don't want to keep him waiting, and Bobby, *you're keeping him waiting*."

"I can't just leave. My friend is in the bathroom—"

"It will be quick, I promise."

I looked from her to the car and then looked back towards the bathrooms. Why the hell was Claude taking so long anyway? And why was this whole situation giving me such a bad vibe?

"If you don't come I'm supposed to start killing people one at a time. Starting with your friend in the bathroom."

"*Wait, what?* Are you serious?"

"Nah, I'm just kidding. I figured it would be a really cool, Super Villain type thing to say. Goes with the outfit, you know?"

"It's a nice outfit."

"I know. I like your suit too. Now are you coming or what?"

Beatrice bounced up to her feet and took a huge bite of the burger I didn't remember Claude ordering. I wondered if I should leave Claude a note, or maybe text him to tell him where I was going, but I was only going to be a couple of minutes, right? After all, the car was *right there*.

Beatrice smiled back at me, and that more than anything convinced me that everything was going to be okay. She had survived Harry and here she was on his behalf, seemingly working for him, so it couldn't be all bad, right?

Right?

Chapter 12
THE JOKER AND THE THIEF

"**Y**ou can hate Harry all you want, but his system works."

This was from Beatrice of course since you'd never catch me having anything nice to say about Harry, especially after the royal fucking he had administered to my life with no lack of glee on his part.

I sincerely hoped that my face wasn't betraying what my mind was thinking. I was making every effort not to run away across the parking lot in a blind panic, mainly because I didn't want to have to deal with Harry right now. Beatrice also made me just a little nervous for all the wrong reasons, and I couldn't shake the feeling that she was watching me and trying to decide if I was tasty or not. Running was looking quite appealing, but I didn't think Beatrice would have any problems catching me even at my fastest running speed. It would probably be best to play along and not show any signs of alarm.

"Um, didn't he just beat the shit out of you?"

Apparently, my mouth hadn't gotten the memo to shut the fuck up.

"Yeah, but I got over it," she said. "He only did it to remind me how much he cares about all of us."

"You're out of your mind," I said hoarsely, not quite believing what I was hearing. This level of crazy was usually reserved for battered wives and cultists.

"Yes I am! Thank you for noticing," Beatrice agreed, and

there was something there, something honest and chilling that said that she knew exactly what she was and that she was very *happy with it, thank you very much.* She continued. "You don't understand, but you will. Without him, there would be only chaos, and we can't have that, right?"

I followed her to the car, completely aware of how little I knew about being a vampire.

***

You don't even notice how much Harry makes it all work, how easily vampire society fits in with ordinary human society. It's only when something breaks that you would notice. You're probably going about your daily routine not realizing just how well the system works and keeps on working. If you're still only aware of vampires as a fictional construct, then congrats: the system is still working very well, and it's because of Harry and vampires like him.

At the time, I still had to experience the entire vampire experience, so I had no idea just how seamless this integration was. I had been able to slip back into my old life while everything was screaming at me that none of this was normal, and somehow managed to ignore that screaming version of myself, because that guy was just all screamy and panicky and nobody wants to deal with that shit. That should have been my first clue and the screamy-panicky side of me was right for a change.

Let me break it down for you, since I have the advantage of hindsight and you clearly lack it.

Harry had integrated almost seamlessly with the city, working out some arrangements for medical, police, security, and especially on the corporate level, to take care of his people. The fact that so many of his vampires were massively invested in large corporations that were critical to the functional aspect of the city, was just the *piece de resistance,* a big part of Harry's plan.

If a vampire got himself killed or seriously fucked up, when the EMTs showed up, there were certain procedures they had to run. It was a testament to the amount of thought Harry and his people had put into the preservation of vampires in the city.

One of the largest manufacturers of medical equipment in the city was run by a family of vampires. They made equipment used by the EMTs and Police Department, as well as in the Emergency Rooms at all area hospitals. This equipment was designed to scan for vampires, and it did its job well. The EMTs, for instance, were essential to the system and were closely monitored. Non-standard equipment was never to be used, *ever*.

Here's where the training and the equipment come in. The EMTs check for vital signs in the usual ways, nothing weird about that, but one extra step they use for all fatalities in the city is the one that stops a vampire from going to the morgue for regular people. Most vampires (call it 100% of them) would not survive the autopsy. It doesn't matter if you're 5000 years old or two weeks old.

Remember what Vern told me when I first came back from the dead? It's all true. When someone cuts open your chest cavity and removes all of your organs, then places said organs into plastic bags before putting them back inside, *you're not surviving that.*

Wait, I'm sorry, I think I said that in a way that you think it's not such a big fucking deal, so let's try again. It's not neat, and it's not pretty what they do, okay? They literally reach into the cavity and yank out your insides, starting from the tongue downwards. If they're really skilled, they can get the entire thing out in one big pull. Remember, part of the process also involves cutting *open the fucking head and taking out the brain*. I cannot stress this enough: *they take out your fucking brain!*

Look me in the eye and tell me that you're immortal and that you'll survive that.

Really? Well, I call bullshit.

The VS-XT200 Scanner is used by the EMTs first to scan the retinas of the deceased and then to take a photo of the face. They don't think of it beyond that, but the rules state that this must be done before the body or patient leaves the scene.

A blinking red light would be all the patient, dead or alive would see. It scans the retina, and that appears to be the end of it, but there is a hell of a lot more going on at the other end of the signal. By the time the body or patient is in the ambulance, the response team already knows that a vampire is coming in and exactly which vampire it is. I don't know if that's a good thing or a bad thing, but I guess the main thing was that they already had a system in place, and more than anything, they instantly knew if it was one of *their* vampires. If you think about that for a bit it tells you highly organized Toronto vampires are.

The next part is extremely low-tech. Vampires get a *red* plastic bracelet with a tracking device. Everybody else gets the *blue* plastic bracelets and sent back to reality. Red bracelet patients like me get to wake up to extortion demands from Vern and then actual extortion from Madame Vera.

***

"That's very interesting," I said as Beatrice finished explaining.

"Hey, it works, right? But the one thing it doesn't prepare you for is the after effects of dying. Occasional flashbacks and panic attacks out of nowhere. If you're into PTSD, that's awesome for you. Otherwise, it can really fuck you up."

"Treatments include therapy and drugs? Except drugs don't work on us, do they?"

"Not the regular ones," Beatrice said with a mischievous grin, and for a second I almost grinned back.

Beatrice pulled open the back door of the car, and I was surprised to find a remarkable lack of Harry in the car.

"Where's Harry?" I asked.

A voice boomed from the speaker system inside the back of the extremely luxurious vehicle.

"Welcome back to the land of the living Bobby. Now get in the fucking car: We're going for a ride."

***

Everything else that happened to me over the year essentially happened because I don't understand jack-shit what being

198

a vampire is about. My flailing around uninstructed wasn't helping myself or anybody else. Maybe Harry had hoped that I would rise to the challenge and would prove that I was worthy to be a vampire or some shit, and to that all I had to say is:

"You shouldn't have taken my drugs."

"You shouldn't have gotten shot."

"Yeah, but me getting shot comes from the fact that *you took my drugs!* Which as I pointed out, weren't even mine to begin with. I appreciate the whole sink or swim argument, that whole 'let's see what he's made of' vibe you got going on, but you don't steal the drugs of psychopaths with guns and leave me holding the bag!"

"He's right you know," Beatrice said, and Harry just grunted. He had a way of grunting that sounded like a glare. Beatrice ignored it. "Well, he is. If they had been my drugs, I would have shot him too."

"Shut your face, Beatrice. You're not helping."

"Happy to oblige," she said rather cheekily. We were in the back of Harry's extremely comfortable town car that had more room inside than should have been physically possible. The seats were welcoming and firm at the same time in a way that told you whoever took care of the car loved the fuck out of it and would definitely object to the way Beatrice had made herself comfortable on the soft leather. Beatrice had somehow found a lollipop from somewhere and was now sucking on it in a way that suggested she was going to start chewing it soon, just taking huge crunching bites and crushing it between her teeth. Strangely enough this was a weird turn-on for me, and from the sly way she glanced at me, Beatrice was fully aware of the effect it was having.

The car accelerated forward, first surprising me and then freaking me out more than just a little bit. The little drive "around the block" had stopped being any kind of "round" shape, and that was making me nervous.

"Can we get back to the 'where were we going' part of this conversation? Beatrice said we weren't going anywhere?"

"She lies," Harry said, and Beatrice nodded happily.

"Yeah. I lie a lot. If I were me, I wouldn't believe a word of anything I had to say."

"You were right," I said to Harry. "She really isn't helping. Are you going to tell me where we're going?"

I had the thought that Claude was probably back at the table and was wondering where the hell I'd vanished to. I reached for my phone to send him a text message, trying to be as casual as I could be. Harry's response made me pause, phone in my hand.

"To the one place I should have taken you instead of sending you out into the world by yourself like that."

"Vegas?"

"You're going to the Hall of the Drunken King."

This announcement was met by complete silence from me, mainly because I was wracking my brain trying to figure out exactly what that was, why it was such a big deal and why Harry thought it was such an awesome thing. From the massive eye roll and heavy sigh, I could see Beatrice had already figured out how clueless I was.

"So definitely not Vegas?"

Beatrice shook the slick-looking flier in front of my face. It was a brochure to the hottest club in town where only top shelf clientele got in, and membership was required. It was a place that mere mortals could only ever dream of attending, a place called HTDK—

Oh, fuck me. The intern at Harry's office had mentioned this.

Beatrice grinned as she saw me finally making the connections.

"That's right, Bobbikins. You're about to meet the rest of the family."

***

You know that scene you always see in the movies where the hero pulls up to the club in the limousine and exits triumphantly because everything was finally coming up aces for him? Yeah, that was me as I exited the limousine, Beatrice close behind and no doubt smirking at me.

"That's right Bobbikins, enjoy it. Just soak it up," she said, and I stood there for a long moment, aware that everybody in the long line of beautiful people was wondering just who the hell I was and hey, maybe I was someone they knew, and maybe I could get them inside.

My phone buzzed in my jacket pocket, and I pulled it out, realizing just how much of a douchebag I must look at that moment. It was Claude.

I briefly considered answering and sent one of the default text messages instead.

-Sorry, can't talk now.

The phone went quiet, and I wondered how long it would take for him to text me back. He was undoubtedly pissed at me, especially after I'd just disappeared again after having been disappeared for a week already. Oh well, since I was already up Shit-Creek, might as well enjoy my stay, right?

The line literally stretched around the block and it was legendary as lines go since HTDK was one of the hardest clubs in the city to get into. I could now remember hearing stories from Sammy about how she'd heard about some guy or girl paying someone to stand in line for them all night, and they still hadn't gotten inside. Sammy herself had been trying to get passes to the club or at least meet someone, anyone who could get her inside, so it was extremely ironic that of all the people she knew, I was likely going to be her ticket inside.

"I think that blonde over there will deep-throat the fuck out of you if you took her inside with you," Beatrice whispered and I looked over to see what she was talking about. An extremely hot blonde chick was making eyes at me, all hot and steamy and pouty… and did she just lick her lips at me?

I broke my gaze away from the horny blonde and took another good look at the club that loomed over us, the club that ruled the desires of all of these pretty strangers on Friday nights. It wasn't a normal converted warehouse like some clubs tended to be. It had been a bottling plant in its former life some twenty or thirty years ago and was all brick walls and steel beams. Someone had replaced the plate glass windows that stood on either side of the gigantic doors with those thick glass bricks that distorted everything behind them and made everything in front of them look even cooler by proximity. Of course, someone had stuck a revolving light behind them, so the glass bricks made pretty patterns on the people and on the sidewalk.

And those gigantic doors? At least ten feet tall and made of solid oak with black metal studs running along the top and the bottom. Those doors said several things to everyone looking at them, things like "you're not getting in here buddy, so go home now" and "turn back now before the dragons get you."

There were two huge well-dressed bouncers holding court at the front of the line and I instantly knew that they were human. They seem to be very committed to their jobs of deciding who made it past them to be allowed to enter that fearsome door, a nice reminder of exactly why I hated clubs with a passion.

My phone buzzed.

-Dude, what the actual fuck? Where are you?

-It's a vampire thing. Harry sent someone for me, but I think it's okay. Mostly.

-You should have waited for me.

-Didn't have a choice. I'll call you when I get out of this, okay?

-I'm not even sure what to say anymore dude. You're an adult. You make your own choices. Don't be a shitty friend. Make sure you call me.

I took another look at the line and decided that the people there either hadn't seen the doors or they were getting a completely different message than I was. Another big reminder of my passionate hatred of clubs: the impossible lines to get in and some of the pretentious and annoying people in said impossible lines.

I still enjoyed the idea of the clubs, and in the past I had spent a good two years drinking hard and dancing harder, but one night, a switch had gone off in my head while I was dancing to some popular song in the midst of a group of girls. It was like someone had zapped all of the electricity from the room and I had stopped dancing, confused by the whole thing and all at once the music had been too loud, too obnoxious. I had walked out then to catch some fresh air and had stood outside the club looking at all of the people outside waiting to go in to share in what was being clearly billed as "fun," but to me had only appeared to be a pointless soul suck. How much time had I spent in those endless lines, facing rejection over and over again at the hands of a bouncer who was waiting for a chance to trip his power all over me or just decided that he didn't like my face?

The oddest thing for me had been walking into my first dive bar and feeling like I had finally come home. Cheaper drinks, music that wasn't trying to become part of you through the sheer act of being loud and there were a hell of a lot less social pressures to impress anyone. The best part of the dive bar was that there were no lines to get in, and that was pure heaven. Plus cheap alcohol for the win. Yay.

I looked back at Beatrice and grinned, feeling a little bit cocky at being one of the chosen few as I noticed the favorable looks being thrown my way. I suddenly remembered that I was also wearing my super expensive suit, and that tonight of all nights I was really looking the part.

"You come here often?" I asked Beatrice.

"I hate this fucking place," Beatrice said and grinned at me. "I was thinking about killing everyone inside and burning it to the ground. Coming?"

I honestly couldn't tell if she was joking.

"But not tonight, right?" I hissed at Beatrice as I stumbled after her.

Beatrice was lost in thought, no doubt imagining the flames exploding out of the building in front of us and the screaming crowds all running from their inevitable slaughter at her hands. She turned to me, a distant look on her face.

"Can't you tell when I'm joking? What kind of psychopath do you think I am anyway?"

"I honestly don't have an answer for that…"

I hurried after her past the crowd and noticed how one of the bouncers practically groveled for Beatrice and opened the door for her, ushering the both of us inside to the largest foyer I have ever seen. The ceiling was at least three stories high and the wall at the far end was all polished mahogany and burnished aluminum from floor to ceiling. The club logo hung high on the wall, a metal and neon monstrosity that made me think that it would be useful to kill a dragon or extremely hard-to-kill bad guy in a movie. It looked cool as shit, is what I'm trying to say here.

"Welcome to the Hall of the Drunken King," a tall, good-looking brunette turned from the sleek mahogany desk that served as reception and met us with a huge smile. She tipped her head to Beatrice in recognition and then looked back to me. "Harry told us to expect you."

"That's great I guess?"

"Sir, please look this way one moment, " the woman said and I glanced over to her. The device she pointed at my face flashed once, not enough to blind me, but just enough to irritate. It apparently gave her the results she desired and she nodded approvingly to me.

"Aren't you going to scan her?" I asked, when she simply stepped aside for Beatrice. There was a flash of nervous amusement on her face as she shook her head.

"We *all* know Miss Beatrice," she said. "You're new here, but you're in the system, so now you're good to go." She waved the device she was holding and I could see an entire profile about me on the screen. Everything Beatrice had mentioned about the system Harry had set up made a lot more sense now. The system went far beyond just making sure bodies went to the right places.

I stepped forward and then something made me spin back around, my heart going from zero to 120 in less than a second as adrenaline surged through me. Two huge vampires in black suits were standing behind me and they may have always been there, or they might have just appeared seconds ago, but I hadn't heard them approach. They were just there and that was scary as shit.

"You're new," the one on the left said. He was about six foot six, black, with a shaved head and in the tradition of bouncers everywhere, very hostile to me.

"We don't like new," the other one said. He was the twin of the other bouncer, equally as tall and broad, except he was the Caucasian model of this particular brand of bouncer.

"Please don't let them eat me!" I squeaked and somewhat managed to put myself behind the woman. She just rolled her eyes and tried to wave off the Ugly Twins.

"He checks out, you guys. Please don't make a scene."

"I don't like the look of him," the black one said.

"Ryan, you remember Beatrice?"

They both turned to look at Beatrice, who waggled her fingers at them while she checked her phone.

"Which one of them is Ryan?" I whispered to the hostess.

"They're both Ryan," she answered, and then to the Ryan twins: "Any more questions boys?"

I slowly backed away, the Ryans watching my every step as I stumbled over to where Beatrice was waiting for me, phone still in hand. She had pulled open the huge door on the right side of the foyer. This door was at least eight feet tall and about eighteen inches thick. There was an identical door on the other side of the foyer, but judging from the way the music was muffled, reduced down to the distant thump-thus-thump of the bass, it was equally thick and very soundproof. I wondered for a moment why music wasn't pouring out of the doorway Beatrice held open, but then I saw the stairs leading up and realized that there were two sets of rules in place here at this club. After all, there were two kinds of people to deal with.

"Just ignore those assholes," Beatrice said. "They're not here for you. They like to sneak up on people. It's the only thing they're really good at. Come on."

I followed Beatrice up the stairs, feeling the *thump-thump-thump* of the music through the walls.

"Regular people are allowed over here by invitation only. It used to be easier to bring 'em in but Harry's been setting down more and more rules recently. I don't think he had planned for the place to become popular with the humans."

"The harder it is to get into a place, the more people want to go," I said. "Basic human nature."

We reached the top of the stairs and pushed through the door. I paused as I looked out over the reality of the club. It was a huge upstairs area that was filled with about one hundred and fifty vampires of all shapes, sizes and ages. I knew they were vampires in the same way I had known that the bouncers downstairs were all human. Except for the Ryan twins of course. It was just a sense, a certainty that these people here were just like me.

That was probably the stupidest thought I'd ever had.

Beatrice leaned close and for the first time I noticed her perfume and how pretty she was, that slender jawline and those piercing blue eyes that always seemed to be searching for something and laughing at everything at the same time. For the moment, they had settled directly on me and there was no laughter at all.

"Don't let them change you Bob," she whispered. "Whatever you do, remember who you are."

"What's that supposed to mean?" I whispered back and she grimaced.

"I honestly have no idea. I just wanted something cryptic and mysterious to say."

"Okay then…"

"But seriously, don't let them change you!" She growled, deadly serious. Then smiled warmly at me. "*Allons-y*! Let's go!"

***

There is a remarkable power in an expensive suit.

Look, people will say things like *"oh it's so totally worth it"*, or *"you'll appreciate it once you wear it"*, but they completely forget the *true* power of an expensive tailored suit, especially if they've grown accustomed to wearing them all of the time. You see, the power doesn't lie in how good it feels, or how comfortable the fit or even how soft the fabric. The comfort is only a *reminder* of what you're wearing, and what you're wearing is *power*.

Or to use another word: *access,* but access equals power and vice-versa, so it's all the same if you really examine it.

A well-fitted custom suit is a *suit of armor* that allows you to walk into the halls of power with the confidence that you belong there. It announces very loudly that you belong exactly where you decide you want to belong and puts any questions immediately to rest.

It would be the understatement of the year to say that Madame Vera knew exactly what she was doing when she had me fitted for the suit. It was almost as if she knew I was going to end up at the club.

"That's a lot of vampires…" I whispered to Beatrice. She just rolled her eyes.

"Follow me and try not to trip on anyone."

I reminded myself that the suit (and the *shoes*, I have so many good things to say about the shoes) was my protection. It was my only armor. I kept repeating that in my head as I followed Beatrice through the crowd of vampires.

I belong here. I belong here. I belong here.

The crowd parted like the Red Sea for Beatrice, and I was glad she was leading the way, since people seemed more than happy to get out of the way for her. It was the most fucked up way of introducing me, since they would see Beatrice first and there would be a flash of something like panic as if they were wondering if she was looking for them. That would quickly turn to relief and they would shuffle aside, glad to be not on her radar and then BAM! there I was, right in their pretty faces, an outsider, an interloper. *An accident.* But here's the thing: they would see me and then instantly see the suit and it was almost as if they then would *see me again* and there was a sense of questioning that maybe I was more than I appeared to be after all. *The suit changed everything.*

A part of me was freaking out, wondering why everyone seemed so intimidated by Beatrice, but a more sensible part of me was yelling at me to *shut your filthy mouth! Don't ask any questions that can get us killed!*

Beatrice looked back at me and smiled reassuringly, eyebrow raised questioningly. I nodded that I was okay and managed a hopeful grin. That was good enough for her and she continued leading the way without looking back at me again.

There was the huge open area with two and four seater tables, and then there were the couches and coffee tables if anyone wanted to be a little more comfortable. All of the chairs were occupied, but there were still a few groups of people standing and talking the way friends do, which of course led to them blocking the main walkway. You know, just like how small groups of friends do at the club. Vampire or not, some human behaviors just don't go away.

There's something you have to understand about these

vampires. Some of you are no doubt picturing a whole goth scene with heavily made-up and pale faces, like lots and lots of pale faces, and yes there were a few of those, but those *weren't* the vampires. The actual vampires, my fellow creatures of the night, apart from their intense blue eyes and overwhelming good looks, were impeccably dressed and discreetly rich in the way that only the extremely rich can be. They weren't cookie cutter vampires like you would find in the movies. There was the occasional vampire with some personal flair and style: a white suit on a short haired Indian woman, a waistcoat and jeans wearing black dude; a goth looking white dude with a Nikki Sixx haircut and dressed in all black who on closer inspection *actually was* Nikki Sixx (and that explained a hell of a lot). You could actually look around the room at the balance of the different races and get a good idea of where all of the money in Toronto was, and a good chunk of that happened to be right there with me. But I guess my main point is that not all of the vampires were white, and none of them were obvious unless they were actually trying.

And yes: there were humans among the vampires. That's all I'm going to say about that for now.

I glanced down at the dance floor of humans fifty feet down below, and was almost mesmerized by the movement of people genuinely having a good time as they were caught up in the group think of dance. It wasn't packed tight, but had enough of a crowd that made dancing pleasurable and not an awkward thing. Nobody wanted to be the only one out on the dance floor after all. Of course, there were girls in glass cages hanging from the ceiling, only part of the experience to make sure you knew damn well you were in a special club and that you should be grateful to be there.

The thick glass that went from floor to ceiling all along the long balcony that overlooked the dance floor did an amazing job of keeping most of the *thump-thump-thump* isolated. This was probably the only area of the club where you could actually hear yourself speak or think, and for me it was a hell of a relief. I imagine the enhanced vampire hearing which I had gotten used to so quickly that I'd forgotten about it, had something to do with it. It was *by design* that we were isolated from the music.

Beatrice stopped walking and I almost walked into her back. I peered around her to see why she had stopped.

"Oh this is so fucked up," Beatrice said.

An extremely good looking man stood next to Harry. When I say good-looking, I mean like ridiculously good-looking to the point that his absolute confidence and perfect hair made me instantly want to punch him. There was only one word to describe his hair and it was "lustrous". Nobody had any business looking that perfect. It was like he had been ripped directly from a magazine advertisement with his slicked back hair, square jaw and pearly teeth, pretty much the quintessential vampire that made women everywhere instantly get all moist in their panties.

Of course he was shirtless, and no I'm not going to describe him, so deal with it.

"If he starts to glitter, just kill me now," I said.

Beatrice just raised an amused eyebrow at me.

"Are you jealous of how his muscles glisten—"

"Oh please just kill me."

Harry spotted Beatrice and then me and the smile on his face was predatory and full of trouble for me.

"Beatrice! Bob. So glad you could make it," Harry bellowed. He indicated the hunka-hunka-burning-man-meat behind him. "I'd like you to meet Sebastien, the newest member of our family." He even said '*Sebastien*' with the Spanish pronunciation so it was more pretentious and grating than I thought possible.

"At least his name isn't Edward," I said. Neither Harry or Sebastien seemed to get the reference.

Harry beckoned for me to come over to him. When I hesitated, Beatrice gave me a not-too-gentle push so I stumbled towards Harry. I glared back at her, hurt by her traitorous actions, but she looked restless.

"Okay, bored now. Call me when you need someone killed or something," Beatrice said to Harry and stalked off into the crowd, leaving me alone with Harry and the glistening Sebastien.

I slowly turned to Harry who smiled magnanimously.

"Bob, we got off on the wrong foot—"

"You mean the foot that you shoved up my ass? That foot?"

Harry gave me a dangerous look and clapped me hard on the back.

"Remember what I told you about interrupting me Bobby?"

"Shutting the fuck up!" I said promptly, and then for added measure, to make sure he got that I got it: "Sir!"

"I've invited you here because Sebastien here also recently became a vampire, and tonight happens to be his invocation ceremony, where he officially becomes one of the family. I thought I would extend the courtesy to you as well, since you only so recently became a vampire yourself."

I glanced over at Sebastien, who was silently glaring at me. That sent any thoughts of congratulation out of my mouth, such an outward show of hostility. You'd think I'd slept with his sister or something. I looked back to Harry, curious about one tiny detail.

"When you say 'ceremony', this doesn't involve virgins and knives and shit, right?"

A older vampire in a white suit came up and whispered something to Harry. I grinned at Sebastien and he nodded and leaned over, a fake plastic smile on his perfect fucking punchable face.

"Excited?" I asked.

"I'm going to crush you," Sebastien whispered to me, still fake smiling at me.

"Excuse me?"

"I've been waiting for this moment for ten years. Ten. Fucking. Years. I'm sure as shit not going to share it with you."

"You'd better take it up with Harry then," I said. Wow, his teeth really were prefect. "He's really open to his plans being criticized."

"When this is over, you'd better run, you prat," Sebastien continued and it was obvious he thought he was intimidating.

I grinned happily, wild thoughts running through my head, and said the first thing that came to mind.

"Has anyone told you that you have a punchable face?"

"No-"

His face was really punchable. I must have gotten in three or four good punches before they dragged me off of him.

***

There was a huge expensive steak on my eye, and I was seriously considering having it grilled for breakfast. The steak was still in a Ziplock bag, and since it was now on my eye, helping tremendously with the swelling, I considered that it was now *my* steak.

The ceremony was going on a hundred feet behind me, obscured by the crowd of people either trying to get a better view of what was going on, or to escape unnoticed. Apparently not everyone was interested in watching Sebastien get his final initiation rites, either because they didn't care or just didn't know him. That was pretty telling on its own, and comforting that the vampires weren't all mindless zombies following Harry's orders. That was either going to be a good thing or bad thing…

A tall good looking black man was walking towards me. He looked vaguely familiar, like he was on TV or something, a celebrity I'd forgotten I'd known about, and to be truthful, it wasn't that surprising to me that he was a vampire. I just wished that I could remember his name…

"Nice one," he said and offered a fist for the obligatory fist-bump. *Of course* I fist-bumped him. I mean I'm not stupid. I might have misplaced his name, but I wasn't completely stupid.

"That was pretty stupid of you," he was saying. "But totally worth it to see the look on Harry's face when you knocked the shit out of Golden Boy over there."

The crowd cheered at something just then and I grinned at my newfound admirer. Something clicked in my head and a name attached itself to his face.

"Glad I could provide a momentary distraction for the King himself," I said. "I even got a free steak out of it."

The King was one of the biggest rappers in Toronto, wildly popular, and when you stopped to think about it, with all of the music videos and public appearances he had to make, he'd actually managed to achieve a perfect balance of lifestyle that made him look like a perfectly normal if eccentric rich human being. If you actually had to live through his schedule, you'd see quickly that he was one hundred percent a vampire.

The King gave me a business card and grinned at me. "Text me sometime. You can come hang with my crew when you get tired of this place. It's not for everyone…"

"Isn't this the official spot for vampires to hang out?"

"Only if you're rich and pretentious. The new ones Harry's got coming out seem to love it, but some of us have been around a little bit longer. We just ain't got the patience for all this bullshit."

"Plus it's full of blood-sucking bastards, right?"

"You said it man." His eyes flickered over to the crowd where Sebastien was no doubt being anointed with oil or some shit to the approval of said crowd. "Be careful here tonight." And with that, the King disappeared down the stairs.

Another roar came from the crowd and I glanced over just at a moment that there was a gap between people. I could see Sebastien sloppily pouring an over-sized goblet of what looked like blood into his mouth and down the front of his shirt. It stained the shirt red, but he didn't seem to care. Sebastien grinned at the crowd and his fangs were huge even from where I was sitting. I subconsciously rubbed at my own mouth where my fangs still hadn't made an appearance.

Someone shoved a beer into my face. I looked up to see Beatrice holding the beer and not even looking at me, her gaze firmly in the direction of the thoroughly bizarre ceremony.

"It's called the *Ritual of Magazi*. For the past fifty years, all new vampires have gone through the ritual. It reminds them of where they've been and what they are… or at least that's what Harry says. I think he just likes to drench these idiots in blood."

Well, that answered that question. Beatrice was really good at the exposition thing.

"Is that real blood then?"

Beatrice looked at me for the first time since she had returned.

"Either take the beer or I'm drinking it myself."

I took the beer and after a brief glance at the label to

appreciate Beatrice's expensive taste in beer, swigged long and hard. Beatrice sat down next to me and poked at the steak on my eye.

"Nice steak. You should grill it up later."

"Oh I have plans for this steak, don't you worry. If I had known there would be free steak I would have started a fight earlier."

"It would have been an actual fight if Harry hadn't had to drag you off of whats-his-face. You should have seen the look on his face—"

"Oh I saw it, right before he punched me. Harry's got a mean punch."

"At least he only punched you once. And it was Harry doing the punching. In his own way he was protecting you."

"How the fuck do you protect someone by punching them so hard that the bruise instantly forms?"

Beatrice glanced at my swollen face and then leaned in close. She pointed out a man in the crowd to me.

"See that guy in the white suit?"

I looked and remembered seeing the guy before. The white suit kind of made him stand out, but he still would have been hard to miss. He had long silver-grey hair pulled back into a ponytail, not a strand out of place, and wore rose-red sunglasses. He was tanned in a way that you knew it was spray-on but that it was also an *expensive* spray tan. I could tell from looking at him that he drove a little convertible with too much power under the hood.

"You mean the Mafia guy?"

"That's Renaldo Demucci. See the white suit? It's ritual for the sponsor to wear white. He's the one sponsoring Sebastien, and his methods of teaching are a little unconventional, but very *affectionate.* He loves the hell out of his proteges, until he gets bored of them and then he's off to make himself a new one. He's also a vicious fuck who is probably plotting to have you gutted in the alley out back when this is all over."

Renaldo glanced our way at that moment and just for a second there was direct eye contact between the two of us. The crowd shifted and the gap closed, leaving me feeling more panicked than I had known was possible.

I stood up, ready to run for my life. Beatrice grabbed hold of my arm and I froze in my tracks. Damn she was strong!

"Oh sit down and finish your beer," she said. "I've already paid for it, so you'd better finish it."

I sank back down and tried to hide behind my hand even though Renaldo could no longer see me with the crowd between us.

"Oh he's not going to be bothering you," she said off-handedly. "Harry wants me to make an example out of that motherfucker. I'm going to murder that sonofabitch in about six, seven hours. I'm going to murder him so good…"

I did a double take at Beatrice, a stupid grin frozen on my face. *She had to be joking right? Nobody walks around saying things like that, did they?*

Beatrice didn't give me a chance to ask. She drained her beer and got to her feet, slamming the bottle onto the table at the same time. She looked around the room, searching for something.

"Look, I'm going to bug out—" I said, or at least started to say. Beatrice glared at me and cut me off.

"You stay right there. I have to do a thing for you."

"I can catch an Uber—"

"Stay dammit!" Beatrice snapped, and vanished into the crowd.

I looked around miserably, wondering if I dared to look in the direction of Sebastien and Renaldo "I'm going to kill your puppies" Demucci. I quickly decided hell no to that, and instead looked over at the dance floor where all of the humans below danced rhythmically to some song I couldn't hear but still had enough bass for me to feel through the walls and the floor. I wondered how many of the people down there even suspected that there were vampires above watching them dance. I wondered what they would say if they could see the bizarre blood ceremony going on in the middle of that crowd.

That reminded me. I looked back at the people on the VIP floor now, the mix of vampires and humans, the question that had been bugging me, popping up and reminding me that yep, it was still there and still wanted to be answered.

There were humans hanging out with vampires, mostly

very friendly, almost equals. But there were a few of them, men and women alike who were bleeding from cuts on their wrists and in a few cases, on the necks, while the vampire they were with sucked on their wounds. Some of the less extreme cases even managed to carry on a conversation, pausing only every now and again to shift position.

It was bizarre and disturbing to watch, more because of the way they just made it all seem so casual, so everyday… so goddamned normal. It made me wonder for the first time why the vampires were even drinking the blood. We could very clearly eat food, so it wasn't a nutritional thing. I hadn't even made the step towards even thinking about drinking blood in my short time as a vampire, even though the thought had occurred to me that I might wake up feeling homicidal one day, thirsting for blood like in the comics. But no dice.

Beatrice came back, two gorgeous young women on her arms.

"So Harry asked me to be your sponsor and I told him he could go fuck himself, but not in so many words because I hate having to grow back the teeth he would have knocked out, so there was this whole back and forth going on. I think he thinks he won, so I might be your sponsor, but whatever."

"What's going on?"

"This," Beatrice presented the redhead and she twirled for me, giggling. "Is for you. It's time you had a taste of blood."

The redhead plopped down into my lap and gently moved the steak from my face. I was stunned and was instantly out of my depth, wondering what the fuck was going on. I caught the eye of another human girl a few seats over, a female vampire sucking gently on her neck and it suddenly occurred to me that I could smell the blood and had *been smelling it all along…*

… And it was *sweet, so sweet,* and so close. Before I had realized it, I had tuned in to the *thump-thump* of the heartbeat of the redhead in my lap, and my breathing slowed, which in turn slowed my own heartbeat until I was in perfect sync with her.

I looked up to Beatrice and she smiled at me.

"Drink Bob. Find out what it means to be a vampire."

I looked back to the redhead and I honestly meant to ask her name, but there was that *thump-thump-thump* of her heartbeat again, not unlike the *thump-thump-thump* of the music downstairs. I *really wanted* to ask her name, to tell her that she could leave and go back to the safety of the humans downstairs, but I didn't.

She knew what I wanted even if I didn't and she held up her wrist for me to suck on, looking me deep in the eye and she may have whispered something like "*don't worry, this is what I want*" but I honestly couldn't tell if that was just my imagination. All there was, was the beat of her heart and mine, that *thump-thump-thump*, that heavy bass, the *smell of the blood.*

When she pressed the wound to my lips, I didn't even think about it. I sucked willingly.

Taste exploded on my tastebuds and it was sweet and rich and heady, and it filled me with absolute euphoria, spreading through my body slowly and instantly. It was just like heroin, but *so much better. Oh, so much better...*

It's in the name you know. It's all in the name of the beast, and I am the beast.

We suck blood because we are vampires.

We drink blood.

We share the blood.

We *are* the blood.

Drink deeply and know your name...

I know my name now, and it is *oblivion.*

Chapter 13
DANCING IN THE DARK

*F*OUR DAYS.

That's how long it took me burn every bridge I had managed to build, and it also included the one I was standing on. I'd love to be able to claim that I don't remember the details or that it was all just a blur, but I'd be lying to myself as well as to you. The fugue of the first night, that complete loss of self and utter euphoria from the taste of that hot, wet blood fresh in my mouth, that was the high I found myself chasing.

To put it simply: *I got hooked.*

It was easy for me, just like falling off a wagon, and I laughed at myself at the sheer irony of the situation. When I had been human, I was hooked on heroin. And now that I was a vampire, there I was hooked on blood. Turnabout is fair play, and fair play is one hell of a bitch. I wondered if I died and went to Heaven, how long it would take before I found the heavenly equivalent of heroin. I guess some people just have to be addicted to something and we just choose badly.

For the first time, I started to enjoy being a vampire.

***

Blink…

I remember limbs. Naked arms and legs and breasts that I may have fought to get out from under for minutes or maybe days or even hours. It was hard to tell in my state of delirium, but there seemed to be more women than I could remember, the bed and floor covered with naked sleeping bodies in different positions of rest.

One of the girls, a slender black girl with the body and face of a model opened her eyes and watched me silently from the bed, but I looked away, confused by all of those beautiful bodies and faces and the smears of blood that seemed to be everywhere in the bedroom. We definitely weren't in the club anymore, but where the hell *were* we?.

Blink...

The fridge was packed full of delicious looking foods with labels I wasn't even going to bother trying to pronounce and what the hell was I looking for again? How had I even gotten there? I could taste the blood on my lips, and was it dried there or was it fresh? Whatever form it took, it was delicious and heady, the taste hitting me with a euphoric high...

Blink...

I couldn't find my clothes and these weren't my shoes were they? I didn't know these pants goddammit. Where were my goddamn pants and more importantly: whose underwear was I wearing?

Blink...

The hoodie was tight and constricting, way too small for me, but at least it covered my head and most of my face which I was desperately trying to keep hidden as I stumbled down the street. The sunglasses were some kind of women's fashion and no doubt looked ridiculous on me, but since I didn't have to look at myself I really didn't care. The point was that they worked, and shielded my eyes from the sun. I kept expecting to spontaneously burst into flame and wondered if I was leaving a trail of smoke behind me, broadcasting to the world or to anyone that cared to look that there was a vampire walking, better clear the streets! Nobody looked at me. Nobody cared. If they did, then I certainly didn't notice them.

What the hell was I even doing outside in the sunlight you ask?

Come to think of it, that was a very good question, one I didn't have an answer to. Thankfully my sense of self-preservation was managing to keep me to the shadows of the building in the morning sun, so at least my drug induced stupor wasn't suicidal. Madame Vera would no doubt have some choice words for me if I showed up on her slab burned extra crispy.

Blink...

If you've ever gotten high, and I mean like really fucking high, and you continuously maintained that level of intoxication for hours and hours, you know what it's like when you finally sober up. Everything is weird and real-but-not-quite and kind of funny if you think of it a certain way. You know you're fucking high and you like that feeling. You'd agree to almost anything and maybe even try to argue a point, but you quickly lose the thread of thought and either drift off or break away abruptly to do something else. You can't focus on anything for too long but that's all right, that's okay, you gotta chase the dragon, gotta feed the monkey and don't call him a monkey, he's a 300 pound ape and will rip your fucking arms off, man...

You'll also know that while you may only remember hazy moments of being high and trying to act sober, it's the moment that you sober up that's the most jarring. It could happen at anytime at all, slowly with a sense of waking up, or in some cases you just...

Blink...

You're cold sober standing across the street from the Art Store, staring into the huge plate-glass window with the canvasses and easels and paints on display to lure any passing artists into the maw of commerce and continual lack of money. You're not staring at what's inside the window though, you're staring through into the store at the love of your life, and you want to go to her and proclaim your love, but even in your former drug induced stupor, you weren't quite stupid enough to do that.

The *you* in this equation is of course *me*, but that kinda goes without saying.

So that was how I ended up in front of Jaime's store in the middle of the day, dimly aware that the shadow of the building I was standing in was slowly getting smaller and smaller. In a minute I would be standing in direct sunlight and parts of my face would no doubt burn exactly like they should, but at that moment, I didn't care. In that moment I was just glad to see her face inside the store. Normally that made me feel a little better about myself to see that she was still okay, but that day I felt even more cut off from her. I suddenly felt less human for the first time and that was no good. *That was no good at all.*

A silver Lexus with darkened windows pulled to a stop in the alley next to me. The front window rolled down and a vaguely familiar looking black woman leaned over and called for me.

"Bob, we've been looking for you," she said. "You shouldn't be out like this. Not in the sun."

"Then where should I be?" I asked, and for the first time I didn't have anything smart-ass to say.

"Come and see, Bob," the woman said.

I took one last look at Jaime through the store window and shook my head.

"Fuck it."

I went and I saw.

***

I still have this vague memory of arriving back at the club. I still had no idea where we had found my clothes, but ye-old-expensive-suit had made a reappearance, so at least I wasn't naked. Yet.

Three of the women whose names I had spent most of the day forgetting escorted me from the back of the boat sized Uber Black, directly into the club. It was fast and efficient and for a while I was wrapped up in my own version of reality. The women were gorgeous and loved to walk around naked, so I had spent most of the day occasionally either sucking their blood or fucking whoever happened to be close by until I was exhausted. The sad thing was that I couldn't even remember the actual sex, or even enjoying it after a point. I was just too fucking stoned to care. I still have no idea how we made our way upstairs, or how we commandeered the corner table with the comfy chairs almost at the back of the room. I do remember some of the other vampires throwing knowing looks our way. Some of the looks were definitely shady, but I really didn't give a goddamn. My personal universe was just

220

me and the girls.

"Enjoying yourself?" Beatrice had appeared from nowhere or maybe it had been from everywhere. It was remarkably easy to sneak up on me. My entire world was made up of beautiful women who treated me like a prince and how the hell could you beat that? An army could have snuck up on me and shoved a rocket launcher up my ass at that point.

"Hey! Beatrice! You vanished on us!"

"Are the girls treating you well?"

"The girls are absolutely amazing. So beautiful. So fucking accommodating." I smiled up at the dark haired girl, she of the long limbs and amazing blowjobs. I wanted to say her name was Connie, but I knew that wasn't even close. I kissed the inside of her wrist and noted the slight puckered scar that was all that remained from where I had sucked at different points during the day. Remind me to tell you sometime about the remarkable healing powers of vampire saliva; I'm still tripping balls that nobody has bottled and synthesized it for sale from the drug companies.

Beatrice smiled at the three women, but it was a smile that wasn't one hundred percent friendly.

"Thank you for your services ladies. Beat it," she said, and all at once the women disentangled themselves from me, fixed their sexy and sparkly little black dresses and walked away into the crowd. I looked desperately from them, back to Beatrice.

"But I love them! Especially the brunette one. Connie?"

Beatrice shook her head "no," obviously not impressed.

I tried again. "Sheila?" No. "Madeline?" No. Fuck it, I gave up and looked at her imploringly. "Make them come back. They're awesome."

"You don't even know their names." Beatrice settled into the opposite chair. She didn't look impressed. "You spent all day in my condo having a grand old party and you never even bothered to learn their names?"

"I can learn. I promise."

"How high are you right now?"

"On a scale of one to extremely?" I grinned, and tried to look somewhat sober, but failed magnificently. "Are you here to tell me to pull myself together? Not to make a scene?"

"On the contrary," Beatrice said and she was already distracted, staring off through the crowd at something or someone. "You're not my responsibility, so I really don't give shit."

Oh damn. That was a bit of letdown. Just when I thought we had hit it off so well too. I tried to gather my wits, but when you're high as fuck, you're also slow and stupid and sloppy.

"You know, Harry said I need a mentor—"

The kiss caught me by surprise, coming out of nowhere like it did. Beatrice's lips locked on to mine, warm and sweet and there was a neediness in her kiss, a kind of desperation that I could almost smell. Her hand circled in my hair, pulling me close to her with force—

WHACK!

If the kiss hadn't caught me by surprise, the slap across the face sure as hell did, all feeling in my skin dulled for just a few seconds before the blood rushed back to wake up my nerve endings, which all wanted to scream at me all at once. I could only stare at Beatrice in shock as my face screamed at the insult; the surprise boner she had provoked wilted in fear that it might be next.

"What the hell was that for?"

"I couldn't decide if to kiss you or hit you," she said.

Oddly enough, that seemed to make sense to me.

"Good luck finding a mentor," Beatrice said and got to her feet. She emptied her drink, still distracted, but managed a smile at me. "I'm not your magic elf dude. Go out there and use your charm. Make some friends. Don't trust anyone. Just don't call me, I'll call you."

"Oh."

"That last one was a lie," She said. "Bye Bob." And with that, Beatrice vanished into the crowd, leaving me to my own devices.

Looking through the crowd, I caught Harry looking my way, just watching me from a distance. He saw me looking and his lips pursed tightly before he glanced away and I knew right than that I was being watched and more than anything else, I was being *judged.* I looked away and there was another look from another vampire, and then another one from a passing pair of trust-fund kiddies. All at once there was this feeling that everyone was watching and waiting for the inevitable, just waiting for me to completely fuck it all up.

I looked away, feeling way too vulnerable, way too sober.

I somehow found my feet and stumbled away to the balcony overlooking the dance floor where clubgoers were still coming in, oblivious to the watching eyes above them and for a moment I was jealous of them, wanted to be one of them again… then I almost slapped myself silly. What the fuck was I even thinking? I'd never been one of them either. The only thing I'd had in common was the fact that we were all human and thought that we would all live forever or at least die trying.

That reminded me: I really needed to ask somebody about immortality. Was that even a 'thing'? And exactly how the hell did that even work?

I glanced over to where my former playmates had gathered. The black girl

(whatthehellwashername?Melanie?)

glanced my way and gave me a wry smile before turning her attention back to an extremely good looking man in a very expensive suit. The message was sent loud and clear and even though I couldn't remember her damned name, it was still a punch to the gut, that sting of rejection. Ow, fucking ow.

I looked away irritated, as I realized my high was fading away and that all three of my former party girls were now going to be unavailable to me for whatever reason Beatrice had decided. I had been cut off and left on my own, like it was some kind of test. A seriously fucked up test that I was now going to have navigate while sober.

Fuck *that*.

***

I found what I needed downstairs.

The girl was at the bar by herself and her behavior was different from most everyone else in the club due to the fact that she couldn't stop herself from staring up at the upstairs area. Everybody else was busy with dancing or posing and preening, trying to show off for each other. Not her, though: she knew there was more to this club and she wanted in.

The girl was fairly ordinary looking, but pretty in her own special way, with her slight upturned nose and full pouty lips. Her lips had on more makeup than they should, but not as much as you would expect from a Goth girl. Jet black hair cut in bangs right across her eyebrows framed her pretty face and ordinary brown eyes; the way she absently reached for her face and ended up having to do something else with her hand told me that she usually wore glasses, but not that night. That night was for contact lenses only. She was dressed in a black mini-skirt with fishnet stockings that would have been distracting on longer legs, but were perfect on her. She had a slightly longer torso that seemed like it belonged to a girl with longer legs and always seemed a little awkward to me, but whatever. She had nice B-cup boobs that she was doing her best to flaunt in the corset that fit her quite well and accentuated her curves. I guess what I'm trying to say here is that she wasn't a knockout like the skinny models we had upstairs, but she was still a damn good-looking girl. She spotted me almost immediately as I made my way over to the bar, feeling very much like a predator on the hunt.

The bartender came over immediately, recognizing my status if not my face. It definitely wasn't the suit, since it was no longer immaculate and I had lost (thrown away?) the tie at some point over the past thirty odd hours or so.

"Are you looking for the VIP bar sir?"

I shook my head and glanced toward the downstairs VIP area in the back of the club where the bartender was trying to direct me. There was some kind of roped off area with one very skinny bouncer. I thought I caught a flash of what could be Beatrice talking to someone, but I couldn't be sure. In any case it was definitely not on my must-see list.

"Do I actually have to pay for drinks here?"

"Not at all sir. Your money is no good here."

"My man!" I said, delighted by this turn of events and then was instantly sad. I finally had a place with permanent open bar and I couldn't even get drunk anymore. "Bottle of tequila por favor! Something expensive but still good."

The girl had been watching me this entire time, and trying very hard to make it look like she wasn't watching me, but she couldn't hold it in any longer. The instant the bartender turned away to fetch the bottle of Tequila, she turned to me.

"Oh my God!" she said, her eyes wide in shock and awe. It was as if she had just seen a celebrity. "You're one of them! You're one of the family!"

I almost smiled at her mention of "the family"; I wasn't about to be having thanksgiving dinner with any of these motherfuckers anytime soon.

"It's the eyes isn't it?" I said, now a little self-conscious. No wonder the bartender had recognized me. There were no contact lenses I knew of that could simulate what my eyes had become. At least not without looking *like contacts lenses.*

"Yuh-huh. So freaking cool! Syndine and Angelyne are never going to believe this. They've been trying to meet one of the family, like forever." She indicated two blondes a few feet down the bar who were engaged in talking to a pair of douchebags who seemed a little too intent on drawing attention to their blue eyes. One of them was pretending to be a little self-conscious about his pointy little nubs of incisors and the girls were eating it all up. Idiots.

"Are those their actual names? They sound a little made up."

"You kidding me? Cindy totally made hers up and Angie insists on using a fucking 'y' in her name now. Says it's more mysterious and that none of you would respect a name like Meredith. That's me, by the way: fucking Meredith."

I grinned and held out my hand; Meredith shook my hand and held on, breathlessly excited.

"Fucking Meredith, I'm Fucking Bob!"

Meredith squealed and held on to my hand with both hands, such nice soft warm hands. I was aware of just how good she smelled, knew that she used Dove soap and had only used a tiny bit of perfume on her neck and wrists. Under all those layers of goth clothing was just an excitable girl who was too thrilled to play it cool.

"You're fucking with me, aren't you?" She laughed and I shook my head, laughing with her. "Seriously? Bob?"

"It's the only name I've got. Technically it's Roberto, but only my mom calls me that."

"I like 'Bob'," she said and now she was flirting heavy, leaning towards me. It occurred to me that she still hadn't released my hand and didn't seem to have any intention of doing so. She looked over her shoulder to watch her friends Cindy and Angie walk away through the crowd giggling and whispering to each other, quite possibly on their way to the bathroom or something. The fact that they hadn't even bothered to drag Meredith with them said a lot about her pecking order in the trio. Their fake vampire douchebros watched them go and then fist-bumped each other.

"Are they friends of yours?" Meredith asked innocently enough. "We could go over—"

I couldn't help myself. I nodded in the direction of the two men as I watched them try to order drinks from my bartender who was taking delivery of a very special looking bottle from one of his staff. It was a tall bottle of *Barrique de Ponciano Porfidio* tequila according to the label, and from the way he handled the bottle, it was extremely expensive. He saw me looking and lofted the bottle with a slight smile. One of the douchebag brothers started to say something, but the other one grabbed him roughly and whispered something in his ear. They both turned to look in my direction as the bartender came back towards me, and their eyes widened just a little. Apparently they also knew what to look for and at that moment, it was me.

"If you know what to look for, you can spot who the posers are…"

She grinned evilly. "Cindy and Angie are going to be so disappointed. I would hate to be the one to break the news."

"So let's not and say we didn't!"

The bartender presented the bottle with a flourish and produced two shot glasses. He smiled as he poured for us and corked the bottle, ignoring the douchebags down the bar who were now arguing amongst themselves. There was apparently a disagreement about how best to be a douchebag.

"Will there be anything else sir?"

"Get a glass for yourself my friend. Have a toast with us."

The bartender produced a glass and poured for himself, ignoring me trying to get a better look at his name tag. OTIS the name read. "Right you are sir. And what are we toasting?"

I gave a glass to Meredith and took one for myself. She looked at it nervously.

"What? No salt? No lime?"

Otis was scandalized. "This costs at least five thousand dollars a bottle and it's worth every cent. You *want* to taste every drop, not obscure it with lime and salt. That's for the cheap stuff."

"Listen to your friendly neighborhood bartender," I noted and Meredith smelled the tequila cautiously. I could see her friends returning from wherever they had gone and they were looking over at us curiously. The douchebros had deliberately turned away from me and seemed to be trying to make themselves invisible.

Otis nodded. "Listen to your friend. He gives good advice. So what are we toasting?"

I raised my glass again. "To new lives and new friends."

We drank deeply and I grinned, relishing the taste. Meredith gasped and smiled, surprised at the actual flavour that didn't threaten to strip the skin from her throat.

"Holy shit!"

I smiled at her reaction, and just relished the warmth of the alcohol and the instant rush that it gave me before it faded away. I was going to need a lot more shots if I was even going to pretend to be drunk. I looked at the stunned Meredith and decided right then that just a little of her blood was exactly what I needed to get the high I was looking for.

"I think the bottle is staying with us Otis," I said and he nodded.

"Right you are sir."

"Damn straight!" Meredith said and held her glass out for Otis to pour. He obliged her and set the bottle down on the counter with a longing look.

"Call me Bob, and have another shot."

"As you wish sir," he said, and poured another shot for himself. "Will there be anything else?"

"As much as I love to see those two douchebags squirm, I won't keep you."

Otis glanced over and allowed a smug smile to come to his lips. He downed the shot. "Some people just don't respect the house sir. Do you want to have them escorted out?"

Whoa! Really? Someone was going to give me *that* much power? Having the ability to not have to pay was awesome enough, but this was really way too much power in my hands. I shook my head and poured a shot for myself.

"Give them some friendly advice before Harry sends someone to talk to them. I'm going to take this lovely young lady upstairs and give her a thrill." I paused and smiled at Meredith. "You do want to come upstairs with me, right?"

Meredith squeezed my hand tight and her eyes widened to the point where I thought her contact lenses were going to pop out. A shudder ran through her entire body and she barely breathed the next words, never taking her eyes off of mine.

"Will you really take me?"

"I'll take you," I said, barely biting back the innuendo.

"What else will you do to me?" Meredith whispered. I stroked her cheek gently, already anticipating kissing those lips and biting her on the neck, or maybe on the upper thigh. I had a flash of the girls from last night enjoying the hell out of that particular trick.

"What will you do to me?" She asked again.

I answered Meredith as honestly as I could.

"Everything."

***

Meredith was awkward and sweet and nervous as hell.

I took her into one of the dimly lit rooms upstairs where she sat on my lap and I drank from her wrist. She hissed with pain when I used the little knife to make the cut, but she kept her eyes on mine the whole way, telling me with every action that she trusted me. *Silly girl.*

I drank deeply and her blood was sweet and was everything I needed in that moment.

I got high and I lost myself for a while.

***

I woke up in a strange bedroom and was acutely aware of how naked I was. The next thing I was aware of was Meredith sitting at the foot of the bed, just staring at me. She was wearing an over-sized Blue Jays jersey and possibly nothing else, but I couldn't immediately tell.

"Hi?" I ventured, not quite sure what to say. I was still playing catch up with last night's event in my head and was not too completely sure what exactly had happened. Judging from my nakedness and the cute possibly half-naked girl in whose room I was in, there had been sex involved.

"Hi," she breathed, shy all at once.

"Is this your dorm room?"

She nodded eagerly and turned a bright shade of embarrassment-red. I looked around at the tiny room and wondered just how loud the sex had gotten. There was no way we hadn't been heard.

"How the hell did we get here?"

"You don't remember much about last night do you?"

"I was in a bit of a state, so no." I saw the crestfallen look on her face and tried to not be a jerk. "But I remember you," I said.

"What's my name then?"

"Meredith," I said and she beamed, her face lighting up. She was sweet, way too sweet and good hearted, and she wanted to be liked so much. Wanted me to like her.

"I should probably get going before you get caught with me."

"But it's the middle of the day," she said shyly. "You're kinda stuck here. With me."

"Oh," I said. I hadn't thought of that. "Well, that's not such a bad thing..."

"Are you really a vampire? I mean, you guys aren't exactly supposed to exist, and yet here you are..."

My eyes met hers and I smiled. "You already know the

answer to that." I replied.

"Do you want me?" She asked.

She wasn't wearing anything under the jersey and she was perfect. It wasn't until I was biting her neck as she rode me, her legs wrapped around me, that I realized that she was possibly the most dangerous woman I had ever met.

I was careful when I drank from her neck, her sweet blood filling my mouth as she orgasmed on top of me, and I lost myself for a while.

***

I stumbled away from Meredith's dorm as soon as the sun had gone down enough for me to leave. She was asleep and I just had to escape, so I didn't care who saw me. Add the fact that I was high off her blood and you can guess just how many fucks I was giving at the time.

As I hailed a cab, determined to head back to HTDK for more, there was a little bit of guilt, but I knew that I could never see Meredith again.

Oh, what? You don't get it? Need me to spell it out for you? It's simple when you really look at it, so I'm surprised you aren't getting it. I know exactly what I am and how fucked up I am. There's a lot of self-awareness here, so bear with me. I know I'm an addict but I actually *like* the addiction and that's the dangerous part of me. Girls like Meredith marry guys like me and they're convinced that we will change for them. They even convince *us* that we will change for them, but deep down inside, we both know it's a goddamn lie. It's the power of love and all of the rest of that bullshit of relationships that we've been fed through movie and television shows.

I could see it in Meredith's eyes that she'd already written a script starring me as the dashing bad-boy vampire who was going to sweep her off her feet for a whirlwind adventure and romance. Even when I was fucking her brains out, I could see it in the way she looked at me like I was the most amazing thing she had ever seen. She wanted so much more.

And me, I just wanted to get high. As much as I liked her, *I just wanted to get high* and that was fucking with my head in a serious way. See how fucked up I am?

So was I going to see her again and break her poor little heart? Fuck no. Better for me to just walk away and let her be disappointed now, rather than be fucked up later. Besides, I'm good at running away.

***

My old friend Oblivion was waiting for me within the walls of the Hall of the Drunken King and I gladly accepted his invitation.

***

Have you ever gotten blackout drunk? When you finally wake up, for a while you have no idea who or when you are and all you know is that you're sober and you don't like it one little bit. Yeah, that was me, and my waking up was problematic to say the least.

See, there's waking up from a blackout and then there's *waking up from a blackout, slumped in a chair in a darkened club and realizing that Harry the motherfucking vampire, has been waiting for you to wake the fuck up.* And then you realize that for the first time in what feels like forever, you're 100% sober.

"Fuck," I said, as eloquent as ever.

Harry was seated in a large leather bound chair that looked like someone had dragged it from the corner specifically for this conversation. It was large and heavy and awkward and moving it had involved a certain level of difficulty that pisses off the person moving it, because they know that they're going to have to be the one to put it back where it came from. It was *that* kind of chair, the kind that can only be described as a "throne."

You know what clued me in to the fact that I was possibly in the worst kind of trouble? There was nobody else around in the club. We were completely alone. Okay, that wasn't the only thing. It was also scary as hell since it was so quiet and dim, most of the light having been turned off and it had that heavy, boomy feel that only deserted buildings tend to have. It's almost as if the building itself has gone to sleep and is just waiting for people to come back so it can be alive again. You know the feeling, right? Well, that was bad enough, especially with the impending headache and slight panic attack I was having as I was struggling with an existential crisis and the fact that I couldn't remember how I had gotten there, yet there was an indefinite sense that a lot of time had passed.

I really knew I was in trouble when Harry slowly unwrapped a piece of gum, ever so delicately.

Just so you know, there is never any situation that can be termed as "good" when you have a dangerous guy like Harry sitting alone in a room with a guy like me. When said dangerous guy is about to eat something, somebody is getting hurt. I was actually glad it wasn't an apple because according to movie rules that would mean I was about to be a dead man.

"There's a saying my da was always proud of trotting out whenever he wanted to be a complete ass," Harry said after a long moment. "I don't remember very much about my da you see, because it's been such a very long time, but this one thing always stuck with me over the decades and then the centuries. 'If you give a man enough rope, he will eventually hang himself.'" Harry paused to look at me, the gum unwrapped, letting the weight of that statement sink in properly. He continued after a moment. "I always hated when he said it, but it's been proven to be true time and time again. I meet someone new, I give them the benefit of the doubt and wait to see how long before they fuck it up."

"Did you just say 'centuries'? How old *are* you?"

Harry popped the gum into his mouth, completely ignoring the fact that I had spoken at all. He had a speech prepared and I wasn't about to steal his thunder. He chewed the gum very deliberately, intent on letting me know that it was me who had fucked up, and heavily implying that he had given me as much rope as he was willing to give.

I gathered myself, desperately trying to remember anything I had done, trying to remember just how bad I had screwed up. All I could remember was how sweet Meredith had been, how good her blood had tasted. There was a flash of a memory of sex in a bathroom, Meredith gasping in orgasm, but with the way my mind was I could have just been making shit up.

"I'm drawing a blank here, but is there any chance I can get a do-over?"

Harry stared at me over steepled finger tips and exhaled slowly.

"What the fuck are we going to do with you Bob? You're an addict—"

"Of course I'm an addict! Remember the bag of drugs that got me shot in the face?"

Harry waved it off and he may have shuddered a little. It was weird to see that I was having this much of an effect on him.

"From what I've seen, you were a terrible human being," he fairly spat at me, "and I think you might actually be a worse vampire!"

"Hello? Addict over here?"

"Your actions over the past days have put us all at risk—"

"At risk of what exactly? From what I understand, you can just about shut down anything or anyone with the snap of your fingers… so exactly what risk can I pose? I'm just an addict, remember? And I seriously doubt I'm the first addict you've ever had to deal with, so respectfully speaking: fuck you."

That was definitely one step too far.

Harry blurred and the next thing I was aware of, my head was ringing and there were dark spots in front of my eyes. I was also twenty feet from where I had been sitting, and apparently had made friends with the glass wall in front of the balcony. I had made friends *really hard* from the way the glass had dented and starred from the impact, the shatterproof coating the only thing that was stopping me from being covered in a rain of glass. Harry was on his feet and my chair was over-turned, so apparently I just met Harry's freight train of a fist and by all rights should be dead.

I tried to move and pain spiked through my chest, the bones and muscles screaming at me. At least I knew *where* Harry had hit me.

"We're going to play a little game Bob. I hit you every time you tell me 'fuck you.' Simple rules."

"At least I know how much I ruined your carefully prepared speech," I said and dragged myself to my feet. "What exactly did you expect from me Harry? *Huh?* It's obvious that you don't like me and as much as you'd like to try fooling yourself and me, this was *never* about giving me a chance to do shit. You dragged me to this fucked up place after I'd gone through a traumatic, and not to mention *normally life ending* event of a bullet to the head, which I survived only because I'm a vampire. Then you shove me in a room full of vampires and without so much as a warning, you introduce me, *the addict,* to the one substance on earth that you *know* vampires are *massively addicted to*. That's not an act of kindness or even *waiting* for me to fuck up. That's literally shoving the fucking needle in my arm and yelling at me because *there's a fucking needle in my arm!*"

I flexed my sore muscles, keeping an eye on Harry, wondering just how much I was pissing him off. I'd actually surprised myself at the sudden clarity of thought about just how much Harry was setting me up and truthfully, it scared the shit out of me. Usually, coming out of a blackout leaves my head seriously fucked up for days, but this wasn't an ordinary sobering up process. Once again Harry was playing a one-sided game and I was damned if he wasn't playing for keeps.

"I was going to have you killed you know," Harry finally said after a long moment.

"That's a little drastic, don't you think?"

"But then I thought that might be a little drastic. Times have changed Bob. It's not like it was a hundred years ago, or even fifty years ago. Even twenty years ago... but here's the thing: I have to think about what kind of message I'm sending. I've spent years changing how we vampires *think*. How we fit into the world. We can't keep on making the same mistakes, and believe me, a lot of mistakes have been made. So I'm going to make an example of you Bob. All of us have personally witnessed your personal brand of assholery and debauchery over the past three days and none of it has been pretty. You are now a prime example of exactly why we don't allow accidentals, so I have to thank you personally for being such a brilliant fuck-up. All of my vampires know who you are now and they don't like you, because you remind them of what they could have been. In a bad way of course."

Well, fuck you too Harry. I made sure not to say that one out loud.

"Okay, that's a little harsh," I said instead. "A lot harsh really, but that only makes me want to ask one question. Do I still get free drinks?"

"Throw him off the roof," Harry said.

I have no idea where they even came from, but suddenly the bouncers Ryan and Ryan were there on both sides of me and had grabbed my arms and hoisted me into the air.

"I thought you said you weren't going to kill me!" I yelled at Harry's retreating back.

"It's not going to kill you," Harry called back.

"It's just going to hurt a lot," Ryan added.

Chapter 14
AFTER THE AFTERLIFE

There are five things you need to know about being thrown off the roof of a four story building. While some of you may scoff and say that this is an easily survivable distance to fall, people have died falling off of the roofs of *one* story buildings. Hell, some people have died from falling off a *six-foot ladder,* so trust me: there are no guarantees. Basic fact is that it's largely a matter of luck in how you land, so good luck with that.

Step one: don't do it. Fight it all the way if you can. Get thrown down the stairs instead or maybe throw someone else down the stairs, but whatever happens, do not let anyone throw you off the roof of a building. It doesn't matter how nice or reasonable they're being about it; you fight it as hard as you can. Crying is optional since it may remind them to be human, but it might just make them mock you mercilessly instead and tell you to man up. They're just throwing you off the roof of the building, after all, so don't be such a pussy, right? Don't listen to them. Trust me: *be a pussy,* embrace it. You want to fight those fuckers all the way to the edge.

Step two: try to find anything to grab onto on the way down that can slow your fall. Any handy branches, plants, window ledges, pipes, pretty much anything at all within reach can slow you down long enough so that you survive the actual fall. The one thing you want to avoid is being thrown off of a roof in a downtown area because there aren't going to be any branches around to grab onto. Plus the act of throwing will send you as far away from the side of the building as possible, and that's not going to end well, especially if they throw you face first. Still, it's better than being thrown backward.

Now some of you are thinking, hey, it's four stories, you can just do a flip or somersault and get into a better position and pull some ninja shit. Yeah, no. You have literally a little less than three point something seconds before you slam into the ground. The human body drops really fast, and you've only really just begun to react to being thrown off the damned roof by the time your very short trip is over and you're bleeding out on the ground, all broken-boned and shattered skull.

Wait… I'm supposed to be telling you how to survive the fall, so let's get back to that.

Step three: accept the fact that you're completely fucked and that this is not something you're going to be walking away from with anything less than a few broken bones. The key here is to relax, let your body go limp and to try to land on your feet, but make sure that your knees are bent just a little. Sounds almost impossible I know, especially after the whole "try to be relaxed" thing, but I got this advice from Wikipedia, and the guys there seemed to know what they were talking about. I mean they had a ton of citations and everything to back them up, so it's more than just some guy on the internet talking out of his ass. So yeah, relax and try to land on your feet.

Step four: land on your side if possible and try to protect your head from hitting the ground. Apparently, some people have managed not to hit their heads on immediate impact, but it was when they bounced or had the secondary impact that things got all fucked up and they shattered their skulls. Don't ask me how the Wikipedia guys know this shit. They just do, and they were very clear about not getting your head all fucked up.

Step five: be a vampire.

***

Three-point something seconds after I had been thrown off the roof of HTDK, I crashed into the windscreen of the limo that happened to be passing below at that exact moment. To say that this surprised the hell out of me was an understatement, but honestly, I think the limo driver and the passengers were a tiny bit more surprised than I was.

The car screeched to a halt, and there was some commotion, but at the time I didn't care. I was embedded ass-first into the windscreen of a limo and was aware that I had also caved in half of the roof of the car. I was also aware that in a few seconds my body would be screaming at me, but at that moment I felt truly alive.

I began to laugh then. It was either that or cry and laughing seemed appropriate to the moment.

"Hey I know you," a voice said, and I craned my head to look up.

The driver of the limo looked at me and then at the car in utter shock, his mind no doubt running through the different scenarios his insurance company was going to try to use to fuck him over. It wasn't him who had spoken to me, though. The King and a tall Japanese woman were standing next to him and both looked down at me.

"Oh hey King," I managed to gasp. "Fancy running into you here." Adrenaline was still running through my body and I could feel the shakes coming on, possibly followed by a lot of pain, but nonchalance was winning out over shock and pain for the moment.

"You know you're traditionally supposed to leave the building by the front door, right?"

I tried to sit up but something screamed in my back and then there was a slight pop that worried the hell out of me.

"That's what I told the Ugly Twins, but they were really insistent. And strong. Really fucking strong."

"The 'Ugly Twins'?" he asked, but I could see him starting to get it.

"Bouncers. Big, tall, ugly. The Ryans."

"The Ugly Twins actually suits them," he admitted, then he grinned evilly. "I'll make sure that name makes the rounds, though. It will drive them crazy."

From my vantage point, I saw the faces of the twins appear over the edge of the roof. I couldn't help myself as I flipped them off with the one hand that was free. The King followed my gaze and upon seeing the Ugly Twins, he grinned and gleefully gave them the full force of both his middle fingers.

"I've never liked these guys either. I think you're the first person they've had to throw off the roof." The King grinned wickedly. "Man, having you around is going to be a blast!"

The twins retreated, and the King looked back to me, still grinning. I think that might have been the instant that he decided that we were going to be friends, but I've been known to be wrong, so don't quote me on that.

"As much as I applaud the thought, I'm in serious pain here."

"Well you did just fall from the roof into my car, so that's kinda obvious."

"I was just being cool about it. But ow, fucking ow?"

"Damn dude, let me give you a hand."

I nodded and laid my head back for a second, aware of just how blue the early morning sky was looking.

"Don't mean to be a bother, but could you hurry? The sun's coming up and I think I'm stuck."

***

When I finally entered my apartment about an hour later, it was as if I hadn't been there in years. The King had given me a ride home and then I'd ended up having to get the building supervisor to open up for me since my keys, wallet and phone had all gone missing at some point. Keeping to the shadows at around eight in the morning can be pretty tricky, especially with the sun trying to assassinate you at every turn, and the fact that I was dealing with extreme pain that comes from being off a roof into a car. I somehow managed it and made sure to give Oscar some serious stink-eye for being Claude's paid informant. Still, I was glad he was around, and I didn't have to find a way to break into my own apartment.

"What the hell happened to you?" Oscar asked, noticing my discomfort.

"Fell off a roof. Thrown actually." I grimaced and accepted the key he held out for me.

Oscar nodded wisely. "Maybe you should avoid rooftops, you know? They don't seem to like you very much."

I escaped back to my apartment.

I hadn't minded losing the keys that much, but losing the

phone stung the most since I was still under contract and wouldn't be able to get a replacement without having to pay an arm and a leg, plus the fact that I didn't actually remember anyone's numbers anymore. I'd probably have to end up getting an Android instead of an iPhone, and after having what amounted to a small computer in my hand, I wasn't sure I was going to be able to give up that last reminder of my former life. You know the life: the one where I actually had money left over after paying bills. The wallet was going to be a pain in the ass because I'd now have to get a new ID card and new debit and credit cards, never mind the other rewards cards I'd bothered to keep on me because at least they filled out my wallet a little better even though I hadn't used many of them more than once, if ever. I wasn't even thinking of the hassle of getting new government type ID cards. Most of the offices that issued those were only open during daylight hours and required some serious running around. It was almost as if the government knew all about vampires and had decided they were going to fuck us over as much as possible, never mind the bureaucracy.

I let the door slam shut behind me and took off the sunglasses and the oversized hoodie the King had so thoughtfully provided, glad to actually see my crappy apartment. It was almost like stepping out of a dream. The past week had felt like such a heightened state of reality, and now reality was anything but real. It was darker and dirtier and just so... ordinary.

The clock over the sink ticked too loudly and arrogantly in the booming silence of my perfectly ordinary apartment and all at once I wanted to smash it into pieces for being so obnoxious.

Coming all the way back to reality always leaves you with a slight desperation and a slow-building but ultimately smothering sensation that you may have fucked up too bad this time. It was the inevitable feeling of being completely and thoroughly fucked.

So there I was, back to reality. I looked down at my bruised body and my expensive semi-ruined suit (but still wearable if everybody around me squinted) and could only shake my head in despair. Reality was depressing as fuck.

Even though I was a vampire, my life actually hadn't changed, and it was going to keep on being normal for the rest of my life, one minute at a time.

The weight of the past few days came crashing down on me all at once, and I think for the first time I realized the full meaning of what had happened and just how badly I had fucked things up for myself.

"FUCK!"

***

I woke up a couple of hours later, the pain from my bruises and cuts now a distant memory, and Claude was already there waiting for me. I opened my eyes, and he was just there like Harry had been. I vowed to myself that I really needed to stop letting people sneak up on me, or at the very least I needed to get a damn chain for my door.

"Call your mom," Claude said and threw an iPhone at me. I caught it and fumbled it, embarrassed to look at him. He continued: "That's an older model, but it's mostly secure. I already transferred your contacts, so be grateful for the Cloud. You now don't have any more excuses about why you can't call people. So with that in mind: *call your mom.*"

"Aren't you going to ask me where I've been?"

"Nope. That's a conversation for after you've called your mom."

"So… never?"

For a long moment, all I could hear was the loud ticking of the damned clock. Was there a volume control on that thing or something?

I broke first.

"Fine, I'll call her," I mumbled, looking away at the shiny white iPhone 4 of which I was apparently now the owner. "How did you even know I was here?"

"Oscar called me. He doesn't earn money if he's got nothing to report. He said you looked like shit."

"I got thrown off a roof, so that's fair."

Claude got to his feet, shaking his head. I realized for the first time that his hair was getting longer than he was used to keeping it and he was a little unshaven, but still managed to make his suit look good. Not for the first time I had the thought that Harry would have probably welcomed Claude as a vampire more than me. Was I jealous? *Yes, of course, I was,* but only because I knew that Claude would not have been getting lessons in how *not* to fly from the Ugly Twins. I knew that he would have been killing it as a vampire and I would have been cheering him on in my role as perpetual sidekick. Instead there I was in the role reserved for the hero of the story, and I was fucking it up massively. Probably royally as well.

Claude paused in the door and pinched the bridge of his nose. I could tell he wanted to yell at me and I think I wanted him to break down and just to get it over with.

Come on Claude, tell me what a fuck-up I am.

"I'm not asking," he finally said, and I glared at him.

"I got thrown off a roof, and you're not even curious?"

"Oh I'm curious, and I know you're going to tell me at some point, but right now I have one job, and it's to get you *to call your mom.* So please pick up the goddamn phone and call her already? *Okay?*"

"She's been callin--"

Claude walked out of the room, clearly done with me.

"And you've not been answering! Call your mother dude. I'm out."

I stared at the phone for a long time. When the front door slammed behind Claude as he exited, I was still staring at the phone.

***

It's funny: I really didn't want to get into the whole "*how I became a vampire*" thing since it's always the first thing everybody wants to know. Personally, I think the whole situation with the vampire support group is a hell of a lot more interesting. I mention the support group and about Stanley and Benjamin and Frankie, and people actually get interested, you know? It's me introducing an aspect of being a vampire that they'd never considered. It seems to make it more real… or maybe to them, more like a story they could sit down and listen to, so I guess it's not *really* real to them?

Argh, too many thoughts running through my brain to process here.

Look: my point is that I never wanted to tell the story of how I became a vampire and especially how I got kicked out of HTDK and became persona non-grata in vampire society. That shit is just plain *embarrassing,* and it's not a story that I can remain dispassionate about. That shit is *my life.* I made a lot of bad choices, many more bad than good and I can freely admit to it, you know? But it still hurts on a deep level to look at myself in the mirror like this and go into detail about exactly how I fucked up.

Besides, the whole addiction thing is seriously fucked up and not funny at all, so if it's all the same to you, I'm going to skip past some of the most embarrassing bits. You really don't want to hear about a sad, lonely vampire suddenly realizing how much he had fucked himself, do you?

Oh, you do?

Seriously?

Goddamit.

***

Sobriety!

Have I mentioned how much sobriety sucks? Well, it does! It was back in my life with the kind of vengeance usually reserved for laying waste to entire cities, and it wasn't taking any prisoners. It made me look at my reality in a completely different light and all of a sudden I had a lot of questions. I mean, like a *shit ton* of questions. The type of questions you don't ask when you're deep in the shit because you're just accepting your bliss and going with it, but for the marginally curious mind, these were questions that just had to be asked.

"How does the whole blood thing *work* anyway?" I asked.

Of course, there was no answer coming forth since I was on the toilet, and Claude definitely wasn't around to ask. If anyone had been around to talk to, they certainly wouldn't haven't been in the bathroom for me to ask since I definitely can't take a shit while someone is in the same room. When using public bathrooms, I usually have to close my eyes and pretend--

What? You were the one who wanted all of the dirty details here.

I actually do some of my best thinking while taking a nice leisurely shit, *in private*, with no one watching or judging me, so you know: *deal with it.* Taking a shit is the most vulnerable act that any of us can ever take. We have no defense against attack, unless some of the more brazen have learned how to weaponize their shit, and that lack of defense tends to open up the mind in ways that it wouldn't usually be. Abstract thought is not just possible, but happening right there, exciting and *alive.* Taking a shower or a bath is similar, but *taking a shit* is where magical thinking occurs. It wouldn't surprise me if Archimedes hadn't been actually taking a bath before he ran out into the streets yelling "Eureka," but instead had been taking a shit. The bath story was just a cover, because last I checked, shit displaces water in the exact same way that dipping a toe into the bathwater does.

There was no Eureka moment for me, just the realization that I was asking a question out loud to an empty apartment and in effect talking to myself. It was a reminder that I had most definitely pissed off Claude to the point where he had no words to say to me. That was something I had never accomplished before, and it was a weird feeling.

I went to text Claude but the phone was still booting up and I had to wait for the "Your Phone Is Now Ready to Use" message to go away. There was an instant barrage of waiting text messages, but I gnored them all for the time being.

-*The blood is a drug.*

I sat there waiting for a response to my text message, wondering if one was coming and desperately hoping he wouldn't just pick up the phone to call me. I hate talking on the phone while on the toilet. I'm always afraid of the other person hearing the echo of the room and figuring out where I was and then from that, assuming I was taking a shit (which I was) and getting grossed out because they now had a mental picture of me taking a shit while talking to them. The last thing you need is a mental picture of your friend taking a shit, especially since no shit is the same and there is the tendency for random loud farts and various bodily noises; they never look at you the same way after that.

My phone lit up as Claude responded.

-So you've been stoned off your ass for the past 4 days? When you call your mom, please don't mention that.

-How do you know I haven't called her yet?

-Dude, please. Have you met YOU? Call your mom.

Well, at least he was still talking to me. Didn't matter if it was going to be yelling or whatever. Talking was much better than silence.

-I'll call her. Just a lot to process. Need to borrow your brain later.

-When you say blood… have you been sucking blood from people? Real actual people?

-Yeah. But I haven't had to kill anyone yet if that's what you're worried about.

-What do you mean "yet"?

-Oops. Haven't killed anyone at all?

-You're stalling. Call your mom. I'll text you later, and we can talk about this whole blood/drug situation. I'll pick you up from work.

Work? Holy shit!

The reality that I probably didn't have a job anymore was what really jolted me out of the headiness of the past four days. I looked at the 56 voicemail messages displayed in the home menu and 144 new emails that had popped up when I had turned it on. I had ignored the pounding heart in my chest that had been inspired by the avalanche of messages from people looking for me and had just texted Claude directly without reading anything. Nobody had the time for that kind of guilt, *amirite?* Yeah… no.

Yes, there was a fair bit of freaking the fuck out as I scrolled through my emails and saw way too many messages from my boss (*"Are you dead or sick?"*) or from Sammy *"where the fuck are you?"* and *"Re: Re: Dude WTF?"*). Then, of course, there was the huge glut of unanswered text messages that finally made me want to throw the phone down the toilet. Instead, I flushed without toileting the phone and went to find something to eat, my heart pounding, hands shaking, headache incoming.

Welcome to Life 2.0, where you don't get to vanish for days at a time with no consequences, especially in this constantly connected world where everyone is telling everyone else what they had for lunch and how everyone should feel moral outrage because of some stupid meme they found on the internet that a little bit of research would have revealed was 100% false.

So I did what anybody else would do in the instance of freaking the fuck out. I avoided facing the situation, spent about an hour brainstorming on stupid plans to save my ass and come up with a convincing enough lie that would explain where I had been and how it was *completely not my fault*. And then I went back to sleep so I wouldn't have to think any more.

Pretty standard right? I didn't even bother reading the emails or messages because even just thinking about them filled me with nothing but panic, and I really didn't need that. You know what I did instead? *Select All and Delete.* It was that simple, and it gave me such relief that I wondered why I hadn't done that sooner.

Don't judge me. I can feel you judging me, so just don't, okay?

I woke up an hour before the sun went down enough for me to go out, but once it reached that point, I was out of the house in a hurry, a vampire on the hunt. Yes I was on the hunt for my old job back, but I was hunting dammit, so don't ruin this for me.

***

"No."

Imagine the stupid look on my face as my Boss very clearly and unequivocally gave me the answer I was not looking for, and all before I could even open my mouth to ask the obviously stupid question. He had been fixing a display by the door when I had hustled in, the biggest shit eating smile I could muster plastered across my face. I had a whole speech prepared and even had my phone in my hand to show proof of how fucked up my entire situation was.

"But I've got a great story this time!" I protested, and his eyebrow had gone up at that.

"Seriously? You've got a *great story*? You've been fucking *gone* for over a week, no calls, no email, even fucking Sammy has no fucking clue where you've fucked off to, and you come in here with *a story*? What are you? *High?*"

"When you put it like that--"

The Boss scratched his scruffy cheeks as some fresh-faced pimply guy brought over a couple of new boxes. He was dressed in the official Staff T-shirt and was actually wearing an apron, so I guessed he was a completely new hire, probably on the endless rotation of ever-changing daytime staff. I had never bothered learning any of their names or faces since they were usually gone so quickly, but I was pretty sure I had never seen this kid before.

"Bob, I don't *not* like you, but you done fucked up. I hired somebody to replace you five days ago. I got a business to run, and you fucked up the rotation."

"What if I told you that I got shot by the neighborhood drug dealer and things just got really weird after that?"

"Why would you even tell me *anything that stupid*? Do I look fucking stupid to you?"

I looked down at the short man that the Boss was and really wanted to tell him how much he looked like a bad Danny DeVito knockoff, but then considered how much I needed the job.

"I really need this job. I mean *really*. This is a seriously fucked up time for me--"

"Goddammit Bob. I'm trying to be the nice guy here, at least as nice as I can be. I don't give a shit about what you got going on, or how bad things are for you. All those considerations went out the door when you fucked off a week ago and didn't do the job I hired you to do. You coulda asked for time off while you *still* worked here. Would you have gotten it? All depends on what we coulda worked out, I mean I'm a reasonable guy, you know?"

The new guy was giving me a weird look, almost pitying, and I wanted to hit him really fucking hard. He must have sensed it, and looked away instead, busying himself with using the pricing gun on the new merchandise from the boxes. The boss turned away from me, and I reached out to him, desperate that he at least listen to the eloquent speech that I had prepared which had somehow failed to register anywhere in my brain. I managed to grab his shoulder, and he turned, scowl already on his face, his thick hairy arms already coming up, ready to defend himself and administer the ass-kicking he really wanted to give me.

I don't know what happened next, but I found myself looking the Boss deep in the eye, and for a moment, it was like I made a *connection* with him, could see how much *he was really going to regret kicking my ass in the alley behind the store, but that it needed to be done because I was obviously not taking a hint and he promised himself not to enjoy it too much but God it would feel so good to just let go and kick someone's ass--*

There was a brief moment that reminded me somewhat of looking down the barrel of my drug dealer's gun

(bang!)

but I was already speaking before I knew what I was going to say.

"Give me another chance. I'm not a bad guy, and at least I've never stolen from you. I need this job as much as you need someone like me to do it, so just think again. *Give me another chance.*"

I blinked then, unsure that I wanted to be holding eye contact with the Boss or anyone else for that long and for a long moment wondered if the Boss was going to kick my ass. He blinked and then gave me a half-smile.

"I'm going to give you another chance Bob."

Holy shit! Seriously? Had I just Jedi mind-tricked him or something?

"But I'm docking you a week's pay and putting you back on probation, so don't fuck it up."

So much for the Jedi-mind trick.

"So just to be absolutely clear, I still have a job?"

"Want me to fire you now, shit-for-brains?"

The new guy was looking at me like I was some kind of wizard. I shrugged and grinned at him as I headed towards the back of the store, not wanting to push my luck.

"And put on a goddamn apron!" the Boss yelled at my retreating back.

I considered giving him the middle finger, but that might have been a step too far. However, I didn't wear the goddamn apron. Only the new guys ever wore the goddamn apron.

***

There was a dildo on the counter in front of me, and there was no fucking way I was touching that thing.

"I told you, man, it's not working," the customer was saying. "You're going to give me a refund."

"Respectfully speaking sir, get the fuck out of the store."

"I have rights! I'm your customer dammit! You don't get to swear at me! Where's your supervisor?"

"I'm the supervisor. I'd call the owner but after getting a call at two in the morning, he's going to tell you the same thing I just told you, but much, much meaner. So please do us all a favor and get the fuck out of the store."

The big problem here wasn't the dildo. Nor was it that fact that we test every single dildo that is sold in the store, according to basic company policy and the powerful human need not to touch any returned merchandise. The problem was that this particular dildo, like most dildos that people have tried to return, had most definitely been inserted into one of many orifices in the customer's frail body. In fact, it was still sticky, and there was the strong raw stench of fecal matter that was currently assaulting my senses and making me want to commit murder, mainly because the stupid fucking customer had reached into his pants and somehow pulled the fucking dildo out of his ass before slapping it down on my fucking counter.

What the fuck is wrong with people?

I'd spent the evening immersing myself in the mundane rhythm of reality and I'm not ashamed to say that I had hated every second of it.

It's only after you return to what most people consider "normal" after going through some extraordinary event that you realize you'd do anything to not have to deal with the ordinary anymore. The rush of the concert that had transported you for a few hours to a state of euphoria, or the excitement of waking up to a new place every morning during your vacation, or even the heightened sense of self and frenzied activity that comes from being on a mind altering substance for days at a time, those were all glimpses into the awesome and the profane, a reminder that life was anything but ordinary. Ordinary was the *grind,* the day to day interactions of being stuck doing the same thing in different ways while your brain shut down out of boredom or desperation.

You want to know why so many retail workers end up smoking crack or doing meth or whatever drug is reasonably available? It's not because they have no direction in life or anything that simple. They get into drugs because their brains are bored from being mired in the ordinary and the drugs allow them to take a break away from the ordinary. That glimpse is enough to keep them going, keep them from getting too bored and getting up to no good, at least until they either accomplish what they needed and can escape or until they settle into their reality of having to survive from paycheck to paycheck, waiting to get their next hit. After all, drugs are more immediate and cheaper than a concert or a vacation, and you have to take your euphoria wherever you can find it.

That used to be my reality, and now my eyes were opened. As the night ground on I settled into the groove at work way too easily. For a while, everything felt normal. Working in the porn store was reasonably mundane from a certain perspective and after working someplace for a year, I'd gotten used to almost anything. The store had its own rhythm and flow that shifted and morphed according to what was going on in the city.

You could tell the mood of the city by what people bought, who was actually coming in to look or buy, and how many minor crimes were committed.

People stole different things at different times of the year or even when the economy sucked. It was predictable that if the dollar was down we'd be seeing a huge number of pocket pussies go missing. We got all types in the store. Sixty-year old grannies who insisted in leaving the batteries in the vibrators after we turned them on to test before they left the store, because they wanted to use them on the way home; straight men in their twenties who came in to buy *amyl nitrate* on the way back from clubbing, who thought they had discovered the newest drug craze and had no idea those "poppers" were used to relax the muscles for anal sex; gay men who knew exactly what the *amyl nitrate* was for and often bought lube and the occasional toy to go along with it; the occasional couple with one person more into sex than the other more prudish partner who considered sex to be dirty and looked at me like I was a peddler of smut (which I was) and was personally responsible for their spouses' particular choice of kink (to be clear, I totally wasn't) instead of me just doing my damn job; the occasional joker who would try to embarrass me by asking loud idiotic questions designed to embarrass me (they didn't) and who would then be puzzled when I refused to sell them their "tobacco" pipe or "decorative glass stem" and had zero qualms about calling them on their shit.

The Boss had one rule about the customer, and it wasn't anything to do with them being right. If you really want to know his opinion, which should have been printed on our staff t-shirts, it was simply "Fuck the Customer (just not literally)." It would have been nice to have that exact phrase embroidered on a doily or something hanging in the store so I could point to it whenever some asshole would inevitably start yelling at me about customer rights and what did I mean no refunds, even though we clearly and loudly pointed it out to them with the sale of every sex-toy.

By the time the new guy (no, I didn't bother to learn his name) had finally clocked out around 11 PM and left me to my own devices before Sammy was due to show up at 3 AM, I was already regretting my return to reality and remembered how much I fucking hated our customers.

Claude texted me around midnight, just when I was wondering if he was still talking to me.

-Dude I'm about to get on a plane to South America. Don't ask for details. Will be gone for a week. Stay out of trouble.

I stared at the phone for a long moment, trying not to feel

disappointed or irritated at the sudden turn of events. Claude's particular expertise had unpredictable travel arrangements and he had a tendency to vanish at times, so this was hardly surprising. I had just been looking forward to talking to him about different theories on blood and vampires and shit.

The phone buzzed as another message came in.

-Call your mother dammit.

And now there was a shit covered dildo on my fucking counter, and I could feel the rage building in me, but with the rage, there was something else that had been lurking through all of my customer interactions over the past hours. A violent urge to rip this douchenozzle's head from his shoulders and guzzle in the spurting blood from his neck—

"GET THE FUCK OUT!" I yelled, and the customer yelped and jumped away from me, scared shitless. He hadn't been expecting that kind of reaction and to tell you the truth, neither had I. He tentatively reached out to grab the offensive dildo from the counter as if I was going to jump over the counter and bite him, then he scurried out of the store.

I took a deep breath, calming myself down as I sprayed the counter with the Lysol we kept under the counter. I wiped up the slimy leavings, utterly grossed out that we actually had to have Lysol and paper towels handy for this exact reason. I was glad that I only had an hour left before I could go home. Maybe I would even swing by HTDK on the way home for the after hours party if I could manage to avoid the Ugly Twins on the way in—

THWACK! A red dildo smacked me right in the side of the face. I jumped back, getting ready to freak out since I was convinced that the customer had returned and had thrown the used dildo at me, complete with fecal matter. I took another look, remembering that it had been a pink Tantus Eaze 5 inch model, and what had thwacked me so solidly in the face was clearly an 8 inch Flexible Jelly with Vibrator which was currently turned on and throbbing its way across the counter towards me.

What the fuck?

I turned—

Sammy was standing by the door, methodically and angrily

unwrapping a *Doc Johnson Double 12 Inch Black Dildo*, which had been marked down to only $19.99 and was apparently destined for an appointment with my face.

Can I mention exactly how happy she did not look?

"Don't you say a fucking word!" Sammy snapped at me, and I felt all of my words immediately dry up, not to mention all the joy in my life. "I still haven't decided on if I'm going to murder you or make you listen to some bad poetry and then fucking murder you."

Through my brief moment of intense guilt that Sammy had triggered, something stood out to me. "Why bad poetry exactly?"

"Because that's what that asshole you pawned me off on made me suffer through!"

Sammy's aim with the dildo was remarkably deadly accurate. Her throwing technique involved just whipping it forward and letting the dildo fling out into the air as an extension of her arm, whipping through the air with hardly any wiggle, startlingly beautiful and graceful in a perverse way that only a flying twelve-inch dildo could be. It actually distracted me to the point where I found myself watching the dildo make its way toward my face before I remembered to duck. The dildo bounced harmlessly off the back shelf—

THWACK!

That one got me up on the temple, and I turned to see a Fleshlight go bouncing through the air. When Sammy had grabbed that to throw, I hadn't even seen since I had been so distracted with the flying dildo, but apparently, she wasn't wasting time. Goddamn, she was accurate.

"You ghosted on me, dude! If you didn't want me around, you could have at least had the decency *to tell me!*"

"Sammy, what the fuck are you even talking about?"

Sammy hurled another pair of dildos, and I deflected them both as I made my way into aisle three which had much better cover from the aerial assault. My mind raced, trying and then ultimately failing to piece together any of the not-remembered snippets of memory from the last four days.

Sammy advanced through the store, unwrapping another piece of merchandise. She brandished it at me, and I flinched, expecting the throw.

"The other night at the club, you *motherfucker*! At HTDK!"

Oh shit. I had run into Sammy at the club? No wonder I was feeling this nagging guilt. What the fuck had actually happened?

Okay, proceed carefully…

"Exactly how high would you say I was at the time, do you think?" I asked carefully and hopefully. Hopefully, because Sammy had stopped mid-throw and was possibly reconsidering the situation. Since she was no stranger to getting seriously fucked up from time to time and regaling me with tales of her partying and subsequent regrets, she was the one person on earth right now who could possibly understand what I had been going through. At least as long as I didn't mention anything about blood.

"Really fucking high," she admitted after a moment. "You were seriously fucked up man. So fucked up, you wouldn't even share whatever it is you were on."

"You totally did *not* want what I was having. Trust me." A thought occurred to me. "Did I at least put you on my tab?"

SMACK! The previously unthrown and still unwrapped P*ocket Pussy(TM)* smacked me right between the eyes. Admittedly I had deserved that one. The following barrage of products, however, was definitely questionable.

"You have a TAB?" Dodge. *Sensual Massage Oil. "*How the fuck do you have a tab at HTDK?" Smack! 10 oz bottle of *Flavoured Lube.* "You don't even like clubs!" Duck. Jar of *Make Me Cum Clit Sensitizer.* "And you're as broke as fuck!" Slap! *American Whopper 8 Inch Vibrating Dong with Harness.*

"It's a thing I'm in! Kind of a secret society thing. Has a great benefits package!"

Sammy paused her throwing, definitely curious.

"Is that what you've been off doing for the past week? We thought you were dead or something. Claude even stopped by looking for you and the Boss hired some other moron to fill your slot." Sammy gave me another look and lowered the giant strap-on she had been about to throw at me. She considered me carefully before she asked the next question. "How the fuck do you even have your job back? The Boss said he was going to murder you if you showed up here again."

"Seems there's a lot of murdering me going around right now. Can we, and by we, I mean you, stop throwing things at me now?"

"Maybe," she said, and then dropped the dildo and breezed past me, glaring all the way. "But this isn't over yet buddy."

"You won't believe the week I've been having."

"Unless you died, I'm really not interested."

"You missed the funeral."

"How was it?"

"Expensive."

"I swear when I die, just cremate me and put my ashes in a ziplock container and throw it onto the first garbage truck you see. The price of a burial urn these days is horrible."

"You got it."

Sammy snorted and looked at me with what I could only consider to be fondness. "I'm glad you're back Bob."

"So does this mean you're going to forgive me for the other night which I swear I don't remember?"

"The only way I might even think about forgiving you is if the King himself were to walk through that door and personally invite you to go partying with him."

Right on cue, the bell rang as someone entered. We both turned, wondering which of the night's particular perverts had decided to pay us a visit. Sammy's greeting turned into a squeak when she realized that the black fur coat wearing, tall black man in the midst of the three gorgeous women in little black dresses was, in fact, the King. The women went through the merchandise while the King made his way over to the counter, sunglasses on and apparently high out of his mind.

"Hey King," I said, way more casually than I had any right to.

The King pulled down his sunglasses and looked at me over the top. He grinned when he recognized me.

"Bobby! My man! I almost didn't recognize you without any general destruction around you." He looked around the store at the mess Sammy had made with her barrage of pornographic missiles. "Close, but no cigar. Still sore from this morning's trip?"

"Teeny tiny bit," I admitted.

Sammy couldn't believe her eyes and ears. She looked back and forth from me to the King and back again.

"You know Bob? Bob, how the fuck does the King know you?"

The King had spotted Sammy now and took his sunglasses off all the way, intrigued. He walked towards her, completely ignoring me, eyes only on Sammy.

"Remember that club I was telling you about before?" I asked as the King closed in.

"You mean the one that sounded totally made up?" Sammy was not looking away from the King for anything.

"Yeah, that's the one. We're both members."

The King towered over her, and I could have sworn Sammy was about to swoon as he held out a hand for her to shake. Sammy put her hand into his, and he smiled.

"Hi there sugar tits," the King said, and I winced, expecting Sammy to spoil the whole tableau and rip his head off. Nothing of the sort occurred.

"Hi back to you. Aren't you going to ask me to dance?"

"There's no music so we might have to skip the dancing."

"I'm not that type of girl."

"What type of girl are you?"

"The type where you'd better make some music up so we can dance. Go ahead and sing. I'll follow along."

The King laughed loud and lustily. He grinned at me, taking his eyes off Sammy for a second.

"I like this one, Bob. She's not yours is she?"

"Sammy's kind of her own person, but I feel I must warn you that she's a predator posing as a house pet."

"Shut the fuck up Bob," Sammy sang as sweetly as she could.

This was getting awkward, being stuck between the two of them.

"Hey, can I move now? Bit of a third wheel thing going on and your friends might need some help, so…"

The King backed up and allowed me to slip past him into the fresh air and away from their lusty stares. What the fuck was happening? I'd never seen Sammy get so weak in the knees over anyone, but from the moment the King had walked in it had been all over for her. It occurred to me to wonder if there was some kind of look that vampires had that could influence people, and then I instantly wondered if the King could teach it to me.

"Hey, King," I interjected when Sammy had sauntered off with a little extra wiggle in her hips. She had gone to get something from her bag, most likely every bit of her contact information. "What are you doing here anyway?"

The King looked around the store to his three lady friends who were looking over the merchandise. One of them was chasing another with an enormous strap-on we had on the shelf for demonstration purposes while they all laughed uproariously. They were into their own thing and obviously didn't care what was going on with the King.

"The girls wanted to make a stop for some toys. Having a bit of a private party. You want to join us?" He leaned in to whisper the last. "You're looking like you could use a taste."

"Just a little craving, nothing I can't handle, but yeah," I nodded towards Sammy. "Are you planning on using Sammy to get your fix?"

The King looked taken aback by that. He looked over to Sammy and the smile on his face surprised me. It looked intrigued and surprisingly gentle. It was the smile of a man who was completely smitten by a woman.

"Naw man," he said, "I'm not going to do her like that. She's a special kind of girl. I mean at least I think she is…"

"Oh good," I said, "because if you fucked her over, you know it's going to be my fault, right?"

"Aren't you going to threaten me or something? About breaking her heart and shit?"

"Nope. Sammy is her own person. Her mistakes are her own to make. She's a big girl."

Sammy was walking over to us. I clapped the King on the shoulder and grinned.

"Time to forgive me Sammy! Guess who's going partying with the King?"

***

Sammy was still swearing at us as we left the store and piled into the King's brand new limo.

As we drove away, I introduced myself to the King's friends, them of the lovely necks and seriously long legs. They were friendly and flirty with me, not that the King seemed to mind, and that was awesome since they all smelled so good. The mixture of sweat and perfume coming off of each girl was intoxicating until I realized that there was something else, musky and sweet that I could smell--

"So you want to bite me or not?" The tall black girl offered, and I smiled, wondering if I should tell her that I could smell her sex, but somehow I think she already knew.

It wasn't until I sucked on one of the girl's necks and the blood had spurted into my mouth, hot and salty and *so, so, sweet,* that I realized just how much I had actually been craving the taste of the blood and the high that it brought me. It was everything that had been missing from my life, was everything I needed and more.

As I felt my mind open up, the high of the blood opening my eyes to the extraordinary once again, I knew I was hooked and that there would be no going back.

I was a vampire and life was never going to be the same again.

Chapter 15
MY OWN WORST ENEMY

There was no way that the King was going to be my goddamn mentor. I know this because he told me so.

"I'm not going to be your goddamn mentor," the King said to me. "No way, no how, sorry, not sorry."

See? What did I tell you? Luckily for me, he waited until we were actually inside HTDK and had gotten past the extremely hostile and overbearing Ugly Twins who had insisted that I was persona non-grata and there was *no fucking way* I was getting inside.

"He comes in here and he's going off the roof again," one of the Ryans had insisted. Personally I wanted to run, but the King seemed intent on making a point.

Have you ever seen a grown six-foot-six man get pimp-slapped into next week? I use the term *"pimp-slapped"* with no sense of irony or political correctness since the King was in full pimp mode even at 3:14 AM on a weeknight. Both of us were pretty damned high since we had both had a mouthful of blood from the girls on the way over. Riding in the King's limo had its perks, for the girls and us. We got high on *their* blood, and the girls got high on the drugs that were readily available in the back of the limo; cocaine seemed to be a group favorite. So yeah, we were all pretty fucking high, and the King was not in the mood for taking shit from anyone, least of all the Ugly Twins.

The two highly attractive hostesses who looked like they had been poured into their dresses, had no problem at all and were kind of cool with us, even a little flirty with me, but the instant Ryan #1 had placed his hand on my chest to stop my entry, it had all been over.

Ryan #1's head spun around so fast, for a second there, I thought that the King had broken his neck. The sound of the slap still echoed through the foyer as Ryan #1 staggered a few steps back. It was only because Ryan #2 had grabbed him that he hadn't gone all the way down to the ground. The two hostesses gasped audibly, but it was the tall Korean-looking one who reached for the phone on the counter.

"You do *not* touch my friends," the King said, a strong African sounding accent showing strongly through his anger, "and you sure as shit don't tell me what to do. Do we understand each other?"

Ryan #1 looked back at the King, his fangs extended in his mouth and good God they were huge. Ryan #2 stepped between him and the King, apparently the more cautious of the pair.

"No disrespect King, but we have orders directly from Harry."

The King didn't look away from them but spoke directly to the hostess behind them.

"Jina, do me a favor and remind these assholes of exactly who I am and if I were you, I'd get Harry on the phone right fucking now. Or you can wait and just call Madame Vera to pick up two dead bodies."

Jina nodded eagerly and dialed as quickly as possible.

I just tried to look as small as possible and grinned helplessly at the trio of stoned girls behind us. I would have struck up some lame conversation but they all had stripper names, Diamond, Amethyst, and Pearlie and I really couldn't remember which name belonged to which girl. My two previous attempts had been completely wrong, and I was sure to fuck it up again.

The King leaned against the nearest wall and calmly rolled a joint. He didn't even bother to look at the Ugly Twins any further, but there was a subtle menace in the very deliberate way he was rolling that joint. For a second there I thought they were going to attempt to grab me, but Ryan #2 whispered something to Ryan #1, and they just shook their heads in clear agreement. Jina, the hostess, listened to the phone, obviously distressed.

"Respectfully speaking sir, this is *the King* we're talking about—" She listened as Harry said something possibly offensive on the other side of the line.

The King raised his eyebrow and offered the joint to me. "You can hit the Green. It's a designer strain developed just for our kind. One of the benefits of being rich. It's got a smooth flavour."

"You can't smoke that in here sir," the second hostess said nervously, and the King gave her an openly hostile look for a split second before he just smiled and waved his hand dismissively.

"Don't worry about it. I'll wait until I'm upstairs with my friend. I'm just not used to being *made to wait.*"

Jina spoke up. "*Apologies* sir. Harry's calling legal to advise on this dispute."

Legal? Holy shit. "Maybe I should just go," I suggested. "I didn't think it would be this much trouble to get in."

The King shook his head and lit his joint, pulling hard and long as he looked at the hostesses, daring them to stop him.

"I'm a senior partner in the Family. You Bob? You're my guest. And all of this *is bullshit.*"

I watched as the King exhaled a long thick plume of smoke into the air. I could smell the thick, sweet pungent odor of the cannabis, and there was something alluring about the smell, something different from any of the common weed I had smoked over the years. I reached for the joint, wishing I had taken the green hit when it had been offered.

"Fuck this," the King said and handed the joint to me. "We're going inside."

Ryan #1 reached out for my shoulder—

The King was a blur. He hit Ryan #1 with a flurry of blows to the torso and then shoved him back ten feet through the air to crash into a corner. It had happened before I had even finished turning around to try to evade being grabbed. One second, Ryan #1 had been there reaching for me and the next instant he was picking himself up from across the room, the King standing in front of me. I hadn't even managed to get the joint up to my lips yet.

Ryan #2 stepped up to the fight, really not wanting to get killed tonight because of his stupid partner.

"*STOP!*" Jina yelled, and the King glanced at her, still ready to fight.

"You have an answer for me?"

Jina nodded and spoke quickly and directly to me, the phone still to her ear as someone dictated to her.

"You're allowed in the upstairs VIP area only by invitation of the King and only in the presence of the King. Failure to stay within the immediate company of the King will result in your immediate ejection for the remainder of the night. As a courtesy to the King, you will also be allowed into the general area downstairs by yourself at any time. While there you will also be granted access to the downstairs VIP areas, where you will be treated as one of the Family. Any attempt to enter into the upstairs area for any reason other than being invited and accompanied by the King will once again result in your immediate expulsion from the premises for the remainder of that night. Your behavior in the general area will be closely monitored, and it will be up to the discretion of HTDK staff to take any immediate action should you break any of the rules. Harry encourages you just to nod your head, smile and I quote: *take it up the ass like the bitch you are.* End quote. Do you understand the terms as I have laid them out for you?"

My mouth must have been agape at the sheer flood of verbiage that had just been hurled at me. The King leaned in to whisper.

"I'll have a chat with Harry later. Just nod and agree. "

I found myself nodding yes.

"I'll need verbal confirmation," Jina said, and held up the phone, so my words would be clearly audible.

"Just so we're clear, still free drinks right?"

Jina smiled tightly, obviously trapped. This was obviously a new situation for her.

"None of the Family are expected to pay, so the answer to that is, yes. Just use your discretion."

I glanced at the King and then nodded in agreement. "I can be discreet. That's a yes from me."

Jina smiled with relief and gestured towards the entrance. "Please enjoy your stay with us."

The King didn't move, even as the three girls made their way inside. He stood there coolly staring at Ryan #1 who was beginning to look extremely nervous.

Ryan #1 broke first. "I would like to apologize—"

The King didn't let him finish. "Bob I want you to come over here and slap this man."

"What?" I said, unable to believe my ears.

"What?" Ryan #1 repeated, and he definitely was unable to believe his ears.

"They threw you off the roof. Into my car. I *liked* that car. I think it's only fair." The King looked Ryan #1 directly in the eye in a very deliberate and telling manner. "Don't you agree that's fair?"

Ryan #1 squared his shoulders and grit his teeth as he accepted his fate and presented his cheek for me to slap with a look in his eye that promised a certain amount of pain later when the King wasn't around.

"Are you fucking kidding me?" I protested. "These guys hold a grudge! If I slap him, I'm signing my own death warrant!"

"This is probably going to be your only chance to get a proper shot you know. Look, he's even standing still."

I didn't slap him. I wasn't that suicidal.

As we made our way up the stairs, my mind racing on just how awesomely cool the King was and how he could teach me so many things and it would be awesome because we could party together, it was almost as if he could read my mind. He had already shaken his head to my unasked question.

"As a matter of fact, I wasn't going to ask you to be my mentor," I lied as huffily as I could. "I was about to say thanks and tell you how awesome that was. Then I was going to ask you how old you were. But now I'm not going to do any of those things."

"You're a bad fucking liar, " the King said.

"I know," I shrugged, "but I'm working on it. Takes time."

"Look, the best I can do is give you a few tips, and you need a few."

"I need the owner's manual is what I need," I grumbled.

"I'll have some pamphlets sent to your place, but that's only cuz I kinda like you. None of this mentoring bullshit, okay?"

I gave him the thumbs up and made a mental note to actually read whatever the King sent for me.

"Dude, let me just give you a tip on the blood. You don't need as much as you've been drinking. A single mouthful is more than enough to get you good and properly stoned. Any more than that is just overkill, and you're going to go from enjoying yourself to being a pain in the ass and believe me, that's no fun for anybody. The girls will like you a hell of a lot better, you'll be a lot more chill, and you won't end up a big fucking mess passed out between the urinals in the men's room."

"Wait, did that actually happen to me? The urinal thing?"

"Not yet, but you were pretty damn close. Just take it easy, okay man?"

I nodded, still picturing myself on the floor between the urinals and then smiled as genuinely as I could. I couldn't get that picture out of my head for the rest of the night. When some new girl cozied up to me, thinking that I was someone special because I was hanging out with the King, and I eventually took advantage of my privilege and drank deeply from her, my drinking was cautious, not as eager as before.

***

Blood…

You know that feeling you get when you can't think of anything else except that one thing you want? For some people, it's waiting the whole day to get home to the X-Box or the PS4 and get back to the game they've been waiting all day to play. For others, it's waiting until they can crack open that bottle of vodka, or light up that cigarette or joint or whatever it is they're aching for. The whole day is spent waiting to get to that one moment. And for the entire day, it's like everything is in black and white. It's less real, less vivid, so much *less there* and the only thing real, the only thing getting you through it, is knowing that the release is coming soon.

I drifted through my commute to work, seeing but not

seeing the people on the bus and not caring so much about anything. I carried the memory of the sharp taste, and the dull musky heat of the blood that had filled my mouth, but more than anything, it was that euphoria as all of my senses had woken up, synapses rapidly firing, my brain going into overdrive with so many possibilities, so much life…

That right there, that was the only thing that mattered and every waking moment I had to wait for it was a quiet torture of just getting through the day.

"Are you staring at my boobs?"

I blinked myself out of my stupor and realized that I had been staring at the neck of the woman on the bus across from me, enough to freak her out. She had one of those long slender necks that made you wonder what kissing them must be like, the kind of neck you could call graceful, elegant, lovely even. I smiled in what I thought was a reassuring manner and shook my head.

"No, not at all," I said. "I was admiring your neck."

"That's not any better," she snapped. "Stop staring at me you freak!"

She, however, stared at me for the rest of the ride, and I valiantly read the posters on the ceiling and looked out the windows instead, and really tried to avoid looking at her neck. Or her boobs.

Over the course of the day, I must have pulled out my phone a dozen times to send a text message to the King, but I'd always put it back, not knowing what I was going to say without sounding too needy, too much like a goddamn junkie.

The King was one of the only friends I'd actually made at the club. I'd been so focused on getting high that I'd either ignored or pissed off anybody else who had made any overtures of friendship, and worse yet, I couldn't even remember who I had pissed off. You don't make friends and then only ask that person for favors. That's just tacky. Besides, he had made it clear that he wasn't going above and beyond to do me any favors and I really didn't want to burn that bridge. He was a wealthy and famous man in his own right, and he already had plenty of hangers-on.

A couple of times during the night I caught myself staring at some customers, actively wondering what their blood tasted like. Smell and taste are very closely connected, so it was only inevitable. Vegans definitely smelled a lot different from regular people, but then again, everybody smelled different depending on what their diet consisted of.

My deep philosophical thoughts on these differences had gone beyond the mere admiration of necks that I had recently taken on as a hobby and had now progressed to noticing in great detail how the blood pulsed through their arteries, the slight *whoosh-whoosh* of the blood perfectly in rhythm with the steady *ba-bum ba-bum* of their beating hearts. The *ba-bum ba-bum* would at times speed up when they noticed me watching them, the beat so loud in my head that I would briefly wonder why nobody else was hearing this, before remembering that this part was something unique to being a vampire.

The older blonde lady with the long willowy and beautiful neck *(what was up with the long necks anyway?)* had been flushed and embarrassed about buying what had to be her first sex toy, and she had turned bright upon turning and meeting my gaze. I had tried to smile, but from her reaction, smiling wasn't working so great for me. She had quickly escaped but had glanced behind a couple of times, one time biting her lip as if trying to muster the courage to do something against her character. The next woman had been short with dark, unkempt hair who just seemed to have a bigger presence than most of the other customers—

"It's the bloodlust you know," a woman's voice said right in my ear, causing me to almost jump out of my pants. I jumped and spun around, my hands grabbing uselessly for the baseball bat Sammy kept under the counter.

Beatrice leaned casually against the wall, a box of Chinese takeout in one hand, chopsticks in the other. This immediately struck me as bizarre, because I've never actually seen anyone outside of a movie ever actually eating out of those containers. Most Chinese takeout I'd ever had usually came in those flimsy styrofoam containers with forks that were always too small and too flexible to allow you to eat your food with any real enjoyment; I'd always had to swap them out for real forks since chopsticks always made my hands cramp.

Why was I seemingly distracted by what Beatrice was eating, you ask? Well, first of all, it reminded me that I hadn't had lunch yet and that I also hadn't eaten any Chinese food in ages… at least not that I could remember. I'd scarfed down some frosted flakes earlier and had spent the day grazing on the Costco-sized box of granola bars that Claude had tucked away in the top cupboard with the stupid sports cups I never got around to using but still collected for some stupid reason. He had either thought I would never find them there or had figured I would eventually find them when I got desperate enough. Either way, I found them and proceeded to pig out, but just a little. Apart from that, there hadn't been any actual real food since I was out of eggs and the bread had gone all moldy on me.

Beatrice was almost unrecognizable as either of the versions of herself that I'd had the pleasure of not being able to avoid meeting. The last time I had seen her, she had been wearing that form fitting white suit that had suited her so well, and she had looked the part of the predatory vampire. The woman eating noodles out of the box in the middle of my store wore gray baggy sweatpants, sneakers and an unbuttoned red plaid shirt that had been thrown on over the top of an old Motley Crue "Dr. Feelgood" t-shirt. Her long blonde hair was buried under a black Beanie, but as always, it was a stark contrast against her dark clothes.

She grinned at me and continued. "Before long, you're going to start wondering how everybody tastes." She slurped up some noodles, keeping her eyes on me, then continued through a mouthful of food, "and then soon after that, you're going to be *finding out.* It's how bad legends and even worse movies get made you know. Some idiot just decides he can't help himself."

"How did you get in here? I didn't see you come in."

"You think I did the Batman thing and just appeared out of nowhere? I only wish I could do that. That shit is hard, all that sneaking around just to be dramatic."

"But you just—"

"I could have brought a marching band with me, twelve trombones and a full drum section, maybe even a hundred elephants, and you still wouldn't have seen me. You're like, totally out of it man."

"You're confusing the hell out of me."

"You want to take a bite out of that lady!" Beatrice yelled and pointed at the short woman with the unkempt hair, who whirled around, fumbling her collection of DVDs of BDSM porn.

"Hi!" she yelled, clearly startled, then her brain caught up with what was going on: "He wants *to do what* to me?"

"Nothing!" I glared at Beatrice. "It's just a little vampire humor."

"Well, she's not very funny. And in my professional opinion, neither of you would make very good vampires."

Beatrice and I exchanged a look that spoke volumes of definite What-The-Fuck, then we both looked incredulously at the small woman who looked more like a frumpy middle-aged housewife who might have a BDSM fetish than any type of vampire we'd actually met. Her mud-brown eyes glared right back at us imperiously.

"You don't even sparkle!"

Beatrice turned sharply to look at me. "Bob, what the fuck is she talking about?"

"You really don't want to know. Hell: I know, and I wish I didn't know what it is that I know. Run now and save yourself."

"Can't I just kill her instead?"

"It won't do any good," I groaned. "There's more of them." Beatrice looked completely lost, and I suddenly realized she really had no idea what I was talking about. "Have you seriously never heard of Twi-Hards?"

The lady was aghast, then her brain caught up with her. *"Are you threatening to kill me?"* She sputtered at Beatrice, and her eyes were darting around the store, desperately looking for a witness, someone to back her up in the empty store. Of course, there was no one since it was 2:03 AM and only the weirdos and drunks were out at this time.

"No. *She's* threatening to kill you. I'm just providing service with a smirk."

"Stay back!" The frumpy lady grabbed the first thing at hand, which of course happened to be the *Belladonna Bitch Fist*. It was good and sturdy and better than her threatening us with a dildo, but still…

Beatrice had had enough.

"The level of stupid in this store is giving me a headache," Beatrice deadpanned. "Since you're not going to let me kill anybody, I'm getting the fuck out of here." She glanced at the frumpy lady and laid on a thick layer of sarcasm that only an idiot could miss. "She might call the police. Oooh! Eeek! Run away… run away…"

Beatrice winked at me as she sashayed towards the door, making it very clear that she was not, in fact, running away from anything at all. The frumpy lady glared at her the whole way. The Belladonna Bitch Fist was still held up like some magic totem to ward off the weird blonde chick and smirksome store clerk.

While I rung up the lady (she decided to take the Belladonna Bitch Fist after all), it occurred to me that I wasn't even thinking about blood anymore.

***

Beatrice was waiting for me when I escaped the store an hour later. She stood on the street corner staring at the sky as light flakes of snow drifted down. It wasn't proper snow, just the light dusting that melts as soon as it hits your face, the type that seems to play with the laws of gravity just so it can look pretty hanging out in the glare of the streetlight. It was the type of snow that happens in early Spring in Toronto; Winter always gave us a reminder that it was still hanging around and could fuck with us any moment.

"I didn't know you were waiting for me," I said, trying to think of something clever to say and failing abysmally.

Beatrice turned to look at me, and there was something lost and completely vulnerable about her. It was almost as if she didn't know where she was for a moment, the way she just stared right through me as if I didn't exist in whatever reality she was occupying.

She looked away from me, back up at the falling snow in the light, and once again I wondered just how long she had been out there. Snow had gathered in her hair and on her shoulders. I only noticed this detail in passing, not like I was doing some Sherlock Holmes shit, just more like one of the tiny details people see about other people without actually thinking about it. In any case, it did get me thinking that she'd been out here for a while.

I tried to see what she was looking at, but all I saw was the snow dancing in the streetlight and the dark building across the street.

"What are you looking at?"

Beatrice snapped back to me, and this time she recognized me. A smile split her face, and there was that slight mania back in her eyes.

"Are you hungry?" she asked. "I bet you're hungry. Let me buy you some food."

***

Beatrice took me to the club. Of course, she did. You don't get someone on the hook for a wonderful new drug and then fuck with the supply. No, what you do is let them know that they have to depend on you and that you can cut off their supply at any time. That was exactly what Harry was doing to me via Beatrice, and I knew it and hated him for it. As I stood in the middle of the downstairs part of the club, watching as Beatrice rode the glass elevator up to the second floor, I knew that I was totally fucked.

I got Otis the bartender to put in a food order for me, the biggest fucking steak they had on hand.

"Hungry sir?" Otis asked as he poured me a gigantic glass of something expensive.

"Like a vengeful motherfucker," I agreed. "Don't worry, I'm taking most of it home anyway."

"I'll make sure the kitchen packs some of my 'special sauce' to go with it, sir. By special sauce, I mean a bottle of something expensive."

"This is still on the house, right?"

"I'd warn you if it wasn't."

"You're a good man Otis."

"Well, you are a good tipper, so there's that," Otis grinned, then something caught his attention. "Redhead at one o'clock and closing fast."

"Regular or newbie?"

"Regular for sure."

I nodded and downed the glass of expensive scotch. I glanced up at the balcony and wondered for a moment if Beatrice was watching from upstairs, then decided that I didn't give a shit. I was getting exactly what I wanted, right? That was all that mattered. Right?

I didn't even ask her name. I took her into a VIP booth, and as I swallowed a mouthful of her hot, hot blood and felt that euphoria spread through my body, I had time to wonder exactly how long I could keep on doing this.

***

Two weeks.

Okay, so it didn't last long, but what did you really expect? I could always lie and say that I held out and kept my shit together for at least two, maybe three months, but I really can't be bothered to lie right now. Hell if I start lying about that, I might as well just lie about everything else and then me telling this whole story would be completely pointless.

So yeah: two weeks.

The easy access to expensive food, the occasional smuggled bottle of booze (thanks to Otis) and the ready supply of blood from a rotation of beautiful and nameless chicks, kept me on a short leash. It also kept me very well fed to the point where I didn't even have to think about going to the supermarket for supplies. I couldn't even remember when I'd had to spend money even once in the last couple of weeks, and as a result, Otis got a bigger tip than I could usually afford. Just because it was "free" didn't mean I had to be an ass and you're never an ass to your bartender. I had my monthly MetroPass, so I never had to hunt for random change when I wanted to take the bus or the train; a $20 Tim Horton's card, that one of our regulars kept leaving for Sammy every week, to handle my coffee addiction; and dinner, booze, and blood were taken care of courtesy of HTDK. I had it made in the shade, living the good life, and for once, I was actually staying out of trouble.

The King started showing up at the store, actively wooing Sammy, but apparently she was playing hard to get and he was acting more like a lovesick 12 year old than a 300 year old vampire or however old he was. Sometimes we'd shoot the shit for a while, but I had the feeling that I was damaged goods, so I didn't really push the issue of hanging out with him as much as I wanted to.

"You could always ask her to go to the club with you?" I suggested to him one night. Sammy was in the back, changing out of a dress that was way too small and too sparkly for our customers to handle, so I kept the conversation low-key.

The King shook his head.

"I kinda wanna keep her away from there."

"Too many vampires for your liking?"

"You know it," he said. "How you holding up man?"

I grinned and deliberately didn't ask him for a ride to the club. Sammy wouldn't have cared if I had split early, but that really wasn't the point. I was actually beginning to enjoy my little routine. The Ugly Twins had mostly been giving me the stink eye something terrible, but they'd left me alone as long as I stayed downstairs and didn't make a fuss. Hanging out with the King would have brought its own brand of trouble, and I was afraid of jinxing it.

"I'm actually doing okay. Waiting for my buddy Claude to get back from a work trip for things to feel kinda normal again, you know? It's still a bit of a trippy experience."

"That's what I keep hearing. One of the reasons Harry likes to string 'em along for ten years."

"That's one hell of an internship program. Designed to keep idiots like me out."

"Something like that," the King smiled. "It's not always successful though. Some psychos are good at playing normal. You need to watch your back."

It was a subtle warning, and unfortunately went right over my head. The King must have thought that I had figured out what he was talking about, since he moved on. I just shook it off and eventually forgot he had even said anything.

***

Of course, I stopped by the club on the way home, but it was getting to be routine by that point. The weather was still unpredictable as the weather tends to be in Toronto and the days were already getting longer, so some mornings I cut it really close getting home, but I was getting the hang of it and knew that I still had at least until 8 AM for the sun to be any proper threat. In summer that was going to be a different story, but for the time being, it was just becoming part of my routine as a vampire.

I'd wake up to my darkened apartment around 1 PM, either from my stomach demanding that I put some proper food into it or from my bladder threatening to spring a leak and flood the bed. I caught myself having one of those dreams one morning. You know the dream I'm talking about. The one where you dream you're peeing and then have to jump up and run to the bathroom because you suddenly felt the rush of hot liquid on your leg or stomach. In my case, I was dreaming that I was peeing into an abandoned swimming pool and it was such a good feeling of relief, the kind of epic pee you could only have in a dream. It was also the kind of pee that required me to have to take an immediate shower. I, of course, had to strip the bed and desperately hope that I hadn't gotten any urine on the pillow and that it hadn't soaked through the mattress cover that Jaime had insisted so long ago that I just *had* to buy.

I vowed to myself that nobody would ever learn of my shame, even though I was fairly sure other people have had near misses. I'd have to ask Sammy about it sometime and see how badly she made fun of me.

It was while I was slipping my shoes on in the kitchen, my soiled sheets in the hamper in front of me, laundry card in my hand, that I realized there was no way I was going to be able to do laundry during the day. The laundry room was across the courtyard, and that was way too much sunlight for me to even begin thinking about.

Fuck.

This is the point all pretense of normal drains away, the point where the panic that has been lurking in the shadows of your mind and fear throws off its horrible disguise of bravado, idiocy or lunacy and wraps its arms lovingly around you in an embrace that only death will break.

Since we've established that I'm going to be honest, I'm just going to keep going with that theme: *I pretty much lost it.*

I don't know where the tears came from, or even the desperate sobs that forced their way out of my chest and surprised even me. I'm an ugly crier, so it's not something I do very often. I mean when I really let go of myself and actually allow myself to cry, it's really fucking *ugly*. There's lots of snot involved, and my crying face is nothing you want to take home to your mother. Some people will say *"Hey it's okay for men to cry,"* but those same people will take one look at me crying and instantly change their minds. It's not pretty is what I'm really trying to drive home here.

It got pretty embarrassing, so I'm just going to skip that part and get to the point.

I have no idea why the stupid fucking laundry got to me like that. I was having the best week of my life in a very long time, things were seemingly going well and I was actually adapting to my new life as a vampire, right? Believe me, I was as surprised as you are right now, but there it was, that raw swell of emotion that completely engulfed me and yanked the tears out from my chest, making me feel every goddamn thing to the core of my being. I felt the loss of my humanity and the overwhelming panic of being completely out of my depth and not knowing how I was going to survive this. And somewhere in there, that deep guilt and anguish that surrounded the question: *"how was I going to tell my mom that I'm a vampire?"*

Riiiiing! Riiiiing!

I almost pissed my pants at the sound of the phone ringing, especially after invoking my mom, and I had a panicked thought that it was actually her calling again and that I would have to answer this time and lie to her. I mean it had to be my mom calling, right? Nobody calls me anymore. It's all text messages these days. The only calls I ever got were usually from my mom or from the phone company threatening to cut off my phone, but even they have switched to text messages. So I wasn't expecting anything good when I fumbled the phone out and saw all it said was *UNKNOWN NUMBER*.

Beep.

"You've reached the line of someone who doesn't give a fuck. What the fuck do you want?"

"*Bob?*"

The level of concern in Claude's voice shocked the shit out of me. Wait, that's a lie. Just hearing Claude's voice shocked the shit out of me. I sat up immediately.

"Dude! Are you back?"

"Are you okay?"

"Definitely not. I'm actively losing my shit."

"Did the Russians get to you yet?"

Russians?

"What Russians? I'm having an existential crisis and losing my shit on my own. No Russians are involved."

"Well, an existential crisis is better than Russians. Kills you slower anyway. Is your crisis because you're a vampire?"

"Something like that, yes."

"Can we skip all of the self-doubt and get to the part where you agree that you're still alive, would like to remain alive, are not mythical and that you're looking outside to make sure nobody Russian-looking is watching your place?"

"Can we spend a little more time on my self-doubt before we get to the homicidal Russians. I don't think I'm emotionally equipped to be murdered today."

"Are you ugly crying? I can hear the snot from here.*"*

"Maybe definitely yes. At least until you called and interrupted. I was really getting into it too. Had a good rhythm going and everything. Epic snot."

"Then you're definitely over it. Wipe your epic snot and look out the window."

"No. Don't want to."

"Why not?"

"Because, according to you, there might be *big mean Russians outside of it!*"

I was already at the window and slipping my sunglasses

on as I climbed onto the back of the couch so I could see through the window. Oh, the joys of a basement apartment. The window was covered with a couple of heavy-duty black foam-core board panels, and they overlapped in the center, only held together with a strip of black duct tape. It was a simple matter of peeling the tape and then carefully and slowly sliding one panel to the side so I could peer outside. Of course, it was only while I was doing this that I remembered I had promised not to be a complete bum and invest in some heavy curtains, especially before summer came.

There was an unsurprising lack of Russians outside my window, scary or otherwise. I relayed this information to Claude.

"You sure?"

"Not really, but I'd prefer not to scorch my retinas any more than I have to if it's all the same to you. It's the middle of the day man."

"Okay. Fine."

I pulled the panel back and looked away from the blazing light of outside, aware that black spots were racing across my vision like vengeful sprites. I slumped onto the couch and tried to avoid looking at the overturned laundry hamper on the floor that was taunting me with its very existence.

"You gonna tell me what's going on?" I asked Claude.

"Can I tell you that when I get back?"

"Well, are you likely to get killed? Because if you are, you should tell me now and I can be oh so sad at your funeral instead of being pissed off."

"I'm in Belize."

Oh. *Damn.*

"What the fuck are you doing in Belize?"

"*Crime.* Don't ask details. But somehow the Russians are now involved…" Claude paused, and I instantly dreaded whatever he was going to say next.

"Don't say it…" I said.

"I think at least one of them is a vampire."

"Seriously?" A thought occurred to me, tinged with a lot of conspiracy. "Do you think it's a coincidence that it's a vampire? Maybe you just know what to look for now, so you're more likely to see vampires?"

"There are no coincidences in this business. You really should keep your eyes open for any Russians. I have a feeling that your new friends make a habit of playing dirty and that somehow they know about me. I'd like to get out of this with my head attached, so please don't piss off anybody."

"Yeah, about that…"

Silence from Claude, then: "I'll be back in a week. Please don't piss off anybody *else*. You can do that, right?"

Of course, I promised to stay out of trouble. I even meant it when I swore that I would keep my head down. I spent a few hours moping around the apartment, which turned into me reading stupid status updates from my friends on Facebook, with their photoshopped selfies of their perfectly happy and ordinary lives, far removed from vampires, Russian assassins and best friends who were in Belize and not there when you needed them. I got particularly spiteful and just unfriended anybody who had posted pictures of their babies, or any baby for that matter. Then I just gave up in disgust, letting that edgy anxiety, *that hunger* creep up on me again until I could take it no longer.

Of course, I still had to wait for the sun to go down, but that's one of the good things about maybe-but-not-quite-spring: I didn't have to wait too long.

As soon as there was no direct sunlight, the sun finally being too low to mess with me, I did the laundry.

No amount of restlessness was going to make up for not having clean sheets to sleep on, especially when the air still had that chill to it that the more adventurous referred to as "brisk". Screw that: I needed to wrap up in my damn blankets, brisk or not.

***

I showed up early at HTDK and in hindsight, I should have known something was wrong. I was early, and they were still getting started for the night. The velvet rope wasn't up yet for the non-members, and the hostesses were idly chatting and laughing. Jina gave me a look but then just shook her head and waved me through. For a second I was tempted to try for upstairs, but it really didn't seem worth it. Besides, Otis was downstairs, and he told some killer jokes as well as being a top notch wing-man.

The club was just settling into the evening routine, the lighting tech and the D.J. still messing around in their respective booths. The waitstaff were all gathered around a booth over in the VIP area, no doubt having the nightly staff meeting before things got going properly. I glanced upstairs, but no other vampires seemed to be there yet. There was a shadow of a single person looking down through the glass, but I couldn't get a good look and truthfully, I didn't care who it was.

There is something to be said about a club or a restaurant that is empty. It feels so wrong when all of the house lights are up, and the music is at a low volume instead of the dull roar that will come later. Instead what you notice is how sound echoes and travels through the space. You can hear every scrape of a chair, every clink, and clank of cutlery and bottles being moved, every sizzle and thud from the kitchen. These were the sounds that were always there of course, but once people start to fill the room, they turn it into something different, something more energetic and alive, something that has its own rhythm and ebb and flow.

I walked toward the main bar, and it was almost as if I could taste the air. There was something already cooking in the kitchen, perhaps an early dinner order for the shift manager or for someone upstairs who I was utterly failing to see. I glanced up again and I wondered for a moment if it was Harry himself looking down at me, *judging me.*

Did I get a sense of foreboding? Hell no. This story might have turned out a hell of a lot less interesting if that had happened.

I settled in at the bar and watched as the staff meeting broke up and Otis appeared, walking towards the bar. I grinned, deciding to ask him if he had seen any Russians hanging around, but I never got the chance. When I saw his face, the words shriveled and died in my mouth.

Otis' left eye was swollen shut, a huge purple and black bruise across half of his face. There were cuts across his eyebrow, and the bridge of his nose and his lip had been split in two places, now held together by stitches. His usually well-tailored white shirt seemed a little too big for him, as if he was wearing someone else's shirt; his knuckles had been wrapped in a number of bandaids, one of them seeping blood right through the brown fabric. The worst part of it was the flat look he gave me that said quite clearly that no he hadn't walked into a door, or fallen down the stairs, no matter what he said. Oh and by the way: *I was the one somehow responsible for his "not-falling-down-the stairs."*

"You should run," he whispered and there was real fear in his eyes. Wait, I'm sorry, that was the wrong word. Did I say fear? No, what I meant was terror.

Oh, fuck no...

"Who did that to you?" It was the only thing I could think to ask, the only way to fight back the sickening nausea of impending doom that was creeping up on me.

"We did that to him," a voice whispered in my ear, and I closed my eyes. The Ugly Twins had finally caught up with me. Something had gone horribly wrong and now they were here to kick my ass. For a moment I wondered if Claude's Russians had anything to do with it, but that was just a fleeting thought.

I tried to buy some time.

"Any chance I can get a running start?"

"Are you kidd—*hey! Get back here!*"

I was faster than I had expected and a lot more difficult to catch than they had expected. As far as I was concerned, I was running for my life and I was good at running, so believe me, I was *slippery as fuck.* I had some vague idea that all I had to do was make it out of the club onto the streets and that I would be safe there, like it was some fucked up game of tag or something. I just knew that getting caught in the club was going to end very badly for me.

I almost made it you know.

Almost.

When I slammed through the huge door to the foyer, it was like the entire world went into slow motion as terror, utter pants-shitting terror, grabbed hold of me and made me its bitch.

The Gentlemen were walking towards me like a long forgotten nightmare.

***

When they come for you, it is always a nightmare.

It's the kind of nightmare that lurks in the corners of your mind, so that even when you're awake, it's always there with you, teasing and swearing at you, reminding you that you're weak and that you're going to die.

Mr. Flynn leads the way, his long black coat flaring out behind him with the appropriate sense of drama, his eyes deep and intently focused. Is he surprised to see me or is that sheer delight in the pain that he is about to bring on me?

Mr. Bryce and Mr. Sinnel are directly behind him of course, flanking Mr. Flynn to the left and to the right, like the world's most terrifying and middle-aged boy-band. The Hackstreet Boys. Boys to Murderers. Fuck Your Life. That sort of thing.

These are the panicked thoughts that fly through my skull in the space of a millisecond, the ramblings of a mind about to be stricken by terror and the blind panic that comes with it.

My body reacts first, its self-preservation mode taking over completely and forcing me to a complete skidding stop, my feet flying up from under me, my body crashing to the ground and my feet desperately trying to run the other way, trying and failing to tell gravity to go fuck itself.

I'm somehow moving backwards and it is like swimming in invisible maple syrup, I seem to be moving so slow. And all the while I'm unable to look away from the Gentlemen and their implacable, unstoppable advance. I know for certain that there is no escape and that I'm about to die and there is nothing I can do about it--

"Oh stop that," Mr. Flynn says. "We're not here for you."

***

Reality returned with a thud, which was instantly followed by me slamming into the floor at full speed, slow motion be damned. That took the wind out of me, along with any momentary relief I was cautiously considering beginning to feel. I did have a moment to feel betrayed by any sense of drama and by my own fears, before a pair of meaty hands clamped onto my ankles and the Ryans started to drag me across the floor away from the door and my failed escape.

"You're getting off lucky, Bob!" Ryan #1 hissed.

"Don't care!" I yelled. "Let me go!"

I fought back, kicking and screaming and caught Mr. Bryce's eye as the Gentlemen made their way to the elevator on some terrible errand which didn't involve me. This time. Mr. Bryce mouthed something at me, which might have possibly been "See you later" or even "Beat you later" but it all depended on interpretation.

The Ryans dragged me by one leg all the way through the club. Fighting them was next to impossible since they both had the same density in body and brain as that of an 800-year-old tree. And was I glad it was them and not the Gentlemen? Maybe just a little, but not much. My attempts to dig my fingernails into the concrete floor, or to grab hold of any furniture in reach, were all in vain.

The rest of the staff just stood aside and pretended not to notice as I was dragged past them. The only person who looked at me was Otis and he sure as hell wasn't going to help me. I wish I could have told him that I didn't blame him, I mean the poor guy had just taken a beating for hanging out with me and that was seriously fucked up.

"What the fuck did I do?" I managed to yell as Ryan #1 literally threw me across the alley. It was an upside-down flight, and I had a brief moment to notice the black garbage bags piled up next to the dumpster and to hope that they weren't filled with bricks or a random set of knives or otherwise sharp objects. Otherwise, this flight was going to be a more painful that I had thought it was going to be. My question was almost cut off when I hit the wall at speed and of course, still upside down. My ears rang as I slumped to the ground, gravity welcoming me with open arms, always ready to be a friend. I somehow managed to miss the pile of bags, so that was a plus I guess.

Ryan #1 was saying something to me. "You're not welcome here anymore."

"Fuck you!" I said as defiantly as I could. I tried to scramble around so I could at least protect myself from the inevitable beating that was coming, but my head decided it didn't like that at all and I sunk down on one knee instead, like I was making the worst marriage proposal ever.

"I followed the rules!" I stammered. "I did everything I was supposed to! I kept my goddamn head *down!*"

Ryan #1 grinned cruelly. "What can we say? The rules changed."

Ryan #2 leaned in. "You pissed off one of the Family, *and* you fucked with the Bleeders," he tsk-tsked at me.

For a second there I was drawing a blank. *Who the hell had I pissed off?* I hadn't even seen any of the family in the downstairs area at all, so what the fuck was going on? Then the other part of the statement hit me. The Bleeders? *Seriously?* All of this was because I pissed off one of the hangers-on at the bar that allowed us to drink their blood?

"You didn't even get their names man," Ryan #1 said with disgust.

"These girls--"

"And guys."

"--give their blood freely to us. In return, all they ask is to be treated special. They get access to our kind, and we all treat them well. And you don't even know their names."

"You bled one of them dry, you know."

"Monica," Ryan #1 said and made the sign of the cross.

"Left her for dead."

Panic seized me then as I processed this bit of information, searching desperately for some fragment of memory that would tell me that the Ugly Twins were seriously fucking with me. The problem with blackouts is that they're often *complete blackouts* and there was no way I knew what the truth was anymore. Anything I might or might not have done was hidden from me, and they knew it.

"That's a *goddamn lie,*" I meant to yell, but it came out as a hoarse whisper. I had the panicked thought that if it were true, then it would have been Mr. Flynn and the Gentlemen spending quality time with me instead of these two assholes, but that was immediately followed by a very cynical thought:

Suppose they only care if it's other vampires you're supposed to have killed?

"We should take his fangs," Ryan #2 said way too conversationally, and he actually started rummaging through his coat pockets. You want to know who the hell just happens to carry around pliers with him in case a random act of torture came along? Yeah, you got it right: *that guy.*

"You kidding?" Ryan #1 gave him a look, ignoring how my hand instantly went up to cover my mouth. "Nobody's done that since Roderick, and you know how that turned out."

"Listen to him!" I pleaded from behind my hands. "I don't want to be like Roderick!" I watched with rising panic as Ryan #2 continued his search. I searched desperately for an escape route but the two men were a wall and were definitely much faster than I was.

Ryan #2 grinned evilly as he pulled out a shiny metal pliers. "You should get this on camera, man. I bet he screams like a little girl."

"No cameras! Or pliers!" I protested. "Look, they're not even worth it. They're tiny, barely pointed. It's genetic I think. My dad has the same tiny incisors."

The Ryans looked more amused than they really should have. Ryan #1 shook his head mournfully and pulled out his iPhone to record the assault. Of course he held it vertical. Fucking savage.

"Look, I'll apologize to the girls! I'll apologize to *everyone*. Make a list and I'll go on a goddamn apology tour. I'll even apologize to your made up dead girl if you want!" I pleaded, but I knew it was too late. Still I had to try. "I'll even get to know their names! Most of them at least. I promise!"

The Ryans weren't moved in the slightest. If you've ever met a bouncer for a strip club, you have a pretty good idea of how protective they are of the girls. Some of them get tipped a little extra, but most of the times they've actually become good friends... the kind of good friends who were ready to rip the head off of that one stupid customer who always has to take things too far.

Damn, I hate being the stupid customer.

The heavy metal door creaked open behind the Ryans and

I looked over, hopeful that it was the calvary coming to save my stupid ass. It was just an empty doorway for a second and then a hand snaked out and a finger beckoned to whoever was looking. It was a well-manicured finger and the arm to which it belonged was wearing what appeared to be a white suit, so it *had* to be a vampire. It was a male vampire, just in case the manicure threw you off. Rich, metrosexual and vampire seem to go together almost as much as you'd assume. It was most likely the vampire I had pissed off, who was definitely not Harry.

"Um, I think somebody wants to talk to you," I said helpfully.

Ryan #2 turned to look, almost convinced I was trying to pull a fast one, but then he saw the hand beckoning. He nudged his partner in crime.

"Don't start without me," he said and slipped away to the door.

I made a run for it, but Ryan #1 was ready for me. He lazily backhanded me and I flew backward to make a re-acquaintance with the wall and then the ground. I was welcomed like an old friend. My ears rang as I somehow stumbled to my feet, my body apparently way too stupid to stay down.

"Who was that?" I mumbled as Ryan #2 returned and whispered something to his partner. I saw that the door was solidly closed now, the white suited vampire gone. From the shared expression on the faces of the Ryans, they had not liked or agreed with their orders.

They beat the hell out of me.

I didn't even see the first blow coming. Something that felt like a Mack truck slammed into the side of my head and I crumpled, wondering where the fuck that had come from. I was distantly aware that I was being pummeled, blow after blow slamming into my poor body. I had the thought that maybe I should pull myself in a ball and just wait for it to be over, but control of my body was only a distant concept at that moment.

After a while it was over and I could move again. My body screamed at me that moving was not a good idea, but I told my body to go fuck itself and moved anyway, glad that the Ryans had at least focused the beating on my body. By all reckoning, my face should have been a disfigured lump of broken bone and swollen flesh, but for some reason the beating had only been to my body. Surprisingly, none of my arms or legs seemed to be broken.

The Ryans leaned against a wall, looking very disappointed. They shared a sole cigarette between the two of them.

I spit out blood and slumped over onto my back. I somehow found the energy to raise my hand and gave them the one finger salute. It hurt like hell, but I did it anyway, just to be a defiant asshole.

"Thanks for not killing me, you fuckwits."

My arm collapsed onto my chest, the muscles feeling more like jello than actual flesh. Bruised jello.

The Ryans weren't bothered by me.

"Do you know the staff is running a dead pool on your sorry ass? Nobody thinks you're going to survive on your own."

Well, that sucked. I was on nodding terms with a couple of the guys and I thought they'd kind of liked me. Typical junkie thinking right there.

"Upstairs has a deadpool on you too. I've got five grand riding on you lasting four days," Ryan #1 said. "Ryan here's betting ten grand that you last at least a week. Do me a favour and kill yourself in four days, okay?"

Ryan #2 kneeled down in front of me, so we were practically nose to nose. His fangs snapped into place with deadly precision and goddamn they were huge and *by the way, how the hell did he even do that?* He definitely had my attention.

"The only reason you aren't dead right now is because Sebastien asked us not to kill you."

Who the fuck is Sebastien? I wanted to ask, but I kept my mouth shut.

Ryan #2 continued: "If we ever see you in here again, we're going to cut your throat and hang you upside down to bleed out. And then we're going to start cutting off body parts. You understand me? It would take a hell of a lot for Madame Vera to bring you back from that one."

"You killed that girl Bob. Melanie--" Ryan #1 smirked.

"I thought her name was Monica," I corrected without thinking.

"Whatever man: I didn't kill that bitch," Ryan #2 said dismissively. "I don't have to remember her name. You killed her: you remember her name."

When they left, they slammed the heavy iron door behind them, and just like that, I was exiled from the Hall of the Drunken King.

Chapter 16
GOING ROGUE

Everybody thinks they know what rock bottom feels like. We all have an idea in our heads of what absolute rock fucking bottom is supposed to be and we spend most of our lives simultaneously running away and congratulating ourselves that we've avoided this horrible, horrible fate. Said horrible fate usually takes the form of that homeless person you just passed and deliberately didn't make eye contact with and the realization that at some point any empathy you'd had for them was just too inconvenient to deal with anymore. You think that's the rock bottom you want to avoid and even as you pat yourself on the back for going back and putting that five dollar bill into the homeless person's dirty and battered cup, (making sure not to touch the sides of course), you're one hundred percent confident that you will never be like that guy. That is not what rock bottom looks like for you, right?

Apparently, my rock bottom consisted of sitting on a northbound bus and trying not to make eye contact with the slightly creepy woman sitting across from me. I was sure she was checking out my phone to see if it was worth stealing but it was kind of hard to see where she was looking through the black sunglasses she wore at night without the slightest bit of irony. I could have told her that it was just a late model iPhone 4 and was hardly worth the trouble, for either of us.

"No, you can't have the night off." The Boss wasn't happy to hear me at all, especially after what I had asked him. "I don't care if your grandmother died: she'll still be dead tomorrow!"

"You're an asshole."

The Boss had already hung up on me, but I said it anyway just to get it off my chest and wished I had called from a phone booth just so I could have something to slam down. Cellphones have killed all sense of drama. Even if you throw the phone across the room, more likely than not you'd still almost deliberately throw it someplace relatively safe, after all, anger is momentary but a broken screen on a $700 phone is still expensive. Yes, I know it's a mixed metaphor: deal with it. In any case, I was on the bus and it was all hard surfaces, so there was not going to be any phone throwing going on, only impotent rage.

Slightly-more-creepy lady was still clocking me, and she might have gone chasing after the phone anyway. I almost chucked the phone right at her face just on principle.

Rage. Rage was good. It was at least an emotion I could understand, actually *admit to,* and was a lot better than the numbness that had taken over since I had left the club. I guess I could only call it a complete lack of purpose, or even more truthfully, the harsh reality of utter and complete rejection—

My phone buzzed in my hand and for a second I just stared at it, wondering when I had turned it to vibrate. It was Sammy calling this time. I flipped the little switch back on and answered the phone.

"What?"

"Boss called me laughing at you. Tonight's your night off, dumbass," Sammy said. I could hear her crunching on what was most likely to be an apple from the way she was chewing. "Go get drunk or something."

I stared at the phone after Sammy had hung up, really not knowing how to feel now that I didn't have the distraction of trying to avoid going to work looming over me.

"Fuck!"

Even-slightly-more-creepy lady was definitely looking at me now. She leaned closer elbows on her knees and made a "come closer" gesture with her fingers. I glared at her as hard as I could and shook my head. There was no way I was getting any closer to her.

"Have you heard the good news?" She asked me, and grinned the lunatic grin of the marginally insane. "The dark lord is risen!"

"And this is where I get off," I said as the bus lurched to a stop. I grabbed the pole and pulled myself upright and towards the door in one smooth motion, my primary goal to get away from crazy as fast as possible.

I exited the bus, and just started walking. I didn't look back to see if definitely-creepy-lady was standing in the bus yelling after me, or if she had settled back into her craziness. It wasn't in my face, so it wasn't my business and immediately became somebody else's problem. The only thing I was thinking of at that moment was finding the closest bar.

Guess what the bar was called. Go on: I'll give you one guess.

It was with no small sense of irony that I entered the bar that called itself "*the Rock Bottom*". I could go on at great length about how it was a sign, that the Universe was either trying to tell me something or just fucking with me, but I won't. No, that's what they call hindsight and like Dave Mustaine says, *hindsight is always 20/20*. What I probably did was chuckle and roll my eyes, too pissed off to be impressed by the Universe showing off how clever it was.

I scanned the bar quickly, determining that it was as shitty a dive bar as I had hoped for and that it wasn't just a hipster dive bar. So far the signs were good. There were tattoos, but no stupid anchor tattoos to be seen, just a motley collection of bad art and badass ink. Guns N' Roses was blasting from the weathered jukebox in the corner, Axl Rose screaming to the world that *You Could Be Mine* and he was right goddamit, and you bet your ass that Motley Crue or Metallica would be playing next. The people were the convincing part of the equation for me though. The sheer authentic age and wear and tear of the bar itself and the random but thick collection of genuinely aged band flyers that plastered the walls in overlapping layers and for some reason the ceiling, told a story that no hipster could fake.

There was the obligatory old drunk guy at the edge of the bar who used to be tough once upon a time and had since graduated to just yelling at people and practically living on beer nuts and alcohol. A couple of normal looking chicks were at the pool table, one of them slightly heavier than her friend in a perfectly normal way that I hadn't realized I had missed seeing. She was pretty, had a nice curvy figure and definitely knew how to rock the cleavage. Her friend was the standard skinny chick, model thin and not as pretty, but you could tell she definitely thought she was the pretty one, with her long dirty blonde hair and slightly slutty makeup. A couple of guys were at the bar talking to the bartender, and they all looked so damn *normal.*

I didn't care at that moment if they had all turned out to be hipsters. They were all real, normal people and I had actually missed this reality, because this was what normal people did. They came out with their friends and got drunk and told stupid jokes and just enjoyed themselves. Maybe the occasional fight would break out for whatever reason... just like the fight that broke out at the table next to me as I walked in.

It was like coming down off that cloud of heightened reality and realizing at the same time that you were a *god* among mortals.

I looked around at all of the people, the regulars checking me out to see what kind of asshole I was, the randoms glancing right past me as they checked out the fight that was now happening behind me and I mentally counted the number of girls who were on their own.

I made eye contact with a redhead at the bar, noted that slight look of amusement on her face that challenged me, checked out the tattoos on her bare shoulders that her scrappy blouse allowed to show off, and made my decision. I nodded to the bartender as the guys at the bar parted to make way for me.

"Vodka on the rocks," I said.

"We don't got nothing fancy here," he said, and I realized he was looking at my slightly scuffed, but still very expensive suit.

I just shook my head. "As long as it's cheap, Russian and you might use it for paint thinner, I don't care."

"You're man after my heart," the bartender said approvingly, and poured me a glass of his cheapest moonshine substitute.

I glanced over at the redhead again and smiled. "Not *your* heart I'm after," I said as I sipped my drink. I slid a five across the bar and watched as some guy sidled over to the redhead and summoned the bartender to refill her glass. Neither the bartender or the girl looked impressed.

I shook my head and squared my shoulders before I knew what I was thinking. *I was a vampire goddammit.* No shame, no pity.

The guy was flailing at talking her up when I got over there.

"So Jenny, what do you do for a living?"

I clapped Doofus on the shoulder and he looked up at me, startled.

"Fuck off buddy," I said. "You're in my space."

Doofus actually looked from me to Jenny, as if expecting her to save him. Poor guy just looked so confused. I almost felt sorry for him. Almost.

"What the fuck man?"

I smiled and didn't give him a chance to finish. I turned my back on him and slid between him and Jenny.

"Hey!" Doofus grabbed my shoulder and I swear my fist went up on its own. I just heard a wet smack and the sound of him collapsing behind me. Jenny was giving me her full attention, the 'what the fuck' look on her face saying everything it needed to. I was aware that the bartender was watching with some concern, trying to judge how far this fight was going to go. I could have told him not to worry: the fight was already over.

"Maybe he should have listened to you," Jenny said and I knew I had chosen well. Jenny was one of those pretty girls with a mean steak and she pretended that she wanted a nice guy in her life, but always ended up with the bad boys. *Perfect.*

"Oops." I shrugged. "He'll heal, eventually."

"Eventually," she agreed and gave me the once over. "What happened to your suit?"

"A fight happened to me."

"Did you win?"

"You're kidding right? I'm a lover, not a fighter," I proclaimed and reached up to take off my sunglasses. Her reaction to my eyes was worth it.

She gasped and leaned closer as if expecting to see contact lenses. "Whoa! Are those for real?"

"All the way."

"You want to waste more time or you wanna get outta here?"

I love loose women.

***

It started with the sex of course. It was the kind of sex that started in the back of the taxi with a heavy makeout session where you're doing everything in your power to not get naked right there in the backseat. Jenny was surprisingly into it and had her hand down my pants for more than half the ride, while she ground her crotch against my leg. I could feel her burning for me even through the layers of clothing and wondered how far into her place we could make it before her panties were off and we were matching body parts.

The couch. We at least made it to the couch, leaving a trail of clothes from the door. There had been a desperate moment while we fumbled with the condom but then she had expertly slipped it on for me and then all bets were off.

It wasn't making love. This was not that kind of sex. This was the kind of sex of two people who just desperately wanted to fuck the shit out of each other. It was passionate and angry and frantic, all full of moans and vigorous thrusting that's designed to last for at least six minutes, max. She knew what she wanted, what we both wanted, and we fucked like there was no tomorrow, sucking each other's tongues and lips and then finally looking into each other's eyes as she started to orgasm, which of course got me all excited and that was the moment that she seemed to understand what it is that I really wanted, knew deep down what I was. She nodded desperately as she cried out her orgasm, and I sank my teeth into her neck, feeling for the first time as my fangs slid into place, small incisors be damned. The blood exploded in my mouth and I came at the same time.

The ecstasy of that moment as I swallowed that mouthful of blood, and pulled my mouth away from her neck, shuddering all over as the euphoria gripped me and the adrenaline of sex ebbed away…

Jenny grinned at me and touched the already clotting wound on her neck, a stunned look in her eye.

"You bit me," she said, but there was no surprise, just acceptance.

I shrugged, conscious that my fangs had already retreated. *Holy shit! Talk about the effects of arousal!* I wondered briefly if my fangs would pop out every time I got a hard-on, and suddenly realized just how easy puberty had been for me in comparison.

"Do you mind?" I asked and looked her in the eye, wondering what she was really thinking.

"Not at all," Jenny panted and smiled. "That was… amazing. Ready for round two?"

Sex on drugs can be fucking amazing, but only sometimes. Now I could get into the details about how heroin affects the libido and is great at first but then you end up lasting too long and generally being bored, sore and chafing. That's just the cliff notes version and I won't get into the hour long mind-blowing orgasms and the truly freaky shit you can get up to, especially if both people involved are equally high. Truthfully though, if you want a fuck that will blow your mind then there are much better drugs, and I had found mine.

I poured Jenny a glass of orange juice from her fridge and left it at the bedside table. I also left a note with my number and a smiley face, but somehow I knew that she would never call me, but I was okay with that.

I stood there in the dark of Jenny's bedroom and looked at the curve of her naked body, inhaled the smell of sex and blood that still hung in the air and realized all at once that I *could do this.* I could survive and thrive, no matter what Harry and the other vampires thought of me.

Things were changing for me and I knew it.

I had taken control of my life again.

Fuck Harry. Fuck HTDK. Fuck all the other vampires and their rules and bullshit games.

I had gone rogue.

Chapter 17
CONFESSION TIME

You know what? I'm just going to stop myself right there and make a confession. *Ready?* Almost everything I told you about the bar and Jenny was a goddamn lie.

Yes, the whole situation with Jenny happened, but it sure as shit didn't happen *that night* or even that soon. I took a few liberties with the actual details and timeline of the story, but it's something I've always done because I don't want to admit just how much I fucked up. To be fair, every single one of us does it at some point since we have to fulfill that need to be the hero in our own damn stories, and *you're goddamn right* I'm going to be as much of the hero as I can be.

So I didn't run into Jenny that night.

That happened later, some other night. Instead I did what every asshole does when rock bottom is heading toward their face at the speed of suck.

I went to see my ex-girlfriend.

I went to see *Jaime.*

Chapter 18
THE TRUTH

"**L**ESSON NUMBER ONE IN stalking your ex-girlfriend? Don't get caught."

Jeremy the Stoner passed the joint to me and held up a finger to indicate that he had something to say just as soon as he was able to exhale. I took a long drag and watched Jeremy let the smoke out after a moment, the thick acrid smoke hanging in the air before it drifted high enough to be caught in the crosswinds above the alley.

"You serious man?"

"I don't mean that kind of stalking," I said, knowing exactly how it sounded. "Not the murdery rapey kind, or even the Edward from Twilight kind of stalking. I just kind of check up on her from time to time."

"Huh-huh. And you make sure not to get caught," Jeremy said with a raised eyebrow and I could see the doubt in his face.

I thought about it for a second and felt deeply ashamed. "You're right: I'm totally Edward right now."

We were hanging out in the alley behind Jaime's apartment, so this confession was a hell of a lot more relevant than you probably realized. Jaime lived over on the Danforth in one of the third-storey walk-up apartments that existed over the storefronts along the street. You know the ones: you can usually only access them via a lonely door at the front of the building that nobody ever really sees among the storefronts which populate the street-level floors of the building. This door invariably leads to a long flight of stairs that takes you up and up and was hell to move furniture up and down. The thing about some of these apartments was that they were also accessible from the back-alley if you didn't mind climbing up a fire-escape to the rooftop of the first floor restaurant. In the case of the Greek restaurant on the first floor of Jaime's place, the entire rooftop was accessible from said fire-escape and led directly to Jaime's weird little back-patio deal. In warmer weather, she tended to use the rooftop as an extended balcony and even had a propane grill and some plastic chairs set up close to the wooden stairs that led to her kitchen. It was kind of cool, especially with the vents, pipes and air-conditioning units that stuck up from the roof.

If I got there at just the right time, I could even see Jaime through the kitchen window without her realizing that I was outside in the darkness sitting next to the mural covered wall that the previous tenant had painted.

Apparently Jeremy had discovered my spot and had decided that it was the perfect spot to smoke a joint. Judging from his cook's whites, he worked in the Greek restaurant downstairs.

"So how long have you been checking in on her, man?"

"Since we've been broken up. She got a restraining order against me and everything, so this is as close as I get."

"*Restraining order?*" Jeremy asked and I nodded, noting that he was giving that look. You know the one: the one where it clearly states that he thought I was the kind of asshole who goes around beating up women. I wish I could have told him that I was the other kind of asshole, but I doubted that it would have made any difference.

Did you forget about the restraining order? Did you think it was some cute little detail that I just glossed over? Do you think it actually had any effect on keeping me away from her? If so, then you obviously don't know the depths to which the humongously rejected will sink.

"She had a cop friend deliver it about a month after we'd broken up. Calvin or some shithead name like that. He was really fucking gung-ho about it too. Probably wanted to get into her pants—"

"You know how some guys are, man," Jeremy nodded in agreement.

"—So you already know he wasn't exactly gentle about the

delivery. Dude beat the shit out of me and almost broke my arm."

"And you still came back?"

"Man, fuck that guy! It wasn't like I'd actually hit her or anything so that whole thing came right out of nowhere, you know?"

"Damn dude," Jeremy said and I sat there for a long moment, feeling that familiar impotent anger and grief welling up again. I was surprised to find that depth of emotion still there after all of this time, coupled with a sense of hopelessness that had been dogging me all night.

"How long you been broken up?"

"Six, seven months." I said, and he nodded. "I'm not checking up on her to obsess over her or see who she's fucking so I can go and make their lives miserable. It's never been about that for me. It started out with me just wanting some answers, to hear from her how she felt. *Maybe* I even wanted a chance just to say sorry that I fucked things up the way I did. Now it's all about just making sure that she's okay. That's not so bad is it?"

Jeremy shrugged, clearly stoned out of his skull by this point. He started to say something and lost the thread, then seemed to catch it again and waggled his finger at me.

"So what are you doing here tonight then?"

"I'm having the shittiest night I've had in a long time and I guess I just needed to see her face, you know?"

Jeremy nodded. He totally got it. Stoned or not, he got it.

"What happened with you guys?"

That one surprised me, since so few people besides Claude and Louise had even bothered to ask. All of the rest of our shared friends had simply made assumptions, bad ones, and then with the rumor of the restraining order, they had picked sides (pretty much everybody chose her side but can you blame them?) and chosen their alliances (her side again). Everybody knows you had to have been a real psycho if your ex had to get a restraining order against you.

The truth was a lot more complicated and frustrating.

"I fucked up the relationship," I admitted and stared at the empty kitchen window as if I could will Jaime into existence.

I continued after a moment. "The thing is, that I knew I was fucking up and I still continued to actively fuck it up. It was like I couldn't help myself, you know? I'd always been so damn proud of the fact that I'd never once hit Jaime, so I couldn't be that much of a fuck-up, right? I never crossed that line so I was able to convince myself that I wasn't being as much of a shit as I was really being. When she decided that she didn't want to be with me anymore and she just walked right the fuck out, I was left with a lot of questions and a whole lot of a lack of closure. So *of course* I showed up uninvited. I mean, she wasn't taking my calls, had deleted me off of facebook and social media, so I knew it was over. That says it all right there man. When *even Facebook* denies that you were *ever* a couple and all of the photos she shared with you are gone, that hurts more than you think it should. So when I showed up, of course we got into it…" I trailed off, remembering just how bad, how embarrassing it had gotten. I cringed at the memory of some of the things I had said, none of them good.

There was movement in the kitchen and I looked up, expecting to see Jaime, but it was just her roommate, Stella (?) pouring herself a glass of tap water and then drinking said water as if they didn't have a perfectly good Brita Water Jug ($49 from Costco and I still missed it dammit) sitting in the fridge. Still no Jaime.

"It just got messy from that point on and then came the restraining order and that was that," I finished lamely. "I'm not to contact her via electronic or telephonic means and I have to stay at least one hundred metres away from her at all times. And if I don't respect the order, I will be arrested and beaten for resisting arrest. And possibly sodomized with a nightstick, according to Officer McPunch-A-Lot."

"Fucking cops man," Jeremy shook his head.

"I fucked up man. Love of my life and I fucked up so bad."

"Just because she's the love of your life, doesn't mean you're the love of hers," Jeremy said, and stood up, checking his pockets for his belongings. I ignored the surge of anger and even patted myself on the back for not kicking him off the edge of the roof. Sure it was only one storey and he would have been okay, but it would have been just a really mean thing to do. He vanished down the fire escape and I was left alone in my misery, feeling sorry for myself—

Pssst!

I looked back to the fire escape and Jeremy was poking his head over the top.

"Don't be Edward. That stalkery thing is just fucking creepy man, especially for a vampire who's that old, so you know man, just *don't be that guy.*"

"You're saying I should go talk to her?"

"Not at all dude. I'm saying maybe you should get the fuck off the roof and stop stalking your ex before you do something fucking stupid. I can't smoke up here if it's a crime scene, you know?"

* * *

Lesson number two in stalking your ex-girlfriend? Don't do anything stupid.

I hadn't planned on doing anything stupid, abysmally or otherwise. I'd actually planned to take Jeremy's good but unsolicited advice and get the fuck out of there. I was even in the act of getting off my ass and thinking about trying to catch the last train over to the west end before I had to eat the cost of an Uber. I was going to get out of there—

But…

Yeah, go ahead and gloat. You knew it was coming.

Let me break it down for you so you can picture it properly. The door at the top of the stairs that led to Jaime's kitchen slammed open with some force and all I could hear was yelling from inside the apartment, before Jaime shoved her way through the door, pausing only to yell back into the apartment.

"Well FUCK YOU TOO!"

Jaime slammed the door behind her and stomped down the stairs, the screen door slowly wheezing shut behind her as if making sure she was gone before it dared to close. Jaime stomped over to the single chair in front of the mural, simultaneously pulling her coat shut over her mismatched pyjamas and patting the pockets as if looking for something. She found the glass pipe she was looking for and just stared

303

at it for a long moment, clearly wondering if it was what she really needed right then.

As for me, I had frozen into place in front of the mural, suddenly too terrified to run and hoping like hell that I would just appear to be another one of the painted figures on the wall. After all, it was dark and if she went through with it, Jaime was about to be stoned, so there was a fairly good chance I could pull this off, right?

Jaime found the lighter and raised it to the pipe—

I have no idea what happened. I swear I didn't make a sound, didn't make any sudden moves, but Jaime had whipped around to look at the mural, a bemused look on her face, then—

"HOLY FUCKING SHIT!"

The glass pipe hit me square between the eyes and I yelped, more surprised then my ex-girlfriend, and now way more bruised and slightly concussed. She had scrambled backward, ready to run even as she threw the pipe at me, but now she paused, something clicking in her brain that this wasn't some ordinary lurker waiting to assault her.

"Bob?" she asked incredulously and I raised my hand, thrilling at the fact that she was using my name and for the first time in a long time it hadn't been preceded with a "fuck you" or "you asshole".

"Please don't throw anything else at me," I said. "I don't think my head can take the beating and your aim is deadly."

"Fuck you Bob!"

Ahh, there it was, like music to my ears.

"Just so you know, this isn't what it looks like."

Jaime just raised her eyebrow and I winced, accepting how caught and especially how guilty I was.

"Okay, fine, it is what it looks like, but it's just not as bad as it looks. I mean, I was literally just leaving, but then you came out… please don't do that…"

That was my reaction to Jaime pulling out her phone and dialling very deliberately.

"Why is it that every time I see you, it instantly goes to you yelling at me—"

"You're on my roof in the middle of the night! Buy a

fucking clue, Bob! I don't want to talk to you!"

"Maybe one more time for clarity?" Yes, I was being a jackass, but it's a defense thing and almost guaranteed at least one tiny smile. At least normally.

"Jesus Christ Bob! Roof! Night! You! Stalker! Get it?"

"Why do you hate me so much?" I pleaded with her.

That one actually made her pause and then this look of what can be only described as pain came across her face for a few seconds. She shook her head slowly and then said rather quietly: "I don't hate you Bob."

"It sure as hell feels like it from over here," I responded and were those tears biting at my eyes, daring me to wipe them away with the back of my hand?

I saw Jaime looking to the safety of the stairs, everything in her screaming that she needed to get the fuck away from me. Normally I would even agree. If your stalker shows up on your roof in the middle of the night, get inside and lock the doors. Don't stand around yelling at them and giving them shit for the sake of drama or whatever. Get the fuck inside and call the fucking cops.

It killed me to see that Jaime thought of me like that, but yet… she wasn't running.

"Why are you here? Is this a thing with you now? Spying on me?"

I shook my head, knowing that there was no way she was going to believe me. "I just needed to see you. I needed to know you were okay?"

"That's such bullshit and you know it."

"I'll never admit it and you can quote me on that."

There was a long moment where we just looked at each other, no yelling, not blaming, just me and her, she and me.

"There is never going to be a you and me ever again Bob. I hope you know that."

"You've been pretty clear, yeah."

"You still have hope."

"You don't hate me, so that's a start, right? And I'll never stop loving you."

"You know I called the cops, right? Just now?"

Ow. That hurt.

"We were in love--"

"I had an abortion Bob. When I left you, I was pregnant. And I ended it."

Fuck.

Oh fuck.

I didn't say that. Maybe I should have, but my mouth wasn't connecting to my brain anymore, and there was just this numbness that was spreading out from my head and working its way down my body. I realized that I was grinning and wondered where that had come from, that uncomfortable and utterly stupid expression that had no place here, no. But there it was, frozen into place, totally disconnected from reality, from emotion, from thought or biology or the slow *beat-beat-beat* of my now frozen heart. Words were forming, but I don't know what they were, didn't know how to think or taste them, only wanted to bite them back and keep them from getting out like the poison that I knew they would be.

I looked at the love of my life and I didn't feel that familiar warmth of love, that familiar flutter of butterflies in my stomach at the sight of her. There was a rush of acid and I had no doubt that those fucking butterflies were dead or at least as stunned as I was.

"You were pregnant?" I finally managed to say, and those were not the words I wanted to scream at her, wanted to howl into the night. They felt so inadequate, but they were all I had, and they could never be enough.

Jaime nodded and I felt it then, the rush of hot tears that would lead to me balled up in a corner giving my best demonstration of a truly ugly cry. I fought the tears back, wiped the back of my hand across my eyes and stumbled away from Jaime, aware that somewhere ahead of me was the ladder and behind me was the woman who had known exactly how best to slay me. How she hadn't done it before was beyond me, but I guess that was one hell of a reason for her not talking to me for six months.

"I'm gonna go," I said, more for the need to say something than anything else, and I don't know if she even heard me. I didn't care at the time.

The numbness hit me hard once I was at the bottom of the

ladder and I blinked into the night, feeling empty and dead inside.

Jeremy poked his head out and he might have said something to me as I stumbled away. I might have punched him, but don't quote me on that.

I don't know what he said. I don't know much of anything from that night.

I had finally hit true rock bottom. The place where I don't have the words to describe how I feel.

That's okay. I don't want to talk about it anymore anyway.

Chapter 19
DAYS LIKE THESE

Okay, flashback's over. You now know everything about my fucked up life, or at least as much as I'm willing to admit to.

So yeah, that's me, the bastard Bob, the same guy I was telling you about earlier who hangs out at your local dive and somehow always manages to leave with whatever chick you happen to be checking out. However, you never get too suspicious about me, since you will see that girl again sometime, so it wasn't like I'm some psycho killer, right?

See, there's a reason Harry has the rules and that his vampires actually follow them. There are people just like you out there watching for people just like me and some of those people are more than actively *looking* if you know what I mean. They just happen to be looking for us in exactly the wrong way.

I had a whole series of awkward conversations about my new adopted lifestyle, the first one being with Claude, but that was a conversation that had been a long time coming, especially with him being gone for so long and me being left to my own devices. He of course, showed up in my apartment while I was sleeping and threw popcorn at my face until I woke up.

"Are you killing people?"

"*What?* Are you fucking kidding me?"

"Let me ask again just so we're on the same page. Have you killed anyone?"

"Hell no! What the hell do you think I am anyway?"

Claude looked me deep in the eye and nodded. He pulled

back from me and sat in the chair at the side of the bed, still carefully watching me. His pulling away was a relief, since he had been right in my face yelling at me and I was desperately conscious that my morning breath tasted like it was about to be condemned by the UN as a weapon of gross destruction. My teeth were feeling all mossy and I knew for sure I hadn't brushed in at least a day, and I could taste it, that rank garbage taste that was a combination of everything I'd eaten over the past forty-eight hours.

"Did you just get back into town?" I asked Claude. "You're three weeks late. I started thinking that you were dead."

Claude grimaced. "What's my number one rule?"

"Don't drink anything from the top shelf?"

"That's a good rule, but that's not rule number one anymore. Rule number one is now 'never work with Russians', a rule which I thought I was following, but somebody pulled a bait and switch on me, and now of course the Russians want me dead, because that's the way these motherfuckers do business."

"Is this going to be a thing now? The Russians?" I asked.

"Only for as long as they're trying to kill me," Claude said, and stood up. "Come on, I grabbed us some McDonald's breakfast sandwiches."

"What time is it anyway?"

"Time to figure out what the hell is going on with you," Claude sighed.

As he walked away from me, I noticed a small detail, something I had never seen with Claude before. There was a bulge at the back of his waist and he was compensating his body movements ever so slightly, the way someone does when they're wearing a gun.

I chased after Claude, jumping into my jeans, glad that I hadn't gone to bed naked like I usually do. I had been going to bed naked more often over the past three weeks and it had become kind of a default state.

"Since when do you carry a gun?" Something occurred to me. "Is that because of me?"

Claude scoffed and rolled his eyes. He tossed me a yellow paper wrapped sandwich from the counter and I caught it easily enough.

"I scoff at the implication that you could hurt me. This is me scoffing." He scoffed and I pretended to be impressed. "Dude, haven't you been following the conversation? We have a Russian problem. Now sit and fill me in on everything that's been going on with you. Starting with what the hell happened with Jaime."

"How the hell do you know about that?"

"She called me and left a very long and very detailed voicemail. Almost as good as texting. Try it sometime."

"Well since you already know what happened, why do you need me to tell you?"

"Because what she says happened and what you think happened are two completely different things. And I need to hear it from you so I know how fucked up you are."

So I told him. I kind of avoided telling all of the truth about my newly acquired habit of hitting the dive bars on my nights off work. Somehow I couldn't let him know the complete truth, but I think he saw right through me anyway. To his credit, he let me get away with it, possibly reassured that I wasn't even allowed back into HTDK and that Harry wasn't actively trying to have me killed, at least as far as I knew.

I was still alive, so that had to count for something.

***

"How you holding up bro?" the King had wanted to know one night. Sammy had vanished into the Boss' office to go change, so we had a few minutes to ourselves.

I had sighed and put down my brand new copy of "Giant Days", my study in British slang put on hold for a second to deal with this traitorous bastard.

"I'm still alive. I hope you put down long odds for me in the deadpool."

"I heard something about that. That's harsh man."

"How much you got riding on me?"

"Nothing! I've been avoiding the club. There are much better places out there to be one of us you know. I mean, we got the whole damn city to work with. Harry's club barely scratches the surface."

"Gee, I wish I had a mentor or somebody to show me around," I deadpanned. For extra flourish, I whipped the open comic book back up to cover my face and my view of the King.

There was silence for a long moment. When I inched the comic book back down to sneak a peek, the King was still there. He raised an eyebrow at me.

"You're seriously going to hold this against me? Me not being your mentor?"

"Damn skippy!"

"You're not going to tell Sammy about me, right?"

I considered this for a moment and let him stew.

"Mentor me."

"No."

"Be my mentor!"

"No!"

"Be my mentor… please?"

"Still no."

"Fuck you then. I'm so telling Sammy when she gets back out."

He called my bluff. I didn't tell Sammy anything, but things changed after that and you could tell. Sammy was really angry for about a week and barely spoke to me, so I assumed that she and the King had broken up or something.

"I hate men," Sammy had snapped at me one day and I had given her an awkward sideways hug. She had retaliated by whacking me with a rolled-up magazine and then ended up chasing me around the store with the magazine since I really didn't want any fresh bruises. After that, we were okay and settled into a new groove, a new rhythm, and life carried on.

***

Most days I tried not to think about Jaime. Some days I was actually successful.

The thing is that pregnant women suddenly seemed to be everywhere I went, their bellies big and round and inescapable like silent accusations. I tried to remind myself how much I actually hated little kids, especially babies. I was the last person on earth who should ever be entrusted with the care of a small child even by virtue of biology and shared chromosomes. I knew it was a bad idea, and Jaime had definitely rejected that idea completely, but still, there I was surrounded by pregnant women on the bus, at the store and even at work.

Do you know that some pregnant women get especially horny as the hormones course through them? I had no idea of that fact either until a very aggressive pregnant woman cornered me in the store and gave me the details.

"I feel like you want me to ask you how horny you get and I'm really not comfortable with that line of questioning."

I really wasn't either. There was something maddening about the smell of her blood and it was driving me crazy. I never thought I could actually smell hormones, but surprise! You learn something new everyday.

"Ask me," the pregnant lady had insisted. "Cuz I'm going to tell you anyway. In great detail."

She did. In great detail. It kind of explained why in the course of the next nine days I sold vibrators and dildos of varying sizes to obviously pregnant women of varying sizes.

Sometimes the universe can't help but shove your pain right into your face.

***

Days went by where I didn't even think about being a vampire, beyond avoiding the sunlight and bitching about the ever lengthening days of the coming summer. And of course there was my new found hobby of picketing the club at least once a week. By the end of May it had already gotten ridiculous to even think about leaving the house before 8 PM and it steadily got worse. Claude took pity on me and started driving me to work, since he was around a hell of a lot more after his excursion with the Russians. Sure I'd have to make sure every inch of me was covered before I ran out to the car, but it was better than having to travel on the bus dressed like that. I think he was a little worried about my bouts of depression that popped up from time to time and he gave me the space and the time I needed, but made sure that I knew he was there for me. Just as long as I wasn't inviting any Russians over to hang out.

I thought about Beatrice and wondered if she'd tell me just how exactly she pulled off the whole "daytripping" thing, before remembering just how much of a fuck she didn't have to give about much of anything.

I spent a lot of time finding new dive bars I hadn't been to yet. A lot of the time was spent with Google Maps just figuring out distances and travel times. I even got an app on my phone to track where I had visited and to take a note of which girl I had picked up that night. It was almost obsessive on my part and I wondered sometimes if the other vampires did something similar. Some level of organization *had* to be at play, otherwise vampires would have made the Nightly News a long time ago out of sheer recklessness. Since I had time at work and I had no intention of being arrested or being the target of some dude's overactive but accurate imagination, I indulged my obsession and tried to plan accordingly.

Anyone following my activities at the bars would have just thought that I was some kind of man-slut who got laid regularly and reliably at least once a week. Lots of guys don't have that kind of average, having to strike out every now and again, but for me, that was a thing of the past.

The bodies hit the bed and the blood flowed.

For a while, I was the king of my own reality.

When I formed the group and actual members started showing up, that's when everything changed.

***

"Hi my name is Bob, and I'm a vampire."

As soon as the words came out of my mouth, I realized just how stupid they sounded, especially since it was supposedly the traditional thing to say at Alcoholics Anonymous meetings, but for this group it just felt so *wrong*.

Natalie coughed in the back of the room and I looked up at all of their familiar faces, all of my fellow rejects and something occurred to me, one of those wild ideas that go off like a flashbulb of intuition, kinda like when you find the last piece of the puzzle under the couch a week after you were last assembling said puzzle. I might have actually said something about it, but then there it was, the sound of someone new, noisily making their way up the narrow staircase.

"Hey guys!" Murray said, practically bursting into the room. "Am I late?"

There was a palpable drop in energy as everyone else shifted uncomfortably, sending a signal to anyone with a brain that Murray clearly wasn't welcome. Murray was either oblivious to this or he had just decided he didn't give a shit.

Murray was also the answer to the question of why it's not such a good idea to post your vampire group meetings to the finest people the internet has to offer via Craigslist. We all knew instantly that he wasn't a vampire. We didn't even have to wait to see his eyes with the fucked up *"Underworld Vampire"* contact lenses he'd ordered from an online costume store. There was a complete difference in the way real vampires carried themselves, even rejects like us. I just hadn't realized how easy it was to spot until Murray came in pretending to be one of us.

I honestly couldn't tell you what Murray's deal was or any of his backstory. I honestly didn't care to listen to anything he had said. He gave off this creepy totally-not-like-Edward-at-all stalkery vibe that made you want to either rip his head off or run very far away as quickly as possible. We just entertained him, nobody wanting to be the bad guy and kick him out, but all of us thinking the same thing: *none of us wanted anything to do with him.* It wasn't like he was the first random dude to show up, but he was the first to give us all the complete creeps.

Benjamin looked around at Frankie and Stanley and then shot me a look as if to say *"do something"* as Murray rooted around for a chair. I shrugged, really not knowing what to say, and Ben finally decided he'd had enough.

"Oh come on you guys!" Benjamin said, then focused his attention on Murray. "Murray, you can't join the group. It's really not the right fit for you."

Murray looked completely clueless and not even a little bit hurt. He gave Ben a look that said that he was not accepting that answer.

"Whatcha talkin' about man? I'm as much a vampire as all

you guys. Is it the fangs? Cuz if it is, I found this amazing deal online. Custom fit. There's a guy here in town who'll even do a more permanent fit."

Natalie had had enough.

"I'm going to take off you guys," she said, and sidled past me to the stairs.

"Natalie! You can't go!" I implored her. "It's gonna be a total sausagefest if you leave."

"Yeah I know. But I don't like him. He gives me the creeps." Natalie shrugged and offered a weak apologetic smile. "Sorry, but you do."

"No offense taken," Murray said as Natalie disappeared down the stairs. He turned to us remaining men in the room. "Bitches, right?"

"Oh my GOD!" Benjamin said, practically having an apoplexy. Frankie grabbed his shoulders and tried to calm him down.

"Don't get so worked up over this Ben. Sammy will kick our asses if we make to much noise."

"He's got to go!" Benjamin turned to me and I knew it was going to be up to me to handle the situation as the leader by default. "You said he'd probably never even come back and if he did then you'd take care of it. So take care of it Bob."

"He's right Bob," Stanley agreed from his chair in the back. He was wearing his security guard uniform since he was heading to work directly after the meeting, and the dark sunglasses made him look like a demented rent-a-cop more than anything else.

"You gonna give me a hand?" I challenged him. "You're the security expert here."

"Pay me fifteen bucks an hour and we'll talk," Stanley said in that cocky way he has and flexed one of his considerable biceps that was supposed to remind me that he was totally worth the fifteen bucks.

"Natalie left because of this dude—" Benjamin protested.

Murray stood up, hands raised in protest. "Hold on guys! Nobody has to throw me outta anywhere. It's cool, man. I get it."

We all shared a look of confusion.

"You do? Really?"

Murray nodded and grinned. "I totally get it. I haven't proven myself or gone through the kind of initiation you guys have—"

"You're not a vampire!" Benjamin hissed, and Frankie gave him a look that made him calm down, but only a little.

Murray continued. "—So I brought you guys a little present to show how serious I am. I mean, not everybody is cut out to be a vampire, right?"

I didn't like where this was going.

"Bob, I don't like where this is going," Benjamin said.

Get rid of him, Frankie mouthed at me, and I glared back at him. I was cautious with my response to Murray.

"What kind of present?"

***

You would think that I would know better than to follow a guy like Murray to his car after the mysterious statement that he had a present for us, and in this case you'd be right. There was no way Ben or Frankie were going anywhere with Murray, so I made Stanley come with me. Sure I had to pay him fifteen bucks for the privilege, but it made me feel a little more secure that I wasn't going to be randomly murdered and dismembered in the parking lot of the store. If there was going to be any murder going on, Stanley assured me that he would at least retrieve my body.

Yes, I had to pay him another fifteen dollars, up front, just in case.

Murray paused by the blue Toyota Corolla while he dug for his keys. It was a 2003 model and still in decent shape, but it wasn't the kind of car I had pictured Murray driving. He looked more like the kind of guy who drove a truck or even better, a white panel van with no windows in the back. There were only three other cars in the parking lot and I would have picked any of those (especially the tan Oldsmobile in the back) over the Corolla. Guess you can't tell with some people.

"Still get decent mileage of this?" I asked idly and Murray looked at me and shrugged.

"Not really. I suppose so. It's my sister's car, ya know, so I don't drive it too often."

Ahh, well that explained that.

Murray found the keys and as he fumbled with the lock to get the trunk open, I had this sinking feeling in my gut that I really didn't want him to open the trunk, not at all, not now, not ever because it was going to be something horrible—

"Ta-da!" Murray sang and all I could do was stare.

It was something horrible.

"I figured that we could take turns drinking from her. She's still really fresh, but she was making too much noise and things kinda got outta hand. Besides I didn't know if you guys liked them still kicking or what. Tell me I did good. I did good, right?"

I was trying to remember the girl's name, trying to see past that look of despair on her slack face, her cloudy eyes telling me a story that I didn't want to read. I just stared at her dead face and all I felt was this deep sadness, this grief rising up and threatening to overwhelm me. And all I wanted to do was remember her name.

Her throat had been slashed and what clothes she had on were soaked through with thick dark blood that had pooled underneath her. Murray had laid out plastic sheets inside the trunk almost a little too expertly.

"How many have you killed?" I asked him almost casually. It was a real effort for me, and I almost whispered it. "I can tell she isn't your first."

Murray tried to look sly as he considered lying to me. I don't know what made him tell the truth.

"She's the third one. She was a fighter, even when I drugged her."

There was something in my gut, a hot ball of rage that scorched my mind with the sheer unfairness of it all, and there were suddenly tears, hot streaming tears rushing down my face. I may have screamed, or that might have been Murray as my arm shot out seemingly of it's own volition to grab that *smarmy motherfucker* by the throat, my fingers clamping down tight like some otherworldly vice.

"*Meredith.* Her name was *Meredith.* She didn't want a fake vampire name like her friends. She was just *fucking Meredith.*"

I growled.

She had laughed at my jokes and she had been nice and real and had such a great laugh, and nobody was going to hear that laugh ever again and *it wasn't fair goddammit!* She'd had no choice in how her life ended and she sure as shit hadn't ever thought it would end like this, slashed and stripped and shoved into the back of a fucking Toyota Corolla.

Where was the justice in that? Where was the poetry and sense of irony or whatever that made life mean something, that made the rest of us fight so goddamn hard to keep breathing so we could eat and drink and fuck and laugh and hope to die in our own beds knowing that close by, someone loved us.

All of the emotions I had been bottling up since Jaime's revelation about her abortion, the one I had never had a choice about, all of those emotions came pouring out of me, glad to have a target for the anger that I had been nursing on a slow simmer over the past few months.

I lifted Murray into the air, not bothering to wonder just when I had gotten so damn strong and realized that my fangs had slid into place, no doubt triggered by my rage. I heard Stanley yell something, but I didn't care at that moment. I slammed Murray into the nearest wall, glad to see the terror in his bulging eyes as he clawed at my arm, desperate for breath.

"You're not supposed to kill anyone you fucking idiot!" I yelled at him. "And you're especially not supposed to kill *my friends!"*

Stanley grabbed me and I turned to him, ready to take him on. What I wasn't ready for was to take on all three of the guys. Benjamin and Frankie piled on and I stumbled back, letting go of Murray.

"Don't let him get away! He's been killing people!" I managed to yell.

Murray wasn't going anywhere. He was on the ground heaving in huge breaths of air, giving me a nasty look.

Benjamin had spotted Meredith in the trunk and his face turned white.

"I think I'm going to be sick," Benjamin whispered and true to his word, he stumbled away to the corner of the parking lot and threw up in the shadows.

I looked at Stanley, expecting him to be reasonable about killing this dude. Stanley had always struck me as being the one more likely to have some random act of violence in his past, but that could have just been me jumping to conclusions.

"You gonna let me kill him now?" I said. "He deserves to die!"

Stanley was just shaking his head, horrified that I was even thinking about it. Had I misjudged him that much?

"Think about what you're saying dude!" Stanley said. "You're not a killer! None of us are!"

"He's going around killing people and drinking their blood. *He thinks he's one of us!*"

"I *am* one of you! We're vampires! Creatures of the night! We kill for blood!" Murray coughed. "Where did you get your *teeth* done?"

"Shut the fuck up," Frankie snarled and I noticed that he had pulled the phone away from his ear. What the fuck was he doing making a call right now anyway? *Come on dude: priorities!*

"Stanley, he's already killed three girls," I pleaded. "You gotta let me kill him."

"Have you ever killed anyone before?"

"No, but I'm willing to change that right now."

A voice came from behind us:

"It's messy, it's sad, they shit their pants and you're left with a lifetime of guilt. You don't want that burden. Kinda fucks with your head."

We all turned around, maybe for the first time realizing just how exposed we were. Beatrice turned from looking into the trunk at Meredith and she looked mildly annoyed as she looked up at me and slammed the trunk closed.

"Who the fuck is that?" Murray whispered hoarsely.

"Beatrice…" Stanley and Frankie breathed, completely stealing my thunder. *What the fuck man? How did they know Beatrice?*

"Hi Beatrice," I said, firmly establishing myself as the resident Beatrice expert in these parts. "What the fuck are you doing here?"

"Oh, I came for the meeting," Beatrice replied looking directly at me. "Decided to stay for the violence. Your ad seriously undersold the murder and mayhem though."

"He brought the murder with him," I jerked a thumb at the prone and now terrified Murray. "We were going to send it right back."

Beatrice looked down at Murray who on second thought seemed to be more enchanted by Beatrice rather than terrified. She considered him carefully and then shrugged.

"Delusional psycho killer who thinks he's a vampire, huh?" She looked at me and sighed deeply, as if she had expected better. "This is what happens when you accept every Tom, Dick and Stanley off the street." She winked at Stanley when she got to his name and that annoyed me for some reason. Beatrice counted us and then counted again, looking puzzled. "Where's Natalie?"

"How do you know these guys?" I finally asked, unable to take the suspense any longer.

"Oh, I made them into vampires," she said way too casually then paused as she looked at Frankie. "Except this one."

"What do you mean *you made them into vampires*?" I asked, the same time that Frankie responded with:

"You can't go around making random vampires!"

Murray chimed in just a second late: "Can you make me into a real vampire?"

Beatrice rolled her eyes and flicked her arm at Frankie. A knife suddenly appeared in the middle of his chest, buried up to its shiny wooden hilt, like some macabre magic trick. Frankie stumbled back one step, trying to suck in air, something vital suddenly not working. The phone tumbled from his hand and landed facedown on the ground with a very expensive sounding thud.

"Shit," Beatrice said. "I meant to tell you to shut up, but I guess that sends a similar message."

Frankie dropped to his knees and I reached out to him, still marvelling at how fast the knife had appeared, still trying to process how things had gone south so quickly. Frankie's hands reached weakly and ineffectively for the knife.

"Oh just pull it out," Beatrice said impatiently. "The faster that it's out, the faster he will heal. In the meantime he won't be yap-yap-yapping in my ear and he certainly won't be making any more calls to Harry."

What the fuck?

"Frankie works for Harry," Benjamin said as he returned from the far end of the parking lot. "He's been reporting on the group."

"Bennie!" Beatrice said warmly. She looked back to me and winked, then said in a stage whisper. "He's my favorite!"

"How do you know any of this?" I asked Benjamin. Then turned to Beatrice. "Does everybody know but me?"

"I didn't know shit," Stanley mumbled. He leaned over the traitorous Frankie and shook his head. "Sorry buddy," he said, and in one move, yanked the knife out of Frankie's chest. I jerked back from the spray of blood from the wound, but you gotta be really fast to avoid sprays of blood and I really wasn't that fast, so half of my face got covered in Frankie's blood.

I had had enough. I wiped the blood away from my face, aware that the right side of my coat had droplets of blood everywhere and this coat was going to have to go into the trash.

"Fuck all of you guys! I'm killing this sonofabitch!"

"Why?" Beatrice asked quietly, and I glared at her.

"What do you mean why? He's a psycho killer and he killed my friend!"

"Dude, you barely even knew her. You met her at the club, fucked her and drank her blood and then ignored her after that. How do you think she ended up with this sick fuck? Downward spiral man, starting with *you*. You can at least be honest with yourself right now. You want to kill him because he's a sick fuck and you want to end him, then admit it, but don't go around trying to claim vengeance for someone you only now choose to call a friend when she's *fucking dead*. When you kill someone, it's for keeps, so you better own that shit."

I really didn't know what to say about that and felt that rage inside dying in the harsh light of the truth.

Murray nodded feverishly. "She's really got a point," he agreed.

"Don't worry, I'm definitely killing him—" Beatrice said.

"Oh goddammit!" Murray said.

"—but at least I know why I'm doing it. Plus I'm a lot better at it and we really don't need to leave a trail. None of this gets back to us. That's the rule. That's how we survive and thrive."

I looked around at the faces of my friends, and wondered just how much we had all been hiding just by not talking about it. I wanted to feel some sense of betrayal, something, anything at all, but somehow my self-righteous switch wasn't working. Unlike myself, it wasn't as if any of them were hitting the dive bars every chance they got to try to get a quick fix to get through the day and then pretending that everything was okay. So they hadn't told me that Beatrice had turned them, but it wasn't like I had ever asked for specifics. The only person who had actually had any other purpose had been Frankie, and the knowledge of that betrayal still stung.

"Fine," I muttered to Beatrice. "Do your thing."

Beatrice was surprisingly gentle with me as she used a finger to raise my chin so I could look her in the eye.

"Chin up Bob. You're doing a lot better than anyone ever expected you to. You're still here and that's gotta count for something, right?"

"Really?"

SLAP! My face stung from the sudden blow.

"Of course you made me lose ten grand when you didn't off yourself last week, so thanks for that." Beatrice turned to Murray and looked him deep in the eye. "You, get up and get in the car. We're going for a drive. And yes, you are going to die."

"Yes mistress," Murray said eagerly and shuffled off to the car, following orders exactly.

"That was way too easy. Somebody's already glammered the shit out of this guy."

Glammered? What the hell was that? I never got a chance to ask.

Beatrice turned to our little ragtag group.

"Oh yeah, Harry wants to shut down your club. You might want to ask Frankie over there for more details."

Beatrice strode off to the car while we all turned as one to look at the bleeding Frankie. When Beatrice drove the Corolla out of the alley and into the waiting night, taking Murray with her, we didn't even notice.

I looked around at the guys, the sudden absence of Beatrice and Murray bringing reality crashing back down around us.

Frankie moaned pitifully, heaving huge breaths that seemed to hurt. Stanley and Benjamin looked at each other in the shy way that men who have just discovered they are brothers do, which is to say: really fucking awkwardly.

Benjamin asked the question we were all thinking.

"So what happens now?"

Chapter 20
STORMING THE CASTLE

Real life does not play by movie rules, not even if vampires are involved. The movies create impossible scenarios and deliberately make people speak in vague sentences just to create dramatic tension. While some drama does exist in real life and people just don't listen, a few intelligent questions can get to the root of a problem pretty damn quickly. So instead of saying completely useless things like *"this isn't what it looks like"*, or *"wait, I can explain"*, to defuse a situation, real people say things like:

"So why were you spying on us for Harry?" I asked.

"Threats, then money, then more threats," Frankie grunted.

"So he's paying you to spy on us?"

Frankie laid back and groaned in relief as he stretched out. He waved a hand weakly in the air as he talked. "Well first Mister Bryce offered to rip my throat out if I didn't do it." He groaned and took a breath as he laughed humorlessly. "That's the threat part. The paying me part... *that* was just to make me feel like I have a choice."

"Carrot *and* the stick," Benjamin nodded. "Sounds reasonable."

"Why would Harry be so interested in us?" Stanley asked, but that wasn't the question that was banging around my skull, trying to find its way into words.

"No idea. I just report what you guys are up to and who comes to the meetings. I think Bob *not dying* has a lot to do with it."

Natalie sidled out of the shadows and Stanley almost had a heart attack.

"Hey guys, what did I miss?"

"Goddammit Nat!" Stanley yelled. "Where did you come from?"

"Ben texted me. I was hanging out with Sammy, discussing the stalker tendencies of our friend Murray and why you guys couldn't just ditch him even though he's a total creep. Sammy wants to kick all of your asses for enabling that creep." She spotted Frankie down on the ground with the bloodstained shirt and slightly seeping wound. "Oh my God Frankie! Is that your blood? Why is Frankie bleeding?"

"Frankie is ratting us out to Harry," Benjamin said matter-of-factly. Natalie looked horrified and there was that question again, ready to burst forth, but not just yet.

"You rat bastard!" Natalie exclaimed, and actually looked ready to put another knife into Frankie's chest.

"For money!" Frankie protested and coughed again, his slight movement causing him pain.

"For money," Benjamin amended, and Natalie looked relieved at that.

"Oh that's okay then," she said. "How much?"

"How much?" I blurted out, seconds too late after Natalie. I spun off in a small tantrum, literally stomping my feet. "Goddammit! So close!"

Frankie shook his head, but slowly. "You guys are terrible," He said, then said the words that I never knew I dreamed of hearing until I heard them coming from Frankie's bloodstained lips: "He gave me a credit card. Mastercard. Black."

I think my jaw might have hit the ground and from the look on Natalie's face, she was hearing the same d*ing-ding-ding* music of a jackpot. Stanley and Benjamin looked suitably impressed, but apparently they didn't have the same kind of wickedly devious mind that we shared.

"I'm not supposed to abuse it!" Frankie was protesting. He had seen the looks on our faces and he apparently *did* have a devious mind, so he knew exactly what we were thinking.

"You can tell Harry it was under duress," I said in what I hoped was a convincing way.

"Well he *does* have a hole in his chest," Natalie agreed. "If that isn't duress, I don't know what is."

"I feel a bar crawl coming on," I said. I was feeling particularly vindictive and really wanted to hit somebody. "If Harry's paying to spy on us, it's about to get fucking expensive."

"Fuck yeah!" Natalie said and then saw how we were all looking at her. "What? I swear. I swear all the time."

Benjamin was the most stunned. "When did you get so… so… predatory?"

She turned red and tried to look demure, but the secret was out. "I'm only shy until you get to know me. I like to watch people until I figure them out. Get a few drinks into me and look out!" Natalie looked back at Frankie. "So… who put the hole in Mister Moneybags over here?"

Stanley was more than happy to oblige.

"You shoulda stuck around for the show. Bob kinda went off on Murray and man it was awesome. Did not see that coming at all, you know? That fucking guy is history now, so I hope you're happy!"

"I'm so confused. So Murray stabbed Frankie?"

"Oh no, not at all," I chimed in. "That was Beatrice."

If Natalie had been confused before, I had just managed to double her confusion.

"Why would Beatrice stab Frankie?"

I raised a smug eyebrow at Natalie and could tell the other guys were thinking the same thing that I was.

"Have you *met* Beatrice? Wildcard doesn't even begin to describe her."

Natalie nodded thoughtfully.

"Like I said Nats: you shoulda been here," Stanley grabbed Benjamin by the shoulder and grinned. "Right little bro?"

I looked back at Frankie, who was slowly pulling himself to his feet, still in pain from his wound. He hadn't even bothered to ask anyone for help and it kinda sucked that nobody was offering to help him up, but to be fair, I don't think any of us knew exactly how to feel about him at that point. It was apparently going to take a while to heal properly, definitely not like the movies where he would be fully healed in thirty minutes and his shirt would be magically fixed and laundered. We were going to have to get him cleaned up if we were going to do any bar crawling. I looked down at myself, aware of how much blood was on me. I was going to have to get changed as well.

"All in favor of forgiving Frankie?" I asked. Frankie glanced at me and gave a weak grin as the other guys and Natalie all raised their hands.

"Frankie is buying us drinks, right?" That was Benjamin.

"He's buying us *all* the drinks!" I clarified.

See what I mean about real conversations?

Watch some moron adapt this story into a movie and instantly add in a series of awkward conversations that go nowhere and do nothing else but play to the whole drama of the situation. A bunch of guys hanging out in a parking lot, one of them with a hole in his sternum, isn't dramatic enough. There has to be angst and a hell of a lot of self loathing, ending with me possibly climbing some utterly ridiculous parapet of a church or something so I could look out on the city and brood. Oh and I would definitely be wearing a trenchcoat.

No goddammit: I wasn't wearing a trenchcoat.

***

After a hell of a lot of drinks, we somehow got it into our heads that it was a good idea to storm the castle. We were literally going to head down to the Hall of the Drunken King and fight our way in to see Harry so we could tell him a thing or seventeen.

In case you didn't know, the term *"storm the castle"* literally means to attack the stronghold. You see it in some of the monster movies where the villagers finally decide that they've had enough of whatever monster is currently terrifying them, and take up torches, pitchforks and other pointy instruments as makeshift weapons. The aim is to take the castle by surprise and force, to drive the evil out of the land forever.

Urban Dictionary has a completely different meaning which details putting the moves on a girl, so since that isn't relevant, go ahead and ignore that. You can come back to it later if you need any tips. We're going to deal exclusively with the monster clearing variety of storming.

As a quick FYI: deciding to storm the castle while drunk out of your mind is usually an extremely bad idea, especially since there were only the five of us and we really had no idea what we were doing.

"You're out of your fucking mind!" Claude yelled from over the phone.

I'd called up Claude to see if he wanted to join us and also, could he maybe call up one of his more disreputable associates and get us a car load of guns and ammo? We had decided that flaming torches were definitely not a good idea, but that we probably needed to be armed to the teeth. Stanley had mentioned that he had a bunch of Tiki Torches and all of us had just stopped and given him a flat look, nobody wanting to say it first, but then Stanley had made the connection and rolled his eyes at us.

"I like to barbeque, okay? That's all!"

We'd moved on, glad that there wasn't a white supremacist hiding in our midst. Since none of us knew where we were going to get any pitchforks, it seemed like a good idea to load up on guns, but since we were in Canada, that was going to be a lot more difficult than you'd expect. It also seemed like a good idea to call Claude with this request but that might have been the whole bottle of tequila talking.

Needless to say: we were all *really* fucking drunk. it had taken huge amounts of alcohol to get us there, but we were giving it the old college try with the assitance of an amazed and well-tipped bartender. Even he couldn't belive how much we were drinking.

"It will be so easy dude! I promise! We roll up, armed to the teeth and be total badasses."

"The word you're looking for is 'arrested' or better yet 'shot'!"

"So no guns?"

"No guns!"

"How about just one? A teeny tiny one."

"I'm hanging up and calling the cops myself and I'm going to beg them not to shoot you *since you're all idiots!*"

Claude hung up and I stared at the phone until Frankie shoved an almost over flowing glass of Whiskey into my hand.

"Drink up! Gotta keep your blood to alcohol ratio up! What did he say?"

"It sounded like a lot like a no," I said, and took a big gulp of the whiskey, appreciating the spreading warmth of the alcohol in my body. "Did anybody call an Uber yet?"

"We're waiting for Stanley. He decided he just had to sing 'Baby Got Back' and he's totally killing it!"

We were in the Fox and Fiddle on Bloor, since it was the closest reputable bar to my work, and Stanley was indeed killing it on the karaoke stage. The Fox had a rotating schedule of Karaoke DJs that came in every night after 10 PM. Apparently this was where Stanley dropped in every Thursday after the meeting, before he headed off to work security a few blocks uptown. If you've ever had to drag a friend who loves karaoke away from the bar when he still has a song coming on, then you know exactly the kind of shenanigans that were going on.

"Fuck it: I'm getting him," I said and stumbled off through the crowd, amazed at how much the alcohol was affecting me. I'd consumed a bottle and a half of tequila over the past two hours, so that in itself wasn't unusual. The bartender had wanted to cut me off a long time ago, but I had looked him *deep in the eye* and given him my best smile and he had shrugged and continued to give us all the alcohol we wanted. It had left me with a weird feeling kind of like a *buzzing in my skull*… but that was easily solved with the application of a couple more glasses of tequila and whiskey. I knew I wasn't that drunk, but I was determined to not be any *less* drunk before this whole storming the castle thing started to sound like a bad idea.

I drunk-shoved my way to the stage and waved to Stanley. He spotted me and waved for me to come join him on stage, so of course I did. I mean, I was drunk, so what do you really expect? Stanley was just as drunk and wrapped his gigantic arm around my neck affectionately.

"We gotta go man!" I yelled to him. "*We gotta go a put a stake through Harry's heart.*"

I wish I could say that I didn't say that at the same time Stanley shoved the mic over to my face for me to sing the next line. I wish I could say that I was sober enough to realize what had happened. Yeah… that's not going to happen.

Everybody was already looking at us, but now they were all paying attention to someone *admitting to planning murder on stage. Fuck!*

"It's okay, though," I said into the microphone. I tried to be as convincing and earnest as possible. "He's a *vampire*, so he deserves it."

The crowd cheered at that for some reason, but there were definitely some weird looks from the more cautious customers. We didn't stick around after that. We got the hell out of there, no matter if Stanley had three more songs coming up that he really wanted to sing.

We hung around outside the bar while Frankie settled up his bill, and I noticed the nervous energy we were all carrying. I wondered if anybody was getting second thoughts yet—

"Are we actually doing this?" Benjamin wanted to know.

"We're *totally* doing this!" Natalie roared a little too enthusiastically, but I was glad to see she was so fired up.

"Storming the castle!" I joined in.

"Is your friend coming through for us?" Stanley asked and took a long swig from a silver flask. "You know, the one with the weapons?"

"We might have to resort to pitchforks," I admitted. "Do it old school. We should get some torches. Can we get torches?"

Natalie raised her hand meekly. "Are we still no-go about Stanley's Tiki torches?"

"Definitely a no-go. No freaking way."

"This is going to be the worst assault in the history of ever," Benjamin said.

"…only if we use Tiki torches, so we're still in good shape," I said, but there was still some lingering doubt in my mind. I just didn't say anything about it. "Come on you guys! Did General Custer let overwhelming odds turn him back? Did Napoleon turn his nose up at Waterloo? Did President Whitmore let those aliens take over the planet after they blew up the White House?"

They were all giving me flat looks that said as drunk as they were, they all still thought stil I was out of my mind. Either that, or fucking stupid.

"First of all," Benjamin said. "Custer and Napoleon lost. And the third one was a movie, so you lose points just for that."

"You guys are getting way too sober, way too fast," I said. "We're going to need another bar."

"Changed my mind," Benjamin said. "*Slowest* assault in the history of ever."

***

Somewhere around the fourth bar (please don't ask me the name), and after an ungodly amount of tequila, the Hall of the Drunken King was only two blocks away. It was a distance that we were relatively confident we could cover and still be drunk enough not to chicken out at the last minute. We had really pushed the limits of drunkeness in vampires and I considered myself among the leading experts on the topic of how long it takes for a vampire to sober up after two bottles of tequila and a fair amount of walking.

"How far was that this time? Four blocks?"

"Three and a half," Stanley said. "Already losing my buzz."

Frankie had his cellphone out, Google Maps on the screen as he reminded himself what the next bar was. "The Woolly Mammoth is just around the corner. We can fill up there."

"Why didn't we just take an Uber?" I groaned. "All of this walking isn't good for us. We're sobering up way too fast! Are you feeling sober Stanley?"

"I'm feeling sober! How you feeling Ben?"

"Can we go home yet? This is taking *forever.*"

"He's feeling sober!" Natalie responded for him.

"One more bar!" I tried to be more enthusiastic than I was feeling, which was anxious as hell and scared as shit. "*We're doing this, right?*"

"Storming the castle!" Natalie and Stanley said almost together, but damn it, they didn't sound as convinced as they had before.

"Don't make me give a rousing speech you bastards!" I growled. "I really, really suck at them."

"Just shoot me now," Benjamin groaned.

We stormed into the *Woolly Mammoth* (the name of the bar has been changed to protect the guilty) and drank ourselves silly. There was no karaoke at this bar, just a lot of over-priced alcohol and a clientele who was dressed way better than we were. For a few moments I wondered if we had somehow discovered another vampire bar, but the lack of those piercing blue vampire eyes anywhere but among our little group, told a different story. It was just rich people who liked to buy expensive drinks because expensive drinks at least kept the ordinary rabble far away from the bar. And yet, there we were among them, rabbling as rabblers do. We got a few looks as we seated ourselves, but they were mostly just innocently curious.

"I gotta piss," I whispered to Frankie and grinned at him. "Don't you bastards go anywhere without me!"

"Storming the castle!" Frankie said without any enthusiasm.

"Storming the castle! Woo!" I echoed, and then stumbled off to the bathroom.

***

I stood at the urinal for a long time, taking a long deserved piss, wondering if I was actively reducing the level of alcohol in my system. It was a stupid thought, the kind you have when you're either drunk or stoned, but it was mostly the type of thought you have when the act of pissing is just taking *for-fucking-ever*.

I noticed the suit first you know. It's funny the things you notice when you're nice and properly drunk. The bathroom walls of the *Woolly Mammoth* held no graffiti to entertain us errant pissers, only little seven inch HD screens placed at eye level to blast us with the specials on the menu or whatever they wanted to show us, and believe me, those are impossible to hold the attention of the properly drunk. So yeah, the suit on the man at the next urinal was definitely the first thing that caught my attention. I hadn't noticed when he had come in, you know, me being caught up in the throes of pissing and everything, so for me it was as if he had appeared out of thin air.

"You all right there?" he asked, with a wry smile on his face.

"I think I just pissed the drunk away," I muttered, deliberately not looking at the dude. I threw a glance his way of course, a slight turn of the head before jerking it back so he would be assured that I wasn't trying to sneak a peek or anything. Some guys can be weird. There was something wrong about him though, even though I wasn't looking at him, but it was just something I couldn't put my finger on.

"I'm sure you'll be able to fix that. This is a bar after all," my strange new friend said and we both laughed that weird hollow laugh, the purpose of which was only to assure the other person that you had a sense of humour even if what they had said wasn't that clever in the slightest. Rules of social etiquette and all.

I finally finished pissing, quickly tucked away and turned away to the sink, still being careful not to look too long or too carefully at my new friend.

"This bar doesn't have *enough* alcohol," I grinned as I reached to turn on the hot water. I stopped then, as for just a split second I caught a better look at the profile of the man at the urinal. I finally realized what had been bugging the shit out of me.

It was *quiet* in the bathroom because nobody was taking a piss. Dude was standing at that urinal and the reassuring *psssssssst* of a stream of urine was definitely missing. Now that I had *stopped* pissing, the lack of sound was even more deafening and for some reason it also scared the shit out of me.

The vampire at the urinal turned to look at me and I could see his eyes now, cold, blue and piercing, and now of all times I realized that I knew exactly who this slightly scary motherfucker was. He had a great head of hair that could only be described as lustrous—

"Hey, didn't I punch you once?" I asked, and that flash of irritation and embarrassment that surfaced on his face was all the confirmation that I needed. What the fuck was his name again? Evanien? Bannion? *Something-something-ien. What the fuck was it?*

"This is not going to end well for you," Dude said, and that would have been disturbing by itself, except I was drunk and distracted trying to remember what his name was.

"Yea, I just figured that out," I said. "But before you fuck me up, could you remind me what your name was again?"

He gave me a look that told me he thought I was the world's biggest idiot.

"It's *Sebastien* you fuck! Sebastien De La- HEY! GET BACK HERE!"

I hit the bathroom door at a run, slamming it open much harder than I had intended. The idea had been simply to run as fast as possible, but somebody should have told that to the two extremely large men waiting outside for me.

"Nyet!" One of them said as he clamped my arm in a hand roughly the size of a manhole cover. An equally large man had grabbed my other arm, and even though he had said nothing, I assumed he was as equally Russian as the other dude.

"Uh oh" did not begin to describe the stirrings of terror in my gut.

They threw me back into the bathroom and as I crashed into the wall, I noticed that Sebastien was still standing at the urinals, his rage barely contained. I looked from him to the two large men who were now very deliberately blocking the door.

"I'm sorry," I said. "You were saying something about killing me?"

"I had a whole speech prepared and I'm going to deliver it!" Sebastien hissed as he turned to me.

I rolled my eyes and settled back into a more comfortable position, glad that my back was at least to the wall. If anything was going to happen to me, I was going to see it coming dammit.

"By all means, don't let me interrupt. I just want you to know you're seriously fucking up my buzz right about now."

"Fuck you Bob. You're nothing but a joke! You think you're so special— *GODDAMMIT!*"

I had made another run for it, pushing off the wall this time and propelling myself forward hard, determined to smash through the Russian blockade, after all they were only human, right?

When the ringing in my ears stopped and I picked myself

up off the floor where I had been knocked to, I sat up and vowed never to do that again. Human did *not* equal soft, at least not when it came to these guys. I glanced at Sebastien, sure that he was going to be just about losing his mind about me not wanting to stick around to hear his stupid speech.

"Are we going to try the speech thing again?" I asked. "I'm really, really interested in anything you might have to say, especially if it involves me not dying. That was a big hint there in case you're interested."

"Oh, you're going to die," Sebastien said quietly.

"You're really not selling this very well,"

"There's no running away from it."

"Watch me."

There was a brief tussle with the Russians again and of course that ended badly for me. Sebastien just shook his head mournfully.

"Where did you get these guys?" I asked. "Are they even human?"

"They're on loan from my Russian compatriots. They don't speak a word of English so I wouldn't bother trying to appeal to their gentler sides."

"Do they even have a word for gentle in Russian?" I took a look at the men and something occurred to me. "They don't know that we're vampires, do they?"

"Not a clue about me, no. But you? I don't know how you can even bother to call yourself a vampire at all. You're a terrible vampire and you know it. You're possibly the *worst example* I've ever seen. It makes me sick to my stomach to think I had to share my initiation with you. It was the worst kind of insult, but then you decided to embarrass me further by *punching me* in front of everyone. I've been waiting ten fucking years, and I put up with a lot of shit to become a vampire, and you just stumbled into it. You should be glad you've had Harry's protection all this time, but now all bets are off after what Harry did to Renaldo. He was my mentor and *they killed him* like he was some goddamn accidental."

Sebastien actually seemed really broken up by this revelation. He turned the full blast of his psycho hate towards me.

"I've been watching you for months you know, just waiting for you to give up and fuck up so badly and get yourself killed, but you're either really lucky or just a goddamn cockroach that *just… won't… die.* You just keep on going and going… and I'm sick of waiting for you to kill yourself. Somebody's got to put you down like the bad dog you are."

"Was that the speech? Cuz it sounded like you've been practicing. Should I be applauding now?"

"It's going to be fun killing you."

"Are you going to kill me here? In this bathroom? Cuz my friends are right outside somewhere. They're probably very drunk, but they're there and probably looking for me."

Sebastien shrugged. "Ahh yes: your Friends of Vlad club. Very enterprising of you to start that. We've been hearing all about it. How's my friend Murray? Do you believe I actually bit that stupid sonofabitch and convinced the poor bastard that he was now a vampire… and he believed me? Didn't even have to glammer him that much. I sent him your way of course. I even gave him one of your little girlfriends from the club to suck on. My little joke."

Oh you sick fuck.

My hand had made a fist all by itself. I have no idea how I managed to keep my rage in check. "Her name was Meredith. And he killed her."

"Not my fault what you vampire rejects get up to. Real or *otherwise*. If you guys are out there actually killing people, it's because you're all so fucked up and undeserving—"

"Beatrice got to Murray," I said, and that hit to shit the fuck up. Good. I was going to have to find a way to kill this motherfucker. I just couldn't figure out how. "I think it's safe to say he's probably not with us anymore, and he's probably telling her everything she wants to know."

"Beatrice?"

"*Beatrice,*" I confirmed, wondering what it was that had gotten him so rattled about Beatrice. I mean she was unstable in a "*I'm going to kill you next and might even enjoy it*" sort of way, but it wasn't like she was the Gentlemen or anything, right? She just did dirty jobs for Harry--

Something occurred to me.

"Didn't she kill your mentor? She mentioned something about murdering the shit out of some Italian guy. The same one you were crying about just now?"

Sebastien looked a little unsure of himself now, and I could see him doing the mental calculations. There was some kind of inner struggle going on which might mean I could actually survive this particular encounter—

"It doesn't matter. She doesn't scare me and you're still going to die."

"My friends will come looking for me."

"*Your friends are already gone,*" Sebastien grinned. "They think you left without them."

"Why would they think that?" I asked, but I already knew the answer, could see it happening in my mind's eye, a full blooded and extremely rich vampire approaching my drunken friends in the bar and telling them that I h*ad run away into the night and that they should all just fuck off.* Part of me wanted to say that they wouldn't believe that, that they would know something was up, but the truth has a way of being really obvious. Of course they had believed it and more importantly, it was exactly the excuse they were all looking for to run away back to their own safe lives where they didn't have to storm the castle in some misconceived plot that dared to dream about actually making it past the front doors of the Hall of the Drunken King.

"You know why," Sebastien said.

"I'm going to fight you," I said, my heart pounding hard in my chest. It was becoming difficult to breathe and I could smell the heat of adrenaline rushing off my top lip.

"You can *try*," Sebastien said and goddamn I couldn't wait to punch him in his punchable face again.

The Russians attacked me then and I fought like a demon. I'd like to say that I won, but this isn't that kind of story.

The last thing I felt was a prick of something sliding into my neck and then everything went black.

Chapter 21
A THOUSAND DEATHS

"The sun is coming up soon, and you my friend, are going *to burn.*"

These are not the words you ever want to wake up to, especially if you're a vampire.

If this ever happens to you, I advise you to get on your feet and run away as quickly as possible. Don't even look to see where you are or anything, *just fucking run*. I wish I could say that I followed my own advice, but I had one teeny tiny problem. I had been laid on the ground in a spread eagle position, my limbs pointing to four different directions; I could feel the coldness of iron around my wrists and shins and knew that there would be chains involved.

Of course, there were chains.

Oh yeah, and there was the teeny tiny fact that except for my socks, I was fucking naked.

There was a tingling, burning sensation all through my body as if my nerve endings had all been set on fire. Even my eyes burned and my eyesight was blurry for a few seconds before clearing up. Maybe I wasn't Weapon-X but damn if fast vampire healing wasn't a nice thing to have.

Oh, did I mention that I was *fucking naked?*

"What the fuck dude?" I strained to look over at Sebastien who had found the perfect position to sit which gave me a nice view of his profile. He was smoking a cigarette.

A cell phone rang and Sebastien tapped the ignore button. It looked a lot like my phone but was gone too fast for me to see properly.

We were on a beach, and judging from the cold wind that blew across the sand and whipped grains of sand at me, while trying to insinuate itself into every inch of my exposed skin, it was one of the more remote beaches. There was not a house or person within at least half a kilometer. They say in space, no one can hear you scream, but they'd forgotten that there are plenty of places on earth that heartily took that statement as a raison d'etre. To say that I had wind trying to force it's way up my butthole would be a slight understatement. Remember, I was spread-eagled, so every inch of me was literally spread and exposed. It's all in the name of the thing. Being slapped about the junk by a particularly aggressive wind is seriously not fun.

It was dark, but the sky (and I could see plenty of sky from my position) had that particularly charming look that indicated said sky was preparing to welcome the morning sun. I turned my head to look around, and pain shot through my head as a reward.

"Don't try to move too much. We injected you with about twelve ounces of bleach, and you're still getting it out of your system. Your body hates it, but it hates being dead even more."

"Remind me to punch you when I get out of this," I quipped and damn if the pain didn't shoot through my skull as if a small and determined gnome was hammering on the top of my head.

"You're going to burn Bob."

I strained against the chains but couldn't get them to move. Whatever they were attached to was firmly rooted into the ground and was purposely thwarting me. *Yep, he was right. I was going to die.*

Ring Ring. The cellphone again and once again Sebastien tapped the ignore button.

"You won't burn up immediately you know," Sebastian said after a moment. "Apparently it takes a long, long time and you'll be awake for the whole thing. Your body tries to heal while it's burning you see, so the fire doesn't consume you like you see in the movies. That's why you're tied down, so you can't run. I've heard it can take at least an hour before your system finally shuts down and you die. It's *really a horrible death.*"

"This is a lot of overkill for me punching you man! Couldn't you just kick me in the balls instead?"

Sebastien gave me a long dirty look and curled his lip at me. "You just don't get it, Bob. I think it may actually be too far out of the realm of your reality for you ever to really get it. You are supposed to be dead by now, and yet here you still are. You go to work like a normal person, you pay your bills like a normal person, and you've gone and somehow gotten yourself some friends who are just like you: a bunch of vampire rejects. You're pretending to be human so hard, it makes the ten years of shit that I put up with actually mean nothing. I look at you and wonder how you can even survive, like *how the hell do you even do it?*" He shook his head. "You being alive is a goddamn insult. *A goddamn lie.* It's a goddamn slap in the face that my whole life as a vampire means nothing and you are a reminder of that. So I'm going to kill you, and maybe at some point in the future I'll forget you ever existed."

"Is it too late for an apology?" I asked. "I'll even try to mean it, I promise."

Sebastien pulled a massive knife from somewhere on the ground, and I strained to turn my head to see what else he had there, but all I could see were the edges of some kind of dark cloth. Sebastien admired the knife a little too lovingly for my taste. He looked like he wanted to French-kiss the damn thing.

Ring! Ring!

"Goddammit!" Sebastien swore and tapped on ignore once again.

"Maybe you should get that. Seems pretty persistent."

Sebastien shook it off and pocketed the phone again.

"You know, I had this whole elaborate plan where I was going to make your life a living hell and make you think you're losing your mind. Purely by chance, I saw you leaving this dive bar with some chick one night, and I figured that you were going to take her back to her place and suck her blood. I was impressed that you'd figured out a way to get your own supply of blood… but what I saw most of all was an opportunity to properly fuck with you. I planned to follow you one night and wait for you and whatever girl you picked up to go to sleep, and then I was going to drain her dry so that when you woke up, there would be a dead chick in the bed with you and you'd think you'd done it!"

"That is seriously fucked up. I kinda like it though. Twisted but I like it." I wasn't completely lying either. I was actually impressed on a certain level. Terrified and uncomfortable yes, but impressed at the lengths this guys was willing to go to just to fuck with my head. You really had to give him credit. "So what happened?"

"Well it was a pretty elaborate plan, and there were a lot of moving parts. I actually made it into the bedroom of that blonde with the shoulder tattoo, you know the one I mean right? About yea tall, thick and curvy, remember her? So I get into the bedroom, and she wakes up but doesn't see me. I spent the rest of the night in the closet listening to you two fucking and moaning and fucking and on and on and on. I almost came out and killed her for being such a screamer, but that would have ruined the whole plan. That night was the closest I ever got. It's a lot of hard work trying to ruin someone's life, and I had other things going on, so eventually, I just couldn't be bothered."

"If you had pulled it off, I would have been seriously freaked out."

"I know, *right*?"

I chuckled, actually enjoying the moment despite myself.

"So, any chance you're gonna change your mind and let me go?"

Sebastien held up what he had been carving so that I could see it properly for the first time. I instantly wished that he had decided to keep it a secret. It was a three-foot-long piece of grayish wood, and the tip had been very recently and almost lovingly sharpened into a long and wicked-looking point. Sebastien got to his feet, apparently loving my response as he lofted it firmly in two hands.

"I'm afraid not Bob," Sebastien said. "I've been looking forward to this all night and you don't want me to go home sad, do you?"

"You're a bit of a date rapist aren't you?" I quipped, and why the hell was I pissing him off even more? It didn't matter if it was probably right, that flash of insight coming to me from his language. The general rule tends to be: *don't piss off the man with the sharp stick!*

"Don't sweat it, Bob! This isn't going to kill you! Just fuck you up a hell of a lot! Now the sun, that's what's going to kill you."

Sebastien reared back, the fucked up stake going high into the air and I knew it was aimed at my heart and in a very short time I was going to feel what it felt like to be a Bob-ke-bab. Or maybe a shishkaBob. It didn't matter that it wasn't going to kill me at all. It mattered that it was going to hurt and that I was going to be the one doing the hurting.

Ring! Ring!

That threw Sebastien completely off.

"Seriously?" he yelled at the phone.

There was a roar of an engine and both Sebastien and I turned to look in the direction, me straining my neck muscles to see properly. I was just in time to see a cherry red Camaro come fishtailing down the beach towards us, a huge cloud of dust rising from behind it. The Camaro fish-tailed to a stop, the driver's door swinging open even before the car stopped.

"You should really answer the phone," Claude said, and for the first time I noticed the huge gun in his hand, the gun that was pointed right at Sebastien--

BLAM!

Sebastien jerked to the left, and I wanted to cheer, wanted to believe that Claude had actually shot the sonofabitch but there was that sinking feeling in my gut because Claude had broken the agreed cardinal rule. It was the one thing that had always driven both of us crazy about characters in movies. They always had a habit of talking too much, instead of shooting first and I guess just not giving the clever one liner. We had always agreed that if it had been us in the situation, we would definitely shoot first. Period. So the elation I had felt when I saw him with the gun had almost fizzled when he had taken the precious seconds to deliver what admittedly had been a completely badass line.

Did he miss? Of course he missed,

Sebastien stumbled and I opened my mouth to yell at

Claude to shoot and not stop until the gun was empty. I didn't get the chance.

Sebastien snapped his head up and looked Claude in the eye.

"You don't want to kill me," he said almost conversationally.

"Yes I do," Claude said, and pulled the trigger.

BLAM!

Sebastien was surprised, but somehow managed to dodge *that* bullet as well. He held out a hand to Claude forcefully and yelled, "STOP!"

For some reason I couldn't see, Claude didn't empty the gun into the smarmy motherfucker.

"SHOOT HIM!" I screamed. "What are you WAITING FOR?"

Claude looked puzzled, but he seemed unable to move.

"I'm trying! I really am! But I can't!"

"Who the fuck are you?" Sebastien growled.

Claude looked at the gun in his hand. "I'm the guy who's trying to shoot your balls off."

"Dude!" I yelled. "*What the fuck is wrong with you?*"

"Shut up Bob! I can't pull the trigger!" Claude yelled back.

Sebastien had figured it out. "Right. You're Claude. The best friend. You know, I've had my Russians trying to kill you for months now. You're apparently really, really hard to kill."

"It's a gift." Claude said.

"Guess I'll have to kill you myself!"

"Claude, *what the fuck man? You don't have to actually listen to this chicken fucker!*"

Sebastien smiled at me and then looked back at Claude.

"Why don't you go ahead and point the gun at your head," Sebastien said, and I watched in horror as Claude obediently pointed the gun at the right side of his head.

"*What the fuck are you doing to him? Stop it!*" I yelled, pulling and yanking at the ungiving chains in absolute panic, but there was not even a little bit of slack anywhere.

"You really need a mentor dude," Sebastien said. "This is what we call *glammering*. Humans like your friend are weak minded and we vampires have dominion over them. We always have and always will. We can control them, make them do whatever we want." Sebastien grinned evilly as something occurred to him. "You've been doing it and you didn't even know. How did you think a loser like you was suddenly getting pussy thrown your way whenever you wanted it? Walk into a bar, pick a girl you want to leave with and next thing you know, she's all hot for you. Nothing makes the panties drop so fast like a little glammer. It's like having a pocket of roofies, twenty-four seven."

The realization of what he was saying hit me hard. There was an empty spot inside my gut, icy cold, dark and filled with a sudden guilt that made me dizzy, made me want to hit something. *Oh Goddammit!* I tried to clear my head, tried to ignore that taste of bile that came with the guilt, *the knowledge* of what I had been *doing*.

"I didn't know! I would never--"

"But you did!" He turned his attention back onto Claude. "*Jump up and down on one foot!*"

Claude complied and immediately started hopping up and down on one leg and Sebastien grinned.

"This next part is going to be fun," he said. "Just not for you."

"Don't do this!" I pleaded. I managed to put aside my guilt about the girls and tried to focus on the danger at hand. On Claude.

"*Just let him go!*" I yelled.

"Claude, come over here and shoot Bob in the chest."

Claude strode over quickly, closing the distance, his gun hand coming down from his head and pointing at me as he walked. I'm not ashamed to say I freaked the fuck out, straining at the chains and cursing myself for not being a better vampire, for not being a better friend, for just not being *better*. My friend was going to watch himself shoot me, and then Sebastien was probably going to make him watch me burn, and there was nothing he or I could do about it.

Claude pointed the gun at my chest and turned his head to me. The panic in his eyes told me everything I needed to know.

BLAM!

I heard the gunshot more than anything, thunderous in

the morning air, and I wondered if Claude had missed and hadn't actually shot me. But then it came, that searing flash of pain that at once throbbed and burned as the damaged nerve endings protested loudly that there was now a *fucking hole in my chest.*

"Fuck," I whispered and felt the searing pain threaten to take over.

Sebastien stepped close to Claude, almost like a lover, flaunting his power, relishing his revenge.

"Shoot him again, Claude," Sebastien whispered to my friend. "This time I want you to shoot him in the *dick.*"

"Dude, seriously?" I managed to whimper.

Claude whipped the gun up and around and pushed it into Sebastien's chest. This time, Sebastien wasn't fast enough. I don't care who says you can dodge a bullet if you're fast enough. Maybe you can if you're far away and you do your best to make sure you're not where the gun is pointing, but when a gun is point blank range, and you can't see it coming, it doesn't matter who you are: there's no dodging a bullet. Even if you're a vampire.

KABLAM! KABLAM! Claude got off two shots into Sebastien's chest, and there was that look of surprise as they ripped through him. He didn't go flying into the air, since as I explained earlier, that's not how bullets work. They just rip a hole through you, just like the holes that had appeared in Sebastien, sprays of blood misting the morning air, blood flowering around the holes in his formerly pristine white shirt.

The thing is, not everybody reacts the same way to being shot. Some people believe what they see in movies, that getting shot is a death sentence, and they just give up on the spot, since if they've been shot, that means they're dead, right? Others don't even notice that they've been shot and will fight you for hours if that's what it takes before they realize that they have a hole in them and somebody really should take a look at that.

Sebastien was one of those kinds of people.

Sebastien reacted, not even feeling the pain yet, and his fist flew out almost like it had a mind of its own and hit

Claude right in the chest. There was a crack that sounded exactly how breaking bone should, and Claude crumpled like a ragdoll, even as he flew back out of sight. There was pain and shock on his face as he vanished from sight, a look that I had never seen before and that freaked me the fuck out, more than anything at all.

"*CLAUDE!*" I screamed, not caring if I was being dramatic, not caring about anything else but that Claude was hurt and I couldn't help him. I turned my attention to Sebastien. "*I'm going to fucking kill you!*"

Sebastien poked at the holes in his chest and looked at the blood on his fingers, surprised.

"That *motherfucker,*" he whispered.

I strained against the chains, the rage that filled me wanting to explode and I was aware that my fangs had slid out for all of the use they were. I pulled and pulled, sure that my rage would do something, anything, after all my grief was raw, and my anger was righteous, and there had to be some kind of good somewhere, right?

You know how I keep mentioning how much real life isn't like the movies? Yeah... it really isn't

Sebastien just watched me and then pulled his stake out of the sand where it had fallen at an angle.

"I have no idea why my glammer didn't work on him and I really don't care. I'm going to fuck up your friend and drain the blood out of him, but first, I'm going to stab you in the dick!"

Sebastien reared up, blood streaming down his chest and stomach and I knew there was no one to save me this time.

"*What the fuck, Dude? Is that you Sebastien?*"

Sebastien paused in the act of my almost murder, stake held high in the sky. "Goddammit!" He yelled. "Can I please just *stab* this guy?" There was a pause as he turned to the source of the voice, and then he said quite simply. "Oh."

Beatrice stepped into my field of vision and barely threw me a glance.

Sebastien stammered, and you could see his brain going into overdrive trying to figure out how fucked he was and if he was going to get to kill me after all. I would have sighed in relief at the brief reprieve, but I had a hole in my chest that felt like it was the size of a football and I just wanted this to be over.

"You actually remembered my name?" Sebastien stammered, and then tried on a smile, just in case Beatrice somehow hadn't noticed me tied naked and spread out on the ground. "What are you doing out here?"

"Same as you actually. Getting rid of a body. It's a good spot for it. I see both of yours are still alive," Beatrice leaned over and waggled her fingers at me. "Hi, Bob."

I strained back to see Claude, grateful to Beatrice for pointing out that he was still alive. I couldn't see him, but I could hear his ragged and strained breathing, plus the occasional pained *"fuck," "shit"* and *"goddamn"* among others. If anything, Claude was thorough with his swearing, even in massive amounts of pain, which was way better than massive amounts of dead. The blow to his chest could have killed him dead. It could have just stopped his heart or even put enough pressure on it for it to rupture and explode in his chest. Clause was tougher than Sebastien had expected.

"This isn't what it looks like—" Sebastien stammered.

Beatrice grinned widely. "Oh good! That's a relief. Because what it *looked* like, at least to *me*, was *you* killing a fellow vampire, and you know Harry frowns on that kind of behavior. We usually leave the killing of other vampires to the Gentlemen, and they hate being denied."

I really wished she would get to the point and save my ass from being impaled before I bled out on the beach. I swear some people have no sense of urgency at all.

"You've got to be kidding, right?" Sebastien said. "Weren't you just *killing someone*?"

"She's not kidding! Definitely not kidding!" I yelled. My goddamn leg had gone numb, and I couldn't feel it anymore. And was the numbness spreading?

"Oh, my guy was only human. *Somebody* convinced him he was a vampire you know."

Oh, fuck! I thought. She knew what Sebastien had done to Murray, and she was letting him know that she knew. I still hadn't figured out what that meant for me since I was still tied up…

"The poor bastard truly, honestly believed that he was one of us, that he was immortal," Beatrice said with a sly look to Sebastien, who had slowly lowered the stake by this point and looked like he was considering using it on Beatrice. *"He wasn't,"* She said in a stage whisper as if it wasn't obvious.

"*Whatever he had to say was a goddamn lie!*" Sebastien blurted out.

Beatrice nodded reassuringly, but you could see she wasn't buying it. Anybody could see she wasn't buying it.

"Of course it was," Beatrice said and patted Sebastien on his shoulder. "It will be our little secret."

Sebastien looked relieved at this.

"Really?"

"Not a chance."

In one swift move that was way too fast for me to see, Beatrice blurred just for a second and stepped away holding something fleshy and gristly in a tightly clenched fist. It was so quick that Sebastien was still smiling and hadn't realized just what had happened yet. The blood hadn't come yet, but when it did as the body got over its shock, it sprayed with every beat of his heart. The arterial blood spurted out into the early morning air and puddling briefly on the sand, in pools of a wasted life.

Beatrice casually threw aside the pieces of flesh that had been the throat of the vampire formerly known as Sebastien and wiped her bloody palm on her jeans. She looked down at me and frowned.

"We really gotta stop meeting like this Bobbikins," she said.

"We've *never* met like this! Can you help me out here?" I groaned. "I think I'm bleeding out here and Claude needs help."

Beatrice made no move to help. She looked down at my limbs and shook her head.

"Oh hush. It's already clotting. It will heal up in an hour."

"Doesn't feel like it. So… little help here?"

"You got yourself into this mess dude. Can't expect me to go around saving your ass every time you know."

"But you just killed dude! You killed Sebastien!"

"Yeah, but that wasn't for you. That was business. Speaking of which…"

With a fluid sweeping motion, Beatrice kicked Sebastien's knife into the air and caught it with one hand. She grabbed Sebastien by the lustrous hair and with one motion, separated his head from his body with barely a sigh.

Sebastien collapsed next to me, spurting fountains of blood onto the sand and I wondered if Claude was also bleeding out in the sand somewhere behind me.

"So this isn't a rescue then."

"Not even close to it."

"You know the sun is coming up right? You do know what's going to happen to me right?"

"Yeah. If you don't get yourself out of there, you're going to burn like a motherfucker."

"That does not sound so great to me."

"Me neither, so you'd better get moving. *Andale Bobbikins! Arriba Arriba!*"

Beatrice held Sebastien's head in both hands and then with a smirk, threw it into the air, and punted it towards the lake. There was a splash as the head entered the water. Beatrice threw up her arms in victory.

"She shoots! She scores!"

"There is something seriously wrong with you," I said.

I strained against my bonds, but there was still no give at all, nothing. I couldn't even move my arms enough to pull the skin off my hands if it came to that. There was zero wiggle room. I looked up imploring at Beatrice, the sharp taste of panic, bitter in my mouth.

"Either help me or fuck off."

Beatrice thought deeply and then grinned. "Tell ya what: you get outta this and I'll buy you lunch. Maybe show you a few tricks. But first, show me what kind of vampire you really are."

"Can you show me how to get out of chains?"

"Oh, that one is easy. First, don't let anyone put you in chains."

Bitch.

"When you do get out of this, and you tell anyone about

this whole mess, make sure there's like a car chase across the desert or some shit. Make it epic."

"Fuck you, Beatrice!"

"Bye Bob!"

And with that, Beatrice was gone. I whipped my head around, looking for Beatrice, completely unable to see her, unable to see anything except the steadily brightening sky.

"Can you at least tell me if my friend is alive? Is Claude alive?"

Silence.

"You can't leave me here!" I yelled. "My legs are numb, and I don't want to die with numb legs!"

There was only the silence of an empty beach at sunrise.

"Claude?" I called.

"Fuck you, Bob," Claude gasped faintly. "Pain. Hurt. Ow."

I strained against the chains, telling myself that my vampire super-strength had to kick in some time and now would be perfect because *goddammit I didn't want to die!* The chains didn't break. No vampire super-strength for me.

"Fuck."

I could see the sky brightening slowly as the sun prepared to cross the horizon and banish the shadows and all creatures of the night with its arrival. It occurred to me then that I couldn't hear Claude anymore.

"Claude, I think I'm going to die, but thank you, man! Thank you for being my friend… even though I got you killed. I'm sorry I couldn't be a better friend man. I'm sorry… I'm sorry I couldn't be better, period."

I was getting hot and could feel the warmth spreading across my body as my nerve endings pricked up, aware that something was going on, aware of the heat of the direct sunlight--

"I love you, man."

And then there was only fire and pain.

I burned.

As Beatrice predicted, *I burned like a motherfucker.*

EPILOGUE

Chapter 22
EPILOGUE

What are you looking at me like that for? Of course, I survived, you silly bastard. But there's surviving, and then there's surviving without any scars. If there's one piece of advice I can give you, it's to take the no scars option.

Long story short, Claude is a fucking *champion*. I wish I had seen him, but I'd been a little busy at the time, you know, with the being on fire and everything. He found out later that he had suffered a cracked sternum and a punctured lung. Sebastien had all but crushed his chest with that single punch and even small movements were pure torture for Claude. Even the act of breathing was agony for him from his chest muscles protesting being used after that abuse. Lesser men would have laid there and waited to die.

Not Claude.

Claude was massively fucked up, is what I'm trying to say here, and somehow he found the strength to pull himself to his feet, fighting through the sheer agony that defined his entire existence at that moment. He did this even as I first began to smoke and then burst into flame behind him, and all the while, I was screaming.

He was focused on two things through all of this fucked up situation: the fire extinguisher and the fire blanket in the trunk of his car which was parked twenty feet away, but for Claude, it might as well have been ten miles.

***

Here's the thing: you don't survive the shit that we went through and come out the same person on the other side. Nobody does. I had changed, and I would eventually find out how much Claude had changed as well. We would both have to come to terms with what those changes meant, but in the moment of me waking up, it was with a relief that I was no longer dead.

Even more importantly, I was no longer on fire.

Is it possible for memories to hurt? I'll save you the bother of thinking too hard about it. The answer is yes. I could remember the pain, the smell of me and how it had seemed to last forever. Even just looking at my smooth unburnt flesh, healed only because of what I had become, I could still remember how it felt when the skin had burned. I remembered how it had once moved and slid off--

I was probably never going to be able to look barbeque in the face ever again.

"Welcome back Robert," Madame Vera said, as she sat down next to my hospital bed. "How are we feeling today?"

"Alive," I tried on a smile, but it didn't feel right. There were suddenly tears burning at my eyes and where the fuck had they come from? The tears burned hot trails down my face, and that was it for me for a while.

When I was in a slightly less embarrassing but definitely damper state, Madame Vera let go of my hand and smiled patiently.

"Claude is in the next room if you're able," she said.

"Claude is alive?" I asked and dissolved into another embarrassing state of blubbering. Another five minutes of emotion later Madame Vera explained that it was Claude who had saved me. He had sprayed me down with the fire extinguisher and had managed to cover me with the fire blanket before collapsing next to me.

"There are going to be a lot of questions later, so you're going to need to prepare yourself for that. Get your emotions out right now and get your mind straight. You have to be strong in the face of what's coming because it's not going to be pretty. While you're here, I can shield you, but you have to leave sooner or later."

"What are you talking about?"

"Harry of course. He has a significant amount of egg on his face over the situation with Sebastien. His entire system has now been called into question considering how unstable Sebastien proved to be. You're going to be prodded and cross-examined by some of the finest and oldest legal minds, some of whom admire you for your role in this. All vampires of course."

"And the rest of them?"

"The rest of them want to see you burn. Again."

"Stuff those guys," I said. Something occurred to me. "Why am I even here? Did I die? I think I would have remembered dying again."

"This is not just the house of the dead. It is also a place of healing, and you, my dear boy, needed a significant amount of healing. You *did* die and that was essential in your healing, but your friend Claude required the use of our *alternate* treatments due to the nature of his injuries. He is doing remarkably well given the circumstances. I've made arrangements to make sure you both get only the finest care. You've been through quite an ordeal."

"How much is this going to cost me?" I asked cautiously. "I appreciate it, but I'm broke as hell."

Madame Vera smiled.

"We're billing the estate of your friend Sebastien. If someone manages to recover his head, he might have something to say about it, but this seems highly unlikely at this point. His body seems to have also gone missing."

"Oh," I said. Then I realized what she had just admitted to. "Oh, wow." Then: "Remind me not to get on your bad side."

"I've been assured that all of my sides are quite good."

"Who called you?" I asked. "How did you guys know to come get us?"

"Beatrice."

"Beatrice?" I was surprised to hear the poison in my voice when it came to Beatrice. I think I had decided how I officially felt about her and hate was too mild a word. Come to think of it, I think I actually hated her more than I did Harry. "She left me to burn! Did she actually care enough to

357

do something other than abandon me?"

The look that Madame Vera gave me was a very calculating one. "Don't take it so personally Robert. I think she quite likes you."

"You're bleeping kidding me right?" Yes, I said "bleeping" instead of some other more colorful epithet. It felt strange to even think of swearing around Madame Vera.

Madame Vera smiled. "You're still alive aren't you? Now, let's go and see your friend."

I went to see my friend.

***

"Pineapple on your pizza? Yes or no?" Claude said as soon as he saw me enter the room.

Of course I instantly scoffed since it gave me a chance to blink away the sudden rush of tears that had spontaneously decided to appear in my eyes. I glanced at the phone in his hand.

"Everybody knows pineapple on pizza is a no go," I said. "But damn it's delicious. Add on some bacon and grilled chicken and you have perfection."

"You're a monster!" Sammy's voice said, and Claude turned the phone towards me. Sammy glared back at me from FaceTime, but only for a moment. Her face cracked into the hugest grin I have ever seen on a person, and were those tears in her eyes? Yes they were.

"Hi Sammy," I said and felt the tears springing to the corners of my eyes. I clumsily wiped them away. "It's good to see you too."

Claude turned the phone back to himself. "So I'm going to expect you here in about thirty minutes with our pizza?"

"Both of you are fucking monsters, I just want you to know that."

"Wipe your tears and bring the pizza."

"It's allergies motherfucker! I will cut anybody who says it isn't."

Claude hung up. "I think she missed you dude."

"You shot me." I said and Claude nodded thoughtfully.

"Yeah, I did that didn't I?" he said, then: "Sorry?"

"Were you faking at the time or were you glammered?"

"Is that what they call it? I couldn't hear what he was telling you."

"Yeah. Glammered. Glammering. Kinda like in the movies, except the eyes go all red and shit. In the movies I mean."

"Red eyes would have been a nice touch."

"So were you glammered?"

"Fuck no. Dude was moving so fast though, I knew I had to get closer, so I played along with what I thought he thought he was doing to me. I improvised."

"*You shot me and you weren't even glammered!* You could have shot him right then!"

"I'm sorry I shot you."

"What if you'd killed me?"

"Seriously? You already took a bullet to the head and you came back from that. I was pretty sure you weren't going to die."

"'Pretty sure'? You bet my life on a 'pretty sure'?"

"Damn skippy. You healed up nicely too. Can't even see a mark."

I just glared at him, embarrassed since I could still see his bruises. I wasn't going to let him off that easy though.

"You could have shot him *right then*," I repeated. "Right in the face."

"Do you know how hard it is to shoot someone in the face?"

"Well obviously you don't!"

Claude shrugged and I tried to glare at him, but I really wasn't feeling it. Maybe it was seeing him lying there in the hospital gown that got to me. It reminded me of what he had also gone through. It reminded me of what he'd had to do to save me.

"So why couldn't he glammer you?" I asked after a moment.

Claude grinned and managed to look cockier than he was already.

"It's obvious isn't it? I'm the man who *cannot* be glammered. I'm the anti-vampire."

"You're going to be impossible to live with aren't you?"

"Damn skippy!" Claude smiled. "It's good to see you man."

"You too. I'd ask how you found me, but I have a feeling it's either going to be that you planted a microchip in my neck or something while I was sleeping—"

"It's the cell phone I gave you. Find My Phone is a wonderful app. Lacks accuracy, but works in a pinch."

All of my conspiracy theories went out the window and left me somewhat deflated.

"Oh," I said. "I was going to say cellphone."

"You're a bad liar."

And just like that everything was okay between us. It was as simple as that. No drama and drawn out angst. I was glad my friend was still alive and still as impossible as ever, and he was glad I had survived it all.

I caught him looking at me a couple of times and I remembered he had been the one who had to listen to me scream as I burned. H had been the one there to put out the flames no matter how hurt he had been, no matter if it had almost killed him.

I'm going to stop before I get all sentimental and shit, so deal with it, okay?

The pineapple pizza was awesome.

***

The next two weeks were not sentimental in anyway and I swear I wasn't responsible for any fires. That was Claude.

***

Two weeks later:

"Have you told your mom you're a vampire?"

"Is there any way I can answer that without lying and still come out on top?"

"So what you're saying is no."

"Is that what I'm saying?"

"Almost in those exact words, yes. Go see your mother."

"Do you know how hard this is going to be? It's not exactly a great conversation starter you know. 'Hi mom! I'm a vampire!' Like that is going to go down well."

"Dude just call her. She's probably the only other person on the planet who would fight a vampire for you. And she would win too!"

"Are we really going there?"

"We're going there! You're bringing this on yourself!"

"I'm scared, dude."

"Be as scared as you want to be. I won't judge you."

"You won't?"

"I'd think you were a complete wuss, but I won't judge you."

"Fine then. Let's do it. Let's go see my mom."

"You're making me come with you aren't you?"

"My mom loves you! Besides, I need you to drive."

"What's the situation with you and the blood?"

"Madame Vera's got me on a program. Therapy and some kind of synthetic blood they cooked up in the lab. At least that's the official story. It tastes and smells just like real blood. No need to go around biting horny young women anymore. Although the sex was really good…"

"Is it helping?"

"Definitely not with the sex. We'll see how it goes. Can't make any promises. You know I'm a shameless recidivist."

"I know you're shameless…"

Silence for a while.

"Let's go then," I said. "Let's go see my mom."

***

We left while it was still dark, hitting the road at an ungodly hour. I looked back as we left the city, the lights, and skyscrapers vanishing into the night and for the first time in a long time, I felt like a real human being. The constant hunt for blood had left a shadow over my life, the obsession making its mark on everything like some rabid dog that just had to piss on your leg right before it bit you.

It was like we were driving away from that cloud and leaving everything behind us, and that was what I needed at that moment.

That version of life might just be waiting for me when I came back, but it didn't matter then. That was going to be a battle for another day.

I drove part of the way until the sun began to come up,

and since we were heading east for a while there, it felt like we were rushing towards a brand new day.

It felt exactly like we were chasing the sun.

END OF BOOK ONE

AFTERWORD

AFTERWORD

That's it guys. Sorry. Story's over, now you can all go home.

I've taken a few liberties with my presentation of the story, so thank you for bearing with me and getting all of the way through. When I say that I've tried to end this novel multiple times, I really, really mean it. My readers on Wattpad can certainly attest to this since the the version that they read is substantially different from what I've presented here. I do have to give them credit for being good fans and asking the questions that I just had to answer in great depth, and they are one of the reasons this novel exists in this current state.

Bob first came to life way too many years ago during a NaNoWriMo when MySpace was still a thing and I still lived in Georgia. I spent the month and churned out my first 50,000 words, reached the part where I could say, "yeah that feels right" especially since I could work the original title "Chasing the Sun" in there ever so subtly. And then I got stuck, which then led to me being distracted and eventually, I just never came back to it. It wasn't until 2012 when my friend Carrie Cutforth introduced me to Wattpad and that spurred me to try to at least complete it. What can I say? There's something attractive about having an audience...

Wattpad ended up being crucial to spurring me to finish the novel, but it wasn't until I changed the name to "So You Might Be a Vampire" and then changed the cover to match, that readers really started to respond. What they found was this ridiculously foul-mouthed character named Bob. The final title change about way later in the process since the book had changed so much that a different story was being told.

Initially the story was formed as a way to explore a character I had developed for a movie I'd been working on just about forever. It was called "The God Stones" and was a road trip about a lesser god walking the earth in mortal form. This was years ago back in 1998 and I was a fan of Neil Gaiman and heavily into the Sandman comic series, so my writing themes heavily reflected that. When Gaiman came out with American Gods, I was floored with how he so easily picked up the theme of immortals walking the earth, but I suppose it was inevitable since that it was exactly the kind of story he would write. I just needed to fnd a new type of story to write.

So I made Bob into a vampire, but a complete fuck-up of a human being, and everything clicked. I wrote out the entire plot and the script and sat there examining my characters and realized that even though I had a pretty good idea who Jaime was... with Bob I didn't have a clue what he had been through and exactly how much of a fuckup he had been. This novel answers all of those questions and I'm grateful for being able to look into his world.

I had a much deeper look once my editor Nikki Barran came on board to help me with the rewrites and editing. Most of this was done via Facebook Messenger at odd hours of the day and the night, but she dragged the rest of the story out of me. All it would take is for her to challenge something I thought had been absolutely clear and then after I had extensively and wittly explained it, her response would be something along the lines of "That's great. Why don;t you write that then?" This scenario happened a LOT. But it was useful in bringing the real story out. What I thought had been complete was actually two stories and that was clearly evident in the editing stages.

Some of you may have read the original story and you're wondering where all the fighting and other stuff is, and I promise you it's still there... just not in this book. This book is about how Bob became a vampire and how much he sucked at it. It's mostly about how he comes to terms with how it's okay to not be the movie vampire and how he has to make his own path and as you can see, that story is very much its own thing.

Mostly though, it's a story of friendship, the ultimate bromance, and that's okay too,

The Second novel "So I'm a Vampire... Now What?" has to go through a heavy edit, but it's mostly done and continues Bob's journey into the world of vampires. It had originally been intended to be part of this novel, but novels have a life of their own and they want to become so much more.

Thanks for reading, and I'll see you back for Book 2 in the series.

- Rodney V. Smith
  Toronto, June 17, 2017

ABOUT THE AUTHOR

Rodney V. Smith is the Barbaods born writer and independent media artist with over 20 years of experience in film and television. He has been writing all kinds of stories most of his life, but in is early teens was most fascinated with horror, fantasy and science-fiction. Heavily influenced by the works of Stephen King and Terry Pratchett, he experimented with short stories, comic books and several attempts at a novel, before being introduced to screenplay writing.

He has filmed and directed a range of short films plus 2 independent feature films over the years. He has found working as Director of Photography on the critically acclaimed web series "Casters" and "Dominion", to be extremely rewarding. His science-fiction series "Out of Time" has been nominated for awards from the IAWTV (International Academy of Web Television) and T.O. Webfest and can be viewed on Amazon Prime.

ACKNOWLEDGEMENTS

I'd like to thank my wife Allison for her infinite patience and encouragement, especially during the month of November when NaNoWriMo takes over.

My editor Nikki Barran, for being my second brain and understanding what I needed to push me through a lazy premise, just so I could really shape it and make it better. You let me talk it out and then you made me write it out.

Evan and Ariel, for somehow understanding that I wasn't really being a horrible dad and that I just needed an hour in my own head so I could write. Also thanks for choosing not to climb into my lap during that hour. Thanks kids.

Andrew Stoute, for the inspiration, the conversation and for just letting me talk. For twenty plus years now.

Carrie Cutforth, for introducing me to Wattpad.

Angie, for being a great reader and friend.

Lindsey Clarke, for all of the good words, written and spoken.

Cristian Giannella and Charmaine Taylor for the great feedback and letting me see the book from a different perspective.

Paul Renshaw, Emily Schooley, Nicole Rosas for always cheering me on and mostly for reading and giving your feedback.

All of my readers at Wattpad who read every word and asked for more. You guys rock.

CHASING THE SUN SERIES

Coming in Fall 2018
Book 2:
So I'm a Vampire... Now What?

Coming in Summer 2019
Book 3:
So You Used to Be Human

Find out more at
www.bobthevampire.com